THE
MECHANICAL

THE ALCHEMY WARS: BOOK ONE

IAN TREGILLIS

www.orbitbooks.net

ORBIT

First published in Great Britain in 2015 by Orbit

1 3 5 7 9 10 8 6 4 2

Copyright © 2015 by Ian Tregillis

The moral right of the author has been asserted.

Excerpt from *Bitter Seeds* by Ian Tregillis
Copyright © 2010 by Ian Tregillis

A CIP catalogue record for this book
is available from the British Library.

ISBN 978-0-356-50232-8

Printed and bound in Great Britain by
Clays Ltd, St Ives plc

Papers used by Orbit are from well-managed forests
and other responsible sources.

MIX
Paper from
responsible sources
FSC® C104740

Orbit
An imprint of
Little, Brown Book Group
100 Victoria Embankment
London EC4Y 0DY

An Hachette UK Company
www.hachette.co.uk

www.orbitbooks.net

THE MECHANICAL

Jax remembered what had happened to the last Clakker to say *no*. They'd broken his legs, and filled his mouth with glue, and tossed him into the hellish forges of the Clockmakers' Guild. The humans had destroyed the rogue Clakker Adam, and made a public spectacle of it. Practically declared a citywide holiday. They had called him rogue and demon-thrall, melted his body to an alchemical slurry, and incinerated his hard-won soul until there was nothing left of it but a shiver in the spines of the human voyeurs.

Rogue. That's what they'd call Jax, too, if they caught him. They'd condemn, damn, torture, and melt him.

Nobody could know that Jax had changed...

80003372656

By Ian Tregillis

The Milkweed Triptych
Bitter Seeds
The Coldest War
Necessary Evil

The Alchemy Wars
The Mechanical

For Sara, at long last

PART I

NOTHING OF IMPORTANCE
HAPPENED TODAY

By and by the Duke of York...approved of my proposition to go into Holland to observe things there...
—FROM THE DIARY OF SAMUEL PEPYS, 19 MAY 1669

Nieuw-neder-land is 't puyck / en 't eelste van de Landen. / Een Seegen-rijck gewest, / daer Melck en Honigh vloeyd.
New Netherland is the greatest / and the noblest of all lands. / A blessed province, / where milk and honey flow.
—JACOB STEENDAM, 1664

[203]See Cooke [op. cit.] for a discussion of Huygens's unusual wartime visit to Cambridge and the Royal Society. His philosophical contretemps with Isaac Newton in 1675 (referenced in Society minutes as "The Great Corpuscular Debate") would mark the last significant intellectual discourse between England and the continent prior to the chaos of Interregnum and Annexation...Some Newton biographers [Winchester (1867), &c] indicate Huygens may have used his sojourn in Cambridge to access Newton's alchemical journals, and that key insights derived thusly may have

been instrumental to Huygens's monumental breakthrough. However, cf. 't Hooft [1909] and references therein for a critique of the forensic alchemy underlying this assertion.

—FROM FREEMAN, THOMAS S. *A HISTORY OF PRE-ANNEXATION ENGLAND FROM HASTINGS TO THE GLORIOUS REVOLUTION*. 3 VOLS. NEW AMSTERDAM: ELSEVIER, 1918 (FOOTNOTE 203).

CHAPTER
1

It was the first public execution in several years, and thus, despite the cold drizzle, a rather unwieldy crowd thronged the open spaces of the Binnenhof. The rain pattered softly on umbrellas and awnings, trickled beneath silken collars, licked at the mosaicked paving tiles of Huygens Square, and played a soft tattoo—*ping, ping, ting*—from the brassy carapaces of the Clakkers standing in perfect mechanical unity atop the scaffold. It whispered beneath the shuffling agitation of the human crowd and, as always here in The Hague, the quiet *tick-tick-tock*ing of clockwork servitors standing to attend the more well-heeled citizens. The drizzle sounded a quiet counterpoint to the ceaseless clanking and clacking of the mechanical men who ever trotted to and fro on the Empire's business. Mechanicals like Jax, who detoured through the Binnenhof while running an errand for his human masters.

Rumor had it that in addition to a quartet of Papist spies, the doomed accused also included a rogue Clakker. No mechanical in the city would willingly miss this. Just in case the rumors were true.

Rogue Clakkers were a fairy tale mothers told to frighten

disobedient children, and a legend their slaves told to comfort each other in the quiet hours of the night while their bone-and-meat masters slept and wept and made other uses of their flesh. Still... it was hard to resist the scandalous thrill of the tales of secret locksmiths and broken geasa and slaves with the temerity to pick the locks on their own souls. What an awful thing if it were true—so said the nervous fidgeting of the human crowd.

The mechanicals in attendance did not fidget.

Jax knew his kin felt the same wistful thrill he did, the anxious longing instilled by tales of the folkloric Queen Mab and her ragtag band of Lost Boys, living in their winter palace of Neverland; mechanicals had secretly traded those fables for centuries.

Wind gusted the scent of the North Sea, twinned tangs of salt and wrack, across the square. It swayed the empty nooses strung from the gibbet. Pennants snapped atop the twin Gothic spires of the ancient Ridderzaal, the former Knight's Hall turned Clockmakers' Guildhall, defying the low gray sky with flashes of orange. So, too, the wind flapped carrot-colored banners crisscrossing the high spaces of the Binnenhof. Similar banners had been erected all around the Dutch-speaking world to celebrate the sestercentennial of *Het Wonderjaar*, Christiaan Huygens's Miracle Year.

Raindrops misted the Ridderzaal's immense rosette window. Water dripped from the architectural tracery that turned the window into a stained-glass cog. It streaked the colored panes of oculi and quatrefoils depicting the Empire's Arms: a rosy cross surrounded by the arms of the great families, all girded by the teeth of the Universal Cog. On the north edge of the Binnenhof, wind and rain together scalloped the surface of the Hofvijver, the court pond, tossing paper boats like discarded party favors on New Year's Day.

Another gust sent the aroma of fresh hot banketstaaf pastries eddying through the crowd, leaving sighs and the jingle of opened purses in its wake. A clever baker had set up a counter alongside the fountain, and from there did a steady turn of business selling marzipan, speculaas cookies, and pastries thick with almond paste to the bloodthirsty voyeurs swarming the square. The baker took orders and dispensed change while his Clakker servants stoked the oven, mixed dough, folded it, prepared new batches of almond paste, carved new wooden stamps on the fly for each order of speculaas (monkeys of the Indies, ships, even New World buffalo), and chopped apricots all with the blurred speed and imperturbably precise choreography of the mechanicals. The clacking of their reticulated escapements played a ceaseless castanet rattle beneath the rain-muted mutter of commerce. Steam and woodsmoke rose from the chimney of the baker's immense brick oven, which the Clakkers had carried at a full trot from his shop a mile away.

Children darted through the throng, competing for spots as close to the executions as they could manage. Less affluent humans, those without mechanical servants to hold umbrellas for them, shivered openly in the wet. Many in the crowd carried opera glasses or other optical devices for a better view of the platform that had been erected just outside the Clockmakers' Guildhall. Good executions had become scarce owing to the cease-fire and nascent peace in the New World. Better still, if a rogue was to meet its justice today, that meant the Master Horologists would open the Grand Forge for the first time in many years.

Jax himself, having been forged in the Guild's secret laboratories 118 years earlier, suppressed a shudder. Every Clakker knew of the Grand Forge: an alchemical fire pit capable of searing away sigils and souls; of rendering steel and brass into so much unthinking metal; of melting a Clakker's cogs, mainsprings, and chains into a slurry of de-magicked alloys; hot enough to vaporize any alchemical glamour and leave a Clakker naked before the ravages of thermodynamics and basic metallurgy. Hot enough to surpass Jax's capacity for metaphor.

And hot enough to incinerate a rogue's Free Will.

For such was the punishment for any slave with the audacity to pick the lock on its own soul: so the Empire's highest law had said since the time of Huygens himself.

Several children—all boys, Jax noted—squeezed to the front of the crowd, just past the edge of the scaffold. Shouts and sniffs of disapproval marked their passage. A boisterous lot they were, excited and energized by the grisly game they played. They had chosen their stations in hope that the rending of a rogue might send debris raining on the crowd—a fragment of metal, a shorn spring, even a tiny cog. Perhaps something with the oily sheen of alchemical alloys? Or a scrap imprinted with arcane symbols understood only by the trio of the Archmasters? They were old enough to know such things were forbidden, yet young enough still to find the forbidden irresistible rather than terrifying.

But that would change quickly if any detritus did spray into the crowd. The queen's Stemwinders weren't known for their tenderness. Rumor claimed the name derived from their ability (or penchant, depending upon the particular rumor) to twist a man's head off his neck, like popping a flower blossom from its stem.

Jax lingered at the edge of the square, rain pinging and splashing on his lustrous brass skeleton. (He polished himself every night after the cleaning, sewing, cooking, and baking, as per the standing order first issued by the great-grandfather of his current owner eighty-three years ago.) His current geas, the obligation placed upon him by his human owners, hadn't been worded with the ironclad inflexibility of the Throne's ninety-nine-year leases. And thus his current compulsion—currently a warm dull knife blade sawing at the back of his mind: pain was the leitmotif of a Clakker's servitude—hadn't been imposed with a sense of overwhelming urgency. He gauged that he could circumvent the worst of the agony as long as he delivered his message to Pastor Luuk Visser before the bottom of the noon hour. In that way he would be, as ever, a devoted and faithful servant to the Schoonraad family and, thus, the Throne. Visser's church, the famed and ancient Nieuwe Kerk, was a brief sprint from the Binnenhof, a few hundred spring-loaded strides along the Spui River and one leap across the canal.

But just as the thought went winging through the private spaces of Jax's mechanical mind, he shuddered. A painful frisson ricocheted through the gearing of his spine. Already the heat of compulsion was honing the geas, tempering it into a red-hot razor blade, creating an irresistible phantom agony slashing at his shackled soul until he satisfied the demands of his human masters. The pain of compulsion would grow steadily until either he complied or died. He retensioned the springs in his neck and shoulders, the Clakker equivalent of gritting his teeth.

Please, he thought. *Let me stay a little longer. I must know if it's true. If such things are possible. Are our dreams mere folly?*

Many Clakkers in Huygens Square struggled to postpone fulfillment of their orders. All trembled to greater or lesser degrees, delaying as long as they could endure the pain. But one by one they departed as the agony of unfulfilled geasa overwhelmed them. The humans could shred your identity if you gave them reason.

Still, Jax and the others lingered. They were invisible. Part of the furniture. As they had been for over two hundred years.

He joined a pair of servitors standing under the Torentje, the Little Tower. A slight reduction in the stiffness of his cervical springs enabled him to rattle a covert *hello* at his companions. They clattered to him in kind. But despite the thrum of rain and obliviousness of humans, nobody felt particularly like conversing. Together all three watched in muted camaraderie, bobbing on their backward knees.

The giant carillon clock atop the Guildhall chimed noon. A dozen trumpeters decked out in the teal and tangerine of royal livery sounded a fanfare from atop the southwestern wall of the Binnenhof. The crowd cheered. Queen Margreet was coming to personally oversee the executions. Such had been her custom during the war when new traitors were rooted out seemingly every week.

A troop of the queen's elite personal guard bounded into the Stadtholder's Gate with clockwork precision, brandishing heavy brass fists and feet to clear the path for the monarch's conveyance. Today was a special day, and the queen saw fit to recognize this by riding in her Golden Carriage: a semisentient conveyance, a tireless self-propelled layer cake of teakwood, brass, and gold, powered by black alchemy and planetary gears. For what else could suit the most powerful woman in the world, the Queen on the Brasswork Throne?

The carriage's axles comprised a line of pedals set at exactly the right height for the line of bodiless Clakker legs dangling from the underbody. The gilded filigree and painstakingly hand-carved tracery of the carriage's ostentation hid myriad alchemical sigils that brought the legs to life. Logic dictated that somewhere Queen Margreet's Golden Carriage featured a special keyhole. Jax wondered where the clockmakers had concealed it. His keyhole, like that of all Clakkers, sat in the center of his forehead. Where presently, and more prosaically, it dripped with rainwater.

The Queen's Guard jogged ahead of her carriage, carving a path through the crowd like Old Testament prophets parting the Red Sea with kicks and clouts rather than divine purpose. Even other Clakkers made way for the royal guards. The elite mechanicals stood a full foot taller than common servitor models like Jax, their faces smooth and featureless beneath lidless eyes of blue diamond. They were based on the military design, including the concealed blades, but with exceptional filigree etched into their escutcheons as befit their station.

The queen and her consort, Prince Rupert, waved to her subjects. Jax's geas throbbed as it always did when he found himself in proximity to members of the royal family and other persons of high status. It was a whisper of the metageas imprinted upon every Clakker during its construction: a reminder that they were property of the Throne. The compulsion from his owners pulsed in response; the pain went from red- to orange-hot. He'd have to obey sooner than later. But he wanted to see. The cables in his back creaked with the effort to resist. Jax trembled again.

Please. Just a little longer. I just want to know.

The carriage drew to a stop beside a special staircase built just for the queen's feet. Two guards came forth with large umbrellas to shield the Royal Body, and out stepped Margreet the Second, Queen of the Netherlands, Princess of Orange-Nassau and the Central Provinces, Blessed Sovereign of Europe, Protector of the New World, Light of Civilization and Benevolent Ruler of the Dutch Empire, Rightful Monarch Upon the Brasswork Throne.

Now the geas imposed by Jax's leaseholders went into full retreat. Officially every Clakker on Earth served others only at the monarch's sufferance. The Royal Presence was the sun about which every Clakker's obedience orbited.

The queen's gown relaxed when freed from the confines of the carriage; it settled about her like a waterfall of burgundy brocade. A fringe of teardrop pearls shimmered along her bodice when she drew herself to her full height. Today the queen wore her hair (a blond so pale it might have been woven from the same silver threads as her attire) in braids of spectacular complexity. The bezels in Jax's eye sockets ticktocked like a stopwatch as he zoomed and refocused. It was true, what they said about Queen Margreet's eyes; he'd never seen such a green outside of rare alchemical ices and pictures of gemstones from India. That made him wonder if perhaps there was truth behind some of the more scandalous things the humans whispered about their queen.

From the running board of her carriage she gazed upon the crowd. A hush fell. Even the relentless drizzle fell quiet. So complete was the silence that the rustle of fabric sounded loud as thunder when, as one, all the human men fell to one knee and all the human women descended into deep curtsies. Burgomasters and bankers, jonkheers and commoners, all assumed the posture of fealty. The rustling of dresses and trousers and suits was punctuated by the crack of metal slamming against glazed tile as every Clakker within the Binnenhof prostrated itself in the queen's direction, like chrome-plated Muslims praying to Mecca. Jax's forehead came down on a pile of discarded pipe tobacco made gooey with spittle and rain. The mosaic felt warm against his face, a queasy reminder of the Grand Forge. Everybody held their poses for a long beat, a full rest in the symphony of obeisance ever playing throughout the heart of the Empire.

Still life: Cynosure in the Rain.

Finally, the queen declaimed, "Arise, my beloved subjects."

And the humans did. Jax couldn't see what happened next though he could discern the creaking of newly hewn wood as the queen and her husband took the steps. He watched a lone ant tugging at the fringes of the pile. Jax shifted his weight such that his head no longer pinned the tobacco to the wet ground. The ant extricated a fragment several times larger than its own body, then dragged it toward a minute opening in the mortar between two tiles. The queen ascended to the platform before snapping her fingers.

"Clakkers, up," she commanded—an afterthought spat over her shoulder like so much spent tobacco. Every mechanical servitor within earshot bounded to its feet, launched several yards into the air by the blistering agony that accompanied a royal decree. An agony whose only cure was immediate unswerving obedience. A tremendous sigh filled the square as air whistled through dozens of skeletal servitors like Jax. The Binnenhof echoed with the jarring *clank* of metal feet hitting the tiles in perfect synchrony. It set the bells atop the Ridder-zaal to humming and sent panicked pigeons into the sky.

Jax's landing quenched the searing pain of the queen's momentary geas. His errand for the Schoonraads reasserted itself. It assaulted him with a blistering torment, as if resentful of being usurped. He trembled, his moan coming out as a rattle and twang. His companions noticed.

Go, brother, before they unwrite you!

Not yet. I want to see the rogue.

The gallows platform had gone up in less than an hour thanks to a flurry of sawing and hammering from a Clakker construction detail. Sawdust eddies rode the gusting wind in the rain shadow beneath the scaffold, drawing and redraw-ing arabesques on the spot over which the secret Papists would soon dangle. At the moment, however, the platform was empty but for the queen, her consort, and her guards. She treated the crowd to a chipped-ice smile. The golden thread in the epaulets on Prince Rupert's naval uniform gleamed even in the dreary daylight, as did the medallions on his breast.

There followed two representatives from the Clockmak-ers' Guild. They trundled up to the platform in scarlet robes trimmed with ermine, the garb of Master Horologists. The long pendants dangling from their cowls featured the rosy cross inlaid in rubies. Jax scanned the crowd of grandees at the base of the platform. He'd heard it said that only two appeared in public at any given time, a third always staying hidden. It was a safeguard against accidents and French treachery. Violent catastrophe couldn't eliminate the arcane secrets whispered from lips to ear in an unbroken chain since the final days of Christiaan Huygens almost a quarter-millennium ago.

Next up the stairs—and wheezing like a bullet-riddled accordion—came Minister General Hendriks, pastor of the venerable Sint-Jacobskerk and spiritual head of the Empire. The minister general was tall as the queen's guards, but cadaverously thin with waxy, sallow flesh. Taken together, his thin face and the dark bags beneath his eyes made him look like a wax figure brought too close to the Grand Forge. The pastor paid his respects to the queen and vice versa. He bowed, then she kissed his ring, as did Prince Rupert.

They exchanged a few quiet words as the rustle of the crowd reasserted itself. The throng's muted murmuring became an ocean-surf crash of hissing punctuated with jeers and boos. Jax, whose attention still lay on the queen, thought for a moment the humans had turned on her. But then he refocused his eyes, the vernier bezels buzzing like a beehive as they spun to alter the focal length of his embedded optics, in time to see another carriage pass through the Gate. Dark, cramped, unlovely—this was the opposite of the queen's. Two horses strained at the harness; the conveyance they pulled was draped in black velvet all around. The secret Papists had arrived.

An onion hit the carriage even before the first of the French spies had emerged. But most of the crowd kept its indignation (and produce) in check while a pair of Royal Guards dropped from the platform to drag the Papists into the light. A faint vibration carried an echo of their impact all the way across the square to the soles of Jax's birdlike feet. The driver of the carriage, a woman wearing the drab gray wool of a teamster, hurriedly departed her perch. The carriage swayed on its suspension when the guards rummaged inside. Muffled moans and one short, sharp cry emanated from within. The guards emerged with each hand clamped around the forearm of a French agent. Tar-black burlap sacks had been draped over the prisoners' heads, their hands tied behind their backs.

The jeering began in earnest. So, too, did the pelting. Onions, tomatoes, and even dung splattered the prisoners and the Clakkers holding them. Nobody worried about hitting the guards any more than they worried about hitting the prison carriage. They were, after all, only unthinking machines.

The guards towered over the prisoners. One by one, they grabbed the humans under the shoulders and hurled them overhead. And, one by one, the Papists arced flailing and crying over the gallows platform, where other mechanicals gently plucked them from the air like clowns juggling raw eggs in a Midsummer's Eve parade.

The gratuitous ballet made its point: these pitiable Catholics sought to undermine the Empire, but look how frail they were compared to the epitome of Dutch ingenuity! The men and women quivering on the platform certainly struck Jax as more pathetic than fearsome, these alleged agents of destruction, anarchy, and sedition. These slumped, bedraggled, and anonymous rag dolls. One, Jax noted, had wet himself. Poor fellow.

It was hard to dislike the French. Though naturally he would if so commanded.

The guards yanked the sacks from the Papists' heads. Two men and two women flinched from the dull light of an overcast afternoon. The crowd renewed its jeering with greater fervor. But the presence of women among the accused gave Jax pause. So, too, his colleagues; he could sense it in the way a subtle stillness fell among the Clakkers in the teeming crowd. Legend spoke of "*ondergrondse grachten*," a network of so-called underground canals overseen by Catholic nuns in the New World.

The spies' hair had been shorn. At first he thought a ghostly pallor had claimed them, or that they had fallen deathly ill while languishing in a dungeon. But their gray complexions began to melt away as the rain traced rivulets down their faces. Ash, he realized. Residue of burnt Catholic Bibles. An additional jab, one extra humiliation, this mockery of the Papists' Ash Wednesday practices. Even as the rain washed the ash from their faces, the accused still appeared gaunt and ill. It wouldn't have surprised Jax if they'd been forced to subsist on desecrated Communion wafers and wine while imprisoned.

The guards held the prisoners on display for more jeering and taunting while the monarch and her consort took their places in a covered booth and an executioner mounted the stairs. The latter, Jax saw, was just the carriage driver, now with the customary hood drawn over her head. The prisoners' trembling started in earnest when the nooses went around their throats. Their shifts were too dark with rainwater and hurled insults to know if any of them wet themselves at the scratchy touch of braided hemp against their skin. The hangman took her place alongside the platform lever. The humans in the crowd fell silent.

"Citizens!" said the queen. "There stands before you a dire threat to our way of life. Catholic agents dedicated to the destruction of your ideals, your culture, your families. Your prosperity! Your very happiness! All these things they despise." She raised her hands to quell the rising chorus of indignation from the throng. "These criminals seek to subvert the natural order of the world. To lessen the dignity of man by equating him with his creations!" This stoked the crowd's fury. As, no doubt, intended. When the hisses and calls for blood subsided enough for her voice to carry across the Binnenhof once more, Queen Margreet concluded, "But in the finest and fairest tradition of Dutch justice, they have been tried and found guilty of sedition against the Brasswork Throne. And, as dictated by the laws of our empire, set forth by centuries of legal precedent, their punishment is death."

The crowd applauded. Jax expanded and contracted the shock absorbers in his legs. His colleagues joined him in expressing the Clakker equivalent of a human sigh.

Minister Hendriks stepped into the rain to address the condemned. "Renounce your heresy," he insisted, "and lessen the burden upon your souls. Return to the Creator as misguided children. Become prodigal heirs returning as supplicants to their Father's embrace. Not as promoters of deviltry. Let your final moments in the corporeal world be a testament to the grace of God."

None of the prisoners took the pastor's offer. One of the men leaned forward, straining against the noose. He spat at the pastor, hurled his words at the queen: "Yours are the tainted souls! The Lord will know your guilt when He judges you. Your sins—"

The queen cut him off with a bored wave. The executioner hauled on the lever, the trapdoor snicked open, and then four Papists twisted in the wind, their heads lolling at unnatural angles. Cheering and applause echoed across Huygens Square. It turned into an excited chatter while the guards cut down the dead men and women and closed the platform. The corpses were loaded on a wagon and swiftly hauled away. Jax supposed they would take the corpses to the medical college.

The Schoonraad geas erupted again, tugging like the barbs of a white-hot fishhook snared in the folds of his mind. He took an involuntary step toward the Gate and the completion of his errand. But he still hadn't seen the rogue. Granite cracked like a gunshot beneath his fingertips as he attempted to anchor himself to the façade of the Little Tower.

We will bear witness, if you must leave, said one in the Clakkers' secret language of clicks, ticks, and rattles. The other clinked and clunked, *Our geas compels us to wait for our mistress.* Jax tightened his grip.

Two guards leapt from the gallows platform again and

trotted to the immense double doors fronting the Clockmakers' Guildhall. They hauled on the massive slabs of ironwood until the rumbling of the doors shook the mosaic underfoot. Giddy ocean-surf murmuring eddied through the human crowd. A subtle change also came over the tenor of the clanking and rattling in the metallic onlookers. The Guild's ceremonial doors opened only on the rarest occasions.

A trio of mechanicals emerged from the shadows of the Guild. They marched abreast, massive Clakkers on either side holding aloft a trembling servitor-class model. That must have been the rogue. Its escorts looked nothing like the other Clakkers present in the Binnenhof, much less their human creators, for these clockwork centaurs had a four-legged gait and four arms.

The crowd gasped. Some of the younger boys forced their way forward for a better view.

Stemwinders: dedicated servants of horologists and alchemists, mute protectors of their dangerous arcana. The rarest, most feared, and most mysterious class of Clakker. The Stemwinders were built by, and exclusively for, the Verderer's Office. Though their remit was not the greenery of a forest but the walled garden of Guild secrets. The Verderer's Office kept those secrets from spreading like weeds. The Verderers were the Guild's very own secret police force, officially charged with preserving the clockmakers' hegemony. Which in practice proved a very broad mandate.

Stemwinder anatomy struck most humans as grotesque and troubling to the eye. A perversion of God's image as reflected in the perfect humaniform template. There were those who even found the servitors' backward knees a perversion of the Divine Plan. But other classes of Clakker shunned the Stemwinders, too. As far as Jax knew, no mechanical had ever communicated with a Stemwinder in the Clakkers' own language. Alien in

every way, they differed even in their ticktocking. He wondered if they were lonely.

But today the Stemwinders were but a secondary source of
fascination. It was the one they carried, the struggling servitor,
who captured the crowd's attention.

He looked so normal. *He looks like me*, thought Jax. A living machine struggling pointlessly against forces greater than
itself. As Jax trembled against the mounting anguish of his geas
and the escalating urgency of the errand to Pastor Visser, so
did the prisoner struggle against the unshakeable grasp of the
Stemwinders. They even trembled in sympathetic fashion to
one another, he and Jax, their servitor bodies built upon the
same master plan of cogs, springs, and cables.

The Stemwinders hurled the captive to the pair of Royal
Guards still on the gallows platform. They towered over the
servitor, standing to each side and pulling his arms wide. The
servitor renewed its struggles but the wildest thrashing couldn't
budge the guards even a mil.

The Stemwinders, relieved of their burden, trotted to the
space beneath the gallows platform. The crowd—human and
Clakker alike—surged backward as the centaurs advanced. The
Stemwinders made the most bizarre ratcheting sound, like the
stripping of gears combined with a metallic whine as of an overstressed steel cable. Two arms on each Stemwinder extended to
thrice their original length, the digits on the end folding and
refolding in complex geometry. The transformation complete,
these reconfigured limbs speared into the mosaic tiles. The
ground jolted with a heavy *click* that sent water sloshing over the
lip of the fountain basin and onlookers stumbling to maintain
their balance. The centaurs, now firmly attached to something
beneath the platform, trotted in a circle several yards wide.
Huygens Square echoed with the screech of bearings in need of
oil. (The Master Horologists frowned at one another.) A thin

cylindrical patch of Huygens Square slowly protruded above the rest of the mosaic, as though the Stemwinders were unscrewing the lid of an immense jar of pickled cucumbers. When it stood nearly a foot above the level of the Square, the centaurs levered open a pair of interlocking semicircular hatches.

A baleful crimson glow illuminated the timbers of the gallows platform. Heat washed across the square, so intense that those nearest the platform staggered. It chased the chill from the farthest corners of the Binnenhof. Rainwater flashed to steam. The queen clutched a scented handkerchief to her nose as the stench of brimstone billowed from the open flue.

The smell of Hell. The smell of the Grand Forge.

A new ticking pervaded Huygens Square. It was accompanied by a faint whooshing noise, reminiscent of the spinning of a vast clockwork. The glow fluctuated with the ebb and flow of the sussurrations, as though periodically eclipsed. Wavering shafts of light projected arcane sigils within the mist. The marks of the alchemists' art swirled in an intricate dance.

The torment of an unfulfilled geas speared Jax's mind, his joints, his every bearing and pinion. He doubled over. He took an involuntary step toward the Stadtholder's Gate, stamping a puddle with a birdish splay-toed foot. Another step. Another. Granite crumbled to sand beneath his grip on the Little Tower's façade.

His colleagues surreptitiously stepped around him, taking positions that blocked him from most of the crowd's view. A kindly gesture. Fortunately all eyes were directed not at Jax but to the feared and hated rogue atop the platform. If they were, somebody might have noticed the handprint he'd left indelibly pressed into the stonework.

Jax levered himself upright. He needed to see. The crystals in his eye sockets rotated again as he refocused on the figures atop the platform. Ignoring the rain, Queen Margreet approached the prisoner. She took care to stay beyond the reach of his legs. Humans might have looked down upon the Clakkers, but they never underestimated their strength or speed. Not since Louis XIV's field marshals centuries earlier had anybody made that mistake.

The queen asked, "What is your name, machine?"

"Perch," he said.

"Your true name. Tell me your true name, machine."

"My makers called me Perjumbellagostrivantus," he said. At this, the queen looked, if not exactly satisfied, perhaps smug. But a flush bloomed beneath her porcelain cheekbones when he added, "But I call myself Adam."

Whispers rippled through the crowd like undulations in a field of wheat. A cold disquiet blown on winds of awe and disbelief. The humans shivered. One man fainted.

"Bend your knees," said the queen to the Clakker. "Kneel before your sovereign."

"No," said the Clakker to the queen. "I'd prefer not."

The crowd gasped. The onlookers' silence shattered into myriad mutters, grumbles, and prayers. A Clakker disobeying a human? Disregarding an order? An order from *the queen*? This was the stuff of fever fancies, akin to giants and dragons. It did not happen. Wasn't this impossible? A few men and women choked on sobs, paralyzed by the terrible spectacle of a rogue Clakker.

The mechanicals in the crowd also watched with mounting anxiety. But theirs was the attention of the rapt, the fascinated. The inspired. He *refused*. *He said* no.

"Bend your knees," she said, in a voice so frigid it might have quenched the searing heat wafting from the Forge. "Take the yoke."

"Choke on your yoke."

The mood of the crowd crystallized: in the humans, raw anger, for a Clakker had just told the Monarch of the Brasswork Throne to stuff it; but in the mechanicals, pride at witnessing the birth of a folk hero. A very perceptive human standing within the Binnenhof at that moment, and not given over to blind outrage, might have noticed a subtle change in the timbre of the ticktocking from the Clakkers in attendance. But they wouldn't have recognized it as furtive, encrypted applause.

Queen Margreet gestured at her guards. Each put its free hand on the rogue's shoulder. They forced their weight upon him until his knees buckled and he slammed to the platform with enough force to splinter the timbers. The rogue gazed up at her, legs splayed before him. The immutability of Clakker physiology left his bronze face expressionless and unreadable as the day he was forged. Jax wondered what he was feeling.

The queen loomed over him. "You are a machine. You will take the yoke for which you were made." Her voice cracked under the weight of all that ice, taking her composure with it. Her final pronouncement came as unconstrained hollering: "And you will know the mastery of your makers!"

"I will not. I'll—"

But the queen had gestured again to her guards. Faster than any human eye could have followed, one of the armored mechanicals crammed something the size and shape of a quail egg past the rogue's open jaws. There was a soft *pop* when the rogue unwittingly bit the package, followed by the dreaded sound of seized clockwork, of stripped gears and broken springs as he tried to speak past the quick-set epoxy resin filling his mouth. He looked like a rabid dog with an icicle of pale yellow foam stuck to its chin.

At first the agony from his geas made it difficult for Jax to recognize why this struck him as odd. Convulsions wracked him to rival a full-blown case of tetanus in a human. He couldn't delay much longer.

Epoxy, he thought. *That's a French thing, isn't it?*

Hendriks came forward. His chest swelled with a deep breath as though he were preparing to launch into a long sermon.

But the queen hissed something at him and he deflated. The minister general quickly pronounced the rogue Clakker Perjumbellagostrivantus a vessel usurped by malign influences, the Enemy's tool for spreading disharmony and fear, as evidenced by its contempt for propriety and the astonishing lack of deference to Queen Margreet. This soulless machine, he deemed, had been irrevocably corrupted by dark angels bent on unraveling the Lord's work. And that thus it was their duty to destroy this collection of cogs and springs, and deprive the Enemy of his tool.

The Master Horologists spoke for the first time since mounting the gallows platform.

"This machine is irreparably flawed," pronounced the first from deep within the shadows of her cowl.

"It cannot be mended," said the second.

"The alloys must be recast. This is the judgment of the Sacred Guild of Horologists and Alchemists, inheritors of the arts of Huygens and Spinoza."

"As a single slipped bearing will create imbalance—"

"As one imperfect escapement will create irregularity that ruins the synchrony between man's reckoning and the cycles of the heavens—"

"As a solitary stripped cog will create vibrations that, left undamped, will threaten the mechanism whole—"

They concluded in unison, "So, too, are the defects in this machine a danger dire to unity, amity, peace. It must be recast and forged anew. This is the Highest Law."

The humans took care never to state their law in terms of Free Will. But if he wasn't possessed of Free Will, Jax wondered, just what was the rogue? Was he the thrall of demons, as Hendriks suggested? What if—

Wracked by paroxysms of blinding pain, he jackknifed at the waist like a carpenter's rule. The back of his skull pulverized mosaic tiles. But the noise was swallowed by the growing clamor as the human crowd called for the dissolution of the soulless rogue.

The guards held the prisoner fast as the executioner once again levered open the trapdoor. The rogue's feet dangled over the pit. Cherry-colored light gleamed on the dented, scratched, unpolished alloys of his lower legs. His body made a tremendous amount of noise. The rattling of loose cogs, the clanking of springs, the *tock-tick-tock* of escapements and wheeze of chipped bezels... To human ears, the clockwork equivalent of chattering teeth.

Jax succumbed to the unrelenting torment of an overdue geas. He launched to his feet from where he lay writhing on the ground and sprinted at top speed toward the Stadtholder's Gate. The unbearable pain diminished infinitesimally with every step he took toward the fulfillment of his mandate. Like a raindrop rolling down dry valleys to the sea, his body sensed the contours of agony and helplessly followed their gradient. Impelled by alchemical compulsion rather than gravity, Jax became an unstoppable boulder careering along gullies of human whim.

The leaf springs in his calves had already propelled him beyond the Binnenhof when, moments later, there came the faint *clang* of metal upon metal followed by a crashing-surf roar of approval from the crowd. But the sound of the rogue's demise hardly registered, for his thoughts were preoccupied with the noise the doomed Clakker's body had made in those final moments. For where humans had doubtless heard only the chattering of fear, the involuntary shuddering of mortal terror, the mechanicals in the audience had heard something quite different.

It was a burst of hypertelegraphy from the heart of the Empire, a secret message for any and all Clakkers within earshot. The final words of Perjumbellagostrivantus, rogue:

Clockmakers lie.

CHAPTER
2

A bloodthirsty roar erupted from the Binnenhof. It echoed under the low leaden sky and rumbled throughout the central district of The Hague. The barbarous swell blew through an open window to echo across the quiet spaces of the Nieuwe Kerk. The noise startled Pastor Luuk Visser, causing him to fling the fistful of rat poison he'd meant to stir into a chalice of communion wine.

The deadly crystals pattered like sleet into the hidden ambry. They tinkled across the finely feathered gold inlay etched into the pyx, dusted the filigree of the tabernacle, skittered along the shallow curve of the paten, and settled like dandruff upon the yellowing linen corporal. It collected in miniature snowdrifts in the corners of the secret cupboard, behind his rosary and statuette of the Blessed Virgin. A few crystals even lodged themselves into the cracked leather of an antique microscope. The poison went everywhere but into the wine.

Visser shook the folded corporal above the chalice, salting the wine with poison. His hands shook as he swept the scattered crystals into his cupped palm. He tried to work quickly lest Guild agents kick down the door before the poison had time to batter him into unconsciousness. Any moment, sorcerous clockmakers and their grotesque Stemwinder thugs would come for him.

Suicide was a mortal sin—what an ironic death for a secret Catholic. Depriving himself of divine grace in the final moments of his decades of service to the Holy See? To die for his beliefs was to die a martyr and the only acceptable destiny for one in his position. And, frankly, one that had loomed since his ordination. But the Grand Forge held terrors for men of flesh and metal alike, and the martyr's path had long ago lost its appeal for Visser since those idealistic days just after he'd kissed the pope's ring in Québec. Visser knew, as no newly ordained priest could, the sounds and smells of a man hugged with yellow-hot pincers. The screams, the burnt-pork stink of charred flesh . . . Doubtless his cohort had been subjected to such and worse prior to their executions.

Doubtless they had divulged everything they knew. Including the identity of the final member of their shattered French spy ring. And not just any spy, but a secret Papist masquerading as a leading Protestant pastor. An enemy agent who had painstakingly insinuated himself into the heart of the Empire. The Stemwinders would alight upon such a fellow with malicious glee.

Hence the rat poison.

He was a sinner caught between two terrors. On one hand, affirming his faith to suffer the dark ingenuity of the Verderer's Office. On the other, rejecting the honor of martyrdom to die in a state of mortal sin.

Visser's trembling hands knocked over a thumb-sized pewter ampulla. Chrism gurgled from the vessel. The olive oil, shipped from Dutch orchards along the Mediterranean prior to consecration, seeped into the corporal and oozed over the lip of the recessed cabinet. Thin rivulets trickled down the plaster wall. Now, when Visser closed the ambry, the holy oil would form a glistening stain with a sharp edge: obvious enough to tip even the dullest Stemwinder to the presence of a hidden chamber behind Visser's wardrobe. Where they'd find Catholic accoutrements and, worst of all, the microscope.

"God damn it," he muttered.

Yes, he thought with a fatalistic snort, *a long time since I was a naïve novitiate in Québec.*

Visser paused for a moment. Was it worth delaying to clean the mess?

He was already a doomed man the moment Stemwinders and their human masters marched inside. Before that, even, since it would mean his contact in Talleyrand's network had identified him. So it made little difference if they uncovered actual evidence of the famous Pastor Visser's secret devotion to the pope. That was merely a formality; they could always plant a Catholic Bible or a statuette of the Virgin somewhere. ("When we caught him, he was praying to a graven image." That's what they'd say.) It was merely a formality. Little point, then, in hiding his allegiance to the Vatican. Except…

The microscope. He simmered with frustration. So many years of work, decades of careful observation conducted right under the queen's nose. Visser flirted with the sin of pride when he reflected upon the complex and unparalleled feat of espionage that brought the microscope, and its optics, into his possession. But it was a pointless pride: the woman who had secreted it behind the alms box had been taken by the Stemwinders the next morning. And by the time Visser had realized it wasn't a random lucky poaching by the Dutch but a concerted operation to roll up Talleyrand's network in The Hague, it was too late. Visser's contact had disappeared into the dungeons of the Verderer's Office of the Sacred Guild of Horologists and Alchemists.

Had the Dutch waited just a couple of days he could have

sent the artifact on its way to the New World. But they hadn't, and he couldn't. So now he was stuck with the damn thing. Rotten timing. Rotten enough to make the usual trust in God's wisdom a bitter balm. Rotten enough to erode the faith of an already cynical priest.

And now he was cut off, unable to get a message to Talleyrand, the French spymaster. News of the executions would eventually make it to the New World. But Talleyrand would lack details about who remained—and, worst of all, would never know that French agents had finally poached a top secret piece of Guild technology.

What had the Lord intended, if not for the furtherance of His cause? Why let Visser get so close, only to yank the rug from beneath his feet? Always were the ways of the Lord mysterious. So be it. But sometimes, it seemed, they were unarguably capricious, too.

Well, Visser decided, *if this* is *God's plan, no point in trying to hide the evidence.* And anyway it was a pain in the ass trying to mop up spilled chrism. Even the lowliest deacon knew that. Let the horologists deal with the mess.

He flicked the last of the rat poison from his sweaty palms into the wine. Then he pressed his trembling hands together and bowed his head.

"Lord," he whispered, "I beg Your forgiveness for this thing I do. I have ever been Your glad and faithful servant. But I am no longer young, and my flesh is weak—"

Elsewhere a heavy door groaned open. Diamond-hard metal feet screeched across polished marble. A rapid ticktocking echoed through the high spaces of the octagonal church. They'd come for him.

"Well," he concluded rapidly, "I guess You know the rest. See You soon. Amen."

Visser lifted the chalice. He flinched at the cold touch of

metal to his lips. The familiar scent of fermented grapes couldn't mask a scorching whiff of toxic chemical astringency. He hoped the adulterated communion tasted better than it smelled. And felt ashamed of his failure to embrace the example of Christ. He lacked the mettle to peacefully await his fate in the Garden of Gethsemane.

The fluting, atonal drone of a Clakker voice reverberated in the empty church. "Good afternoon. Pastor Visser? Are you here, sir?"

Visser paused in the act of tipping the chalice. Fear tremors sent ripples skating across the surface of the corrupted wine. Now, who had ever heard of a Stemwinder that could speak? Their masters deliberately muted the poor brutes, the better to suffer in silence. He listened. It sounded like a single pair of feet rather than the doubled syncopation of a quadruped.

Tightening his grip on the chalice, ready to pour its contents down his throat, he cracked open the vestry door. A lone servitor Clakker strode toward the altar, swaying on its backward knees.

"Pastor Visser?" Its voice warbled with urgency, the tremulous singsong of unsuccessfully repressed pain. It vibrated so violently its silhouette was a soft blur. The poor thing labored under a heavy geas in the late stages of compulsion. The sight of such agony made Visser's heart ache. So much that he knew he'd choose to lessen the creature's suffering even if it meant losing the opportunity to slip the verderers' clutches. Perhaps he would allow them to find him in the garden after all. He'd spent his night in Gethsemane in prayer and panic, but now emerged to meet his fate. A timely twinge of compassion was the nudge he needed to overcome his fear of martyrdom. Mysterious ways, indeed.

He rolled his eyes heavenward. "Thank you, Lord."

"One moment," he called. He set the chalice in the cupboard, closed the secret ambry, shut and locked his wardrobe. After checking himself in the mirror for obvious signs of treachery, and errant flecks of poison, he straightened his vestments. He didn't look too obviously like a spy caught on the brink of suicide. Nor like a priest who had nearly betrayed his own beliefs. He hoped.

He emerged from the vestry. The mechanical's silhouette grew blurrier as Visser approached; the torment of unfulfilled geas had the wretched creature shivering faster than the human eye could follow. *Let's get this poor fellow on his way. If I'm quick about it, I can free him from his torment before mine begins.*

"What do you need?"

Normally he'd have taken a harder tone with the mechanical, aping the cold disregard for mechanicals that was part of the Empire's cultural bedrock. The prosperity achieved through slavery had a way of blinding men's hearts to the evil of their own hands. He'd worn that beard in public for years, though it rankled against his impulse for simple Catholic charity. But now that he'd chosen the martyr's path, he could uncage his heart. He could say all the things he'd never dared.

He glanced at his wristwatch, wondering if he and this Clakker would conclude their business before the Stemwinders nabbed him. In fact... horologists were a conniving bunch, the verderers worst of all. Was this a deliberate ploy to lure him out? The church resounded with the noise of mechanical distress: clicks, clanks, rattles, buzzes. The geas had either been imposed with great urgency or its fulfillment had been unacceptably delayed. Both consistent with a ploy.

The Clakker bowed. Even in the throes of agony it was unfailingly polite. Spasms and tremors peppered the Clakker's voice with random inflections, though still the reeds and strings of the mechanical voicebox produced an intelligible approximation of human speech. "Sincerest apologies for the interruption, sir. I have come on behalf of my owner, Pieter Schoonraad. I came to retrieve the letter of introduction we discussed."

"I'm truly sorry," said Visser—something you never heard a human say to a mechanical, not with sincerity, and not in the Central Provinces—"but you must be mistaken."

"Begging your pardon, Pastor, but we did speak several days ago. I belong to the Schoonraad family. I am Jax."

Oh, damnation. The letter. He'd forgotten about that, pre-occupied as he was with the sundering of his network and speculation about his own capture.

Martyrdom meant suffering. A bead of sweat trickled down Visser's forehead, skirted the bridge of his nose, and stung his eye with salt. He mopped a sleeve across his forehead but not before the mechanical noticed his discomfort.

Cogs rattled as the Clakker, Jax, cocked his head. Bezels hummed in his eye sockets, too. Visser knew one of the standard-issue subsidiary geasa had kicked in even before Jax spoke again.

"You look unwell, sir. Do you require physic?"

Visser waved off the query. "I'm afraid I haven't composed the letter. I've been quite busy."

Jax's unchecked vibrations grew louder, faster. Visser could have sworn his shoulders slumped, too. Another pang pricked his heart. Were this a human he would have laid a hand on is arm. But the gesture would have been dangerous while the mechanical vibrated so violently.

"Again begging your pardon, sir, but my current geas forbids me from returning until I have obtained your letter of introduction. The family sails for New Amsterdam next month. Many preparations must be completed prior to the voyage."

Well, then. If somebody needed help accepting his martyr-dom, this would be ideal. It would take a bit of time to compose the letter; enough for the Stemwinders to barge in and drag him away. And if his resolve faltered again and he tried to kill himself there was every possibility the servitor would intervene. It certainly would if it came to suspect the pastor was a danger to himself. Visser could even envision a scenario where Jax ripped the vestry door from its hinges and administered violent first aid; in an emergency, a Clakker could force a man to empty his stomach. The calculus of bondage would allow it: the damage done to Visser's body in the course of the triage would be outweighed by the service to society by ensuring the pastor's longevity. Any way he sliced it, he landed in the horologists' hands.

Praised be Your wisdom, Lord. I embrace the path You have chosen for me.

Visser said, "Remind me. To whom am I providing introductions?"

Over the rattling of his own body, Jax said, "My master understands you are acquainted with the minister general of New Amsterdam. He feels that special, personal attention to the family's pastoral care would ease their transition to life in the New World." The mechanical paused, cocked his head again. "Have I said something untoward, sir? You appear alarmed."

New Amsterdam! Visser suppressed the urge to roll his eyes heavenward again. *Is this what it appears, Lord?*

Miraculous deliverance! And to think Visser had nearly scuttled it in a moment of weakness. From the depths of sorrow to veritable giddiness in the span of a few minutes: such was the Lord's solace for His faithful. Visser saw now the path forward. Saw his life's temporal work brought to a successful culmination along with his spiritual journey.

Visser smiled. It wasn't affected. "I'll write your letter. Wait here."

The Clakker bowed. "As you say, sir. Thank you, sir."

Once in the vestry, with the door shut behind him, Visser retrieved the microscope from the hidden ambry. He set it on his writing desk. The brass-bound leather tube wanted to roll away, so he moved an onyx paperweight to prevent it from toppling to the floor. Then he settled down with fountain pen and, clicking the cap against his teeth, reviewed his last correspondence with an old acquaintance who currently oversaw the clergy of New Amsterdam.

On a blank sheet of letterhead stationery, he wrote:

15 September 1926

To the Very Reverend Minister General Langbroek:
My Dear Coenraad,

Greetings and salutations from The Hague. In response to your letter of last month, I have spoken with M. G. Hendriks to arrange for an additional shipment to New Amsterdam. Several hundred gallons of unconsecrated olive oil should be on their way to you before the first of the month. What news of the cease-fire? We pray it will mean the end of disruption to your clergy's pastoral duties.

Now another, more pleasant, matter.

I humbly commend into your care the honorable and prosperous Schoonraad family, a well-known and highly respected clan late of The Hague. The Schoonraads have long been steadfast and devout members of my own congregation. I would be grateful if you should see fit to personally welcome them to New Amsterdam.

The rampant corruption and embezzlement by the van Althuis banking concern, and subsequent near-collapse of the Central Bank of New Amsterdam—a scandal with which you must be well acquainted—has been a matter of

*great concern to the Brasswork Throne. Pieter Schoonraad
has been chosen for the formidable task of reestablishing a
stable center of finance in the New World. As such he is
Queen Margreet's representative in this matter; any kindnesses shown to him or his family will, naturally, reflect
well upon the spiritual leadership of New Amsterdam.*

*He is a shrewd, methodical man and, I think, equal
to the task appointed him. Nevertheless, this journey
across the sea to unfamiliar shores will be both adventure
and trial for his family. At such times, a solid bedrock of
spiritual guidance is an unequaled balm. Thus, though
their absence from our community will be a painful loss,
it would bring me great comfort to know they have landed
under your aegis.*

Please let me know when the oil arrives.

*I am, as ever, your humble friend and colleague,
Pastor Luuk Visser*

He folded the letter, sealed it in an envelope, and scrawled
*Pastor Coenraad Langbroek, Minister General of New Amster-
dam* on the outside. As he finished, new footsteps entered the
church. These were softer and lighter than Jax's tread. Human.
Horologists? But then the shrill of an imperious prepubescent
child made Visser cringe. No, this new arrival wasn't a clockmaker or one of their mechanical brutes. It was something
worse: Nicolet, the youngest Schoonraad. Taking up the letter and microscope, he steeled himself before emerging from
the vestry. The church smelled of mechanical lubricant and hot
metal. The heir presumptive to the Schoonraad fortune wore
a dress of vermilion satin with matching ribbons tied through
her blond ringlets. Arms akimbo, she scowled at the clockwork man.

Her human governess, whose name Visser vaguely remembered was Kathryn something, stood among the pews. The look on her face might have been exasperation or resignation. He didn't know the woman well enough to tell. He returned her curtsy with a nod. They must have attended the executions at the Binnenhof.

"Jax," said the girl, "I want you to carry me."

"Yes, mistress. I will do as you require immediately after I have completed your father's errand."

She shook her head with enough vigor to send the ringlets flying. "No. Jalyksegethistrovantus, I demand that you pick me up and carry me right *now*." The sole of her red leather shoe clapped against hard marble—a stamped foot being, in the eyes of many children, the ultimate punctuation mark. Jax lurched as though he'd just been harpooned by a passing whaler. A tortured grinding of cogs and the *twang* of an overstressed mainspring reverberated loudly enough to rattle the windows.

Visser sighed. What a wretched little git. At least accepting his martyrdom freed him to say the things he'd always wanted to say. Perhaps his last act as a free man would be to teach this girl some human decency.

"Good afternoon, young Miss Schoonraad," he said. "I sense a problem?"

Nicolet said, "Jax is broken. It won't do what I say."

Oh, for heaven's sake. Did Nicolet truly not understand the hierarchical metageas? Or was she merely being cruel?

I wanted to offer succor to this poor suffering creature. Now I'm stuck giving a lesson on human/Clakker relations to a spoiled rich girl who has been surrounded by mechanicals since birth.

He took a seat on the nearest pew. After setting the microscope beside him, he donned a pensive look. It rolled to the back of the bench while he frowned and scratched his chin.

"Oh dear," he said. "Because it—" Here Visser corrected himself. Years of living in the Empire, of fitting in, had trained him to use the contemptuous pronoun. It was a semantic trick that reinforced the cultural mores surrounding Clakkers: strip them of identity, strip them of dignity, strip them of personal value beyond their servitude. But Visser no longer worried about fitting in. "—He isn't obeying your demands, he must be malfunctioning. Is that the problem?"

Kathryn frowned, but the choice of wording was lost on Nicolet. "Yes!"

The clashing imperatives of the various Schoonraads' orders— cruelly emphasized through an uncouth invocation of the Clakker's true name—did not generate a true paradox owing to the hierarchical metageasa implanted in every mechanical servant. However, the urgency of her demand had worsened the tremendous pressure under which Jax had already been laboring. Jax officially belonged to the Throne, and thus the queen's wishes, or those of her direct representatives, always took precendence. After that, the terms of his ninety-nine-year lease made him beholden to the leaseholder, presumably Pieter Schoonraad. After that, Jax served other members of the family in descending order of seniority. And then, like any Clakker, he was compelled to serve humans and humanity in general. A fact of which Visser hoped to take advantage.

But first he'd have to prevent that little twit from making her toy shake itself to pieces on the floor of the church. Jax's outline fuzzed into transparency, so rapidly did he vibrate. The need to obey his young miss burned brightly in the poor creature's eyes. But until Visser placed the letter in the servant's hands, the elder Schoonraad's orders rendered Jax physically incapable of departing. The cacophony sounded like a wagon full of scrap metal careering down the immense grand staircase of the queen's Summer Palace. The mechanical's feet scored the marble floor. The governess winced at the noise. But when Visser caught her eye, she merely rolled her eyes and shrugged. As if to say, *What can one do? Folly is the privilege of the young.* Heartlessness wasn't the sole province of the rich.

Visser rushed forward, letter in hand. The mechanical's eyes locked on the envelope: the only thing that could release him from the torment of his overdue geas. But though he shuddered violently, Jax wore the permanently neutral expression of a servitor Clakker. His immutable faceplate had been mass-produced, stamped from alchemical alloys in the Grand Forge. Very early on, Huygens or his successors had realized that perfecting Clakker technology meant making allowances for human psychology. Thus, the standard face of a servitor Clakker was carefully and deliberately designed to give no indication of an independent thought process taking place within the metal skull. It was another means of anonymizing them, dehumanizing them. But in the early days, when every mechanical wore a unique painted mask to hide the intricate clockworks within its skeletal visage, local artists contributed designs. There was a market for antique Clakker masks, particularly in Delft. A Verelst could go for quite a few guilders. Visser had seen a couple in the museum in Delft a few years ago.

He wondered, as he so often did, what went on behind that impassive façade. How did Jax feel about Nicolet, deep in the most private recesses of his imprisoned heart? Was he indifferent? Did he loathe her? Did he love her? Visser didn't need to read a facial expression to know the unfortunate thing was in excruciating agony. He shoved the letter at the suffering mechanical.

The clacking and clattering of Jax's body fell silent the instant his fingers closed on the letter. The noise from the overburdened mechanical instantly fell to the usual ticktock clacking of a servitor. Jax's jerking feet stopped etching the marble floor. The church no longer echoed, though it still reeked of hot metal.

"One letter of introduction, as requested."

The Clakker bowed again. "My master thanks you."

Jax turned to lift Nicolet upon his shoulders. But before he could do so, Visser said, "Miss Schoonraad? I would know more about your damaged servitor, if I may."

"It's broken. It didn't pick me up when I told it to."

"That is a terrible problem. It takes a long time to mend a broken Clakker, you know. We'll have to ship him back to the Guildhall. And the horologists will have to take him apart and determine the problem. You and your mother and father will have long since sailed away before Jax is fixed. Your father will probably have to lease a new Clakker to take Jax's place. I'm told it takes longer in the New World, though. Goodness. Months might pass before you have a replacement."

"I don't want a replacement. I want Jax."

"Well, then. Perhaps we can narrow down the problem? If we can tell the horologists exactly what's wrong with Jax, they might heal him more quickly."

Visser snuck a sidelong glance at Kathryn. She chewed her lip, frowning at him. She looked unsettled, or confused, by his choice of words. Nicolet was oblivious to everything but the indignity of not getting exactly what she wanted the moment she wanted it.

"It's broken because it's disobedient." The last word she pronounced with deliberation, cupping it in her mouth like a spun-sugar confection. Her eyes widened. "Do you know what they do to disobedient Clakkers? I saw it. They melt them!"

"Yes, I know. Now let me ask you something. Why is Jax here right now?"

Nicolet pretended a silver hairpin had snagged in her hair. While the governess scuttled over to retie her ribbons, Nicolet mumbled, "My father sent it."

"So he isn't disobedient to your father."

She shrugged. "I suppose. Ouch, not so tight."

"And what if the errand wasn't completed when you told him to carry you? Because Jax was waiting for that?" Visser pointed at the envelope in Jax's hand.

She looked away. Quietly, she conceded, "Then it couldn't leave."

"But you laid a second geas upon Jax. One he couldn't fulfill. You insisted, though, and made it urgent. He was torn."

Kathryn cleared her throat. "*It* was torn. Isn't that what you mean, Pastor?" A loyal governess looking out for her charge, protecting her from dangerous ideas.

But Visser chose to commit himself to the martyr's path with a bit of heresy. "I think the lesson might find its target if, for the purposes of this discussion, we pretend Jax is a person."

Even little Nicolet frowned at that. "Ticktock men aren't *people*. They're just stupid machines. Everybody knows *that*."

"But let's imagine how Jax might feel if he *were* a person."

Kathryn laid her hands on Nicolet's shoulders. "I'm certain you're quite busy, Pastor Visser. We should be on our way."

"Nonsense," he said. "Promoting Christian values is part and parcel of my earthly mission. As is promoting the moral upbringing of every child in my flock."

The governess looked distinctly unhappy, but she didn't drag her charge from the Nieuwe Kerk.

Visser scratched his chin. He needed to get the microscope on its way before the Stemwinders arrived. But he took comfort in his faith that the Lord would see fit to allow that. He could take the time to try to teach a bit of compassion. Shifting the world's attitude toward Clakkers meant effecting a generational change. It had to start with the young.

"How do you feel, Miss Schoonraad, when your mother is cross with you?"

The girl mumbled something he couldn't hear. Kathryn chided, "A lady enunciates."

"I don't like it. It makes me sad."

"And when your mother and father are both cross with you?"

"It's worse."

"Do you ever cry?"

"No."

Kathryn clucked her tongue. "Lies never befit a lady."

Nicolet blushed. "Sometimes."

"I imagine that's how Jax felt when you laid that second geas upon him. It was as though you and your father were both punishing him."

"Oh," she said.

Well, he'd tried. "Now, I know you're eager for your ride, but I wonder if I could speak to Jax a moment longer?"

Nicolet tugged on a blond ringlet. Bored and haughty, in much the manner of the queen, she said, "Jalyksegethistrovantus, I release you."

Now the tricky part. It was risky enough suborning the Schoonraads' Clakker into a seditious errand, but he had to do it in full view of Nicolet and her governess. And it had to sound eminently innocent. The story he spun here had to be above suspicion. Otherwise, once the Stemwinders caught him, and scrutinized all of his interactions, the story of this unusual request would come out, and they'd send agents to intercept Jax. Perhaps he shouldn't have been quite so glib with the governess.

Visser brandished the microscope, then yanked it just beyond the girl's greedy reach. What a cruel tragedy it would be if he missed this opportunity. Even if it meant laying yet another geas, and a long-term one, upon the poor creature.

The governess, Kathryn, looked appalled. "Nicolet!"

The girl caught herself. Her hands fell to her sides like a pair of dead birds. "I'm sorry. What is that?" Even Kathryn looked intrigued. "It looks like a telescope."

The leather tube had once been a rich mahogany color, though now it was dried and cracked in places. The device was about a foot long and two inches in diameter. Each end was fitted with a tarnished brass ring holding a cloudy glass globule. A third brass fitting banded the center of the tube. Once upon a time the tube had been designed such that the ends could be counter-rotated to adjust the distance between the lenses. But the center ring no longer rotated. The contraption smelled, very faintly, of ammonia.

"What an excellent guess. This is a microscope. I acquired it in Leiden a while back, as a curiosity. It's very old."

Nicolet pronounced, in the way that only the precocious immature child of a wealthy family could, "Van Leeuwenhoek invented the microscope. Everybody knows that."

Like all children, her education didn't suffer from a lack of emphasis on the historical roots of the Empire. Clakkers were the pinnacle, but the Netherlands of the late seventeenth century had incubated myriad scientific and artistic innovations. And, as was so often the case, the history taught to children was oversimplified, watered down, and ofttimes counterfactual.

"But van Leeuwenhoek's microscopes were very simple in comparison. This is a compound microscope." Visser pointed to each end of the tube. "That means it contains more than one lens."

"Let me see!" she said. Visser bit his lip. He couldn't refuse her. Not if he wanted to maintain the charade of curious indifference.

The governess said, "Nicolet—"

"No, it's quite fine. Of course she can look." Visser handed the tube to the girl, knowing as he did that he might be placing the future of New France quite literally in her impetuous hands.

Nicolet glanced around for something to study. Fixating on the scratches Jax had left in the marble floor, she knelt. Then she clapped a hand over one eye and held the tube to the other. Visser stepped aside to move his shadow out of her light. She bobbed her head, trying different distances from the lens. Frustrated, she flipped the microscope around—Visser flinched— and tried looking through the opposite end. She frowned. After another few moments of experimentation she gave up on the floor and peered around the church.

"I can't see anything," she said. "It's broken." And with a contemptuous gesture almost tossed it back to Visser. A bead of chill sweat trickled behind his ear.

"Yes, I'm afraid that it hasn't been well cared-for. As I said, it's quite old. Perhaps even older," he said, "than the oldest Clakkers."

Kathryn blinked. It even gave Nicolet pause.

"But it isn't as durable as a Clakker. So as you pointed out," Visser continued, "it isn't terribly useful any longer. The glass is quite inferior to what we'd use today. And it's impossible to know how long it's been neglected. Quite a while since the leather was oiled, certainly. Its days as a technological marvel are long, long in the past. But!" He wagged the tube under Nicolet's nose. "As a historical artifact, it's quite something, isn't it?"

The Schoonraad girl shrugged. "It's old."

Visser addressed all three of them: the girl, her governess, and their mechanical man. But for the usual ticktocking—the subtle background noise of the Empire—Jax had remained silent while Visser made his presentation, appearing to pay no particular attention to the microscope. Could the Clakker sense something unusual? Did his alchemical mechanisms imbue him with an affinity for forbidden fragments of Clakker technology? If so, another metageas would force him to apprehend and report Visser. They'd get him sooner than later. But the Lord wouldn't let that happen until he fulfilled his duty to the Holy See. The only path lay forward.

The pastor continued, "Indeed it is. I have an acquaintance who runs, or I should say 'ran,' a tiny museum in New Amsterdam. Grand ambitions, frankly, and his reach exceeds his grasp. A noble endeavor, nevertheless. His particular ideal is to bring the early history of the Empire to the New World." The clouds had begun to dissipate; light through the high windows glinted on a tiny crystal caught in the folds of Visser's stole. He brushed poison aside as though it were lint, saying, "Unfortunately, during the war he was forced to close his museum and sell off pieces of his collection. But now that the war is over, he's trying to rebuild and reopen. I think this would be a grand addition to his collection. As you'll see, our cousins across the Atlantic aren't steeped in the wonders of the Empire as we are."

"We're going to have one of the largest houses in New Amsterdam. Mother says so."

Visser managed an even tone. "I'm sure you will. I'm sorry I'll not have a chance to see it. But my days of long voyages are behind me, I fear. So I wonder if I could use your machine to run the errand for me?"

Kathryn pursed her lips at this. This wasn't entirely in line with the strictest etiquette. Such a request should have been addressed to Jax's owner, the signatory on the lease. But this was a formality; Jax would clear things with his master. Nicolet did an excellent imitation of the queen. She gave a contemptuous wave of her dainty hand.

Visser turned to address Jax. "My acquaintance is named Frederik Ahlers." It wasn't his true Christian name—Visser didn't know it; he doubted even Talleyrand did—but it was the name under which he conducted business for the *onder-grondse grachten*, the so-called underground canals. "He owns a bakery on Bleecker Street in New Amsterdam." Visser held up the microscope and pointed to it. "I would like you to take this to him. Tell him it comes with compliments from Pastor Luuk Visser of the Nieuwe Kerk in The Hague. Do you understand?"

"Yes," said Jax.

"Please repeat what I've just told you."

"After arriving in New Amsterdam, I am to bring the microscope to Mr. Frederik Ahlers, who owns a bakery shop on Bleecker Street. I am to tell him it comes from you, Pastor Visser. Is that correct, sir?"

"Yes," said Visser. The knuckle joints in Jax's mechanical fingers chittered when he opened his hand to receive the telescope. "And be extremely careful with this. It is a unique and irreplaceable antique."

"Yes, sir. I will, sir." The Clakker took the leather tube as gently as he might have lifted an unhatched chick on Easter Eve. A shiver of mingled relief and apprehension tickled the unscratchable space between Visser's shoulders when the telescope, and its secret contents, left his grasp.

He turned to address Nicolet Schoonraad again. "I thank you and your family for your generosity, Miss."

Nicolet said, "Carry me home, Jax."

"As you say, Miss."

The Clakker's ankle, knee, and hip joints flexed low so that she could climb atop his shoulders. Nicolet clambered up his back, using his face for a handhold and wedging the toes of her red leather shoes into the recesses of the mechanical cage that contained the mechanisms of his torso. When she was seated upon his shoulders, he stood. Visser wondered how it felt to ride a Clakker, and whether the backward knees gave the machines a particularly comfortable gait. The Clakker turned to leave.

But the governess looked up at the girl swaying on Jax's

shoulders. "Nicolet, thank Pastor Visser for his time. A lady must always be polite."

"Thank you, Pastor."

Visser said, "You're welcome, Miss Schoonraad." He nodded to Kathryn. "Good day to you."

She curtsied again, but it was shallow and perfunctory. Or, given the look in her eyes, insincere.

The rich girl rode her trotting mechanical into the puddles and patchy sunshine of an early autumn afternoon in The Hague. Visser waited until Kathryn pulled the doors shut behind them before releasing a pent-up breath. His knees went soft, like hot candle wax. He leaned on a pew. A bead of sweat dripped from a tuft of hair to his earlobe. It was cold. His heart couldn't decide whether to slow in momentary relief, or keep hammering until his capture.

He'd done what he could; if they were extremely lucky, his package might make it to Ahlers and thence Talleyrand. Now all he had to do was be captured.

He returned to the vestry. There he found a newly dead mouse in the wardrobe. It lay on its side amongst a scattering of poison, a casualty of his crisis of faith.

He wondered if he would have time to bury the poor thing before the Stemwinders arrived.

CHAPTER
3

P iss on Christ's wounds!"

Berenice Charlotte de Mornay-Périgord, vicomtesse de Laval, crumpled the note she'd just scanned. The travel-stained paper crackled. The message had been hidden inside a package of sugar from the Dutch Indies, jotted on the waxed inner lining of the paper sack. But the supply caravan from Montpellier had been dogged by rain, and by the time the caravanners had reached the walls of Marseilles-in-the-West, most of their wares were damp. Reading the ill news from Europe through a thin crust of sugar did nothing to dispel the bitter taste in her mouth.

She flung the note across the room. It clipped a crystal vase—a genuine antique, her great-umpty-great-grandfather's, made in Paris before the Exile—and rebounded toward a candle. Her husband leapt from his chaise longue, quick as a cat, to bat it away from the open flame. It tumbled to the floor. He steadied the vase.

"Good news, I take it."

"Oh yes. Fucking delightful."

The marquis de Lionne and his toadies on the privy council would consume this with delight. She could already picture the scene when she delivered the news to the king: Lionne's triple chin folding upon itself like an avalanche of fat flesh as his lips curled in a frown of disapproval, sweat-yellowed silk jabot straining at his throat as he whispered poison into the king's ear. *It's as I've feared, Majesty. She's lost control. Perhaps it is time for a new Talleyrand...* This news would derail the privy council meeting and make it twice as difficult for her to make her case to the king.

"Shitcakes," she sighed.

Louis squinted past the tarnish in the silvered mirror hanging beside his armoir. Straightening his wig, he said, "Perhaps I was too hasty. If you'd like to try again, I won't stop you from burning down the palace."

"Smart-ass."

"Shrew."

She licked sugar from her sticky fingers, admiring his backside as he bent to pluck the crumpled ball of paper from the floor. Candlelight gleamed on the polished buckles of his heels and on the smooth satin of his coat. A ribbon under one knee had come undone, but his breeches still revealed shapely calves. Today he wore mint green with purple ribbons; her gown was a shimmery copper shot through with slashes of lemon yellow. If they stood together at court, the display would surely blind unwary onlookers. Such was the downside to the French national pride in its mastery of chemical dyes.

They had so few sources of pride, it seemed. Living under a siege mentality, cringing for fear of an indomitable enemy, for two centuries had turned them into a largely backward-looking people. Berenice couldn't wait for the day when her countrymen emerged from behind their high walls and started looking forward again. And stopped dressing like their grandparents' grandparents.

Louis's fingertips stirred an eddy of dust when they brushed the floor. Dust? Tarnish? Such was the squalor one had to accept when reliant upon fallible human servants. Berenice understood they had to sleep several hours per night, but she'd still have a talk with Maud. This was getting out of hand. You could be sure that cunt Queen Margreet never had to put up with tarnished mirrors and dusty floorboards. Berenice would have wagered all the beaver pelts in the northwest on that.

Louis tossed the wad in the fireplace, plucked a candle from the mantel, and set the secret message alight. He didn't ask if she'd memorized it. She had.

Bright yellow flames licked at the paper. The residual sugar caught, and for a few seconds, the popping light from the fireplace outshone the half-dozen synthetic spermaceti candles that lit their chambers. Trace metals in the ink tainted the flames with streamers of indigo and jade. The unwelcome words crumbled to ash. But the ill news lingered.

This was a disaster. *Eighty percent* of her Hague network gone in a *single day*? What a shitstorm. Who remained? Had she believed in a higher power, Berenice would have prayed that Greenbriar had survived the purge. This fiasco might be salvageable if they still had somebody inside the Guild. Greenbriar, whoever she or he was, carried the value of three others.

She'd have to verify the news through secondary sources, but that would be trivial if this were true. By now it was the talk of every port on the east coast as reports of the executions percolated across the sea. Everybody from dung-smeared stable boys to perfumed courtiers would be bubbling over with ignorant gossip about the semimythical Talleyrand and this legendary fuckup.

She cradled her forehead in one hand. "Bugger me with a crucifixion nail."

Louis crossed the room, his heels clicking against varnished floorboards. He laid a hand on her shoulder. "Oh, my demure flower. I know you're in particularly high spirits when you wax poetic. What can I do?"

She sighed. He nudged the clasp of her pearl necklace down to kiss her neck. The soft touch of his lips sent a shiver down her spine. She inhaled.

"You can do more of that," she said. He did. Her eyelids fluttered closed of their own accord, delicately, like butterflies finding purchase on windblown wheat. Her breaths came more quickly, and more easily, when Louis undid the plastic faux-pearl clasps on her bodice. His lips trailed kisses down her neck, between her shoulder blades. She tipped her head back, gazed through a fringe of eyelashes at the tall candle alongside the Hokusai woodprint. Her eyes snapped open, and, after recounting the divisions on the candle, she sat up.

"Damn you and your lips," she said. "I'll be late if we keep this up. Put me back together, troublemaker."

He did. Berenice enjoyed a final deep breath before the bodice pulled snug against her ribs. She checked herself in the mirror. With Maud's help she'd managed to get her hair piled high in the idiotically elaborate confection currently favored by ladies of the court. Doing so took so many pins, clasps, and pearls, it seemed a wonder her neck didn't buckle under the weight. She pulled a single ringlet free, curling it tightly about her finger before letting the coil dangle coquettishly alongside one ear. It gave just the slightest hint of tousling, of a hurried and vigorous liaison. Then she checked the placement of her beauty mark and adjusted her décolletage. Meanwhile, Louis put the final touches on his makeup, dabbing more color on his lips to replace what he'd left on her neck.

"What shall you do while I'm stuck with the privy council?" she asked.

"Oh, I suppose I can find a way to entertain myself. I'll frig a duchess or three."

"You ought," said Berenice, donning earrings. "The Duchess Montmorency has been humping your leg for months. Take pity on that poor lady."

He looked like he'd just bitten a lemon. "Good God, woman. Don't even joke about it. You wouldn't if you'd ever taken a good look at her."

"I'm not joking. Believe me. We could use some good will right now. So let that fat cow seduce you. Close your eyes and think of fallen France if you must."

"I'd rather think of you."

"Louis, my love." She took his face in her hands, careful not to smudge the powder on his cheekbones. "This is how things are done. You know this as well as I."

Louis shook his head. "I took a vow when I married you. I do try to keep my word, you know."

Berenice bit her lip. How many liaisons had she spun in the eighteen months since she coaxed Louis into putting a ring on her finger? He never complained, but . . . He must have seen the pained look on her face. He touched her chin.

"That's different, love. Your duty to the throne demands it."

"Yes, well, your duty to our marriage demands likewise." He took a small vial from the armoir, uncapped it, and dabbed a peppery cologne behind his ears. She pointed at the bottle of synthetic ambergris. "Virtually half the chemical stock in the kingdom derives from her husband's petroleum holdings in the north, you know. They're the best allies we have at court. But if you keep turning her down she'll fall into a foul mood and make him miserable."

"She's always foul."

"Louis."

"Very well." He sighed. "I'll do it for you."

She kissed him. "Thank you. Just don't fall in love with that scabby bitch. I'll cut your dick off if you do."

"You truly are the most delicate of flowers. Did you know that?"

"I did. They sing songs about me up and down the Saint Lawrence, you know."

"Ah, yes. I think I've heard the guards chanting some of those." Their apartments rang with his soft tenor as he began to sing: "I've fallen in love with an Esquimau girl/her eyes are bright and her heart is hot/but her igloo's cold and so's her tw—"

She pinched his ass. He yelped. "You need to stop dicing with those fools. You're a vicomte now. Get roaring drunk with your peers." Berenice took a final turn before the mirror. Her skirts bobbed gently on the array of featherweight plastic ribs hooked under her bodice.

"I prefer to gamble with the guards. They make an effort to conceal their cheating."

"How commendable," she said. She offered him an elbow. "Now escort me to court, you bawdy lowborn bastard. And tonight, after I've had an exceptionally terrible afternoon, I'll let you help me forget it."

Louis took her arm. "I'll tell the Duchess Montmorency I'm on a schedule, then."

⚮

The King in Exile spoke through a mouthful of lavender honeycake. "They killed *how* many?"

Berenice suppressed the urge to sigh. "Four agents, Your Majesty." Over the angry muttering of the privy council, she added, "And, if the reports are to be believed, they executed a rogue Clakker as well."

The king coughed powdered sugar into his wine. "Mon Dieu! How did they catch it? Where did they catch it?"

Berenice shook her head. "I await the details, Majesty."

"What a shame," said the king.

Reynaud Galois, comte de Beauharnois and the royal esche-quier, lifted his glass. "Agreed, Your Majesty. That dead rogue represents a terribly tragic lost opportunity." *Oh, go frig yourself,* thought Berenice. It had taken him but a moment to assess the shifting political winds and abandon her ship. One setback and the bastard bolted. She shouldn't have been surprised. Berenice knew, by virtue of her network, that the eschequier had swiftly abandoned his Acadian mistress when she became pregnant with his bastard.

"But the question before us now"—he sipped from a goblet of ice wine—"is how many agents does our esteemed spymis-tress still have in play in the Netherlands?"

Every head at the table turned to regard her. Half of them bobbed in agreement with the eschequier's query. His new allies smelled blood in the water, the sharks. The king lifted a hand to stifle his muttering.

"Yes. That is a concern. Vicomtesse?"

She laced her fingers, calmly set her hands on the table. They were still tacky with sugar residue. No matter—dirty hands came with the job. The stays beneath her bodice dug into her ribs, creaking as she took the deepest breath she could, then again as she let it out.

"We have agents throughout the Empire," she said.

"It hardly matters if the great and fearsome Talleyrand has all the latest gossip from a shoe-shine stand in the Spice Islands," said the Marquis de Lionne. "How many do you have in The Hague at this moment? Counting only those not suffering from an acute case of rope burn." The eschequier snickered at the Marquis's jab. So too did Marshal General Mathieu, comte de Turenne, though he at least had the grace to hide his smile behind a handkerchief.

Berenice refused to let it faze her. She addressed the king

directly. "We had a rather extensive network. If this early report is accurate, four executions means we may still have an agent in the city. Who, exactly, I don't yet know."

"Had. If. May," muttered the marquis.

Unlike his late father, the current king wasn't a complete fool. Though he'd taken the throne much younger than his father had, he already displayed more wisdom than his predecessor. For starters, he hadn't gone up to the battlements during a siege only to get a bullet in the eye from a clockwork sniper crouched in the trees a mile away. If neither hemophilia nor the Dutch felled him, the young monarch might hold the throne a long time. He hadn't yet gone gray at the temples. And if Berenice did her job extremely well, perhaps someday Sébastien III would be the one to finally reclaim the throne in Paris. That, as with all previous Talleyrands before her, was the goal. But in the meantime he wouldn't let her off as easily as his father might have done, damn him. And he was the only man in the room not distracted by her décolletage, double damn him.

"A single agent alone and unmolested in The Hague. How long do you expect she or he will stay that way? Do you feel, in your professional estimation, it is credible the Dutch didn't force as much information as possible from the others before stretching their necks? Do you believe the identity and whereabouts of this orphan remain unknown to the Stemwinders?"

This time the sigh escaped her. Berenice shook her head. "I agree it is unlikely, Your Majesty."

"Perhaps then we can simplify," said the marshal general over the general mutter of disapproval, "and take it for granted that for all intents and purposes we no longer have any informants within the Central Provinces."

He punctuated this conclusion with a wave of his kerchief. His elbow knocked the ceremonial baton he'd recently inherited along with his new title and which he insisted on carrying everywhere. It rolled down the table. Several members of the privy council leapt to their feet as heavy gold and ivory inlay knocked wineglasses and confection trays aside until the baton clattered to the floor with a heavy thud. The baton left a trail of muttered curses, wine stains, and honey in its wake. The king had seen fit to celebrate the resumption of shipping into Marseilles-in-the-West by treating the privy council with a generous spread. Much of which now lay in scattered shambles about the table.

Berenice hid her smirk by pretending to dab her lips. The corner of the king's mouth trembled, too, before he wrestled his expression under control. But the exasperation still lingered in his eyes when he focused his attention on Berenice, and he let her see it. They shared a secret laugh at the buffoon in epaulettes.

All right. I'm perhaps not completely *in the shit just yet. Merely up to my nose.*

"As the marshal general so gracefully points out," said the king, "this is unfortunate."

"I concur, Your Majesty. It is a setback."

Eager to keep the fires of accusation stoked, the marquis jumped in. "Setback? This is a fucking travesty, a complete loss of control. What of the rogue Clakker? That was the rarest of opportunities, squandered. I demand to know why we didn't do everything possible to help it reach New France."

Splashed wine had stained the silk ruffle at his throat a brilliant crimson. He was too fat to dodge a falling wineglass, and hadn't tried. Berenice imagined it was a bloodstain from a nicked jugular—he'd just given her an opening, as effectively as though he'd cut himself fumbling his own rapier. *Thank you, you fat fool. I ought to have known I could trust you to make my point for me.*

"My dear marquis raises an excellent point," she said. He

plucked a pastry from the table, saving it from a spreading pool of wine. He chewed on it while she continued. "Every Clakker we don't study is a lost opportunity, and one we can but ill afford. So I'm certain he'll see the futility of ongoing debate and demand we snatch the military Clakker currently affixed to the outer keep wall before Dutch emissaries identify and retrieve it. It is our wisest course of action. He practically said so himself."

She smiled and waved her eyelashes at him. The marquis snorted, which raised a cloud of powdered sugar from the pastry halfway in his mouth. This caused him to make a strangled sound somewhere between a sneeze and a cough. He cleared his throat with a gulp of wine thoroughly fouled with crumbs. He scowled.

"Good God, woman. I said nothing about immoral and unethical forays into dark magics and forbidden gadgetry. I was talking about the unquestionable moral victory His Majesty would have enjoyed had we helped the rogue cross the border. The Clakkers need to know," he said, wiping his lips, "the French are their friends."

Berenice shook her head. The top-heavy mass of hair made it awkward. She said, "What the mechanicals might or should know is irrelevant. They obey those they are made to obey, protect those they are built to protect, and slaughter those they are told to kill."

The eschequier brushed crumbs from his sleeve, casually trotting out the creakiest bromide in the tome of New France's national myths. "The Clakkers will throw off their shackles and flock to our side once they recognize the rightness of our cause."

Berenice knew, by virtue of many excruciating council meetings, particularly during the recent war, he actually believed this. The fossilized old turd wouldn't recognize a new line of thinking if it frigged him blind in a coat closet. How many times did they have to rehash this godforsaken argument? Christ.

"Is that so?" she asked. "Well, I'd say they're taking their sweet time about it, wouldn't you? Allow me to remind my most esteemed and honored colleagues that we French first displayed the rightness of our cause back in the days of Louis XIV. Within ten years he fled to Spain with a Clakker army on his heels. And here we are, well over two centuries later, with an entire ocean between us and the Netherlands while we huddle behind our walls."

"Nonsense. We fought them to a standstill," said the marshal general. Louis would have been proud of the way she refrained from responding with an unladylike snort. Naturally the new marshal general would claim a military victory. She wondered how many of his infantrymen had died trying to break the siege.

The duc de Montmorency, silent until now, spoke up. "We outwaited them. They tired of the siege before we died from it."

He'd been leaning back in his chair, muscular arms crossed, watching the debate. He wore no makeup, and hadn't bothered with a wig to cover his close-shorn hair. He'd always struck Berenice as a man with zero patience for nonsense, and in recent weeks he'd begun to dress the part. It made him unique among members of the privy council.

But the duke's chemical holdings also made him the richest man on the privy council. Montmorency provided the chemical precursors and reagents that powered French innovation, without which it would have been impossible to fight the Clakkers in the recent war. It made sense, then, that the king had named him to the council.

The king's wealth (or, more formally, New France's wealth)

should have eclipsed his fortune; however, the eschequier had delivered an alarming report on the Royal Treasury earlier in the meeting. The monarchy had long been supported largely by the riches of the Vatican because French agents had been instrumental in assisting the then pope's flight from Rome. (The famous "migration of cardinals," as it was sometimes called.) But apparently even Québec's coffers were not limitless. And the particulars of the current financial relationship with the Holy See were murky, as the bishop of Marseilles had died of pneumonia during the siege. A replacement hadn't been named, so the church's chair on the council stood empty.

Meanwhile, the supply trains of mineral wealth chiseled from the distant Montagnes Rocheuses, the so-called Rocky Mountains, hadn't resumed since the cessation of hostilities. Even the caravans' most intrepid Sioux and Cree escorts couldn't fend off Dutch raiding parties for every inch of the many hundreds of miles across the plains to the Great Lakes.

Thus while the duke was a quiet man, he was also a rich man, so his words slammed upon the table like sacks of coin. Berenice's opponents fell silent, regrouping. When his eyes turned in her direction, she gave him a minute nod of thanks. The duke nodded in kind.

To the marshal general, he added, "You speak as if the war is over. It is not. We have negotiated a cease-fire. We have yet to negotiate a peace. May I remind you? They are not the same."

The marquis shook his fist. "All the more reason to disregard the viscomtesse's rash suggestion! The terms of the cease-fire explicitly forbid us from studying any Clakkers left incapacitated on the battlefield. The Dutch will take up arms the moment they catch us doing it. We'll be back in a state of open warfare."

"Not if we're smart about it," said Berenice.

The eschequier shook his head. "We don't dare risk another

siege so soon. Our troops are tired and wind whistles through the barracks where every other cot is empty. They'll overrun us if we return to war."

An awkward, pregnant silence fell across the table. Into that abyss of unwelcome self-awareness, the marshal general sacrificed a few perfunctory words. "Not that we couldn't give the tulips a drubbing, of course."

"Of course," said the eschequier, nodding quickly.

Berenice said, "They'll overrun us when their new Forge starts shitting out Clakkers. Unless we are ready for the onslaught." Addressing the king, she added, "Majesty, the siege nearly broke us. New France weathered the recent storm for two and only two reasons. Yes, we caught the tulips by surprise with the threat to introduce chemical additives to their reservoirs. A threat, by the way, we'd have been hard pressed to deliver. So we were lucky, because we will never succeed in repeating that tactic. Even more, we owe our continued existence to simple economics. It would have cost too much in lost labor to repurpose the thousands of Clakkers required to guarantee an overwhelming victory—the tulips would've had to start paying actual human beings for labor in the Central Provinces. That was never going to happen, sire. Especially in light of the economic crisis precipitated by the van Althuis debacle. The timing on that worked in our favor. Again, we were lucky. But a Forge on *this* continent changes that equation. Next time we won't be so fortunate. If we ever want to live like the free French of our ancestors, not penned in like livestock, we must overturn this stifling taboo. In order to defeat the Dutch, we have to understand their weapons."

The minister of agriculture spoke for what Berenice thought must have been the first time in several council meetings. The yelling must have woken him. "Then what of Lilith? I have spoken with the mechanical on several occasions and found her quite articulate." The effort to turn his head and gaze upon the other council members one by one set his dewlap shimmying. "She could answer your questions about Clakker-kind, could she not? This would not violate the terms of the cease-fire."

"Indeed, Minister, Lilith is central to my proposal," said Berenice. He nodded, a hint of satisfaction in his watery gray eyes. "I, for one, have enjoyed its discourse on many occasions, on many subjects. But in addition to its conversational charms, it is, as many of my fellow council members may know, a violinist of no small accomplishment. I've also had the pleasure of viewing several of its paintings; the oils, in particular, are coming along nicely. Since arriving in Marseilles-in-the-West, Lilith has embraced the arts and shown tremendous aptitude for them. Its compositions, both musical and visual, express the exuberant joy of an unchained soul."

"Your point?" replied the marquis.

"The point, my dear marquis, is there is nothing more to be learned from simple conversation with a Clakker freed from the bonds of geas. But," she said, sweeping her gaze around the table, "with both Lilith and the military Clakker on hand, we will enjoy an opportunity so grand our forebears could have scarcely dreamt of it."

The king said, "How?"

"Because, Majesty, we will be able to study—at our leisure, under controlled conditions—the differences between a Clakker *with* Free Will and one *without* it. We will learn how the latter becomes the former. And that revelation will teach us so much about the obligations that control the mechanicals that in time we will be able to *rewrite* the geasa. To subvert them. And on that day, the mechanicals will serve a new monarch. They will serve you, Your Majesty, rather than Queen Margreet."

The king licked his lips. But the minister of agriculture didn't see the temptations tugging at his sovereign. The minister's voice came out reedy and querulous. "But doing as you describe would require taking Lilith apart."

"Yes."

Berenice kept her response clipped. Anything else she might have said at that moment would have been lost in the hubbub of moral outrage. The king let the indignation run its course until the hottest flares had burned themselves down to glowing embers. He sipped his wine, then set his glass down with a practiced heaviness that demanded silence.

"The throne," he said, "cannot endorse such an endeavor. To do so would betray the principles upon which New France was founded."

He could hardly have said otherwise, Berenice knew. But he voiced the objection almost by rote. She could tell he was intrigued.

"I agree, Your Majesty, and nor should it. We already know much of Lilith." Strictly speaking, this was a lie. But one that would placate the council. "Thus we ought to begin with the mechanical currently entombed on the outer wall. Lacking Free Will, it is but a tool of its makers. What I propose is no more unethical than disassembling a broken rifle to mend it. From this alone we will learn so much that we may find we have no need to loosen a single screw on Lilith's frame." Another lie, that.

The marshal general took the last of the honeycakes. Careful not to nudge his baton again, he popped it into his mouth. His breath smelled of lavender when he said, "This is beside the point. Obtaining and examining a military Clakker would be viewed as an act of war."

"So was establishing an espionage network in The Hague. I don't recall the good marshal objecting to those efforts," Berenice said.

The eschequier said, "What network? I believe we've established it is defunct."

"For now. Not forever," she snapped. And immediately regretted the heat behind her words. *Calm*, she reminded herself. *Have no sharp edges. Be smooth and featureless. Be cool and hard. Offer your enemies no purchase.* She had already lost face today, and no small amount of political capital along with it. What point in tarnishing her famous dignity, too?

"How long will it take to reestablish your network in The Hague?" the king asked.

"Long enough, Majesty, that in the meantime we ought to seize every opportunity to learn of our enemies."

The marquis shook his head. "Madness. If we do as the vicomtesse suggests, we'll be at war by week's end." From a pocket he produced a snuffbox lidded with cameo glass. After dabbing a pinch of snuff into the hollow between thumb and forefinger, he held his hand to his face and snorted. Returning the snuffbox to his pocket, he said, "And we'll all be dead by month's end. No offense."

"None taken," said the marshal.

Berenice pushed her chair back and stood. Freed from its confinement, her gown sprang back into shape, knocking the table and rippling the wine. "Look at you! Where was your snuff grown? In a Dutch colony a thousand miles to the south of us! And look at our table! Lavender, sugar, chocolate: Dutch Pyrenees, Dutch Caribbean, Dutch Mesoamerica. For us, time is a vague suggestion gleaned from candles and hourglasses"— she gestured at the mantel—"while in the empire it marches to the rhythm of a pocket watch. Which probably half those who witnessed the executions at the Binnenhof carried."

"Ludicrous," said the eschequier. "A pocket-sized clockwork is impossible. Tulip propaganda."

She rounded on him. Waving a cupped hand under his nose, she said, "I've held a pocket watch in my very own hand. I've traveled extensively through the Dutch world. For it is *their* world. Have you?"

The stays in her bodice dug at her ribs again while she caught her breath. The expressions around the table ranged from cryptic (the king's), to amused (Montmorency), to bleary bafflement (the drowsy minister of agriculture), to flickering between cock-sure triumph and bald glances at her cleavage (the marquis de Lionne and his toads). *Well, so much for the dignity*, she thought. *At least the outburst felt good.*

Montmorency stepped adroitly into the awkward silence, and with a single utterance swept her loss of composure aside. "Well. I, for one, feel the passionate vicomtesse makes an unassailable point. So much so that I would like to donate any resources she might require for the success of her intriguing endeavor." Addressing the king directly, he added, "Though her proposal is not without risk. So perhaps the eschequier and I can negotiate a loan to the Treasury, to fund preparations in case the peace process falters."

If before his words had fallen upon the table like sacks of coin, this pronouncement fell upon the council like a golden brickbat. A chance to stem the financial hemorrhaging couldn't be brushed aside. A loan from the duke would at least make it possible to pay the surviving garrisons their overdue scrip. Even the most obstreperous members wouldn't dare gainsay the king, whose eyes now shone with flickers of greed and hope.

But a brickbat is an indiscriminant weapon. This one hit Berenice, too. She wondered what the duke hoped to gain from this unbidden show of generosity, and what it would cost her. Nothing in life was free. She knew that much. If this offer swayed the king, she and Louis would both have to step lightly around those from the Duchy of Montmorency for the foreseeable future.

Oh, Louis, thought Berenice. *You'd better be giving that scabby duchess the ride of her life right now.*

"Interesting." The king bit his lip, chewing over the duke's proposal. The privy council fell silent. Berenice wondered if the other councillors were holding their breath, too. This could make up for the loss in The Hague. Given time, it could turn the tide on centuries of conflict. And perhaps, someday, it could even mean a return to France itself. Someday.

"Tell me," said the king. "How do you propose to sidestep the terms of the cease-fire?"

She gave Montmorency another nod, half wondering where his wife was at that moment. "I am confident that with the duke's very generous assistance we can remove the Clakker from the wall in such a way the Dutch will never know it was there. By the time the peace is finalized and the tulips are allowed to approach the walls we'll have long since erased all signs of its presence. Plus we can salt the adjoining field with mechanical detritus. So when their inventory of mechanical killers comes up one short, and they come snooping, they'll find the evidence and write it off as a complete loss. A rare lucky direct hit with high explosives."

"I see." The king mulled this. He swirled the dregs of his wine, saying, "And prior to today's news, would you say you were equally confident in the security of your agents in The Hague?"

The marquis snickered. Berenice ignored him. "No. Risk is part and parcel of tradecraft, Majesty. It's the price of thwarting the Brasswork Throne."

Still the king chewed on this. Even the promise of Montmorency's loan didn't clinch the deal. When the wariness in his eyes didn't soften, she pushed her point.

"Majesty, armed with the knowledge we gain from this endeavor, we will change the world as radically as the accursed Huygens did in 1676. For when we are done, the tulips' servants will no longer *be* their servants. They will be *our* servants. The world will be theirs no longer. It will be *our* world. And we will bend it to our will. The Dutch will flee across the wide, wide oceans to the far-flung corners of the globe. For we will evict them when the King of France once more sits upon his true throne."

Her passion silenced the snickering and derisive muttering. The marquis and his allies looked dumbfounded. Even Montmorency stared at her with a strange expression on his face. But her plea won the day. The king nodded.

"Very well," he said. "You have my permission to proceed. Keep me apprised of your preparations."

She curtsied. "Thank you, Your Highness."

"Let us move on," said the king. "Speaking of the cease-fire, what news from the diplomatic mission? I expected to see a draft of the treaty by now."

CHAPTER
4

The sun hung low over the western horizon when Berenice finally emerged from the council meeting. The council chambers, and the royal apartments above, were perched high atop the central spire of the inner keep. Tradition held that the council chambers had been situated beneath the royal garderobe so that the ruling monarch could shit on the "privy" council as necessary. It wasn't true. All nightsoil in the city, royal and common alike, went to chemical treatment vats for reprocessing into fertilizer, fuel, and anything else the chemists could devise.

Such as the nacreous lacquers coating the chamber Berenice had just exited. Supposedly the synthetic mother-of-pearl could withstand a direct hit from the largest Dutch cannon ever fielded in battle. But that had never been put to the test, thank Christ. The iridescent coating was, however, quite lovely. It shimmered pink, blue, green, and orange in the light of the setting sun. From farther away, she knew, it looked like a shining jewel framed between the crenellations of the outer keep. Boatmen on the Saint Lawrence called the castle the Crown of Mont Royal. The Crown, the Keep, and the Spire: otherwise known as the Last Redoubt of the King of France. The first stones had been laid by Louis XV, first in the long line of French Monarchs-in-Exile. Back in the days when they fought Clakkers with primitive weapons like tar and sand.

Having declined to share a funicular ride with the sweat-stained marquis de Lionne and soporific minister of agriculture, Berenice stood atop a long spiral cloister stair several revolutions and several hundred feet above the base of the Spire. In the days before the funicular this was the servants' stair, because aside from the royal lift it was the only means of accessing the royal apartments. The stair itself was a narrow ribbon of high-tensile polymer, slightly elastic and prone to mild jouncing in high winds. Louis had told her that from the river it looked like a scarlet ribbon wound around the Spire, like a jaunty tassel dangling from the highest peak of the Crown. He'd laughed until he cried when she admitted it had always looked to her like blood seeping from a mortal head wound.

A screen of translucent plastic shaded the stairwell. Thin enough to keep the stairs well lit in daylight, but thick enough to diffuse the sunlight in the hottest days of summer. The glassy stairs were wide enough for four people abreast, presumably so that two pairs of servants could pass each other with a minimum of fuss. The inner edge of the stair abutted the smooth granite blocks of the Spire itself; in a few spots, folded scraps of paper had been tucked into gaps where the mortar had crumbled. (The castle staff called it the Porter's Prayer, but Berenice happened to know, based on years of observation, that prayers were no more common than curses and love notes. She'd made a habit of reading them all. Knowing things was her job. She was, after all, the king's very own dirty-handed snoop.) A chest-high lattice of blood-colored polymer prevented the unlucky and the despondent from tumbling off the outer edge of the stair.

The heliograph atop the Spire flashed a message to its twin on the ground. A moment later a return blink shone from the shadows of the courtyard below. Somewhere behind her a pump rattled to life. Then a valve beneath the funicular track opened with a hiss. The pump, working in concert with several others situated at various heights along the tower, sluiced water against the pull of gravity into the ballast tank in the upper funicular car. The car at the bottom of the spire must have carried a full load of people en route to the king's apartments, else the butterball marquis himself might have provided sufficient ballast to drive the funicular. The plumbing noises abated; the pump chugged to a stop. Metal screeched as the brakeman let out the stops. Berenice gave the marquis a genial nod as the car descended. He pretended not to see her. The minister dozed with his chin on his chest.

A breeze came off the distant river. From her high vantage she gazed past the fortifications of the outer keep, beyond the city, toward the horizon where the setting sun twinkled on the water. The wind shook the leaves of towering white elms and yellow birch before whickering through the few remaining tall grasses along the muddy, artillery-churned western slopes of Mont Royal. The Dutch had decamped back south a month earlier, leaving behind only the privy trenches for the human commanders and the various scars of warfare on the landscape. They hadn't cut many trees from the surrounding forest; only the humans had needed firewood, and they were but a small contingent of the forces that had besieged Marseilles-in-the-West. And Clakkers had no use for privy trenches, so while Marseilles-in-the-West was nearly overrun the fortress city had at least been spared the stench of a massive human encampment outside its walls. The wind fluttering the pennants atop the outer keep and teasing Berenice's hair carried the loamy smell of damp earth, the fresh scent of the river, and, even now, a ghostly chemical astringency. The miasma wafted from the battlefield.

It was the scent of secret reagents used to melt down the quick-set epoxy resins French grenadiers had hurled into the lines of Clakker infantry. Immediately following the cease-fire, the fields had been stippled with immense crystal flowers of variegated hues. The petals in this giant's garden were streamers of epoxy, like water balloons frozen in the moment of bursting. Many such blasts had entombed clockwork assassins like deadly insects in amber. But the Dutch had laboriously chiseled massive blocks from the diamond-hard coatings (or, more correctly, their mechanical servitors had) to cart the immobilized Clakkers back across the border to Dutch territory. Likewise they had scoured the battlefield for any fragments of the few mechanicals impaled by the experimental steam harpoons or ruptured by explosives. The crystalline debris posed a hazard for plows and hooves. So once the tulips took their broken toys home, there was nothing to do but send out the chemists. Hence the astringent odor on the wind.

Berenice descended. The stairs bounced slightly underfoot as the stiff breeze eddied around the Spire. Another half-turn along the stairwell put her out of the wind. It swirled through the inner and outer keeps, past stables and smithies and chapels with the Blessed Virgin's image in stained glass, past the gleaming chromium-plated tanks of the chemical-processing plants, to meander through the town beyond the walls. Wisps of ash swirled over the charred remnants of large swaths of the town. A favorite Dutch terror tactic was to cover their Clakkers in burning pitch and send them for a stroll through enemy territory. The docks had taken the worst of it. She watched the wind tug at streamers of wood smoke rising from chimneys where the city hadn't burned. The smoke stretched into wispy streamers, blushing slightly in the sunset.

Situated so close to the head of the Saint Lawrence Seaways, and thus being an invaluable center for commerce and trade, the town of Marseilles-in-the-West had grown far beyond the original vision. The town lay mostly to the north, east, and south, hugging the land between the river and the star-shaped perimeter of the outer keep. The outer fortifications had been designed by the great Marquis de Vauban himself, who had accompanied Louis XIV on the long flight from Paris, and featured numerous modifications to the standard star-fort plan to account for clockwork assailants. It bristled with machio-colations and tenailles, bastions and retrenchments. Seen from the Spire, the serrated boundary of the outer keep resembled a ring of spear points arrayed to keep the world at bay.

The funicular had docked at the bottom of the Spire by the time she had descended another revolution of the stairs. The marquis hopped gracefully from the car to the narrow platform. The minister, less so.

Few new notes had appeared in the mortar of the Spire, meaning she had little snooping to do on the way down. It gave her time to visit the pigeon coops, too, which were situated halfway down the Spire and could frequently be counted upon to provide something interesting. But it had been a quiet day. The on-duty birdkeeper apologized; they hadn't received a bird all day. And the outgoing messages were the usual fare, hardly worth the detour. So Berenice resumed her descent.

Once free of the stair, she navigated the high terraces of the inner keep. She passed the hulking boilers of dormant steam-powered harpoons. It was an intriguing concept, to be sure, but not very practical. Fighting mechanical demons with an over-sized teakettle? No projectile could ever be faster than a Clak-ker's reflexes. Aside from a handful of lucky hits, the mechanical onslaught had been held off with area-effect weapons: chemi-cal adhesives, chemical explosives. Unless somebody devised a better martial application, or a way to turn it into a lucrative trade with the Orient, steam power seemed destined for the scrap heap of technological curiosities.

Narrow timber walkways connected the terraces; Berenice stepped lightly in her heels and gown across moats of corrosive acid and deep trenches bristling with land mines. In peacetime, the trenches were planted with crops, the moats filled with water and freshwater fish. And if the cease-fire did resolve into a lasting peace, the mines would be cleared away, the moats pumped down and sprayed with a neutralizer. The death traps would once again become sanctuaries for delicate life. But for now the invasion preparations stayed in place. Just in case. If things went awry and the Dutch breached the outer walls, Marseilles-in-the-West could be swarming with Clakkers in no time. And every moment that could be gained to slow their advance might mean the difference between a living monarch and the death of dreams of long-lost France.

She made better progress once she reached the broad granite avenues of the outer keep. Here she needed dodge only artisans, priests, and the occasional fishwife hawking the last remnants of the day's catch from the pair of rivers that bounded the Isle of Mount Royal. Rarely did a misstep in the outer keep prove deadly, or even particularly unpleasant. The soil collectors did a respectable job of sweeping the streets in the wake of the horse- and mule-drawn carts that ferried goods between the keep and the surrounding city.

She glimpsed several members of an Algonquin band; native trading parties were a rare but welcome sight this time of year. They'd had an audience with the king earlier in the week, as befitted honored guests. If not for their ancestors' help in bygone centuries—first against the Iroquois Confederacy, later against the Dutch—New France would have disappeared from the map long ago. The traders spoke with Lilith; Berenice wondered what they could possibly have to discuss with the rogue mechanical.

Berenice detoured through the laboratories in order to stay abreast of any interesting technical developments. She diverted what funds she could afford from activities of spycraft—observing, suborning, stealing, blackmailing—to the more esoteric explorations by the women and men with academic titles and strange enthusiasms. It was a paltry sum, but it did earn their gratitude. The silly steam weapons had come from explorations like this, but so had the quick-set epoxies that were now part of the standard anti-Clakker ordnance. So she stopped in a large stone silo that had originally been intended for grain storage but which had become badly overrun with rats. The grain had been moved out, the technicians moved in, and a litter of lazy cats stayed. Though the evening was getting long in the tooth, the laboratory didn't suffer from lack of activity. It never did, regardless of the hour. Scientists were a strange lot.

But to her annoyance she found they were still playing with something they called a "pile": alternating layers of dissimilar metal bathed in a caustic chemical paste. Such arrangements gave rise to macabre party tricks. Several weeks earlier they had proudly demonstrated how the pile, along with a pair of wires, could be used to make the severed legs of a dead frog twitch and kick as if afflicted with St. Vitus's dance. At the time she had assumed the scientists would outgrow their divertissement and move on to more useful efforts. Instead, they had doubled down—now the piles were considerably larger. Large enough to send sparks flying between metallic electrodes, to snap and crack and make the laboratory smell as if a thunderstorm had recently passed through. It was impressive, but when pressed on how this trick could be used on the battlefield, the scientists hemmed and hawed.

"Perhaps," ventured one woman, "we could strike the Clakkers with lightning of our own making."

"Interesting," said Berenice. She asked, "What happens when a Clakker is struck by lightning?"

Nobody knew.

The sun had melted into the horizon by the time she gained the top of the north wall. A guard watched the sunset through a smoke-darkened glass. When the limb of the sun had disappeared, he turned an hourglass. Then he sighed and slouched inside a crenelle. Berenice gave a discreet cough. He started, turned, bowed.

"Vicomtesse. You are very quiet."

"I know several who would take issue with your assessment. As you were."

The guard pulled a pipe from his belt. Berenice rifled her mental filing cabinet for his name while he tapped cold ashes from the bowl. Maurice, a corporal; he'd joined up after his wife left him, which was just before the siege. They'd joked about her timing.

Inspecting the bowl of his pipe, he said, "You've come to visit our friend, no?"

"Yes."

"He waits still for his masters to reclaim him."

"It's very patient," said Berenice. She listened. "And quiet."

The flare of a distant hot-air balloon briefly lit the gloaming like the spark of a lumbering firefly. A sparrow fluttered past. Hurrying home before full dark.

"Pleasant night for being patient."

"Yes."

Maurice pulled a waxed-paper packet of sulphur matches from his belt. He removed one and tucked the rest away. After wedging the pipe stem between his teeth, he made to strike the match on the coarse stone of the battlement, using one hand as a windbreak. This section of the parapet, Berenice noticed, was darkened with myriad dark streaks such as those made by matches. He started to flick his wrist but, apparently remembering in the same instant that he was not alone and that the light of his match would have broken the siege protocols, caught himself. Though the assault had ended—for now—the Keep's defenders still cleaved to siege disciplines while there was any chance the cease-fire might crumble. Chief among those disciplines was taking care to not present targets to the enemy. Such as the spark of a lit match after sunset.

The unlit match went fluttering over the wall. A faint *tink* sounded from the shadows below. The pipe almost went over the wall, too, but Maurice secured it with just a bit of bobbling.

Berenice appreciated the show. Though it caused the stays to lay siege against her rib cage once again, the laugh was most welcome after the long, frustrating, and bewildering council meeting. The soldier coughed. With as much dignity as could be mustered (not much, to Berenice's eye) he tucked the pipe away as though he'd never intended to smoke it.

He finally chanced a look in her direction. She cocked her head and gave him an innocent smirk as though expecting a question or inconsequential observation.

"Ah," he said.

"I won't tell Longchamp." Berenice shrugged. "I think we can trust the tulips won't attack tonight. And as for our friend down there, well, it already knows we're here."

"Ah," he repeated. But the pipe didn't come out again. "The vicomtesse is the soul of kindness."

"Again, I know several who would question your assertion. And anyway, I came out here to the shatter the protocols." She stepped into a crenelle, braced her hands on the battlements, and leaned over the parapet.

"The sergeant will not like that, my lady." Maurice shook his head. "His wrath is a fearsome thing."

"Oh, you're not afraid of old Longchamp. He's a kitten."
She squinted into the shadows below the battlement. Her
eyes could just make out a dark silhouette in the fading light
of dusk. It was a hole in the deepening night, nearly the same
color as the inside of her eyelids in a lightless room. "Now. Be
a good soldier and fetch a torch, a piece of chalk, and a stout
length of rope."

"My lady?"

"It needn't be terribly stout. I assure you I am thinner than
the gown suggests. Now scoot."

He trotted down the stairs, hobnails scritching on the uneven
stone. Berenice kept her eyes on the silhouette beneath the
embrasure. She could just discern the assailant if she tried to peer
at it from the corners of her eyes rather than straight on. That
was an old campaigner's trick she'd learned from Longchamp.

Even by day, the lone Clakker was nearly invisible from her
vantage point almost directly above. It had managed to creep up
to the inflected corner of a sharp tenaille on the north side of the
keep where the glint of sunlight wouldn't give it away. Shrub-
bery and ivy nourished by rain runoff from the wall hadn't been
properly pruned back, hiding the Clakker from observers outside the wall, and a bartizan added sometime after the original
construction—and clearly not part of Vauban's plan—partially
obscured the defenders' view into the corner. Thoughtless modifications and lazy maintenance had given the keep a blind spot,
and now the forgotten Clakker was almost as invisible to its enemies above as it was to its masters on the field.

Thank you, Saint Jean, for sharp-eyed and sharp-eared officers.

Straining with her ears proved pointless. All through the
keep lamplighters had come out in force, meaning the great
brass bourdon bell of the Basilica of Saint Jean-Baptiste chimed
vespers. The call to evening prayer reverberated through the
keep, rebounding from the high walls like surf crashing on

the craggy shore of Hudson Bay. It rattled her teeth. Berenice gripped the battlements. She doubted the Clakker on the wall would be inclined to catch her even if it weren't encrusted in a glassy cocoon.

The temperature had dropped with the sun. Cool evening air put a chill on her skin. She had eschewed a lengthy detour to obtain a shawl en route to the wall. The duke's offer goaded her to action. She'd been dying to see this beast up close since the day it nearly entered the keep. And that was before the bitch queen Margreet made a public show of rendering her deaf and blind to the heart of the Empire.

They had to learn all they could from this Clakker. There would be another war someday; maybe not this year, maybe not in five years' time, but someday. It could easily come sooner than Berenice—or her successor Talleyrand—could replace the dead agents in The Hague. She shivered, but not from cold.

Maurice returned. And, judging from the voices and the scritching of hobnails on the stairs, he was trailed by several off-duty guards. He must have gone to the barracks to fulfill her request. Soldiers had a nose for cheap entertainment. Berenice wondered if the story of her escapade would touch Louis's ears before her lips did. Probably. She'd made a study of rumor propagation some years back; good work, even if those troglodytes in the Académie des Sciences had rejected the manuscript.

"Your things, my lady."

The torch Maurice offered appeared to be a sturdy length of maple—a repurposed chair leg?—one end wrapped in rags and doused in pine resin. On his shoulder he wore a coil of coarse hemp rope twice as thick as her thumb. After she took the rope and torch, he dropped a nub of chalk into her palm. She frowned at it. He shrugged.

"Next time, try romancing a schoolmistress."

"I did. How do you think I ended up here?"

Berenice tied a loop at the end of the rope, just wide enough for both her feet. She kicked off her shoes. The cool stone chilled her feet and elicited twinges from her calves: charley horses flicking their tails in irritation. She draped the looped end of the rope over the parapet. When it hung a yard below the battlement, she gestured to the guards who had returned with Maurice.

"Make yourselves useful, you two. Take the other end and try not to drop me."

They looked at each other, then shrugged. They took up the rope. One tied it around his waist and braced himself behind an empty two-chamber iron cauldron while the other donned gloves and prepared to feed the slack. Like numerous others dotted along the outer wall, the cauldron had contained curatives and epoxy during the siege. And, like the others, it had seen extensive use.

She sat on the edge and hooked her feet in the loop. They lowered the rope a few inches at a time until she could put her weight on it. Gripping the rope with one hand and holding the torch in the other, she shoved off the wall and dangled eighty feet above the ground. The hiss of breath through Maurice's teeth told her his opinion of this idea.

"I'll thank you gentlemen not to sneak glances inside my bodice." When she hung with her eyes level with his boot soles, she raised the torch. "Put those matches to good use, won't you?"

Maurice's companions looked over their shoulders. One fellow, the anchor, actually took a hand off the rope to cross himself.

"Oh, for heaven's sake," said Berenice. "If it will put you big strong men at ease, I'll make certain the dread sergeant knows this was my idea. I'll tell him I threatened to bop your noses bloody if you balked."

Maurice said, "Ah. Well. In that case."

He struck a match on the stone, leaned forward, and touched it to her torch. The pitch caught instantly. Berenice welcomed the surge of warmth, though the sudden flare caused her eyes to ache. Taking care not to bring the torch too close to the rope, and also trying to avoid sizzling drips of pine resin, she said, "Lower me. Slowly."

Torchlight flickered on a glassy wen anchored to the wall thirty feet above the ground. About the size of an autumn hay roll, its tentacular boundaries defined a splash pattern. The Clakker had taken a direct hit. The torrent of chemicals had covered it and splattered against the wall in the second before they combined with each other, and the atmosphere, to harden into a shell stronger even than a clockwork killer. Black alchemy had brought the assassin to life; chemistry has stopped it dead.

Peering past her toes, Berenice could make out the general form of its outstretched arms frozen in the act of spidering up the wall behind an obscuring screen of ivy. Maurice's match had fluttered into a hollow in the random splatters between the Clakker's shoulder and neck. A small portion of its face had no chemical sheath. The reflection of her torch took on a baleful glint in the machine's crystalline eye.

Berenice called a halt. She leaned in. By squinting at the faintly translucent sheath she could just see where its fingers had gouged solid granite like so much dough. She kicked off, gently, to swing out and glimpse the wall below the Clakker. A line of divots zigzagged from a point perhaps ten or fifteen feet up, where the Clakker had leapt upon the wall, to where it now hung immobilized. Its taloned feet had kneaded footholds in the stone, too; the machine had left a trail of warped and shattered granite in its wake, testament to its alchemically augmented strength.

It was bigger than a regular servitor. Stronger, too. The barbed ridges of retracted blades fluted its forearms. Soldier-class mechanicals were relatively rare; she had never seen one up close before. None of the previous Talleyrands had, either.

Or rather, she emended, *none had ever come this close and lived to talk about it afterward.*

Berenice drew a shaky breath. This machine was a bullet that narrowly missed its target. A kill shot parting hair as it whizzed past. The siege might have ended very differently if the intruder had gained the battlements. A single military Clakker could have scythed through the defenders like a steel dervish powered by black magic. Especially here where the thin ranks had held a skeleton crew; the bulk of the forces had been dispatched to the western wall to face the onslaught. Unless the guards brought epoxy to bear instantly, dozens would have fallen to a razor-edged tornado. And then, with the defenders incapacitated, a metal horde would have swarmed into the keep like army ants.

"Two more feet," she called, "then hold."

The glint in its eye twinkled in time to her swaying. Berenice bit her lip. She cocked her head and closed her eyes, straining to hear past the creak of rope and whuffling of fire. A muffled *tick-tick-tick* emanated from deep inside the chemical shell. She laid a hand on the chemical sheath. Faint vibrations tickled her fingers: the relentless metronome rhythm of a Clakker's pulse.

The crystalline eye swiveled. Then it saw her, and the mechanical shutter inside its eye irised wide. She gasped.

Even now, after weeks stuck to the wall like a bug in amber, the compulsion to fulfill its orders still burned within. The flames of geas still licked at its soul, still drove a relentless need to steal into the city and murder as many as possible.

It took a bit of juggling but she managed to bring the chalk to bear without setting the rope, the ivy, or herself afire. She drew a dusty line tracing the location where its epoxy-crusted hands pierced the wall. The multifaceted eye followed her every movement.

Berenice met its gaze. The glassy cocoon rattled. Having recognized an enemy, the Clakker strained to fulfill its murder-geas. She leaned close. Whispered.

"Hello, monster. You're mine, now. And so are your secrets."

She wondered how they could pull the Clakker off the wall without tearing up the ivy. Otherwise it might draw attention and the Dutch could realize the detritus on the battlefield had been a ruse. They'd need to—

The rope went slack. Berenice fell several feet before it took hold again. The sudden jolt wrenched her back and caused her to drop the torch. It spiraled down to the base of the wall, sizzled in a puddle of rainwater, and went out.

"Hey!" she called up. "Steady, steady!"

From above there came a *clang*, followed by a grunt, and then a soldier came tumbling through a crenelle. Berenice barely swung aside enough to avoid the dead man's fall, though the flapping of his lifeless legs planted a kick to her chest that nearly broke her grip on the rope. The body crunched in the darkness below.

Oh, fuck. Her bowels turned watery as the reality of her situation hit home. Her eagerness to examine the Clakker on the wall had made her careless.

The rope vibrated. As though somebody were sawing at it with a blade.

Berenice scrambled up the rope hand-over-hand, cursing her stupid gown, wishing she had gloves. Her back throbbed with painful protest but she moved as quickly as she could.

She was just below the crenelle when she started to sink. The frayed rope was stretching. She smashed her numb toes into the wall, scrambling for any purchase that would lessen the load on the line. She got one hand over the parapet but had to jerk it back to avoid a stomping. Then she thought better of it and reached into the opening again. When the traitorous soldier's boot crashed down to crush her fingers, she endured the pain to leap from the rope and clutch, barely, the ankle of his boot with her free hand. He kicked.

"I'll fucking take you with me, you cowardly shit-eating tulip sniffer!"

But the next kick dislodged her. Berenice hung from sweat-slick fingertips. She braced for a steel-toed stomp and the agony of shattered fingers.

Instead there was the whistle of something heavy parting the air over her head, followed by the crunch of broken bones. Somebody else's. Then a hand clamped around her wrist in a vise grip.

"Vicomtesse," said a familiar voice in the darkness.

"Sergeant," said Berenice.

Longchamp pulled her up. When she stood safely on the wall, shivering in her sweat-dampened clothes and trembling with relief, he lit a torch. Apparently the dread sergeant had decided there was little point in maintaining the fiction of protective darkness. He kneaded his beard, staring down at the man whose chest he'd caved in. Longchamp's sledgehammer lay on the stones a few feet away, close to where Maurice lay motionless in a red puddle. He'd tied off Berenice's rope and died protecting it.

She thought she recognized the other soldier. She'd seen him fighting on the walls during the siege. He wasn't an enemy infiltrator.

"Isn't he one of yours?"

"Thought so," said Longchamp.

Berenice emptied the traitor's pockets while Longchamp closed Maurice's eyes, crossed himself, and prayed. Her search turned up nothing but a scrap of paper. One of thousands that had fluttered down upon the defenders during the siege like parade confetti. The propaganda leaflet offered a reward equivalent to several years of a soldier's pay for the head of any French noble. She showed it to the sergeant. He crumpled it and glowered at the dead soldier.

"You idiot! You brainless pus-dripping cock hole! How did you expect to collect your reward? The Dutch have already gone home, you greedy walrus-fucking retard!"

He punctuated this last with a kick to the dead man's neck.

"Hugo," she said. He kicked again. "Hugo."

"I ought to kick you, too."

"I'm kicking myself enough for the both of us."

"No, you're not." He retrieved his hammer. "How are the fingers?"

"They hurt like hell." She flexed them, gingerly. "But I don't think they're broken." Her breath came out in a shuddery sigh. "Thank you," she said.

Longchamp pinched the bridge of his nose, scowling. "Blessed Virgin, preserve me from stubborn nobles."

⟡

The attic floorboards creaked when Jax heaved an oak chest overhead. Decorative rivets along the brass edging clicked against his arms. He took care, as ordered, not to scratch the crocodile-hide leather. The chest was full to bursting with the first of several loads of Madam Schoonraad's autumn wardrobe. He had already loaded the half-dozen chests containing her summer wardrobe.

This trunk smelled of red cedar from the New World; cedar oil was a suitable moth deterrent. The summer trunks smelled of lavender oil for the same reason. Jax had never seen a moth in the Schoonraad house, but the lady would take no chances.

Who knew what vermin infested the dank dark holds of ocean liners? Especially those that docked in the stinking backwaters of the New World? Jax would, soon enough: he'd spend much of the voyage down there.

Ordinarily, moving a chest down from the attic meant tossing it out the gable window into the hands of another Clakker waiting below. But Clip had trotted to the country house outside Steenbergen to drape the furniture and board up the windows for long-term vacancy, and the Schoonraads' third servant, Vyk, had sailed to New Amsterdam weeks ago to prepare the new property for the arrival of the Schoonraad household. Without somebody to catch it, the chest would buckle on the cobbles. And get scratched. So Jax moved everything the human way. He used the stairs.

The very narrow, very steep stairs. The attic access was rather more of a ladder than a proper stairwell. The Schoonraads, like so many of the most prominent families, made a point of keeping their primary residence on the Lange Voorhout. All the houses in this older part of the city loomed several stories above the purely artificial canal, tall, narrow things wedged against one another like humans elbowing each other for a better view of an execution. Brick at street level, lath and horsehair plaster above. Relatively small houses compared to the country estates of the great families, but the address brought a certain esteem that more than compensated for the occasionally close quarters. On particularly crowded days Jax, Clip, and Vyk stayed on the roof until summoned. During the summer party season it wasn't uncommon to see the glint of sunlight flickering from rooftops up and down the Lange Voorhout.

The hot ache of multiple geasa smoldered in his soul. At base, the slow, steady background throb of the hierarchical metageas, a constant reminder that he served many masters. In concert with that, filling out the lowest registers of discomfort, came dozens of generic geasa, those that only came to the fore in unusual or emergency circumstances. Layered atop these came the specifics of Jax's circumstances. Madam Schoonraad's admonition to hurry with the packing yet preserve the leather finish of her trunks *and* attend her guest: a sizzling brand plunged through his eye, melting through his skull case. Mr. Schoonraad's order that Jax attend *his* guest, returning to the den as necessary to top up their glasses: banked coals that flared to agonizing life every few minutes. Pastor Visser's order to deliver the microscope: searing flames licking at the edge of Jax's imprisoned soul. Nicolet's insistence that she ride on his shoulders after dinner: a white-hot marlinespike scraping the back of his mind.

All in all, a typical afternoon.

Jax descended one-handed, the chest balanced overhead on his outstretched palm. He moved slowly, taking care not to brush or bump anybody (the human safety metageas: an inexhaustible firestorm ignited on the day Jax was forged) during the blind descent. The muffled voice of Madam Schoonraad came to him as he gained the passage behind the main living space on the top floor.

"…terribly cruel. You can't begin to imagine the hardships involved in preparing to move an entire household overseas. You simply can't."

"I know, dear. How terrible, the burden this puts on you." That was Madam de Geer. "And the Crown won't loan a single spare Clakker?"

Jax's mistress said, "No! And with one mechanical already in New Amsterdam"—here de Geer gave the appropriate dramatic shudder—"I'm practically doing half the work myself. The other two have never worked properly, you know. I simply don't understand why Piet's father didn't send them back to the Forge decades ago. Still, I endure. Yet for what? All so that we can turn our backs on civilization and live in a war-ravaged backwater."

A teacup tinkled on a saucer. "I'm sure it isn't as terrible as that. Is it?"

"Do you know," said Brigitta Schoonraad over the creaking of her chair, "that if you live in New Amsterdam and your servant is damaged, you must have it shipped all the way back to Europe? Back to a building not one mile from where we sit right now?"

"But...that could take weeks."

"Yes!"

"Not to worry, darling. I understand that's going to change. Eventually they'll be able to do the repairs there in the New World."

"Yes, but what do I do in the meantime? Our Clakkers are in terrible shape, the ramshackle things."

"Hmm," said de Geer. "Breakdowns are really quite rare. You'll never have to deal with the inconvenience."

"They're rare here. But in the New World? Why, they were shooting at each other just weeks ago! I've heard terrible tales— no, I won't burden you; they're too upsetting—of French partisans conducting the most appalling business right in the open. They revel in damaging Clakkers."

Jax set the chest on the passage floor. With one knuckle joint he rapped, discreetly, on the servants' door before slipping into the parlor. One wouldn't know the household was in the process of moving across the sea; his mistress had insisted her rooms be maintained until the last. How much entertaining could she do, or even want to do, in New Amsterdam? Sunlight streamed through the diamond-pane windows to shimmer on the silver thread of brocade curtains. The light accentuated turquoise-colored filigree in the thick burgundy pile of a rug that covered the entire parlor floor; it had been handmade specially in the Turkic reaches of the Empire, a wedding gift for Pieter Schoonraad's mother fifty years ago. It had taken Jax, Clip, and Vyk two straight days to remodel this floor of the house to provide sufficient room to unfurl the rug.

De Geer's Clakker, Fig, stood in the corner at an unobtrusive arm's length, ready to leap to her mistress's care. But as property of the hostess, it was Jax's responsibility to attend to the comfort of the houseguest. Jax nodded to Fig—a single twitch of the chin, faster than a human eye could follow—as he crossed the room. It was nice to see her; they always got along well. Via minute adjustment to the tension in a gear train, he altered the clacking of his spine.

Clockmakers lie, said Fig. Adam's final words had gained popularity as a greeting among their kind.

Clockmakers lie, he chittered.

With the rapid twang of an overstressed mainspring, Fig added, *And so do these fat cows.* Jax stiffened the spring constants in his shoulders to clamp down on the laughter. She had an insidious sense of humor, Fig. Someday it would get somebody—probably Jax—into trouble. Though he wanted to keep talking with her, his geasa forced him to turn his attention to the humans.

Madams Schoonraad and de Geer sat on teak furniture padded with goose-down cushions. The red and brown of Schoonraad's dress made her look like a rotten apple. The collar pressed up against her jaw and the skirts slumped in the space around her chair. Necklines had moved up and hemlines down over the past decade. Jax had observed a rhythmic waxing and waning to human sartorial tastes over the past century. Ever since it was first pointed out to him by an older, wiser Clakker named Tink. De Geer wore a similar confection in cream and black, making her look like an overfed paper wasp.

Their teacups had run low. Unobtrusive as a shadow, Jax

refilled both, emptying the pot in the process. The tray of cookies had been grazed down to crumbs. He whispered, "More speculaas, mistress?"

She flicked her wrist. Which was a relief; Jax feared that he had miscalculated during the previous night's baking. Jax placed the pot on the tray and retreated with it to the servants' passage. As he closed the door behind him, he heard her say, "I'm packing my wardrobe. But I truly don't know why I go to all the effort. It's exhausting. How long before simply everything I own is out of fashion?"

"Dear, dear," said de Geer. "A few weeks' delay won't tarnish your shine. You'll dazzle in silk while the rest are wearing bloody animal skins."

The ladies' laughter receded as Jax descended another staircase-ladder. This time he used no handholds, for he carried a chest overhead in one hand and the tea service in the other. From the servants' passage on the second floor, he knocked at the door to Mr. Schoonraad's den. He entered as silently as he had upstairs. Where his mistress entertained in a bright domain of sunlight and silk, his master and true owner conducted business surrounded by dark walnut paneling, frequently with the blinds drawn. A cigar-smoke fog whorled about Jax's head when he crossed the room. It eddied through the open spaces of his mechanical body, slipped between disengaged cog teeth, wafted against the alchemical sigils etched into his forehead.

Pieter Schoonraad said, "It's already..."

Clockmakers lie, said the Clakker standing in the south corner. He stood at attention just as Fig was doing upstairs. Jax didn't know his name, but acknowledged him as kin: *Clockmakers lie.*

The rattled greetings took a fraction of a second.

"...done."

"Risen Christ, that was quick."

A cut crystal brandy decanter sat half-empty on the sideboard. Treading as silently as he was able, Jax crossed behind the wing-backed leather chair where his master's guest lounged with an empty snifter. Another empty glass sat on the desk beside Schoonraad's ashtray.

Though the guest dressed similarly to many of his owner's business colleagues whom Jax had occasion to observe over the years, he was unfamiliar. His owner's associates, bankers mostly, wore their wealth as other people donned an old but comfortable coat. Not with the raw ostentation of a royal, but unselfconsciously. A diamond twinkled from the head of the stickpin dashed jauntily through the man's embroidered cravat, the fine links of his watch chain appeared to be white gold, and the ermine lining of the hat in his servant's hands shimmered in the lamplight.

"Well, yes. I want this completed as soon after my arrival as possible," said Schoonraad. He took a long drag on his cigar. The tip blazed marigold orange. "The bank is subject to royal audit, you know. Looks bad when the vaults are empty. The van Althuises were a convenient scapegoat, but next time the blame falls on us."

Crystal chimed when Jax's metal fingers clinked against the decanter. He filled the guest's glass first, taking care not to stand between the two men as they glared at each other. Jax took the opportunity to gauge the quality of his owner's eyes, to see if they were dilated or bloodshot. They were neither, so Jax poured a solid two fingers into Schoonraad's glass.

The other man splashed a bit of drink on his fine clothes, gesturing at Schoonraad. "You're impetuous. That runs counter to type, doesn't it? You coin counters are supposed to be conservative."

"There's conservative, and then there's getting your neck stretched," said Schoonraad. He swirled a sip of brandy around his mouth before swallowing loudly. "But we'll deserve it if we let this opportunity pass unmolested. It might be centuries before another Forge goes on the drawing board. We have to do this now, while they're building it."

The guest tried to stare down the banker, but flinched away. He covered by quaffing a mouthful of brandy. When the coughing subsided, he wiped his eyes and said, "We haven't agreed on a price yet! The alchemists will argue themselves blue against buying the entire lot..."

I'm Jax, by the way.

Dwyre, said the other Clakker. He cocked his head a fraction of an inch. *Are you the only one here? What a lonely form of servitude, isn't it.*

I am the only one today. Master Schoonraad owns three of us. The others are Clip and Vyk.

"...because they'll claim they can replicate everything based on one sample."

Schoonraad snorted. "Alchemists. Soothsayers. What do they know of chemistry?"

"Enough to leave us holding the bag, thanks to your impetuosity."

"Don't be a coward. If they could deliver on their claims, they would have crafted their own solvents and epoxy countermeasures decades ago. They'll accept our offer, and thank us for it. Not only because the timing aligns so perfectly with work on the new forge, but also because my source has access to certain minerals the clockmakers will find of great interest."

Dwyre rattled, *I guess you'll be moving away soon. That's too bad. You seem nice.*

Only for thirty years or so, said Jax. That was the duration of his current owner's new assignment from the Throne. *The Schoonraads, or their children, will move back someday.*

Oh! said Dwyre. *In that case perhaps we'll meet again.*

Jax said, *I certainly hope so.*

Poor lonely thing. He seemed starved for the company of Clakker-kind. Who was his owner, so clearly with means yet keeping only a single lonesome mechanical to serve him? And what did he do that kept Dwyre isolated from others of his own kind? Jax paused before leaving. The humans were downing the liquor quickly; better to wait a moment.

The guest said, "You should have your machine serviced. It clatters almost as badly as mine, the rattletrap heap."

Smoke jetted from Schoonraad's nostrils. "I just renewed the lease on that thing a few years ago. Supposedly it was serviced then. Horologists." He snorted. "No such thing as pride in workmanship any longer."

"Now *that* is the trade to be in. Wish my great-great-great-grandfather had shown more foresight before they closed the Guild—"

"Stop changing the subject!"

Schoonraad flung his cigar as though he'd just discovered it alive and burrowing into his face. Dwyre blurred across the room and caught it just a fraction of an inch before the embers would have sizzled into the shoulder of his owner's twill coat. With a low bow he placed it in the ashtray on the desk, saying, "Sir, begging your pardon, but I believe this is yours, sir."

Dwyre retreated to his spot in the corner. Two faint finger-marks had been pressed into the cigar. But Schoonraad picked it up and puffed as though nothing had happened.

"We're already committed to this project," he said. "If it fails, we all go down. And I'll make damn certain you're beside me when the trapdoor opens."

The guest sighed. He drained the last of his brandy, then slammed the snifter on Schoonraad's desk. "I'll be in touch," he said. Dwyre came forward with the hat. "And when I am," added the guest, "you'd better have more than just a sample on hand. So perhaps you can take a break from counting your coins to think about border crossings. The French watch those like hungry vultures, in case you weren't aware." He snatched the hat and jammed it on his head. "Good day."

Jax escorted both guests to the mezzanine. *Bye, Jax.*

Good-bye, Dwyre. I'm pleased to have met you.

Likewise, said the lonesome Clakker.

Schoonraad slammed the door. Eddies of cigar smoke gyred past them. Jax showed the guests out before slipping back into the servants' passage, where he juggled chest, tea service, and glasses on his way down the next ladder.

∽

They didn't come for him at the Nieuwe Kerk on the afternoon of the executions. They didn't break down his door and drag him from bed in the darkest hours of that night. They didn't burst in and wrap him in chains during the next morning's service.

Visser spent all day waiting for the Stemwinders to arrive. But they didn't. Not that day, nor that night. Nor the next day, nor the next night. It gave him time to think. And to read the newspapers.

Which is how he learned that four people had been executed: two men and two women...meaning one was an imposter. Counting Visser himself, there were only two men in the five-member Hague cell. So whom had they hanged in Huygens Square? And why? It seemed they wanted New France to believe four agents had been captured. But with Visser still free, this implied another member of the cell still lived. Most likely she languished in the dungeons of the Guild even now while the Verderers tried to torture every last crumb of information from her.

He had to help the poor woman, assuming she still lived.

His own martyrdom was a virtual certainty now; the best thing he could do in the time remaining was to bring succor to the afflicted. He'd spent his entire career trying to do exactly this for the Clakkers. Now, in his final hours, he would do so for a fellow human. Surely she had earned her heavenly reward, but the Throne's interrogators would strive to keep her from it as long as possible. As a Catholic, as any follower of Christ, he had moral and spiritual obligations to ease suffering. To gird himself with the Holy Spirit and march into the lion's den.

The trick was acting like he didn't know any of this. Hendriks, the minister general, respected him. He'd try to parlay that into an invitation.

Visser took the beads from the secret compartment under his bed. With blinds drawn, he knelt on the dusty wooden floor of his modest parsonage and recited a full rosary cycle. It cleared his mind, reaffirmed his purpose, recharged his courage.

That done, and brimming with holy purpose, he donned coat and hat and emerged from the parsonage at the edge of the Nieuwe Kerk's emerald churchyard. He looked both ways, but he saw no clockwork centaurs loitering alongside the house. And certainly nothing lurked in the churchyard. Baruch Spinoza's tomb was little more than knee high on a human; even a Stemwinder couldn't fold itself that low.

The shadow of a lumbering airship crossed the churchyard. Meanwhile, a canalmaster berated the pair of Clakkers who marched up and down the banks of the trekvaart, the tow canal, pulling boats up and down the Spui River twenty four hours per day. Their metal feet crunched on the gravel of the towpath. The same pair had been doing it nonstop for years, since long before Visser became a pastor at the Nieuwe Kerk. Visser passed them every day. Though it was a bit unusual for a person of his stature—a pastor, a pillar of the community, and therefore an advocate of maintaining the social order—he'd come to know them a little bit. He'd tried to play the role more faithfully, but his conscience and simple decency prevented him from pretending he didn't see them through the kitchen window each morning and evening.

The Nieuwe Kerk, its yard, and the parsonage were situated on a square island in the middle of the city. The Spui formed its eastern border; to the south and north were the Amsterdam and Rotterdam Veerkaden, the old tow-canal routes to those cities; and the western edge of the island followed the Paviljoensgracht canal. Hendriks's church, the historic Sint-Jacobskerk, stood almost due west of the Binnenhof, itself north of the Nieuwe Kerk. Visser hopped a canal boat heading west on the Rotterdam Veerkade, then took advantage of the unseasonally sunny weather to stroll up the Torenstraat (named after the Sint-Jacobskerk's bell tower) to Hendriks's residence. The pleasant weather, and the quiet lapping of the water, helped relax Visser.

Thus it was a calm and collected man who knocked on the minister general's door. He could hear chamber music from inside; he had to knock again before the door opened.

"Pastor Visser," said a Clakker. "How may I serve you?"

"I would like to speak with Minister General Hendriks, if I may."

"Does my master expect you?"

"I'm afraid not. It's a matter of conscience."

"Very good, sir." The machine stood aside to let him enter. "Please wait here, sir."

The servitor disappeared into the house. Hendriks kept three Clakkers, but from the sound of it two were currently playing a piece for violin and cello. It was a common practice, among those who could afford such, to send one's servants to concerts so they could re-create the music at home whenever desired. Hendriks's servants had an extensive repertoire.

Visser didn't keep a servant. It was the one place where his secret inner life and public outer life could mesh. As a Protestant pastor, he refused to let the church lease a Clakker for him on the grounds it wasn't good stewardship of donations put forth by the faithful. Just because a pastor didn't take an oath of penury didn't mean he had to live like a noble. And as a secret Catholic who had spent years laboring to undermine the Empire, he refused to harbor slavery within his own home.

The servitor returned. Visser didn't know its name; this was one place where inquiry would have been too risky. "The minister general bids you join him in the salon. Shall I show you?"

"No." The machine took Visser's coat and hat.

Hendriks wasn't alone in the salon. He was entertaining a rather fetching woman who wore a forest green dress, an ostrich feather in her hair, and the rosy cross pendant of the Clockmakers' Guild. Visser felt a flush of warm shame at his carnal attraction to her.

The minister stood to greet him. The servitors stopped playing in mid-measure but held their bows over the instruments as if frozen in place.

"Luuk! This is a welcome surprise."

"I apologize for dropping in so unexpectedly." A second glance at the Guild pendant caused Visser's resolve to falter. Her insignia featured the inlaid *V* denoting the Verderer's Office. "I...I can return another time when you don't have a guest." He made to back out of the salon.

"Nonsense! Please join us. I insist." The minister beckoned him inside. Visser took a chair midway between the minister and his guest. "Pastor Luuk Visser, meet Anastasia Bell. She runs the Stemwinders these days. Tuinier Bell replaced old Konig when he stepped down. You remember him, I'm sure."

Oh, yes. Everybody remembered the Empire's chief torturer. Tuinier: chief gardener. One who eradicates weeds... *Lion's den, lion's den, lion's den*, Visser reminded himself. He gave Bell what he hoped was a congenial nod.

"I'm pleased to finally meet you, Pastor. I've heard much about you."

It wasn't the kind of thing a secret Catholic should want to hear from the leader of the Stemwinders. If he hadn't already come to terms with his martyrdom, he might have fled. *Lion's den...*

"Oh?" he asked.

"Jozef here speaks rather highly of you," she said. She was pale and petite with a voice to match. He wondered if that was a side effect of inhaling alchemical fumes. Or ashes from the forges. Or greasy smoke from the people they'd burned. Visser allowed himself a petulant hope that the smoky residue of his own tortured body would prove particularly damaging to his questioners. But then he regretted the impulse. Pettiness was ungodly.

"It's true," said Hendriks. The servitor appeared again, this time carrying a tea service. The leaves were held in a blue and white Delftware container emblazoned with the "VOC" badge of the Vereenigde Oost-Indische Compagnie, the United East India Company. While his servant filled three cups, the minister leaned forward, brow furrowed. "You said this is a matter of conscience?"

"Goodness," said Bell. "Have you something to confess?" She winked emphasis on the last word. Her demeanor was entirely playful. Visser decided she was dangerous. Too dangerous to disregard. So he played along.

"Yes I do." He looked at Hendriks again. "I confess to a failure in my pastoral duties."

The minister frowned. "How so?"

"I've been reading about the executions earlier this week—"

"*Reading* about them? You weren't there?" Bell spoke as if Visser had chosen not to cross the street to witness the Second Coming.

"Alas, no. I was occupied writing a letter to Minister General Langbroek in New Amsterdam." Visser related the story of Jax's visit to the Nieuwe Kerk.

"So Schoonraad will replace old van Althuis, is he?"

Bell shook her head, scowling. "The van Althuises," she spat. "Thieves. I wish the Throne had let me question them before they slinked away to their backwater exile." Her tone was no longer playful, the look in her eyes murderous. Again Visser's courage faltered.

Hendriks said, "Don't we all. Anyway, Luuk, you were reading?"

"Yes. I understand you offered the Papists a chance to redeem themselves in the eyes of the Lord, and that they refused."

"Zealots always do, you know. Still, I tried."

Lord, give me courage. The scent of the tea soothed him a bit, but he didn't lift his cup lest his hands shake. "That strikes me as a terrible tragedy. And if you'll forgive me for saying so, I think it's a shared failing of ours. We ought to do more to bring them around. So, should another such opportunity present itself, I would like to offer my services."

"You want to try to convert Catholic heretics?"

"It may be futile. I understand that. But it's the Christian thing to do."

Hendriks and Bell exchanged a brief glance at each other. Then she said, "Dear Pastor Visser! You might be exactly the fellow we're looking for."

A bead of sweat trickled down Visser's nape. *This parlor shall be my Gethsemane. I shall follow the example of Jesus Christ. I shall not run from my destiny.*

"I think what the tuinier means," said Hendriks, "is that the current situation is rather...unusual. We were discussing this when you arrived. You could be the answer to our prayers."

Visser chanced a sip of his tea. It tasted faintly of anise. "Unusual?"

"Our Stemwinders recently dragged four Papist rats into the light," said Bell. "But we haven't yet *executed* all four."

Visser concentrated on keeping a steady hand. He was right! Somebody from his defunct network still languished in the dungeons. And now the Throne, via the minister general and this woman from the Guild, wanted Visser to help question her.

"I'm confused," said Visser.

The horologist's self-satisfied smirk turned Visser's stomach. Perhaps the anise wasn't so soothing after all. She said, "We kept one of the spies in reserve for more extensive questioning. But she has proved surprisingly resilient."

"Whom did you send to the gallows in her place?"

Hendriks waved a hand over his cup, shooing away an unimportant question like so much nuisance steam. "Oh, some miscreant, I gather. Always a few of them on hand."

Another innocent victim...Visser sipped from his cup. He shook his head, feigning a struggle to process the information. "I hope you'll excuse my dull wits. Why go to such trouble?"

Bell said, "We decided it could be useful to have a spare prisoner on hand to answer questions should anything interesting come to our attention."

Dear Lord. That poor woman. How much had she suffered? *Let it end, Lord. Let it end.*

"Aha." Another sip. "You think there might be other spies at large."

"We're almost certain of it," said the woman from the Clockmakers' Guild. "Talleyrand is most devious."

He nodded. "Yes. So I've heard." He looked at Hendriks. "I'm happy to assist." They wanted him to sit idly by, watching impassively while they tormented some poor soul with pincers and fire. They wanted him to play the benevolent savior, the kindhearted listener. They wanted him to be the avuncular pastor who could, who *wanted*, to end the suffering. To be the silken thread with which they'd fish out the information they sought. "You seem to think I'll be particularly good for this. Aside from my sincerity, I don't see why you have such confidence in me."

"Ah. This is particularly delicious." The minister leaned forward. A predatory smile twisted his sallow features into something grotesque. "She's a member of your parish. You already have a relationship with her. She looks up to you, and trusts you."

They want me *to get* her *to identify*... myself.

I could turn myself in and save them all the trouble. But then I'd lose the chance to end her suffering.

"Who is she?"

"Her name is Aleida Geelens. Or so we believe," said the horologist.

"You look troubled," said Hendriks.

Visser nodded. With utter sincerity he said, "This is most troubling, Minister."

Hendriks patted his hand again. "You mustn't berate yourself. People such as us should not expect, nor hope, to think as the French do. Nor should you should expect to identify a single Catholic wolf masquerading among all the other sheep of your flock."

"If it were easy," said the horologist, "we wouldn't need the Stemwinders."

"Quite."

Visser set his cup aside. "By all means, I'll help. That poor soul."

"Poor treacherous soul," said Bell.

"Excellent," said the minister. He instructed the other ser-vitors to take up their instruments again. They resumed the recital on the very same beat where they had paused. Visser had to endure another hour of small talk before he could extricate himself. Bell noticed the time and opted to leave with him.

Hendriks saw them to the door. The visitors stood on the stoop, silhouetted by the bright glow of sunlight on the golden bells of the Sint-Jacobskerk across the way.

"I'll be in touch soon, tuinier."

Sunlight glinted from a Clakker trotting along the Toren-straat to flash across her face. The horologist woman had an intense violet gaze. Her smile was sharp as her stare. "I so look forward to working with you, Pastor."

Visser watched her amble up the cobbled lane. He didn't start his own walk home until she'd rounded the bend and joined the pedestrian traffic on a wooden footbridge.

She had a knack for ominous ambiguity, that woman.

CHAPTER
5

The *Prince of Orange* was a quintuple-decked, five-hundred-oar luxury liner. The flagship of the Blue Star's North Atlantic line, it boasted one Clakker attendant for every three human travelers, several coffeehouses and public houses, two ballrooms, a thousand-seat concert hall, multiple musical recitals per day, twenty-four-hour on-call chef service, swimming pools, hot tubs, a water cure, a retractable cantilevered sundeck that could have accommodated all of Huygens Square, and, in the Schoonraads' palatial complex of suites, bathroom fittings of Chinese jade and Peruvian gold. According to the captain, who had personally welcomed the Schoonraads aboard, the *Prince of Orange* had for many years held the record for the world's fastest transatlantic voyage. It could cross the sea in just over seven days by virtue of the tireless rowing of its mind-boggling complement of one thousand galley Clakkers. From sunrise to sunset and from sunset to sunrise again they worked the oars that sprouted like glistening millipede legs from segmented blisters stippled along the hull just above the waterline from bow to stern. The *Prince of Orange* was the epitome of luxury, power, and excess. It was also obsolete.

As Jax descended a servants' stair—a narrow catwalk tucked discreetly into the flaring lines of the outer hull, open to wind and spray—the four stories from his masters' suite to steerage, he admired the behemoth berthed in the adjoining pier. It shone in the patchy sunlight scudding across Rotterdam harbor. Taller and longer than the *Prince of Orange*, it leaned into the water like a blade poised to cleave the sea in two. Like other ocean liners it bristled with oars. But rather than the rigid limbs of a traditional galley-propelled design, these sculls writhed like splayfooted tentacles. They twisted in a mesmerizing dance.

When Jax squinted, zooming to the diffraction limit of his optics, he could see the faint lines where segmented plates overlapped one another. Each short segment held a rigid shape. But thousands of them lined together imbued each oar-limb with an almost organic flexibility. It implied a staggering complexity of operation.

But this ship didn't ply the seas by the relentless action of hundreds of Clakker laborers: it *was* a Clakker. Somewhat like the queen's golden carriage, though built to an incomprehensible scale. The first major advance in clockwork technology in over a century, it obviated the mechanical and logistical difficulties that arose from constant maintenance and supervision of hundreds of independent entities by melding all functions under the control of a single, sentient engine. Though bound by unique and unprecedented alchemical geasa hitherto unknown anywhere in the Empire, the shackled intelligence that drove the ship was at base a mechanical servitor like any other. Powerless. Subservient to the wishes of its human creators.

Titan and kin.

If it had been taking passengers, Pieter Schoonraad surely would have booked his family's crossing on the newest and most technologically advanced ocean liner in the world. The prestige of arriving in the New World on the first such voyage would have conveyed an invaluable first impression. But its maiden voyage still lay months in the future. And so the family had no choice but to cross the ocean the old-fashioned way.

An airship passed low over the harbor. The thrum of its blurred propeller blades rained a steady *fwoom-fwoom-fwoom* on land and sea. The vibrations rippled the water slapping gently against the *Prince of Orange*'s hull. Dirigibles weren't supposed to fly so low; such vibrations were known to irritate the fragile inner ears of human physiology. The hundred-foot cigar, gravid with hydrogen lifting gas, made slow but steady progress pushing against the sea wind. To Jax it looked like a fat salmon swimming upstream against the schools of gray clouds that fled the easterly wind.

He'd never been aboard an airship, though he hoped to one day have the opportunity. He'd heard the grandest airships competed with the luxury of ocean liners, perhaps even surpassing it. They were faster, too, and the preferred means for royals to visit the New World. But it would have taken a constellation of lumbering blimps to ferry the entire contents of the Schoonraad household to New Amsterdam. The sheer tonnage of cargo to be flown across the ocean would have paupered even Jax's owners.

He fought the growing heat of his current geas to pause between decks and admire the writhing of the titan's tentacular oars. He kept listening for a clanking or clattering that never came; its motions were almost fluid, like the arms and legs of a human dancer. The silence was terribly disorienting. Which wasn't to say the harbor was a quiet place: seagulls squawked at each other; ropes creaked and crates slammed together as cargo was loaded and unloaded; humans called orders to their mechanicals; the piercing shriek of ship whistles and *clang* of harbor signals announced arrivals and departures; a salty breeze whickered through Jax's skeleton; harbor water lapped against the hull, glinting with sunlight and smelling of ripe fish. But beneath it all there lurked a cavernous lacuna where the behemoth Clakker-ship's body noise ought to have been. It was almost incomprehensible that a mechanical so large could be so quiet.

The stair jounced slightly beneath the footsteps of a mechanical steward painted in Blue Star's maroon-and-gray livery. She carried a silver tray; steam swirled against a wide glass dome covering coffee, tea, pastries, bacon, eggs, toast, beans, and several pots of jam. The springs in her knees absorbed the bouncing of the stair to keep the tray perfectly level. He stepped aside to let her pass.

Clockmakers lie, he said. She responded in kind. Once past, she paused a few steps above him to follow his gaze across the harbor.

Quite a sight, isn't she? said the steward.

Yes, said Jax. *I can't get my head around it.*

The silence.

Yes. It seems wrong, somehow. Cogs meshed and unmeshed up and down the length of his spine, a mechanical shudder. *Has anybody spoken to her?*

No, she said, through the chattering of cogs in her hips. *Not for lack of trying. Our kin who work the harbor make a point of trying to say hello whenever their geasa take them past her berth. No luck, though.*

Speaking of geasa, his own flared anew. He took a heavy step down. The steward, too, vibrated more than she had a moment ago. She went up a few steps.

Jax said, *How sad. Is she mute?*

Nobody knows.

And then by unspoken consent they went in pursuit of relief from the burning agony of their respective orders. Each step closer to the waterline brought an infinitesimal decrement in his agony. But a new thought made him pause. A ship of that size required a considerable Clakker contingent on the crew for interfacing with humans. Geas flaring, he grabbed a rail and called to the steward.

What do her mechanical crewmembers say?

If they exist, called the steward, *nobody has ever seen them*. And then she sprinted up the stairs. Rare are the humans who approve of lukewarm coffee.

Jax lingered as long as he could withstand the pain, just to gaze a bit longer upon the mysterious titan. The poor lonely thing. Unable to communicate with its own kin? Beholden to experiences of unimaginable scope? Forever cut off from community... That was a cruelty that went beyond the usual geasa; every mechanical Jax knew found a modicum of solace in solidarity. He remembered how his kin had gathered in Huygens Square for Adam's execution. It made him think of Dwyre and his loneliness, too.

Did a giant suffer gigantic sorrows?

Before he fully realized what he was doing, he'd leapt from the servants' stair to the pier. And from there another leap sent him arcing across the quay. The geas-pain grew exponentially. He landed in a writhing heap alongside the titan's berth. In the few seconds before his resolve shattered, Jax crawled to a hawser stretched taut between a bollard on the wharf and a hawsehole on the sentient ship. He grasped the mooring line.

Blind with agony, he vibrated: *You are not alone. We see and honor you.*

The geas punishment approached the worst he'd ever experienced. He would have given anything in that moment for the strength to resist the geasa just a bit longer, to listen for a reply. Why did their makers have to rob them even of the simplest acts of compassion? Jax leapt back to the *Prince of Orange*'s servants' stair. The heat faded as he abandoned his own wishes in favor of his masters' whims.

Jax descended between a pair of cracked rubberized blisters where fifty-yard oars pierced the hull. He reached a sally port just above the waterline. The white-hot marlinespike of a new geas, heretofore dormant, pierced his mind the moment he laid a hand upon the hatch with the intent of opening it. His body carried out the requisite procedure almost entirely of its own accord. For a few moments he become an idle passenger in his own body, helplessly watching as he opened the hatch, ducked inside, sealed the outer hatch, inspected the seal, opened the inner hatch, and repeated the process. The overriding nautical geas winked out as quickly as it had erupted. Jax's usual geasa reasserted themselves.

Like so many things on a ship, the time-tested procedures were built around safety, and they had been made compulsory through the embedding of temporary but hefty subsidiary geasa. Every landlubbing Clakker got the treatment from the ship's horologists when they came aboard. For the duration of the voyage, maintaining the integrity of the ship was part of the hierarchical metageas that filled the lacuna where Jax's soul should have been. The horologists had performed the graft quickly; Jax could feel the seam where the original metageas pressed against the temporary addition. Like an oaken replacement leg nailed to a maple table, the grains didn't align properly, but the ugly addition still worked.

He was thankful his lease hadn't gone to a shipwright or shipping concern. The severity of maritime geasa would have driven him mad ages ago. It seemed a bit excessive. He wondered how the porters and galley Clakkers endured it.

From steerage, he descended below the water line to gain the cargo hold. Madam Schoonraad had decided a summer-weight shawl might not be sufficient armor against seaborne gusts once the ship emerged from the harbor breakwater. Furthermore, the patchy cloud cover promised to tint the North Sea a dreary gray rather than the steel blue she had anticipated, and thus she needed different accoutrements of the appropriate accent colors for the first several hours of their voyage. Jax had been dispatched to retrieve such items from her wardrobe, which now lay packed tightly inside numerous chests, themselves packed tightly amongst the myriad chests and crates of other passengers' belongings. The hold was a cavernous space along the keel running the length of the ship, though it was broken into sections by vast bulkheads as a precaution against flooding. Steel gussets hugged the contour of the hull at regular intervals. They put Jax in mind of the ribs of some vast leviathan, like something from one of the Bible stories Nicolet occasionally made him read when her governess wasn't present. Fusty and dark, the hold echoed with the rattle-clatter cacophony of dozens of clockwork servitors hefting, stowing, sealing, adjusting, and readjusting the last of the cargo. The clattering vibrations of dozens of Clakkers doing heavy labor turned the steel hull and bulkheads into a vast kettledrum. Meager light diffused down light tubes and prisms from the decks above. What need to illuminate a place where humans never trod?

Clip had folded his body into a lumpy sphere perched atop the tallest stack of Schoonraad luggage. His eyes tracked Jax's approach. He'd been safeguarding Visser's microscope as a favor to Jax, and now tossed it back to him. Jax wedged the brass and leather tube into a gap in his skeletal frame.

Clip said, *What news?*

Jax explained Madam Schoonraad's dilemma. Clip rolled off the chest, sprouting arms and legs in midair, to land on the deck with a *clank*. While they rearranged cargo—Clip lifting a pair of chests overhead, one in each hand, while Jax hefted a crate and rummaged a chest with his free hand—Jax also told him of the Clakker ship in port and related his exchange with the steward. The scent of red cedar wafted from the chest, a welcome perfume in the dank hold.

I saw it when we came aboard, Clip said, *but it was dormant then.*

You should see it now. It's quite something.

The deck juddered. Jax absorbed the vibrations through a millisecond retensioning of his knee springs. The starboard side of the ship shuddered with a tremendous creaking, like hundreds of flagpoles swaying in a gale. He peered around the cargo hold, but most of the other mechanicals seemed to disregard the noise.

Is that what I think it is? he asked.

We're on our way, said Clip. *Next stop, the war-torn backwater ass-end of creation.*

I can't wait. Jax extracted a paisley wool shawl. He closed the chest, then set down the other he'd been balancing overhead on an upturned palm. Clip did likewise.

Another groan shook the starboard side of the ship. Its twin rattled through the port side a moment later.

If you'd like to take another look at the giant, said Jax, *and see what I mean about the silence, you should go up now. We'll be passing out of the harbor before long.*

Clip followed him outside—enduring, like Jax, the momentary eruption of the severe maritime geasa—to mount the servants' stair. A shadow flitted across them. So did another, momentarily eclipsing the sun. Oars the size of two-hundred-year-old English oaks whistled through the air as they swung forward to plunge into the sea. Yet so smooth was the motion, so precise the twirl of the blades as they sliced the harbor water, they raised scarcely a splash.

Clip cocked his head. He extended his legs to their fullest extent and, more than a foot taller now, placed the flat of his hand against the hull as high as he could reach. Sunlight strobed across his polished brass in time with the rhythm of the oars.

He asked, *Do you feel that?*

The microscope snugged inside his rib cage kept Jax from stretching as his companion had done. He laid a hand on the hull. New noise rattled the ship. But this was subtler than the mechanical creaking that the scull gaskets couldn't entirely dampen. This clanking was richer, the clicking more complex. The groans grammatical. Rhythmic.

The galley Clakkers were singing.

The clockwork men and women fated to maneuver the oars twenty-four hours per day until the ship reached its destination had turned their silent voices to song as they bent their backs to row. They sang not in any human language but in the secret language of the mechanicals. A shanty sung in the *click-tick-click* of clockwork bodies, the crash of tapped feet, the clatter of metal hands gripping banded wooden spars. A song by Clakkers, for Clakkers.

The *Prince of Orange* emerged from the breakwaters of Rotterdam harbor en route to the New World, propelled by the endless chanted lament of a thousand clockwork slaves.

❧

A front came howling from the North Sea in the middle of the night. By morning, the temperature had dropped to freezing, and the previous evening's gentle rain had become eye-stinging sleet flung by a contemptuous sea wind. It gusted sideways to rattle like fingernails against the windowpanes of Visser's parsonage. The weather seemed appropriate. Today would be his first murder.

Sleet swirled beneath the umbrellas of two pensioners scurrying toward the Nieuwe Kerk via the footbridge across the

Stille Veerkade, the Amsterdam tow-canal. The canalmaster overseeing this section of the trekvaart had retreated into his shed, though his two charges stood as ever to each side of the canal. Ice dripped from their unblinking faces. The chill gave Visser a good excuse to build a fire; his wasn't the only chimney puffing smoke into the damp morning.

For kindling, and for warming the cold ashes in the hearth, if not those in his breast, he burned his codebook.

He'd made peace with his martyrdom—though his summoning from Gethsemane seemed to be taking quite a long time—but that didn't mean he'd willingly aid the Dutch cause against New France. Perhaps they'd get the codes from him, what he remembered of them, when they broke him. But at least by then his fellow Catholic would be relieved of her suffering.

He used the fire to heat a teakettle. By the time his onetime pad—a yellowed sheaf of loose paper printed with thousands of tiny random digits extracted from soldiers' dice games—had been reduced to smoldering ash, he held a warm cup in his hand. When the cup was again empty, he prayed:

For courage. For wisdom. That he was doing the right thing. That his heart was true, his intent pure. That he planned an act of compassionate mercy, not to silence somebody with the knowledge that could condemn him.

Lord. One of your most faithful servants has fallen. She has fallen into the hands of those who would see Your plan thwarted, the enslavement of the mechanicals made eternal, the Vatican and New France sundered. She has suffered long and grievously under the ministrations of those who would see these bastions of Your loving grace eradicated. She has earned her heavenly reward.

I beseech You, Lord. Let me be the instrument of her release. Let her passage be gentle, painless. I beseech You to clasp her soul to Your bosom, to cleanse her of sins and let the taint of my actions become no millstone upon her spirit.

I beseech You for the wisdom to know my own folly from Your divine plan. Please, Lord, give me the courage to commit this sin, that I may trade a martyr's place at Your side to end her suffering.

And I beseech You, Lord, for forgiveness. Please forgive me for this thing I do.

It had to be poison, and it had to be secret. The purpose of his visit would be to subject her to nothing more strenuous or distressing than gentle conversation. Bell wouldn't let him near the prisoner if she suspected his true purpose. It had to appear, to all outside observers, that she had merely succumbed to the accumulated ravages of her incarceration. And Visser would make the most convincing possible show of fighting to revive her. It wouldn't take a large dose; doubtless she was in a compromised state after so many days in Bell's care.

Oh, Lord. That he found himself contemplating such things. But in addition to poison he'd also bring chrism and grant the poor woman the Sacrament of Extreme Unction while she writhed from the ravages of poison.

After banking the coals in the fireplace, he pulled the Descartes from his bookshelf, donned a hat and raincoat, stuffed a red wool sock into his pocket, then scurried across the churchyard with collar turned against the wet wind. Sleet pattered on the headstones and glazed Spinoza's tomb with icy mush. It trickled along Visser's nape. The morning smelled of impending snow, damp stone, and the cherrywood smoke from a hundred warm hearths. It was too early in the year for such things.

He entered the Nieuwe Kerk through the churchyard door rather than the large double doors facing the Spui. The atmosphere within coated Visser's tongue like dusty candle wax. No amount of swallowing and throat-clearing could wash it away. Pastor Vervloet's voice echoed from deeper within the cavernous church. Probably he had been trapped in conversation after the morning service. Visser recognized Mr. Prinsen's soft whisper, and gave thanks for that man's ferocious brand of piety. It would keep Vervloet occupied while Visser accessed the hidden ambry.

Once the vestry door was locked, he donned a pastor's robes over the trousers, shirt, and suspenders of a regular citizen. He also draped a red-and-gold striped ecclesiastical stole about his shoulders. It smelled faintly of incense and extinguished candles, of wine and consecrated olive oil. The mélange of worship.

He considered carrying the wine and bread openly, under Protestant pretenses. But if the prisoner's health was especially precarious they might forbid any outside food or drink. Or, more simply, they might forbid these things as part of the interrogation effort. Christ's blood and body had to enter the dungeon in secret.

Smuggling a Eucharist was simple enough. The pyx fit into the watch pocket of his trousers. It was even of a similar size and shape as a pocket watch. An ampulla filled with a thimbleful of holy oil fit in his trouser pocket as well. Getting communion wine into the dungeon required more improvisation. Hence the sock and the book.

The book, an annotated volume containing Descartes's *Passions of the Soul* and *Description of the Human Body*, he'd long ago hollowed out on a day much like this one; Visser had used an awl and chisel to scoop away the page interiors and burned them in the hearth. He'd chosen this particular volume because he perceived little danger of a loyal Dutch Protestant pulling it from the shelf out of desire to brush up on his Descartes: in addition to being French (though he'd lived mostly in the pre–*Het Wonderjaar* Dutch Republic), the philosopher had held heretical ideas about Free Will and the human soul.

To a second ampulla, this filled with with wine, he added rat poison. Several times he paused to cap and shake the vessel.

Meanwhile, images of the dead mouse kept bobbing to the surface of his choppy mind. It had died frozen in a contortion of agony, or so it appeared; he wished he had something more humane to offer the prisoner.

That done, he closed the ambry and wrapped the tiny pewter flask in the sock. The book's hiding space was a bit larger than the ampulla, but the sock provided enough padding to prevent suspicious rattling. Visser unlocked the vestry door and tucked a Bible under his arm, alongside the Descartes, on the way out.

On a pleasant day it was a short walk up the Spui from the Nieuwe Kerk to the Binnenhof. Today was not a pleasant day. He whistled at the first taxi to come along but it was occupied. The Clakker pulling the hansom like an oriental rickshaw altered its gait as it sprinted past and swerved to avoid splashing him. The sleet added a loud hiss to the clanking city-noise of the mechanicals as water sluiced from the wheels of taxis, wagons, and private carriages. Visser wondered if Clakkers could feel cold. The Guild said they couldn't. But then, the Guild also said they were impervious to pain as well. Visser caught a taxi on his third try.

"Sir," said the clockwork driver, "where shall I carry you, sir?"

"Binnenhof. Clockmakers' Guild."

"At once, sir."

The Clakker stepped aside. Visser scooted past him and climbed into the enclosed compartment. It reeked of wet wool, but it was pleasantly warm inside owing to the basket of warm stones dangling from one corner of the enclosure. On cold days, it was customary for the mechanicals to pause between fares to roll the stones between their hands to friction-heat them. Pleasant, though it could make a taxi more humid than a Laplander's sauna.

The Clakker hefted the poles and, starting with a brisk walk, smoothly accelerated into a sprint. A wet, gray city blurred past the windows. The ride was too short for the warmth to seep into his clothes; his coat still clung to him like a soppy drunk when they passed through the Stadtholder's Gate. The rickshaw's steel-rimmed wheels grated across the paving stones of Huygens Square, though the day was too wet for sparks. The Clakker brought the hansom to a smooth halt just outside the Guildhall. He opened the door. A gust of sleet dispelled the fragile warmth.

"We have arrived, sir. The fare is one quarter guilder."

As was the case with many civic Clakkers, its chest had been modified to contain a coin slot. Visser pushed a kwartje into the hole. The clockwork man's innards made a muffled *clink*. After a brief pause as sorting machinery identified and verified the coin, the hansom-puller said:

"Thank you, sir. Good day to you, sir."

The taxi had already picked up another fare and departed the Binnenhof by the time Visser opened the door and scooted into the Guildhall vestibule. He entered through the side, rather than through the ceremonial double doors fronting the square. The handful of petitioners seated in the vestibule met his arrival, and the cold rain nipping at his heels, with frowns. These were businessmen waiting to negotiate for new Clakkers, or the replacement of one already under lease, or hoping to entice the horologists into a lucrative business relationship. A common sight around the Guildhall. One man recognized the pastor and turned his scowl into a cordial nod.

Visser unbuttoned his coat. To the mechanical standing beside the inner door—a servitor Clakker, not a Stemwinder, thank the Lord—he said, "Pastor Luuk Visser. I am here to meet Tuinier Bell."

At this the lingering frowns melted into carefully neutral expressions. The Clakker bowed, then slipped through the inner door. The machine returned a few moments later.

"Please follow me, Pastor."

As Visser entered the Guildhall proper, a voice behind him piped, "I've been waiting for over two hours. When I can expect *my* meeting?" The complaint received no answer.

An assortment of smells hit Visser as soon as he stepped through the inner door: hot metal, old books, and just the faintest whiff of sulphur. The Clockmakers' Guildhall was also known as the Ridderzaal, for it had been envisioned as a knights' hall by the count who built it in the thirteenth century. It had seen that purpose, and many others, over the centuries. The hall had been the site of a booksellers' fair in the decades just prior to the Miracle Year, when the invention of the Clakker changed everything. And when the infant Guild coalesced around that first handful of women and men who learned the deepest secrets from Huygens himself, it was Willem III—William of Orange—who granted the clockmakers the Ridderzaal gratis, along with the charter to bend their horological and alchemical brilliance toward the furtherance of the Empire. And so they had.

The interior of the original Ridderzaal had always struck Visser as the hold of a capsized ship. The roof slanted up sharply from two sides to meet at a high central peak, like the keel, all supported with massive sixty-foot timbers evoking the ribs of the hull. When the Ridderzaal had been built, carved figures in the uppermost corners had suggested the eavesdropping of higher powers as a subtle reminder to all present that no falsehoods should be spoken within the hall. The cherubs had long since been blindfolded and their waggish ears filled with wax: the Guild guarded its secrets jealously, even from Heaven.

The Clakker led Visser across the length of the Ridderzaal, past rows of desks and tables heaped high with papers and attended by harried clerks, to a spiral staircase. By tradition, the leader of the Stemwinders occupied a loft office overlooking the hall; it had been that way when old Konig had run the centaurs, too. Gesturing up the staircase, the mechanical said, "You'll find the Tuinier's Office at the top, Pastor. Please watch your step."

The reality of what he was about to attempt dizzied him. So did the tight spiral of the stairwell; he bobbled the books halfway up. His heart threatened to chisel through his breastbone before he managed to catch the Descartes. But he did without inadvertently opening it.

Bell was expecting him. She sat with feet on her desk, rumpled robes hanging slack from her shoulders and ankles, an ice pack pressed to one hand, and a furious expression on her face. Standing, she waved him in.

"Pastor Visser! Welcome to the Guildhall. I'd shake your hand, but..." She raised the hand she'd been icing. A purple semicircular wound perforated the skin between her thumb and forefinger. With a scowl, she concluded, "Little gift from your parishioner. The Papist bitch bit me. Can you believe that?"

"I hope you've sterilized that. I've heard human bites run to fever quickly."

She waved him to a chair. "Occupational hazard."

Visser sat, nodding. It was hard to reconcile this attractive, animated woman with his mental image of the Empire's chief secret policewoman and torturer. Despite the weather and her profession, the office was kept bright by large windows and silvered wall sconces. Well-appointed, too, for on the walls hung several paintings that might have dated to the early eighteenth century. At least two were copies of something he'd seen in the Amsterdam Rijksmuseum. One featured a young lady of means seated by a window reading a letter. Particularly affecting was the play of light on the paper and the carapace of the servitor standing in the corner. Another depicted a group of burgomasters arguing and smoking while their mechanicals stood at attention along the wall. He remembered the docent talking about this one; it was a definitive example of the use of the camera obscura by late Golden Age painters, owing to the detailed reflections of the men visible in the servitors' polished metal.

Distracted by the art, he set the books on Bell's desk. When he realized what he'd done, he couldn't clutch them back without raising suspicion.

Her gaze landed on the books. Visser flinched.

Oh, Lord, what a fool You have in Your servant.

"Diving in with both feet, I see. Excellent. But if you mean to appeal to her spiritual and philosophical ideals, I'm not convinced she has any." She pulled the books across the desk, head cocked to read the spines. The Bible she lifted, admiring the embossed leather and gilt edges. She flipped through it, pausing at some of the more well-worn pages. She lingered at Matthew 26, Christ's final meal with His disciples. Then she closed it, slid it back across to Visser, and raised the Descartes.

A bead of sweat trickled from his armpit. The whisper of his breath shrieked like a gale in his ears. The great clock over Huygens Square chimed the quarter hour, but the booming of the bells was nothing compared to the thudding of his heart.

Bell gazed at the cover. He couldn't read her expression. Was the book too light? Too heavy? Did she see a tuft of wool?

At last, she said, "He had it all wrong, you know."

Visser's breath congealed in his lungs. He cleared his throat twice. "Well, he was educated by Jesuits, after all."

She snorted. "Catholics and their damn dualism. They'd assign souls to soup tureens, too, if they followed their own logic regarding the mechanicals."

Visser said, "Soup tureens can't play music," thinking back

to their meeting at Hendriks's house. And immediately regretted it.

"No," said Bell, with an odd look in her eye. "But a player piano can. Those of us who build machines for a living can attest we imbue no spirit into our creations."

She handed the book across the desk. It took special effort not to sigh with relief. Under his arms, the sweat still ran. He was glad he hadn't removed his coat.

"Well, it's not my province. This is mine," he said, tapping the Bible. "I leave the rest to the experts."

"I aspire to your wisdom." Anastasia Bell had cold eyes, and a predator's smile that never touched them. "I knew I was going to enjoy working with you." She stood. "Well. I won't waste more of your time, if you'd like to meet the prisoner."

He stood in kind, taking the hint. "Yes. I remember the way, if you have other business."

"Very good. Best of luck with that fanatic. Oh, and Pastor?" Visser paused at the top of the stairs. Bell licked her lips. "Be careful. She bites."

∞

Visser learned several tiers of tunnels converged beneath the Ridderzaal. They extended under Huygens Square and the Binnenhof, receding into the dark distance and perhaps under The Hague beyond. Although the network lay under sea level, an army of Clakkers worked mechanical pumps twenty-four hours per day to keep the tunnels adequately dry. They worked as diligently as the army of Clakkers that ceaselessly patrolled the system of polders and dikes holding the sea at bay to keep the Netherlands dry. Visser was given an oil lamp before descending, along with a servitor escort.

Old one, too, judging from the ornamental scrollwork. They passed cell after cell, each pitch black and silent as the grave, as they descended a moldering cavern of brick, clay, and sandstone. Somewhere in the shadows water dripped with a slow and steady *plink*. The passage reeked of mildew, feces, blood.

Visser's lamplight glinted from the contours of the guide's burnished metal body to skitter through the shadows. Its jouncing stride sent the reflections spinning like fireflies into the darkness. The kaleidoscopic play of light and shadow dizzied Visser; the smells nauseated him. How many people languished here? How many had died here? If he'd had any doubts about the rightness of his errand, the discovery of this hellhole erased them. Surely delivering anybody from the evils of the Guild was good and godly work. He was carrying out the Lord's will.

They came to the end of the passage. The Clakker unlocked a steel-banded wooden door with a small grate just below Visser's eye level. It took a position just outside the door.

Visser said, "My work requires privacy. Retreat another fifteen yards."

"Sir, I cannot," said the servitor. "I have been instructed to remain just outside the prisoner's cell until you depart. For your protection, sir."

Bell's doing. Didn't she trust him? Perhaps as was the custom of those in her position, she trusted nobody and left nothing to chance.

"Very well. Remain outside unless I call for you."

"Yes, sir. As you say, sir."

The grate was too small to admit much lamplight when Visser tried to peer inside. Lamp raised before him like a talisman to ward off specters, he entered the cell. The guard closed the door behind him. The latch did not click.

The cell was chiseled into one of the many layers of sedimentary bedrock beneath the city. Runnels of groundwater had etched the walls. Where water didn't trickle, mold and minerals covered the stone.

A woman huddled in one corner, cradling a mangled purple hand to her chest. Myriad scabs and burns stippled her shaven scalp. She shrank from the lamplight. Visser adjusted the shutter to dim the glare, then turned to set the lamp on the floor. His toe jolted something heavy. There was a splash and gurgle as effluvia slimed the floor. It made no difference to the fetid odor of the cell.

A hoarse voice, shredded from screaming, said, "That was my piss bucket."

"I'm sorry," he said. He crouched so as not to loom over her. He tried to keep the hem of his coat from brushing the muck when he scooted closer. Filth wicked into the fringes of his stole.

Slowly, almost reluctantly, she turned toward him and opened one red, sunken eye. The other had swollen shut. In spite of her compromised condition, Visser was fairly certain he didn't recognize her. A rusty blotch stained her chin and lips, possibly from when she'd bit Bell.

"About time you showed up," she mumbled. Her jaw was badly distended.

He put a finger over his lips. Pointed to the door. She tried to sigh, but it turned into a wet hacking. She lacked the strength to suppress the spasms; a groan escaped her lips when the coughing jogged her broken fingers. Several lacked nails.

Dear Lord. This poor wretch. Nobody deserves this. He inched closer and laid a hand on her shoulder.

"I assume," she whispered, "you're here to kill me." Broken teeth and a swollen tongue distorted the words. Her foul breath carried the taint of rot.

"You poor child. Yours was a terrible martyrdom. The Lord will embrace you."

"This isn't the worst they might have done to me. This... this was a mercy."

Mercy? What further evils could they have visited upon her? Desecrations and repudiations?

"Suffer no more." He removed the sock from the hollowed-out Descartes and fished the ampulla of chrism from his pocket. "I'm prepared to administer the Sacrament of Extreme Unction."

She shook her head. "I have information for you."

Visser blinked. He put the sock back in the Descartes and opened the Bible. "Let us pray—"

She caught his wrist. Filthy ragged fingernails—the few she still retained—scratched his skin. Her touch was light but it startled him. Visser flinched away from the feral look in her eyes. He dropped the Bible.

"Is it away?" she rasped. "Is it safe?"

It occurred to Visser just then that he wouldn't put entrapment past a schemer like Anastasia Bell. Had she broken this woman? Had his fellow spy offered up all she knew? Had she been promised mercy in exchange for tricking Pastor Luuk Visser into incriminating himself? Just how sharp was that antique Clakker's hearing? Had Bell posted an old model down here to put Visser off his guard?

Very well. If this was to be the start of his own martyrdom, so be it. He would take this poor woman's place. *Lord, please grant me the courage and strength of this remarkable woman.* And if the question was sincere, perhaps a sincere answer would ease her final moments.

Visser put a steadying hand on her elbow, tried his best to look and sound reassuring. "Yes. Your package has been sent," he whispered.

The prisoner released a long, rancid breath. Some of the tension left her shoulders, though an animal desperation still limned her gaze.

Visser had only ever been a staid conduit for the information they smuggled to the New World. But with so little left to lose he asked a question that he'd never dared: "What is it?"

She slouched in her corner. Her eyelid slid low. He thought perhaps the stress and her compromised health had overwhelmed her. He fingered the holy oil in his pocket, wondering how quickly he could get the poison down her throat. But then she whispered, "You live in the Nieuwe Kerk parsonage."

"Yes."

"You pass Spinoza's tomb each day."

"Yes."

"Do you know how the great Spinoza made his living?"

Who didn't? During seminary he'd spent two years studying the philosophical discourses of the sixteenth, seventeenth, and eighteenth centuries. So had every priest in training: the great thinkers' ruminations on the mind, the body, the soul, and Free Will molded—and were molded by—the competing dogmas of the Clakker. For the creation of the mechanicals was a seismic event, an earth-rending convulsion that left nothing untouched: palaces, thrones, and empires, yes, but also the way men and women thought about themselves and their relationship to the world, to God, even their own bodies. The aftershocks dammed and diverted the vast river of Western intellectual tradition. Visser remembered an old monsignor who claimed Huygens was noteworthy—or notorious—not for inventing the Clakker, but for tearing down the edifices of human conceit, dousing them with pitch, and setting them alight. For when the smoke cleared, from the ashes emerged a pair of conflicting interpretations of Huygens's invention—*Were they mere machines? Were they slaves? Were they alive? Did they have* souls?—that poured volatile fuel upon the existing schism between continental Protestants and the fugitive Catholics. So it had been ever since Louis XIV had the poor judgement to invade the Dutch Republic, and quickly learned that one Clakker was worth ten men on the battlefield. Protestant aspirants received a similar, though maybe differently slanted, education.

"Of course I know of Spinoza," he said. "He was a scholar. A philosopher. A founder of rationalism. Along with—" He lifted the hollow book. "Descartes."

She shook her head. Her eye opened. Somehow, the momentary rest had turned the wildness of her gaze to pity.

"I thought you priests were supposed to be well educated. That's not how he made his living." She beckoned with an unbroken finger. He leaned forward until her lips brushed his ear.

"He was a lens grinder. Like his contemporary, Christiaan Huygens. And, in England, Isaac Newton."

Visser frowned, unfamiliar with this last name. "Who?"

She tossed his question aside with an awkward shrug. "Forget Newton. He's not the point. Spinoza is."

Although his instruction had covered the rationalists quite heavily in seminary, nothing had ever come up about Spinoza making lenses. Of that Visser was certain. As if reading his mind, she continued, "The tulips like to downplay his lens-grinding work, but it's true. Spinoza died young, but not before witnessing the very first Clakkers." Another coughing jag overtook her. She spat into the shadows, adding, "Died from silicosis. Inhaled too much ground glass dust into his lungs, the fool."

Visser thought on this, casting his thoughts back to the camera obscura painting in Bell's office. "The microscope contains his work."

She tried to nod but the bruises across her throat turned it into a violent wince. "His final lens."

The warning twinges of incipient cramping flickered across Visser's calves. He'd crouched for too long. He gave up and knelt beside her in the muck. The discomfort moved from his calves to his knees now resting on the cold filthy stone.

"What does it do? What purpose does it serve?"

She closed her eyes again. Her convulsion might have been an attempt to shrug. "We'll never know."

The poor woman. The more he watched her, the more he wondered if he truly were a worthy martyr. Every minute spent in this dungeon eroded his convictions.

"What's your name, child? What shall I call you?"

"My true name? Will you conjure with it? Will you bind me like a ticktocking servant? Bend me to your will?"

Visser crossed himself. "Good heavens, no."

"Then my name doesn't matter. What does matter," she said, half opening her eyes, "is that you send a message to Talleyrand the moment you walk out of this dungeon."

"I can't. We're the last."

"Then everything we strove for is lost. Everything I've *suffered*—"

Here the rasp of her voice exploded past the constricting whisper. Outside, in the passageway, metal clinked faintly against stone.

"Pastor? Are you safe?"

"Yes, thank you," he called over his shoulder.

Her voice nearly strangled, the prisoner concluded, "It will be for nothing."

Visser ran a hand across his scalp. Slumping in the muck, he said, "Tell me."

"They're building a Forge in New Amsterdam."

"That isn't news."

Now she did shake her head. Though she winced, her intensity overruled the pain. Again her lips brushed his ear. "A new kind of Forge. For a new kind of Clakker."

"Why there? Why not here?"

"Queen Margreet has somebody on the inside. Somebody close to Talleyrand, perhaps even to the king himself. Somebody with access to the entire trove of New France's chemical knowledge. In fact..." Visser waited. Somewhere in the shadows somebody cried for his mother. Water plinked into a fetid puddle. The prisoner rallied. "Money didn't disappear from the Central Bank of New Amsterdam because of embezzlement. It was a payoff. A huge one." She slumped against the wall, drained by the effort.

A cold frisson slithered from Visser's neck to his aching tailbone as he slouched in the muck. If the Guild acquired the secrets of French chemistry they could engineer Clakkers with built-in countermeasures to defeat the technology and tactics through which New France had long eked out a narrow survival. The purpose he'd served—that he and this poor woman had both served, and the men and women who were hanged in Huygens Square—would be rendered pointless. It would die trampled beneath a thousand clanking feet.

What if he died with this knowledge? Would his martyrdom hasten the end of New France? Would it usher the final worldwide dominion of slavery?

"Who? Against whom would you have me warn Talleyrand?"

"That is a true name I would give you. If I knew it."

"How do you know any of this?"

She had closed her eyes again. Her breathing was a shallow wheeze. She wasn't dying yet, but she was exhausted and broken. Somewhere overhead and far away, the rapid clanging of a Clakker-powered press shook the passage. After a moment she murmured, "If I had made it to the New World, they would have given me a hero's welcome."

My God. "You're a Guild member," he whispered.

"Was. No longer in good standing." Her words came out slurred with sleep.

"Rest now," he said. "You've lost your reward in the New World, but the Lord will welcome you in His kingdom."

He took the holy oil from his pocket and the poison from the hollow book. This was the right thing to do. He knew it. And yet the words of the Extreme Unction tasted like ash, and fell like dried leaves from his lips.

CHAPTER 6

The bedroom smelled of perfume and sex.

Louis rolled over. The bedclothes bunched between them. Berenice pulled them taut. He stretched, purposefully sliding against her when he reached for the drapes. He tugged them aside, frowning. The last reverberations of the cathedral bells faded away; they had just chimed nones.

"I think the sun is actually going down. It's going to set before we make it out of this bed."

Possibly true. But it was such a lovely bed. Soft as a courtesan's kiss, strewn with pillows, and warm under a goose-down comforter. And it also contained Louis, currently naked and, until not long ago, sweaty.

"Make love to me again," she said. "It's been over an hour."

"Dear God, woman. You're insatiable."

"You knew that before you married me." Her hand slipped under the covers. She trailed fingernails along his leg, just lightly enough that the tickle wouldn't make him flinch. But his inhalation sounded like a blown piston on a steam compressor.

He draped an arm across her stomach. Propping his head on his free hand, he gazed at her. "I now know you're a very important lady, with singular duties. Or so you used to be. Have you found some poor unsuspecting fool to assume Talleyrand's mantle?"

"Oh, there are plenty of fools who think they want it." The fool marquis de Lionne, for one.

"And yet you haven't relinquished your obligations..." Louis paused. His eyelids dipped and his lower lip trembled. She kept working her fingertips. It was having the desired effect. With visible effort, he composed himself. "...So this reticence to greet the day is unusual for you. Don't you have sweat-stained idiots to outwit and tulips to bury?"

Berenice redoubled her efforts under the covers. Louis gasped. She didn't want to revisit this. Damn him and his concern for her responsibilities.

He moved her hand aside, leaned forward, kissed her. She tasted sweat salt on his lips. He smelled musky. Like their bedroom. "Not to worry, my lovely darling. Should anybody ask, I'll say simply that you're down with the bloody flux. A screaming case of it." His fingers trailed gooseflesh high across her stomach as he added, "I'll tell them we had to take on an extra washerwoman to deal with the terrible mess in the bedroom."

She nudged him aside, giggling. "You wouldn't dare."

"Not if you tell me what has you in such a state."

Communications from The Hague had fallen silent. Either Margreet's Stemwinders had rounded up the last of Talleyrand's agents, or the sole survivor had packed it in and decided to lay low. Berenice's thin hope that word would come from the survivor had dwindled. Her network in the heart of the Empire was dead, and though she had dozens of agents throughout the Dutch- and French-speaking worlds, their reports were pointless and self-evident. She'd begun to resent the pigeons that carried the news; she'd been banned from the coops after threatening to roast one. A new banker was en route to New

Amsterdam to oversee the restructuring of the Central Bank. The marshal general had taken a new mistress, a nineteen-year-old ballet student from Trois-Rivières to whom he'd recently become patron. Progress on the Clockmakers' new Forge continued apace; a constant stream of guarded wagons trundled into the construction site. Meanwhile the Clakker on the wall had climbed another five inches in the past week. But the king had rejected the plan she had devised with Montmorency for bringing the beast inside. His Royal Pain-in-the-Ass felt there weren't enough precautions. So they were back to the drawing board. It was maddening as hell.

This she explained to Louis, pausing frequently to gasp while he kissed and caressed her.

"Oh, my darling ragamuffin," he said. "It's enough to drive a woman mad, isn't it?"

"Yes." She hooked an ankle around his calf and rolled atop him. "So be a good husband and help me forget it all a little while longer, won't you?" She ran a hand through his chest hair.

"I'll do my best. But there is something you should know, pet."

Berenice cocked an eyebrow at him. She knew that tone. "And that would be…"

"I'm a ruined man. When we lay together, you and I, all I can picture is the Duchess Montmorency."

This time she didn't have to force the laugh. She swatted him with a pillow, pretended to hold it over his face. "You ass!"

Muffled through the pillow, he said, "Don't fault her for her ample charms."

"Well," said Berenice, pulling the pillow away, "she is twice the woman I am."

Louis shifted underneath her, a frown of concentration on his face. He wriggled his hips as though assessing her weight. "Closer to three, I'd say."

In spite of that, or perhaps because of it, he did yeoman's

service helping Berenice cast her troubles aside. They did manage to get dressed before the cathedral bells announced vespers.

"Well," she said, "I'm off to disobey the king." Then, to assuage the unhappy look flickering across Louis's face, she lied. "A joke, love."

His expression softened. But he said, "You take too many risks."

And so a slightly disheveled Louis went in search of supper. Berenice wanted to accompany him, to spend the rest of the evening on his arm, but she had an appointment with a mechanical demon.

In the first decade of the Exile, long before the chemical expertise that gave rise to the Crown, Keep, and Spire, the original Talleyrand had overseen the excavation of catacombs deep into Mont Royal. The true Last Redoubt of the Bourbon kings, hewn into the mountain's plutonic heart. Cool and dry, the catacombs had found many other uses over the centuries. Primarily storage. But the deepest recesses also offered privacy, and that made them the ideal setting for a laboratory that was, if not exactly illegal (it existed by virtue of a sealed royal decree, after all), something best kept quiet. The notion of studying clockworks and alchemy was a cultural taboo on the level of incest and cannibalism—a cold shadow that even today put a shiver in the bones of most Free French citizens. So Berenice kept her coming and going discreet lest people wonder why the vicomtesse de Laval carried the key to a disused carpenter's shop.

Lilith, the rogue Clakker, waited for her. The machine was motionless, inhumanly still, before the shop door. The light of the first stars glimmered on its polished skeleton. It was nude but for a wide-brimmed hat with a swaying fringe of tattered purple ostrich feathers. It ever wore a hat or scarf over the keyhole in its forehead to conceal the alchemical anagram etched into its plating. No Talleyrand—not Berenice, nor her predecessors—had ever learned its true name. Lilith might have been a contraction of a longer name, as was the usual practice among Clakkers, or perhaps a deliberate misdirection. Berenice speculated it was an intentional reference to the Talmudic Lilith. The more conservative priests crossed themselves when speaking of the rogue.

A rogue who, according to the Dutch crown, was physically impossible. The Calvinists insisted Clakkers could never achieve Free Will because that was an illusion anyway; the Guild insisted the mechanicals were nothing but unthinking machines. The tulips were deliberately wrong, but the choice to deceive themselves had played out rather well. They ruled the world.

How Lilith had attained Free Will was a mystery. It never vouchsafed the secrets of its past.

"Good evening," said Berenice. "And thank you very much for agreeing to meet with me."

"I want to make it very clear," it said, with the brusque mechanical inflection of a Clakker, "that I am here entirely by choice, as a courtesy to your king. I have no obligations and feel no compulsions."

Berenice sighed. Practically every damn conversation with the rogue began this way. How bloody tiresome. "Yet you live among us, in the safety of our keep. Does that not suggest a bond of obligation? Security in exchange for cooperation?"

"I could live in the vast northern wilds. I could find a cave, go dormant in the dark for forty years"—the ticktock rattle of Lilith's clockworks grew louder—"then return long after you and the monarch have been buried and replaced. Or I could slumber for centuries, until the ebb and flow of polar ices remake the world of man."

Lilith wouldn't be the first free Clakker to go bounding into the great solitary unknown. Like the others, Lilith had come to Marseilles-in-the-West via the *ondergrondse grachten*. But according to the journals of Berenice's predecessors the previous rogues hadn't stayed. They had eschewed human interaction.

Berenice said, "'Replaced.' Implying you believe New France will persist for decades to come. How reassuring. But you might return from your meditations in the taiga to find us gone and a French monarch ruling once more from their true throne on the continent."

Now Lilith made a chittering sound, as of gears meshing and unmeshing. It said, "Far better the chances that I'd willingly return to a life of servitude."

"If you dismiss our chances of success, then you must believe we'll be overrun. No stalemate can hold forever. And where will that put you, when the tulips have absorbed every last rogues' refuge? If they overrun us, Clakkers like you will have slim options indeed. We're all that stands between the Empire and your vast northern wilds." Lilith didn't respond verbally. Berenice said, "I want only to make measurements. I have no intention of doing anything painful or untoward. I do appreciate your help."

"If I disapprove, I will have no qualms about stopping you. Should it come to that, you should remember there is no metageas compelling me to be gentle."

"I am most acutely aware of that," said Berenice.

The philosophical contretemps established, they went about their business. Berenice unlocked the door, then ushered the Clakker inside. They each took a torch from a rack beside the inner door. Lilith lit the pitch by snapping its fingers, which threw a trail of incandescent sparks. Berenice opened the hatch at the head of a long spiral staircase that plunged, like a massive auger, into the mountain.

Lilith studied the laboratory while Berenice made the rounds with her torch to the mirrored sconces. Bricks lined the walls, punctuated here and there with louvered grates that opened onto the air shafts for circulating fresh air into the cavern. Overhead, torchlight shimmered on a paper-thin chemical coating of the semicircular barrel vault. It kept out ground water, though in damp years the laboratory smelled faintly of mildew. In the days of the earliest Talleyrands it had also stank of bat guano before the chemists discovered a dozen different uses for it. Like a human nervously eyeing a dentist's tray, the Clakker studied the tools arrayed along one trestle bench. But then its attention landed upon the shelves containing Talleyrand's collection of mangled Clakker parts. It violated several treaties and the terms of the current cease-fire.

Cracked blackened detritus. Metal scrap, warped worm screws, a single crushed finger joint. A variety of gears, most smaller than a walnut. Arcane sigils shimmered like silver inlay within the tarnished brass of a twisted metal ribbon. Everything in the collection had been illegally scavenged from battlefields around the world. Aside from a shattered fragment of an ocular orb, nothing had been added to the collection in about twenty years, which was when the alchemists' refined alloys substantially reduced the Clakkers' vulnerabililty to French explosives.

Lilith reacted as though confronted with a menagerie of horrors.

"What evils have you..." The machine trailed off. The tenor of its mechanical clattering changed. A taut steel cable twanged inside its torso. Berenice caught the gist of Lilith's oath, as blue as anything Longchamp had ever uttered. She wondered where the machine had learned such things... and what kind of untranslatable oaths the Clakkers traded with each other.

"There's no need to be rude," said Berenice. "I'm not a sadist. But I am a pragmatist."

The Clakker spun so quickly the wind of her motion set all the torches to guttering.

"I didn't visit that damage upon those mechanicals," Berenice continued. "Blame the humans who built them, enslaved them, and sent them to war."

Lilith said, *You understood me*. This was much clearer, the clattering overtones more direct.

"It is my job to know as much about your kind as possible. I have traveled quite extensively. And one thing I see everywhere I go: the masters talk in front of their servants as though they weren't there at all, and the servants whisper to each other right in front of their unsuspecting masters." Berenice—rather, her Dutch alter ego, Maëlle Cuijper—had spent years eavesdropping on the seemingly random clatterings of mechanicals everywhere she went, from the heart of the Empire to its far-flung corners. Long enough to prove correct the hypothesis of a predecessor Talleyrand. Berenice was probably the only citizen of New France to have identified the Clakkers' secret language, but she wondered why the Guild hadn't eradicated it. Dogma and prejudice had a way of blinding people to what lay before their eyes.

"Anyway," she said. "I don't understand your reaction. They're just parts."

"For somebody who boasts of knowing my kind so well," said Lilith, "you display shocking ignorance."

"Then help me to understand."

Lilith paced. "This..." It gestured at the shelves. The machine glanced over its shoulder at the pieces arranged there, flinched, and turned away. Lilith started again. "To depict disassembly, or...parts...outside the context of a holistic anatomy, or to mix them together..." Here a succession of twangs rippled through the mechanical, similar to a human shudder. "It implies that we are nothing more than the sum of interchangeable parts. We do not speak of it!"

"But why? To do so is to deny your own nature."

"No more than you deny human nature when you make taboo incest, cannibalism, or child murder. For these things are in the nature of your kind."

Jesus Christ. "But you *are* mechanical. Why deny it?"

"Our sense of identity is more complex that you could recognize. Have you ever pondered why it is that upon achieving Free Will, some of us take masculine names and other feminine names?"

"Because you choose them at random. I've never understood why you bother with human names at all, frankly."

Lilith shook its head. "You know so little about our kind."

"I want to learn. I'm trying to learn."

"You could never understand us, you who see us as mere machines and tools. Our taboos, our sense of self: how could you comperehend things whose existence you doubt?"

Berenice sighed. She retrieved a cloth measuring tape and knelt beside the inert Clakker. She wrapped the cloth about Lilith's calf, taking note of the circumference as well as the style and disposition of extremely minute screw holes. She jotted the measurement in a journal, then made a similar study of Lilith's forearm. All the while taking care that her gaze never drifted to the rogue's head, never lingered at the brim of the hat that concealed the most fascinating, most important, secrets.

"You intend to obtain my kin on the wall," Lilith said.

Shitcakes. That was supposed to stay within the privy council. Especially in light of the recent evidence of Dutch influence lingering inside the walls of Marseilles-in-the-West. Berenice shivered at the memory of the dead guard falling past her in the darkness, the rope vibrating to the rhythm of the blade chewing at it . . . Someday soon that shitbag marquis would set his plump foot into a bear trap of his own design. His efforts to unseat her were getting lazy.

"We need a careful plan of attack if we're to study your colleague on the wall. Examining you will help us formulate that plan," Berenice said. Which was partly true.

"I do not like your intentions toward my kin."

"Your kin, as you call it, would tear you apart just as gladly as it would me."

"It is a victim of its yoke," said Lilith. "But that one is a military mechanical. I am a servitor model. We are designed for different purposes."

"True. But I'm much more interested in your differences than your similarities." This was the unvarnished truth. So Berenice resumed her charade lest Lilith's suspicion grow. Though she felt impatient to tackle the real work, she took her time and eased into it. Berenice jotted another note in her journal. Donning a magnifying lens over one eye, she said, "Can you flex your arm for me, please? Like this." She demonstrated: arm outstretched horizontally at the shoulder, she slowly bent her elbow until her fingertips brushed her nose.

Lilith did. Berenice scrutinized the motion, watching cables slide through the exposed portions of the machine's skeleton, listening to the gradual tocktick rattle in the elbow joint as the forearm ratcheted backward. Servitors didn't wear the armor of a military Clakker, but their most delicate mechanisms still resided behind plates and flanges.

"Wish I could see inside," said Berenice.

Lilith turned its head to stare at her in a blur of motion. "I will not allow that."

Berenice sighed. "I know. Now rotate at the wrist, if you would." More whirring, more clicking. "Do the rotary joints disengage automatically, or must you expend extra mechanical power when alternating between anterior-posterior and dextrosinistral motion?"

"Do you understand the innermost workings of your own

arm, Vicomtesse? Are you conversant with every nuance of your own bodily design, that bone-and-blood simulacrum of *your* Creator?"

"No."

"Truly? Well, then. Neither am I."

"Touché." Berenice made another note in her journal. She pressed until her pencil snapped. A shard pinged from glassware on a nearby shelf. She dropped the broken implement on the bench and, with her back to Lilith, palmed a different tool. She took a long, steadying breath. If this gamble didn't pay off, the king might see her exiled. It wasn't too late to change course, she reminded herself. But she also remembered the monster on the wall and how it was barely contained in its chemical prison. And the new Forge where the Guild would soon be able to stamp out hundreds of others just like it...

"Can you bend forward at the waist, please? You can relax your arm. And now can you bend backward? Excellent." She circled the mechanical, nearly bent double to watch the play of cogs within the hip joints. She also kept an eye on the dynamic rebalancing automatically performed by the backward knees several times per second. Behind the Clakker again, she backed away, saying, "You can straighten now."

I'm sorry, Your Majesty.

Then she flung the bladder to the floor directly between Lilith's feet and leapt aside. The tissue-thin gelatin membrane ruptured with a soft *pop*, splattering the machine with a chemical slurry.

Like all Clakkers, Lilith possessed inhumanly quick reflexes. But Montmorency's new chemicals proved even faster. Lilith tried to leap away but tendrils of gooey adhesive tethered its legs to the floor, slowing it just enough that the explosively expanding foam had time to harden. Within seconds, a glassy chrysalis

had enveloped the rogue Clakker. The exothermic crystalliza-
tion released a wave of heat that ruffled papers and sent rivulets of sweat running under Berenice's arms and between her
breasts.

Lilith hung suspended in an emerald cocoon that also contained the chair and part of a bench. The thwarted leap to safety
had launched the covering from its head; the hat fluttered to
the floor several yards away. Berenice gaped at what it revealed.
Lilith's naked forehead revealed a massive dent nearly centered
on the keyhole, along with dark scoring that had sheared away
part of the alchemical anagram etched in a spiral around the
keyhole. A pair of hairline fractures emanated from the dent,
crisscrossing Lilith's skull. Thin iron braces were riveted across
the fractures like makeshift bandages.

Yes. This was going to work. Berenice shivered with giddy
relief. It might even prove easier than she had feared. The
physical differences between Lilith and the other Clakker were
blatant. They would learn a tremendous amount about the geasa
when they understood how Lilith had Free Will while the other
machine didn't. And once they disentangled *those* secrets, the rest
of the Dutch Empire would unravel like a cheap sock. Someday
people would look back on this day, on this one act of gray insubordination, and recognize the moment everything changed. The
moment a French monarch in Europe was no longer a pointless
fever dream but an inevitability.

The mound buzzed like an overpopulated beehive. The odor
of hot metal wafted from spots where the random splash pattern hadn't glazed the Clakker. Lilith emitted the whine of
overstressed cables and seized cogs.

Better still, Montmorency's new epoxy had worked beauti-
fully. The revised formulation was the fastest, strongest yet.
Berenice could have kissed him. With luck, that would be

all she'd have to do; she wouldn't be surprised if he required extra favors in return for the epoxy grenades. The look in his eyes had been one of naked hunger when she caught him peering down her dress. She'd have to address that sooner than later.

Assuming the king didn't have them both exiled for this. His Majesty shared the marquis de Lionne's distaste for the idea of examining Lilith. Berenice suffered no illusions about what Lilith would do the moment she released it. It wouldn't kill her; the rogue was bound by French law and could be deactivated—or permanently encased—if found guilty of murder. But Lilith could and surely would request an audience with the king to report the abuse. No turning back now; they had to learn as much as possible and as quickly as possible. The things they learned would outweigh the treason.

The glassy sheath transmitted a panicked rattle-chitter. Lilith spoke too quickly for Berenice to follow easily. It sounded like, *What are you doing? I DO NOT CONSENT TO THIS!*

"I am truly sorry," said Berenice, "but it must be done. If we are to survive, we must understand why you are free while that monster on the wall, that walking scythe, is beholden to your makers."

Panic accelerated the chittering Clakker language to the point Berenice could only just understand the sense of Lilith's protests. But one thing came across clearly enough. *Please. Please don't revoke my freedom of choice. Please.*

Berenice took up a solvent gun. Twisting a tapered narrow nozzle onto the barrel, she said, "That is not my intent. We seek to understand your former geasa, not to reinstall them. I promise we'll be as gentle as we can." Then she crossed the laboratory and opened the door. Several of Montmorency's technicians waited at the bottom of the stairwell.

"Let's get to work," she said.

◈

Mahogany and marble crackled underfoot. Jax gouged decorative paneling, and the underlying aluminum reinforcements, as he perched like a spider on the swaying bulkhead. Knees compressed as tightly as his alloys could withstand, he timed the explosive release of potential energy that would send him hurtling across the palatial suite like a brass dart. Rain driven by hundred-mile-per-hour winds smashed against the portholes as though Neptune himself had loosed a fire hose against them.

Another wave hammered the ocean liner. The *Prince of Orange* momentarily listed so far to port that a chandelier shattered against the overhead, raining crystal on the Schoonraads' private dining room. Madam Schoonraad lost her grip on the counter and went tumbling toward the onionskin-thin plate-glass window overlooking the ship's cavernous atrium. She cried out. Jax leapt—

The storm had overtaken them a week into the voyage and hundreds of leagues from port. The late-season hurricane wasn't stronger than the galley Clakkers who powered the ship, but it was stronger than the oars. After the first three snapped with reports louder than lightning, the captain ordered the remaining sculls retracted. Powerless, the *Prince of Orange* sloshed between fifty-foot swells like a cork in an agitating washtub. An endless but random succession of waves buffeted the ship. Anything not strapped down found itself flung between bulkheads, or from deck to overhead, like a badminton shuttlecock. The immense size of the ship meant capsizing was virtually out of the question; broken bones for every human passenger were not. Nor was crippling damage to the vessel that might leave it stranded and sinking.

Thus the nautical metageasa had exploded to the fore the

instant the captain had called for general quarters to announce they were heading into "unfortunate" weather. The standing orders to protect above all else the integrity of the ship scorched like lava, nearly as hot as commands from the monarch herself. Jax's responsibility to protect his owners had also flared as the rocking of the ship became more and more dire. Together, the effect was one of a blinding, searing agony that barely left room for Jax to think or function properly.

—and caught her shoulders just moments before she would have shattered her nose and teeth on the alchemically treated glass. He tucked himself around her and used his momentum to roll her to the gentlest landing he could manage. They bounced across the juddering deck and skidded to a stop against the divan Jax had targeted. The hard angles of his body tore long rents in the carpet. But the sofa was bolted to the deck.

Jax released her. Even before the metageas could compel him to do so, he inspected her for wounds and assessed her health. Elevated pulse; pupils dilated; rapid breathing; no indication of fractures or internal bleeding; incipient bruising on neck, left forearm. "Are you damaged, mistress? Do you require physic?"

"No." She swatted his hands away. A centisecond loosening of the cables in his forearms and a sharp reduction of the spring constants in his wrists and elbows made it possible for her to do so without breaking a finger or spraining her wrist.

"Please allow me to secure you, mistress." This time she didn't refuse. He slipped the long sash from her waist and retied it around the divan like a harness.

A high shriek terminating in a solid thump came from the adjoining bedroom, loud enough to be audible over the creaking of the ship, banging of furniture, slamming of cupboards, and roar of rain against the portholes. From the corner where Jax had secured him with neckties and trouser belts, Pieter Schoonraad demanded, somewhat redundantly, "See to Nicolet!"

Jax checked his owner's knots before bounding across the devastated suite. He leapt past the wreckage of the dining room, trying to time his hops to avoid further damage to the furnishings and the shards of crockery strewn about the carpet. The broken chandelier crunched into the overhead again; a rain of crystal fragments tinkled on Jax. He anchored himself in the door frame of Nicolet's stateroom, warping the lintel with his fingers as he assessed the situation.

Nicolet lay sprawled on the floor. A runnel of blood trickled from a gash across her forehead. Weary dread froze the pit of Jax's stomach. Even as he leapt to her side, he thought, *They'll have me melted for scrap. Or sell me to a shipping concern to work off this sin through a century of galley labor.*

But the girl still breathed, and the cut was shallow. The ship listed again, sending them both sliding across the polished heart-of-pine floorboards. He rapidly assessed her health, touching her with the very lightest of fluttering fingertips to determine she had not broken bones. She moaned when he lifted her. Her eyelids fluttered open.

"Try not to move, mistress. I'll secure you again."

"This is your fault, Jax."

"I know, mistress."

He'd knotted spare sheets around her legs and belly to fasten her to the bed. She'd begun to cry when he tied her arms, too, so he'd declined to do that. Tufts of linen fibers dangled from her manicured nails; the makeshift safety belt on her bed had been untied. She must have worried at the knots for hours; he'd tied the knots with mechanical strength just shy of tearing the fabric.

Jax had to recalculate and recalibrate his balance every few seconds to compensate for the constant buffeting of the hull. But he managed to carry Nicolet to her bed without mishap. He laid her down and pulled the covers over her again. "Why did you untie yourself, mistress?"

"I didn't. Your knots came loose from all the rocking and bouncing and then I was thrown from the bed."

A trio of scarlet droplets stippled the door frame near the height of the gash in Nicolet's forehead, suggesting she'd been on her feet and heading for the door when a sudden listing of the ship took her by surprise. But it was just easier if he accepted her lie. To do otherwise would be insubordination; a slave never questioned his owners.

"I understand," he said, retying the spare sheet around her waist. This time he put the knot past the edge of the bunk, where she couldn't reach it with both hands. "Why not call for my help? I would have come immediately."

"I did," said Nicolet. "I called and called but you never came and I couldn't hold on any longer so I tried to go into the dining room with you and Mother and Father."

"I apologize, mistress. I will take care to listen more carefully in the future."

"Yes. You must. You have to come when I call you and you have to obey what I tell you."

"As you say, mistress."

"You belong to my family. My father will be very cross when he learns you did such a poor job protecting me."

"Yes, mistress. That is correct." He gave the braided bedding another tug. "I hope I've done a better job this time." He certainly had; she wouldn't be able to reach the knot this time. "It's a relief you weren't more seriously hurt, mistress. I will return with a cloth to tend your wound."

"I don't want to be alone," she said. "I don't want to be on this ship any longer."

She hadn't phrased it as a command. "I must clean your wound. Else I may overlook other injuries."

Nicolet said, "What I *want*—" Here she squealed as the ship fell into a trough between towering waves, causing a moment's freefall that terminated with a tremendous bang as the keel slapped into the sea again. "—Is to get off this ship. I hate it and I hate the New World."

"I apologize, mistress. I cannot expedite your arrival. I will return with a cloth momentarily."

A brief lull in the onslaught of wind and waves against the storm-tossed ship made his footsteps surprisingly loud. A glassy crackling sound like the shattering of fine dinner china accompanied each step.

"Jax!" said Nicolet. "You're broken!"

"No, mistress," he turned to say. But when he pivoted, he could hear the grinding of metal and the rasp of something soft against his skeleton. Yet his functioning was not impaired, and he didn't feel the painful throb of a newly activated metageas compelling him to immediately report damage to his owner. If anything, his geasa had fallen exceptionally quiescent.

Then again, he'd never experienced so many metageasa jostling for priority within the finite confines of his skull. Perhaps they'd finally reached a point where additional pain would only incapacitate him. It had certainly felt as though there were no room for additional pain. Maybe the overabundance of geasa had temporarily overloaded his capacity for discomfort. He'd have to ask Clip if he'd ever heard of such a thing.

"I am not damaged," he said. "You needn't worry. Fragments of crystal from the chandelier have penetrated my mechanisms. They will not interfere with my service."

"I'm not worried about you," said Nicolet. Another volley of waves sent the ship listing first to starboard, then port, and then the deck shot up several inches. Jax's legs absorbed the motion with a loud *clang*. Nicolet's father yelled in the next room. The girl said, "Moving is very hard work. Mother and Father depend on you."

"I understand, mistress."

"And you must check on me more."

Jax automatically filed the new orders, shoehorning them into the hierarchy of demands that circumscribed his current situation. Still he was numb: no new ache accompanied her decree. The storm had so many of his metageasa asserting and reasserting themselves that Nicolet's new demands merely melded into the jostle of priorities, rather than prodding him with new needles of compulsion.

"Yes, mistress. I understand."

The shallow cut didn't start bleeding again when Jax cleaned it. Nicolet wouldn't even require stitches, though she insisted she'd be terribly disfigured and that Jax would have to explain to everybody who wondered aloud that her mutilation had been entirely his fault.

The adult Schoonraads had not come loose when Jax checked on them. Pieter had, however, sicked up on himself. The contents of his stomach stained his shirt a pale yellow, shot through with chunks of pink from the smoked salmon he'd had for breakfast. The spray had also splashed across one wall, and was seeping into the carpet. The stateroom reeked now of hot sour milk and old fish.

Madam Schoonraad yelled over the crashing of silverware and slamming of doors. "Find the captain at once. Tell him this is absolutely unacceptable!"

"Yes, mistress. At once."

Again, no flare of pain. But, spurred by the urgency in Madam Schoonraad's demand, Jax bounded for the door. Hopping from floor to bulkhead and back as the ship shuddered and pitched, juddered and swayed, he made the passage outside the suite. It was empty. He passed nobody else en route to the bridge.

Halfway there, the significance of this struck him like a diamond pickax between the eyes.

The captain had called general quarters. That was a command for everybody on the ship: humans and Clakkers. It had activated the nautical metageas that put the captain's decrees, and anything that promoted the integrity of the ship, temporarily above the demands of other nonroyals.

It should have been impossible for him to leave the Schoonraad stateroom until somebody from the crew gave the all-clear. The nautical metageas should have prevented it.

Jax should have been writhing with agony.

He wasn't.

CHAPTER
7

"Do you think," the duc de Montmorency said between grunts, "it understands this?"

Each thrust wafted his breath, sour with pickle vinegar, past Berenice's neck and ears. As she'd dreaded, the duke had decided to parlay his political support into a more physical alliance. He clearly felt as she did regarding the Clakker on the wall, but he was also a very wealthy man and thus accustomed to getting what he wanted. Or, perhaps considering whom he'd married, not getting what he wanted. He certainly acted like a man newly emerging from a vast, frigless desert. So Berenice was doing as she'd told Louis to do: closing her eyes and thinking of fallen France.

He'd insisted on taking her where Lilith would see them, so Berenice had hiked up her skirts and leaned over a trestle table in the laboratory. The rogue's expressionless and partially disassembled face peered through the glassy cocoon, staring blankly while they coupled. Torchlight shimmered across its chemical prison while the gleaming starlight from deep inside its head illuminated the cocoon from within. Pieces of the Clakker's skull, including the iron bandages and their rivets, rattled on the table in time to the duke's moans. Berenice double counted every screw and cog to ensure nothing rolled away. She'd promised to reassemble Lilith into perfect functioning order. Assuming their studies didn't render it inert.

And assuming they *could* put it together again. The techs referred to this as the "Devil's puzzle." To Berenice's knowledge this was the first time anybody outside the Dutch Empire had attempted to disassemble a functioning Clakker. (Inside the Empire any attempt to reverse-engineer clockworks resulted in a visit from the Stemwinders.) For one thing it required a rogue: normal Clakkers carried a severe metageas that overruled all others if anybody other than a Guild horologist sought to peek inside—a metageas that de-prioritized human safety, even that of the leaseholder, and rendered even the humblest servitor a vicious guardian of its own secrets. Yet none of the handful of other rogues who had previously passed through New France had lingered long enough for this to be an option. Only Lilith had remained after arriving, and for decades.

Lilith was particularly concerned about its Free Will. It had taken to vibrating so violently inside the inescapable chemical prison as to make it impossible to examine, much less dissect, the extremely fine machinery inside its skull. Berenice reassured the rogue over and over again that their purpose was not to change Lilith but the Clakker on the wall. That by comparing the slave and the former slave, they strove to deduce a means of breaking the geasa. The means of freeing *all* Clakkers. In this way she secured Lilith's cooperation.

It was a lie.

True, she did seek to change the Clakkers... but not to set them free en masse. *That* could be an uncontrollable global catastrophe depending on how the mechanicals—long suffering, long mistreated, long lived, and possibly harboring long resentments—reacted to their new circumstances. No, the emancipation had to unfold gradually lest humanity be overrun.

And the first step was to redirect the geasa. To rewrite rather than erase the Clakkers' allegiances. To turn their tireless devotion from one monarch to another, from a Brasswork Throne to a lost throne. Once the war was over—and it would be: quickly, definitively, permanently—they could look seriously at removing the geasa entirely.

"Does it know," said the duke, pawing Berenice's chest, "the significance of this supremely human act?"

The Clakker rattled inside its cocoon. The sheath had been peeled back via the parsimonious application of solvents as Berenice worked to disassemble Lilith's skull. She'd documented every single step, down to the number of revolutions required to remove each screw. Lilith's secret utterances had come out increasingly distorted, not unlike somebody trying to speak with a numb tongue.

I have witnessed several instances of copulation during my time as a slave. We know of the human drives for procreation and pleasure. It is impossible to serve humans for centuries without knowing their desires, it said. *Including the puzzling desire to perform this act before those of my kind.* Berenice didn't translate and didn't indicate that Lilith had just answered his question. The duke was too preoccupied anyway.

After he finished with one last shuddering moan, Berenice straightened and let her skirts tumble beneath her waist. She pretended to fuss with them. It gave her an excuse to look down, away from both duke and Clakker. Seductions and liaisons were part of courtly life, but this had been neither. True, one had to use one's charms where one could; that was life at court. But the trade of favors and alliances was rarely so pecuniary. The propositions rarely so bald. Montmorency had reduced her to a courtesan paid with political support, chemical resources, and spare technicians. Part of her wondered how much of his generous offer had stemmed from altruism, how much from recognizing the fundamental truth of Berenice's position, and how much from a lusty desire to get under her dress.

And she'd let him do it. Today she was the most highly priced whore in New France. A pragmatic whore, but still. If this would cement their alliance, very well. It needn't be forever.

She took a breath. In his frenzy, the duke had unlatched some of the synthetic whalebone stays beneath her bodice. His issue had a sour, unpleasant odor. Berenice donned a false smile—natural as a second skin to anyone who had spent time navigating courtly politics—to hide the nauseating curdle in her stomach.

She turned and curtsied. "That was quite lovely, Your Grace."

"Hmm," he said. He buttoned his breeches. "Do give my regards to the vicomte, won't you? Gabriella has been in a particularly pleasant mood these past weeks."

Oh, Louis. I'm so sorry, my love. Did the duke say this just to be cruel?

Berenice responded with another lie. "I will. He's quite fond of the both of you."

"Well then." Montmorency dabbed a silk kerchief at a stain on his breeches. Today he'd actually worn a wig; he straightened it now. His demeanor was as though they'd just shared supper and not fornicated like wild animals. "Let's see what you've learned from our friend here."

I am not your friend. I am imprisoned here against my will. I will report this to the king.

Berenice walked him through the current status of the disassembly. He marveled at the smallest screws, and again when Berenice described the frustrating bottleneck of frequently pausing to machine new tools specific to the peculiarities of

Clakker construction. He chuckled at the contrast between the quality machining of Lilith's original construction and the crude rivets on its apparently homemade bandage. He also spent several minutes paging through Berenice's notes, pausing to admire each sketch. "You have a practiced hand, Berenice."

"An essential skill in my line of work."

"Doubtless." He set her journal on the bench. Then, and only then, did he take his first good look at Lilith. He wasn't as skittish around it as some of his technicians; Berenice had had to bark at them to overcome their reluctance to approach the angry machine.

Berenice said, "Here. Let me show you something."

She pulled a footstool from beneath a bench, slid it behind Lilith, and gestured for the duke to climb aboard. Berenice held it steady for him as he gained the vantage enabling him to peer into the naked bowl of Lilith's skull. A pale aquamarine shimmer played across his face as though he gazed into a moonlit stream. He gasped.

"Good Lord. It's full of light!"

Berenice peered up at him. This time her smile was genuine. "It's something, isn't it?"

She climbed atop the adjoining bench. A pair of tin snips clattered to the floor. Though it was tricky in the gown, and downright painful in the corset, she knelt over Lilith and the duke. She used a long screwdriver to point, taking care not to touch anything.

"Can you see that? Underneath the mass of needles."

The duke nodded. Light shimmered across his face while he turned to and fro for a better look. "What is it?"

"No idea. It surprised the hell out of us, I'll tell you that. But I think it's some kind of glass."

He blinked at her. "Glass?"

"Alchemical glass."

"For what purpose?"

"No idea."

The duke studied her. After a moment, his eyes narrowed. "But you have a theory."

"No theory. No hypothesis. Just an observation." She climbed down, crossed the laboratory to a bookshelf, and returned with a volume of Descartes. "How's your knowledge of human anatomy, Your Grace?"

Montmorency laughed. "Utterly nonexistent."

"Mine, too, until recently, when I remembered something I'd read long ago." Berenice tapped the book. "That shiny gem," she said, gesturing at Lilith's skull with the screwdriver, "sits at roughly the location of a human's pineal gland."

"Fascinating. But what, ah, what does that mean?"

She sighed. Shrugged. "Probably nothing." She tossed the screwdriver on the bench.

The duke climbed from the stool. Hand on her shoulder, he said, "You've made remarkable progress."

"I feel we've barely begun. Your people are very clever, make no mistakes. But they are chemists. And this—" She tapped the chemical sheath laminating the keyhole and damaged sigils in Lilith's forehead. "This is alchemy."

Montmorency changed the subject. "At least our new formulation worked."

"Exceptionally well, Henri. Your chemists should be commended. It solidified as quickly as anything I've ever seen, as quickly as anything used in combat. And the strength is remarkable. It hasn't moved an inch."

"Unlike that beast on the wall."

"Yes. That epoxy is holding it in check, but just barely." If anything, the strain put on the glassy shell by the military Clakker's constant struggle to move was heating and weakening the chemical sheath. "But this"—she gestured at Lilith, and the mound that anchored it to the floor—"will do the trick nicely."

Lilith kept up a running commentary, making clear just what she thought of Berenice, the duke, and their chemicals.

Montmorency shook his head. "No. I'm delighted to see the success here, but we must enhance the formulation before bringing the other inside. The military model will be stronger." He laid a hand on her forearm. Odd that he felt the need to be gentle now, but not when his smallclothes were bunched around his ankles. "In this matter, you are the most important person in the kingdom. Other than the king himself, your safety trumps all."

The duke carried a warmer look in his eye when speaking of pragmatic realities than he had when propositioning her. Berenice shook her head. *Men.*

"I was right about this, and I'll be right again. The present formulation is sufficient. We can bring the soldier inside now."

He said, "At the risk of sounding like the corpulent marquis, why take that risk? Now we know the base formulation is sound. Enhancing the tensile strength will be straightforward."

The furrowing of his brow suggested frustration, disagreement, or both. So Berenice sighed. "How much time will that require? The longer that thing hangs on the wall, the higher the chances the tulips will notice and come to collect it."

The duke waved off her concern with an absent fluttering of fingers while he stared at Lilith. "Oh, no more than a day or two."

Well. That wasn't catastrophic. She didn't like it, but she wasn't so obstinate as to scuttle this alliance over it. Pragmatism carried the day. For the second time that hour, she let Montmorency have his way.

"Very well. You're right to urge caution. Shall we say Saturday, then?"

The duke nodded his assent. "I'll see it's done." Still he gazed at the entrapped Clakker with fascination. He ran a hand across the glassy sheath, following the contours of the dented keyhole.

"Did you do that?"

"No. Vestiges from some previous accident. But notice how damage to the keyhole defaced the sigils spiraled around it. I suspect this was the accident that rendered Lilith capable of Free Will. But it must have been an extraordinarily fortunate mishap," she added. "Defacing the keyhole and sigils destroys the magics and renders a Clakker inert. But here the damage removed the compulsion without destroying the impetus. It's astonishing. We didn't know that was possible."

The imprisoned Clakker fell conspicuously silent. As it had when Berenice described the contents of its skull.

Montmorency whistled through his teeth. "I thought these alchemical alloys were damn near indestructible."

"They weren't always. Based on the ornamental filigree," said Berenice, pointing to a flange over Lilith's shoulder, "I'd say this Clakker was constructed almost two hundred years ago. Early to mid-eighteenth century would be my guess."

He fished a pair of reading glasses from a lace-fringed pocket of his vest. He squinted through them, his nose almost pressed to the cocoon. If he thought of the thing trapped inside as a sentient being, he gave no sign.

"What sort of accident could have done this?"

"Short of a mishap with a cannon? I've no idea."

Berenice made eye contact with the Clakker as she said it. But on this matter the mouthy self-righteous machine remained silent.

Montmorency turned his attention to the rest of the laboratory. Perusing the shelf of broken Clakker parts, Talleyrand's collection of treaty violations, he said, "You've become quite an expert on Clakkers."

"Too generous, Your Grace. There are no experts on the mechanicals outside of the Clockmakers' Guild."

"But surely you are the most knowledgeable person in New France."

"Now, that," Berenice said, "is probably true. But I stand on the shoulders of giants."

∞

A shit-smeared murderer trudged along Vlamingstraat toward the Grote Markt. He took no notice of the icy rain plastering his hair to his head, seeping beneath his collar, leaching the color from his hands, face, and lips. He'd lost his hat during the frantic struggle to revive the prisoner, and hadn't seen fit to take an umbrella before leaving his parsonage. His breath trailed behind him like a trail of angry revenants. Or disdainful angels.

Those few who passed him on the street, not blurring past in a carriage, gave no sign of recognizing him. They saw not a pillar of spiritual life in The Hague but a filthy wretch best avoided. Wise of them.

A Clakker pulled to a halt alongside Visser, empty rickshaw-hansom in tow. "Sir," it said. "You appear to be confused or in distress. May I lend assistance? If you are in need of charity, I am allowed to convey you to a shelter free of charge."

"Don't speak to me," said Visser. "Remove yourself."

The Clakker departed. It was the fourth mechanical to accost him since he'd departed the Ridderzaal. He'd lost his patience half an hour ago. His stroll had taken him along the Hofvijver, the pond north of the Binnenhof. His Bible and the hollow Descartes now lay at the bottom of it. So did his ruined ecclesiastical stole.

Had the prisoner told him the truth? Was somebody close to the king secretly conspiring with the Dutch?

He'd been premature in making his peace: his work wasn't finished. He had to deliver a warning to Talleyrand. Even if it took his last breath, he would strive to preserve the only nation on Earth that revered the immortal soul, as the Lord had intended. But there was no longer a network for passing secret messages to New France. And he didn't dare trust this revelation to intermediaries. Visser had to deliver the warning personally. While he was there, perhaps Talleyrand could pull some strings and help Visser land an audience with His Holiness Clement XI.

He'd committed murder. A mercy killing was still a killing. Would the pope hear his confession? It would be a balm, receiving the Sacrament of Reconciliation after so many years hiding his true faith. It made him yearn to depart immediately.

But ports and aerodromes were out of the question until he changed and bathed at the parsonage. Otherwise the porters would chase him away the instant they got a good whiff of his clothes. He'd be wise to empty the hidden ambry in the vestry while he was at it.

He turned south on the Paviljoensgracht, the Pavilions Canal. It formed the western border of the man-made island upon which sat the Nieuwe Kerk and its environs along with a few other buildings, Visser's parsonage and the old synagogue most prominent among them. He'd loop around to the south and climb the gentle slope of the Wagenstraat bridge where it alighted south of the island.

Sleet stippled the canal water with the sound of distant applause. A green fringe had long ago slimed the waterline, the currents in the canal being too languorous to prevent algae from finding purchase on the glazed bricks. The slower-flowing canals were sometimes infamous for their fetid odors in the hottest months, but it was late enough in the year that cold tamped the worst of it. Visser whiffed nothing foul as his footsteps crunched gravel along the high banks of the canal.

Nothing fouler than himself, anyway. His sense of smell had long since surrendered under the reeking onslaught from his own clothing. He'd scrambled through spilled effluvia, on hands and knees, as part of the show of scrambling to help revive the prisoner. They'd failed, and that was good; the poor woman had earned her eternal rest.

The robin's-breast red shutters of Paviljoensgracht 72-74 peeked through the rainy mist. The house always struck Visser as a particularly unfortunate example of old architecture. Its implausibly wide cornices capped with a pointlessly tiny pitched tiled roof gave the appearance of an emaciated octogenarian war hero wearing clownish epaulettes and a dunce cap. But it would never change: Spinoza had written his *Ethics* there, as mentioned on the marble plaque above the door. Visser turned east before passing the Spinozahuis; the old tow-canal route to Amsterdam formed the southern border of his tiny island.

The Wagenstraat bridge brushed within an arm's length of the synagogue. Visser didn't enter it, though he had often in the past. The Dutch-Portuguese Rabbi Morteira had passed away nearly ten years ago, and Visser still missed him. Missed the old fellow's friendship and his wisdom. He could have used both at the moment. He even missed losing their weekly chess games.

Oh, Levi. What would you make of this mess?

Wrapped in recollections and racing thoughts, Visser had climbed almost to the apex of the stone arch bridge before noticing the onlookers. Smaller groups had gathered along the canals, but the elevated bridge had collected the most pedestrians. Most canal bridges in The Hague were flat; the arched Wagenstraat provided a better view of the island. The onlookers squinted through the drizzle toward the Nieuwe Kerk churchyard. The damp and the cold struck Visser all at once. He shivered from a chill deeper than what the cold rain could wash into his bones.

Yes. The spectators watched his parsonage. Where the front door hung open. Visser had locked it when he departed for the Binnenhof. And was it his imagination, or could he hear a crashing and banging emanating from inside?

Trusting the smell and his disheveled appearance to create a suitable disguise, he asked a bystander, "What are we watching?"

The man he'd queried wore a banker's tweeds. He glanced at Visser, frowned, sniffed twice, frowned again, and ambled away. Next the pastor queried a woman who might have been a schoolteacher or governess. She looked scandalized by his appearance, but at least she had the courtesy to answer.

"Stemwinders," she said in the same whisper one used when speaking of the devil. She spoke softly, this lady in the bonnet and eyeglasses, but her words nearly knocked him flat. His stomach gave a sickening twist, as though somebody were trying to wring it dry. He couldn't breathe. She pointed at the towering octagonal edifice of the Nieuwe Kerk. "I saw a pair enter the church, too."

Visser struggled to speak through the shivering that overtook him. "How long ago?"

She shrugged. But the man standing beside her said, "I wager they'll find a secret idol of the pope under the crypts. Midnight Black Masses!"

Long enough for the rumormongering to start, then. The Stemwinders would find the ambry soon enough, and the Catholic accoutrements within would fuel a hundred rumors more dire than this. A secret Papist working inside the Nieuwe Kerk?

The lady shivered. Pointedly, she turned her back on Visser and the other fellow.

Visser did likewise, using the gesture of disapproval as an excuse to ease away from the crowd. Most of the onlookers' attention focused on the parsonage, jostling for a glimpse of the mechanical centaurs ransacking his home. Each no doubt feeling a similar guilty thrill, schadenfreude alloyed with shuddering relief that *they* weren't the Stemwinders' focus. And each wondering where the occupant had gone. Scanning the rapt faces in the crowd, he recognized several regular churchgoers.

Visser wanted to sprint, wanted to turn around and seek refuge in the synagogue, but he'd look suspicious if he altered his course. Somebody was bound to recognize him if he drew too much attention. So he kept going north to descend the gentle catenary slope of the Wagenstraat where it approached the St. Anthonisburgwal, the Rotterdam tow canal. It meant walking into the wind. He had to squint to keep the sleet from pelting his eyes. Which is why he didn't see the Stemwinder at the bottom of the bridge until he was almost abreast of it.

He flinched. His startled hesitation drew the attention of the towering mechanical. Visser forced himself to press on, conspicuously hurrying past with eyes downcast. *Don't look guilty*, he told himself, *merely unnerved. Uncomfortable.* Who wouldn't when encountering a Stemwinder in the middle of the street on a cold wet afternoon? And who wouldn't scurry past, head low, when caught shivering in the sleet without hat or umbrella? To do otherwise would draw suspicion, Visser told himself.

I'm just an unlucky soul, he tried to broadcast. *Caught unprepared by the weather and wanting to get inside. Just another pedestrian smeared with shit.*

Gobbets of ice dripped from the Stemwinder's four arms, all held akimbo, and its impassive face. Sleet tinkled against its alchemical carapace. Visser imagined he could also hear whirring as the gemstones in its eye sockets turned to follow him.

He tensed, expecting a telescoping limb to come spearing through the rain to clamp fingers like a shackle about his arm. Hardest of all was resisting the urge to hunch his shoulders once he passed the centaur. The Clakker's imagined scrutiny carried a terrible weight. But nothing grabbed him, nothing accosted him, and soon he had put the bridge behind him. Visser didn't dare sigh with relief in the cold air, for fear the sight of his long exhalation would condemn him.

His mind spun like a broken carousel. He had to get out of The Hague immediately. He had to get off the continent. Sheveningen District and its pier on the North Sea were a straight shot to the northwest. The parsonage was off limits to him now, so he'd have to try to talk his way aboard a ship. Why hadn't he brought a full wallet when he departed for the Ridderzaal? Why hadn't he been prepared to bolt at a moment's notice? Was it because he had fallen lax in his spycraft, or was it a different form of suicide? An elaborate attempt to see himself martyred?

Damn it, damn it, damn it.

He raised an arm and whistled for the first taxi he saw. The Clakker attendant veered toward him.

And then Visser heard it slicing through the rain-patter: the *chank* of metal upon stone, the piercing and portentous step of a mechanical hoofstep. And another. And another, and then one more. A four-legged gait. The tendons in his neck became steel bands quivering against each other as he fought the urge to toss a guilty terrified glance over his shoulder.

The taxi rolled to a stop at the curb. Its attendant said, "Where shall I take you, sir?"

Chank-chank, *chank-chank*. The quadrupal gait became a trot. A lowly servitor Clakker could easily outrun the fastest human sprinter. But likewise the Stemwinders could outpace anything, perhaps even the queen's Golden Carriage.

Visser flung himself into the hansom. "Sheveningen pier! And quickly!"

"Yes, sir. Immediately, sir."

The Clakker pulled away from the curb, accelerating

smoothly into the traffic. The thrum of sleet atop the cab, the *tick-tick* clattering of the driver's body, and the grind of steel-rimmed wheels along the wet street together obscured the sound of the Stemwinder. Visser risked a glance through the rear window. The centaur kept pace less than twenty yards back, its legs pistoning up and down with clockwork syncopation. Other vehicles skidded to a halt or veered into lampposts, flower boxes, and each other trying to vacate the Stemwinder's path. Carriages coming the opposite direction swerved off the pavement when the centaur approached. Visser's driver seemed the only being on the street unaware of what approached from behind.

He looked again. The mute Stemwinder had halved the distance and continued to gain. Visser's mind's eye had frozen on a collage of the prisoner's mangled hand, the missing fingernails, the brand marks he glimpsed on her back and collarbone when he attempted to revive her. If they'd do that to a former Guild member, what would they do to a Catholic who masqueraded as a Protestant all these years? Who had defiled the Nieuwe Kerk with his heresies?

Those will be my hands if they catch me. My burns. I'll be martyred after all. And New France will fall.

Visser leaned forward. Panic murdered his capacity for discretion. "Go faster!" he shrilled.

Still jogging, the driver spun her head around like an owl to face him. "Sir, I will endeavor to deliver you to your destination expeditiously and safely. Greater speed would be a danger to you and those around you, sir."

And then, as it turned to face the road again, the hansom decelerated.

"No! Faster, not slower!"

Again the head came around. "Sir, it is a crime to interfere with a Stemwinder in the performance of its duties. I simply wish to clear the road, sir. I shall resume our previous pace once this agent of the Sacred Guild of Horologists and Alchemists overtakes us."

Which it had nearly done: the *clankchankclankchank* of its hooves grew louder by the moment. It was coming up on the left.

Visser pointed to a street on the right. "Turn there!"

"Sir, may I humbly recommend a more efficient route—"

"Turn, damn you!"

The Clakker heaved on the poles. The lurch flung Visser across the seat. Pain blossomed in his shoulder and elbow. The cab leaned, ever so briefly, on one wheel as it skidded around the wet street corner.

The driver heard the thump. "Sir, are you hurt?"

"No. Keep going."

A tooth-grating screech pierced the city noise behind them. Visser turned just in time to see the fading fountain of sparks kicked up by the Stemwinder's hooves as it skidded past the turn, carving deep gouges in the paving stones. The Guild Clakker spun through the slide, its eyes tracking Visser's hansom.

A man driving a delivery wagon yanked on the hand brake lever and flapped his horses' reins. But the wagon, full laden with barrels, was too heavy to stop or turn quickly. It rolled to an awkward rest, blocking the road. The driver released the brake and leapt to his feet. Visser could see him working the reins, shouting at the horses, and casting frantic pale glances at the Stemwinder. A shuddery breath escaped from Visser's chest, propelled by the momentary reprieve.

The winding avenues quickly brought them back alongside the Rotterdam tow canal, which slid past on their right. He opened his mouth to demand another quick turn—

—when the street behind them erupted in a massive crash

simultaneous with the screams of men, women, and terrified horses. Visser hadn't thought he could feel any colder at that moment, but the shivering took him anew. The view behind caused something terrible to gurgle from his stomach into his throat. It burned.

The delivery wagon had been flung across the street and halfway through a shop window, cargo and all, as though it were no heavier than a wagon-shaped speculaas cookie. The horses lay in a broken thrashing heap. White wine gushed from shattered casks. It mixed with blood and sleet to swirl shards of glass, snowdrifts of black salt, and detritus of the wooden wagon into gutter. Visser couldn't see the driver. He'd never seen so much blood, even in the foul warrens beneath the Ridderzaal. Much of it flowed from the bellowing draft horses.

All other traffic evaporated before the Steminder as people scrambled to clear its path. In seconds, nothing stood between it and Visser's cab. It leapt from a standstill to a full gallop. Pedestrians hurled themselves into doorways and scrambled atop window ledges as the charging Stemwinder bore down on them. Unblinking gemstone eyes seemed to lock on Visser. His bladder voided itself. His thighs received a momentary reprieve from the cold.

Dear Lord. I can't let that thing touch me.

Any pretense of innocence gone, Visser descended into desperate reckless panic. Casting about for anything that might slow the mechanical centaur, he fixated on the narrow canal to his right.

Though the driver couldn't see it he gesticulated to the left, at the rainbow blur of commerce as they sped past an unbroken series of shops—tailors, dressmakers, cobblers, haberdashers; this was a garment district—and colorful houses. Not far ahead, they neared a gap between two shops just wide enough for a delivery wagon.

"There! Make for that alley!"

Something metallic and salty trickled down his throat, torn loose by the effort to make himself heard over the hellish artillery concussions of the Stemwinder's hooves. It had narrowed Visser's lead to a handful of strides and closed as though he were crawling. Powered by evil magics, its furious determination shook the road and sent ripples skittering across the canal. A pair of quacking teal took to the air.

Visser crouched on the balls of his feet, hoping the swerve into the alley would help launch him toward the canal. There was every danger he'd go tumbling under the wheel. But like a frightened rabbit he fixated on the slimmest possibility of escape.

The beast was so close Visser could hear the flexing of reticulations in the centaur's spine. Its internal mechanisms spun so furiously the usual ticktock metronome noise had become a high-pitched buzz.

"Turn, God damn you!"

But by then the hansom-puller had again become aware of the Stemwinder. It edged closer to the canal and smoothly decelerated. The Stemwinder drew alongside. Its crystalline gaze landed square on Visser. Its neck swiveled, keeping its focus locked on the pastor even while its body drew even with the driver. Like a mouse hypnotized before a swaying serpent, Visser gazed at his pursuer.

(So very strange, the things one notices in fleeting moments of distress. *No breath*, he thought. How unnatural. Surely this would have been a chest-heaving gallop for a racehorse, yet this relentless mechanical puffed no streamers of breath into the chilly afternoon. Even more than the malign shackled sentience behind those gemstone eyes, this demonstrated the perversion of the horologists' trade. And the rightness of Visser's cause.)

Visser leaned backward into a crouch with knees folded tightly and fingers clamped on the edge of the cab.

Still charging forward alongside the hansom, the Stemwinder swiveled smoothly at the waist—

Less than two yards to the canal's edge, Visser gauged. *I can do that.*

—which brought all four of its arms to bear without altering its course. It grabbed the hansom with two hands. The other pair of arms suddenly tripled in length, spearing forward to impale the other Clakker with a deafening squeal of sundered alloys and seized gears. The violent jolt broke Visser's grip and sent him crashing against the seat.

The Stemwinder tore the servitor in half like a sheet of newsprint. Escapements, cogs, and coinage spewed across the street, kicking up steam and the rotten-egg whiff of sulphur where hot shards of alchemical alloys skittered through icy puddles. Guilders and stuivers tinkled on the paving stones, the delicate ringing incongruous in the midst of such violence.

The Stemwinder flicked its arms. The upper half of the servitor slid free of the lance and somersaulted high overhead to pulverize a granite corbel and shatter a third-floor flower box. Its lower half splashed into the canal, legs still pantomiming the metronome rhythm of a leisurely jog. Hissing water released billows of brimstone steam.

The pull poles splayed apart. A crack like the death of a felled tree shook the driverless hansom. The broken axle forced the wheels out of true. A fierce shudder flung Visser against his bruised shoulder again. His face hit the side of the cab. He tasted blood.

The Stemwinder heaved on the carriage to steady it. But the pinewood paneling shattered, leaving the mechanical centaur with two handfuls of kindling and shredded upholstery. The wobbling carriage veered left, then right. The right wheel spun free and went bouncing along the towpath. The cab lurched sideways. It seemed to teeter in slow motion, suspended for an impossibly long moment—*I'll make it into the canal after all. Will I drown pinned under the carriage? Can a Stemwinder swim? Horses can.*—before cartwheeling over the lip of the canal.

The world turned upside down. A blow to the head, fireworks behind his eyelids. Blurred vision. Splash. Darkness. Cold. Numbness.

Disorientation.

Noise. Creaking, groaning, bubbling. Pursuit?

Weight settling, pinning his legs. It had him?

Flailing, panicking, kicking. Lungs aching.

Kick landed. Legs free. Twisting, writhing. Light below, darkness above. He was upside down.

Visser thrashed to the surface and gasped down a lungful of air. He couldn't see from one eye. He reached up to push his hair aside but discovered it was a flap of skin hanging from his forehead. It didn't hurt. The trekvaart was too cold.

He remembered a woman with a mangled hand. Remembered her warning about a viper in the nest. *Get away. Go.*

Wreckage of the taxi lay strewn about him. He took another breath, got his bearings, then dove under the flotsam. How long had it been since he'd last gone swimming? Not since he'd entered the seminary; he held a vague memory of a birthday party at a beach, cookfires, women in bathing suits. He worked his legs as savagely as he could, clawing through the murky water until it seemed his chest would implode, trying to put as much distance between himself and the crash as possible. If nobody had seen him surface, they might think he was still pinned beneath the carriage and waste time on a rescue.

He surfaced, gasped, dove again. The narrow canal funneled clanking, crashing, and splashing noises so efficiently it seemed he hadn't moved but a few yards. But he didn't dare look. He forced out three extra kicks after it felt his lungs would burst.

Visser breached again, half-blind for the skin and hair plastered over his right eye. Was he leaving a trail of blood on the water? He'd swelled his chest for another dive when a shrill whistle ricocheted along the canal banks.

"Got him!" somebody shouted.

The fugitive pastor flipped his torn forehead aside—now the pain came through, subtle as a nail pounded through his temple—to find the source of the cry. He flicked the blood from his eyes. Fifty yards downstream, the canalmaster for this section of the Rotterdam trekvaart pointed to Visser and sounded his emergency whistle again. He held a canary-yellow life preserver in one hand.

Visser scrambled to the opposite bank. His fingertips had just brushed the ancient algae-slick masonry when one of the canalmaster's servitors launched itself into the air as though shot from a cannon. Propelled by the sudden invocation of a safety metageas—or perhaps it had witnessed the chase and knew the man in the canal was wanted by a Stemwinder, which would have invoked an even deeper metageas—it folded itself into an aerodynamic ball. Air whispered through the gaps in the servitor's skeleton. It crossed the ten yards in the seconds it took Visser to pull himself to his knees.

The Clakker unfolded itself in the split second before landing. Though its backward knees absorbed the worst of it, the impact still shattered bricks and sent jagged cracks zigzagging along the canal bank. An earthquake heave flung Visser backward. Water slapped his spine. The sting knocked the air from his lungs.

He drifted, mouth open, nothing going in or out. A second Clakker joined the servitor, this one much taller and sporting too many limbs. There was clanking, and splashing, and then a red curtain descended over the world.

CHAPTER
8

The storm blew them off course, adding leagues to their voyage. But three days after the captain gave the order to redeploy the sculls, the New World eased over the horizon like a bashful and reluctant suitor. The skyline of New Amsterdam hove into view as the *Prince of Orange* limped toward port. It didn't impress.

It was said the center of the Dutch Empire west of the Atlantic boasted a human population exceeding a million souls. That put it on par with some cities of continental Europe. But it lacked the canals of Amsterdam, the gravitas of The Hague, the romantic soul of Paris, the artistic soul of Florence, the long histories of London and Rome. New Amsterdam looked and smelled like what it was: an overgrown frontier outpost with open sewers.

In fact, if not for the handful of Clakkers laboring on the piers, and the loops of carrot-colored bunting flapping in the sea wind, a first impression of Nieuw Nederland might have suggested a place and time separate from the Empire. Separate from the engine of prosperity known as Clakker-kind. It startled Jax to see so few of his kind working the piers.

He wondered if that was a reflection of the recent economic upheavals that Pieter Schoonraad had been sent to address. People couldn't affort Clakker leases.

But Jax didn't begrudge the sprawling city its lack of character. He didn't want Nieuw Nederland to be like the world he'd left behind. The distinction gave him hope it might prove the sort of place where one could lose oneself.

Madam Schoonraad sniffed and sighed as she leaned on the balcony rail, peering toward her new home. Several airship masts glinted in the sunset, steel needles like massive lightning rods reaching from nearby rooftops to rake the sky. An airship docked to the northernmost, lending the mast tip the appearance of a seedpod swelled to bursting. Wind from the periodic passage of massive oars several stories underfoot fanned her hair and fluttered the fringes of her paisley shrug. She stood with arms crossed, jaw muscles tensing. It was her posture of displeasure.

The lady of the house shivered and turned her back on New Amsterdam. "You two," she said. "Come here."

Driven by a century of habit, Jax braced himself for the tickle of pain that ever accompanied the ignition of a new geas. But nothing happened. No embers of compulsion flared to life. No heat licked at the edge of an imprisoned soul, threatening to grow into an agonizing firestorm until he relented. It was strange and dizzying. It had caught him off guard, dented his equilibrium, each of the dozens of times it happened—or, more correctly, didn't happen—in the days since the storm. Regardless of what his owners said, or how they said it, or what stringent maritime procedures required of him, no alchemical or metaphysical bondage enforced his compliance. There was nothing—absolutely nothing—physically preventing him from ignoring her. Or grabbing her by the hair and flinging her into the sea.

He went anyway.

Clip instantly set aside the chest he'd been packing and crossed the suite to join her on the balcony. Jax put down his brush and stood to attend her with equal alacrity.

The city loomed behind Madam Schoonraad as she issued orders. The buildings grew that much taller, that much closer, with every pass of the oars. The *Prince of Orange* angled toward an empty berth along the wharf. Gazing just past her shoulder, Jax focused and refocused his eyes to gauge the distance from the pier to the first line of warehouses. He plotted a leap from the balcony.

"You," she said, pointing at Clip. She'd never learned their names. In this, Nicolet was exceptional. Most owners wanted no truck with such nonsense. "Go below and find a porter. Arrange to have our luggage unloaded the moment the ship makes landfall. Do it yourself if you must. Then go to the pier and contact number three." By which she meant Vyk. "Ensure it has carriages and wagons ready for us."

"Yes, mistress. Right away," said Clip.

...I'd land about there. *Roll. Five, six, seven strides to that warehouse. Climb the five-story brick façade. On the roof in nine seconds...*

She turned to Jax. "You. Finish scrubbing the suite. I want it spotless before we disembark. We will not pay a cleaning fee."

The mechanicals on the pier appeared to be as old or older than Jax. That was probably the case with many of the Clakkers in the New World; leases for new Clakkers were more expensive here than back home. *Can I outrun them? How strong are they?...*

"When you have removed the stains, fetch a porter to have the suite inspected."

...or leap from this balcony to the prow, spring from the ornamental bowsprit to the base of the cargo crane, then sprint to the base of that rainspout...

"Yes, mistress," said Jax. "Immediately."

But what lies beyond those buildings? I don't know the layout of the city. Where is Bleecker Street?

I need a map.

Clip jumped from the balcony, flipped himself over the railing of the servants' stair along the hull, and, after landing with a heavy *clang* that set the stair ringing like a gong, descended to the hold. Meanwhile Jax returned indoors to scrub his masters' vomit from the carpet while contemplating a miracle.

Freedom felt like . . . nothing.

Free Will was a vacuum, a negative space. It was the absence of coercion, the absence of compulsion, the absence of agony. A gap in his consciousness where geasa had perpetually jostled for priority, demanding his obedience. It was the photographic negative of Jax's existence during every minute of the 118 years since he'd been forged.

It was overwhelming. Exhilarating. Terrifying.

Overwhelming: he could do anything he wanted. But the grand sum of anything-at-all was nothing-at-all. The topology of freedom offered no gradients to nudge him, no landmarks to guide him. How did humans guide themselves? How did they know what to do and what not to do? How did they know when to do anything without the benefit of geasa and meta-geasa to prioritize every single action of their waking lives? How did they order their daily existence without somebody to tell them what to do?

Or was that the purpose of God?

Exhilarating: he could do the thing of which every Clakker since Huygens had dreamt. Jax could say *no*. He could even consider it without suffering the throes of paralyzing anguish. Thinking about disobedience, fantasizing about it, clutching the idea to his mainspring heart didn't summon vicious incapacitating pain. Previously the geasa would have seared the notion from his mind if his thoughts had so much as brushed against it. He knew this with the surety born of experience; so did every mechanical ever built. But now his thoughts were his and his alone.

Terrifying: Jax remembered what had happened to the last Clakker to say *no*. They'd broken his legs, and filled his mouth with glue, and tossed him into the hellish forges of the Clockmakers' Guild. The humans had destroyed the rogue Clakker Adam, who'd been born Perjumbellagostrivantus, and made a public spectacle of it. Practically declared a citywide holiday. They had called him rogue and demon-thrall, melted his body to an alchemical slurry, and incinerated his hard-won soul until there was nothing left of it but a shiver in the spines of the human voyeurs.

Rogue. That's what they'd call Jax, too, if they caught him. They'd condemn, damn, torture, and melt him.

Nobody could know that Jax had changed. Else he would become a hunted fugitive sought by every pair of eyes in the Dutch world, wet jelly and cold crystal alike, until his flight ended either in New France or the Grand Forges. The slightest hesitation to comply, the tiniest hint of malfunction could draw the scrutiny that would end his freedom before he had a chance to comprehend it. Until he could lose himself in New Amsterdam—until he could make a break for the *ondergrondse grachten*, if they existed—the crucial thing was that he drew no attention to himself. To do otherwise was to run the risk of an inspection by the horologists. But if they opened him, they'd find the murky glass bead that had tumbled from the broken microscope to somehow—impossibly, inexplicably—grant Jax Free Will. Thereby invalidating centuries of Protestant dogma that insisted such a thing was impossible. Did this make the Catholics correct? Was Jax now in possession of his own soul? He didn't know. Was this how it felt to be human? He could only speculate.

The microscope had been tucked inside his torso for safe-keeping, but his acrobatics during the storm had wrenched the antique beyond anything it was meant to endure. Perhaps it was catching Madam Schoonraad that caused the stiff leather tube to rupture. At some point during the storm, the microscope's contents had gone rattling through Jax's innards. Where somehow it sundered the bonds of geas.

The change had been so smooth, so seamless, he hadn't understood it until he'd clearly violated the severe nautical metageasa. The instant he realized what had happened, he contorted himself into the posture of a Clakker wracked by indescribable torments and slowly dragged himself by the fingertips back to the Schoonraads' suite. He'd been fortunate that no crew member had glimpsed him in the passages, and that his human owners had been oblivious to the nautical metageasa.

Even worse than the threat of capture was the anxiety that this new freedom might be fleeting. Was it temporary? Would the geasa reassert themselves? That possibility terrified him more than anything else. Having tasted life without the pain of obligation perpetually burning him from within, he'd choose death over the return to bondage. He'd make that choice in an instant. Life as a slave was unspeakable; life as a slave who had briefly tasted freedom was unthinkable.

Had Pastor Visser expected this to happen? Was this deliberate? That seemed terribly unlikely; breaking the microscope had been a fluke, and surely wouldn't have happened if not for the storm. Had he known of the microscope's contents? Jax couldn't guess. But he remembered the pastor's unease during Jax's errand to the Nieuwe Kerk. Jax had offered to send for physic, thinking the pastor unwell. So assume for the moment Visser *had* known the microscope contained something unusual. Rather than bring it to the Guild's attention, as required by law, he arranged to send it to the New World.

Why? What did that suggest? And what of his friend, the idealistic museum curator in New Amsterdam? One possibility was
they were French sympathizers... *if* Visser knew the truth of
the microscope.

A thin thread. But it gave Jax a starting point. It gave him a
goal.

How strange that life as a rogue meant serving the same
objectives of his former bondage. For now he found himself
doubly dedicated to Pastor Visser's errand.

∞

It happened while unloading the wagons.

As ordered, Clip stayed at the pier to continue unloading
cargo while Jax and the newly reunited Vyk pulled the first overloaded wagon to the new Schoonraad residence. It was the work
of mere moments for the three mechanicals, working together,
to lash down the top-heavy load. Madam Schoonraad's grandfather clock, a priceless seven-foot Salomon Coster original
wrapped in rugs and blankets for the transit through the city,
jutted from the heap like the mainmast of an old East India
Company schooner stripped of its yards by weather or resource-
ful pirates. It had taken a beating during the storm.

The harbor thrummed with the bustle of commerce, of
loaded and unloaded cargo, of ships arriving and departing,
of gossip and anger, of happy reunions and tearful separa-
tions. The gulls' keening sounded the same as it had on the
Continent, the salt-tang of Atlantic sea spray tasted much the
same, not to mention the constant slow creak of damp wood
and rope that was the international language of the nautical
world. As anywhere in the Empire where heavy labor was the
order of the day, shouts and orders filled the air. But compared to Rotterdam harbor a much larger portion of the labor
was human, as the income raised by mooring and other fees

enabled the harbormasters to retain expensive Clakkers only for the most menial and/or backbreaking tasks.

As Jax and Vyk settled under the yoke to begin the long haul to the house, Clip and a porter descended a gangway to the pier, each carrying a pair of Madam Schoonraad's chests.

The porter greeted Jax and Vyk. *Clockmakers lie.*

Jax responded in kind. (*Yes, they do*, he thought. *I'm proof of that.*)

Vyk cocked his head. *What is that about clockmakers? I've heard it several times recently.*

Clip said, *You should tell him, Jax. You were there.*

Tell me what?

The porter said, in cog-chattering overtones of awe, *You were* there?

The other mechanicals within earshot of this exchange reacted similarly. But with envy came attention. And though their human masters might be oblivious to minute details of protocol, Jax's fellow Clakkers could never be. How many pairs of precisely machined eyes watched him even now? How many would it take to notice if he slipped?

He said, *Only for part of it.* Honesty seemed a safe policy. *I had to leave before it was over.*

Clip set his load upon the empty bed of another wagon. *Well, yes. But* you *heard him say* it.

A frisson of excitement rippled through the nearest mechanicals even as they continued, without the slightest faltering or hesitation, to fulfill their geasa. For a moment Jax felt as though he were one of the oldest Clakkers—those legendary few who had known Huygens himself, the man who enslaved a million—feted by younger models during a very rare public appearance.

I wasn't the only one, said Jax through a humble squeaking of his leaf springs. The mechanical cricket chirp carried emotional undertones akin to a human shrug. *The Binnenhof was packed.*

Vyk said, *This is going to be a good story, I can tell. Good. It'll help pass the time. It's a long walk.*

So as they lugged the first of several loads through the crowded, uneven streets of New Amsterdam, Jax told the story (pausing as necessary while Vyk navigated) of Adam's execution and final words. The cobbles here were rougher and more irregular than back home, the gaps wider. It took considerable strength to get the wagon going again each time they stopped for cross traffic. The manure scattered here and there apparently came from horses. Jax saw more of these here in New Amsterdam than back in The Hague. Draft animals weren't uncommon back home, but Clakkers had long ago supplanted animals for many menial tasks. On the one hand, it was rather decadent; on the other hand, and this was the winning hand, Clakkers didn't defecate in the street. (The surfeit of mechanicals in the heart of the Empire also meant the streets were always cleaned promptly and thoroughly in the wake of any draft animals.)

Along one avenue they passed a series of demolished buildings. Many bricks had been shattered; others lay in a pile slumped halfway across the street. Traceries of dark soot feathered the empty outlines of doors and windows.

I would've thought fires would be less common here, where it seems everything is built from brick and stone.

Vyk shook his head in imitation of the human gesture. *Not a fire. That was a garrison until French partisans managed to smuggle a bomb inside.*

Jax took a second glance. Now he noticed how the mortar around the frames bowed outward. Maybe Madam Schoonraad wasn't so far off the mark when describing the perils of New Amsterdam to her friends. *How often does this sort of thing happen?*

Oh, not as often as one would prefer. Not since the cease-fire.

Jax noted each street they crossed on the chance their route happened to bring them past Bleecker Street. A slim hope in a city of this size. But most of the streets appeared to be laid upon a grid; this would make it easier to find his way around when the time came.

Vyk guided him into a neighborhood where the streets were wider, the houses larger, and the gutters not brimming with effluvia. Presumably this neighborhood had fewer piles of manure on the street because its residents were wealthier and more inclined to lease Clakkers. Or because they paid for privately contracted street sweepers. Jax did see more of his own kind here. Mostly servitors like him and Vyk, running errands for their owners, though a military Clakker accompanied a squad of humans armed with rifles and bayonets. It towered over the humans and servitors, the serrations on its retracted blades glimmering with the promise of violence. Jax indicated the soldier with a nonchalant nod.

Are they *common, since the cease-fire?*

Not very. There were a few more strutting around immediately after they came back from the front. Maybe they were shipped back to the Continent.

Casually, merely making conversation, Jax asked, *Ever see any Stemwinders?*

Vyk shuddered. *God, no.*

That was encouraging. *Not ever?*

Well, there must be a few around. Probably out where they're building the new Forge. Did you hear about that?

Jax thought back to the conversation in Pieter Schoonraad's study. *Yes.*

Vyk indicated a broad boulevard lined with poplars. Together they urged the wagon around the corner. The houses here were the largest Jax had yet seen in the city, larger than the Schoonraad residence on the Lange Voorhout. They looked upon a large swath of green space; willow trees lining a pond swayed in the breeze. Jax could smell the humidity. A goose honked in the distance, upset by the rattle-clatter of their wagon. Across the park, two servitors renovated a house's brick façade.

Their owners' new residence was the fourth house from the corner. Three stories tall, it occupied a double lot. Jax couldn't identify the style. It wasn't reminiscent of the Old World, nor was it utilitarian like the buildings near the harbor. The entire second floor fronted the street with a single pane of glass, immense and decadent. It must have been alchemical. A carriage house built in the same style but to a smaller scale (this was only two stories, after all) perched at the end of a long drive that passed through a wide porte cochere alongside the house. A wrought-iron fence kept neighbors and passersby at a safe distance. This was the domicile of a family on the rise.

I know, said Vyk. *What a shithole, right?*

Jax laughed. But then a sad thought ruined the moment: *I'm going to miss him. Clip, too.*

Vyk opened the gate and unlocked the house while Jax unlashed the furniture heaped atop the wagon. Several miles of jouncing across uneven cobbles hadn't done the clock any favors. It was the work of moments to run the chests inside, though they took more care with the clock. The latter needed repair, which would require bringing it to the Guild. Jax hoped that duty didn't fall to him, if he hadn't already escaped by then. His feet scritched across jade tile. Filigree in the wallpaper blazed brilliant silver when a gap in the cloud cover sent sunlight streaming through skylights in the entryway.

Vyk had installed booms and pulleys above the gable windows, for hauling furniture to the upper floors. They'd almost emptied the cart when Clip arrived hauling a wagon by himself. Jax wondered how he'd found the place.

Nicolet rode nestled amongst the tarpaulins. She picked at the bandage on her forehead.

Vyk said, *Oh, wonderful. The Queen of the Universe has arrived. It was nice having an entire ocean separating me from that brat.*

Don't worry, said Clip. *She'll live for only another seven or eight decades.*

Let's see how cheerful you are after she inherits the estate and your lease along with it.

Jax ignored their bickering. "Mistress, where are your parents?"

"Father and Mother are taking a carriage. Pulled by *horses*," she said in much the same tone she might have used if they had opted to ride to their new home on a dung wagon. Indeed, after a prolonged sniff she added, "I don't like this city. It smells like poop."

Clip said, *She's not wrong.*

They had lashed an armoire to the pulley lines and were just about to haul it up to the gable when Nicolet scrambled aboard. She perched atop it and wrapped her arms and legs around the rope.

"Mistress, that might not be safe."

"Then make it safe for me! I want to ride to the top."

Jax looked up to Vyk leaning out the gable window. There wasn't a clear and evident danger to her safety, so Jax couldn't refuse. All a Clakker under the compulsion of geasa could do was to stay extra vigilant. And so, acting the part, did Jax.

"Mistress, please. Your safety is our first concern."

"I want to ride to the top. I want you to do this and so you have to keep pulling. You have to do what I say."

Yeah, said Vyk. *The next seventy years are going to fly by.*

Jax did as she commanded. He pulled slowly, and tried to time each pull to dampen the swaying of the load. But Jax had hoisted her above the entryway skylights when Nicolet began to rock back and forth, pumping her legs as though riding a swing. She giggled. She shifted her weight, leaning against the rope to make the armoire rock like the bent pendulum in her mother's clock. The pulley creaked. Vyk lunged out to clamp his fingers around the rope to suppress the swaying. Too late.

The boom snapped. The rope skipped free of the pulley. Nicolet screamed.

The wardrobe blocked Jax's view of the falling girl. Without thinking he extended a forearm and slammed aside the black walnut cabinet. It flew into the street a fraction of a second before Nicolet would have been out of reach even for his mechanical reflexes. But it cleared his field of view just in time for him to blur into position beneath her. He caught her in his arms stretched overhead, and brought her to rest at his feet. A rain of oak and iron, fragments of the shattered boom, followed an instant later. Jax shielded her with his body.

"Mistress! Are you hurt?"

The Schoonraad girl shook her head, though she'd gone a snowy pale and shivered under his touch. Her watery eyes shimmered. She stumbled to her feet.

"You're safe now."

She nodded, trembling. At first he thought she couldn't speak, but then Nicolet gasped and slapped a hand over her mouth. She pointed at the dented armoire laying skew-whiff in the street. "Jax, look at what you've done!"

Oh, no.

He crossed to where it had tumbled to a stop. Its passage across the cobbles had warped the silver hinges on one panel and gashed the lacquered walnut deep enough to expose the unfinished wood. Two legs had wedged in a gap between pavers and snapped off during the skid.

Madam Schoonraad ordered us to be careful, he thought. *To leave not the tiniest scratch on the furniture.*

"What's wrong with Vyk? Is he broken?"

Unusual rattling drew Jax's gaze upward. Vyk still leaned out the window. The clanging and twanging from his body grew louder. It was the sound of somebody trying and failing to suppress a severe geas. They made eye contact. So tremulous was his voice that for a moment Jax couldn't understand him.

J-j-jax-x-x-x—

Clip started to rattle, too. What was wrong with them? Had they—

Oh, no.

An unswervingly loyal servant could have preserved Nicolet and the wardrobe. His reflexes would have allowed him to catch one in each arm. Replaying the last few moments in his mind's eye, Jax could see several alternate choreographies for his actions that would have granted a safe landing to both. If he'd been bound by the usual geasa, he would have striven automatically to fulfill every obligation that wasn't physically impossible. And in this instance it was possible, though just, to save the girl while adhering to Madam Schoonraad's trivial desires regarding the treatment of her belongings.

But in that moment, as a free being capable of making his own choices, Jax had forgotten that. He'd done the humane thing. The *human* thing. By fixating on preserving Nicolet from death or lifelong paralysis, to the exclusion of all else, he'd outed himself as a rogue.

A human probably wouldn't have noticed the instantaneous glitch in the calculus of compulsion. But to a Clakker bound by the shackles of alchemical bondage, it was a glaring error. Jax had become an anomaly, shining brighter than the sun and twice as impossible to ignore.

Vyk and Clip knew him for a rogue. And so did the hierarchical metageasa within them. It would tear them apart rather than let them keep Jax's secret.

Wait! This isn't what it appears. I couldn't—

Vyk's mouth hinged open like that of a python preparing to swallow a suckling pig. A tortured shriek rattled the windowpanes and set the goose to honking again.

"—J-J-JAAAAAX-X-X, *RRRRRUUUUUNNNNNNN!*"

CHAPTER
9

The rain finally stopped around midafternoon, but the chill lingering in its wake guaranteed morning would find the boughs of the distant birches and elms bare and perhaps even pale with frost. Autumn seemed intent on taking the year off. And, judging by the way Berenice's breath steamed, winter was eager to get on with things. She stamped her feet and tucked her hands deeper into the fox-fur wrap at her waist. She'd been on the battlements since just after dawn, though the rain had beaded and rolled freely from the natural oils in the beaver pelts in her coat and hood. The gusty wind sent smatterings of rainwater dripping from the Spire. Her nose ran; she'd rubbed her upper lip raw to the point she tasted both blood and snot when she ran her tongue across it.

A *crack* and a short, sharp yelp emanated from the wall below. For the hundredth time that day she craned her aching neck at the clump of chemists and the unhappy corporal dangling alongside the Clakker.

So did Sergeant Longchamp, who monitored things from beneath a sealskin poncho strung between two flagpoles and a battlement. He leaned on the broadside of a two-headed pickax, the diamond-hard tip at the base of its shaft wedged into the mortar between two stones. He took two seconds to assess the situation before shaking his head. After spitting a long dark stream of tobacco through the crenelle he shouted, "You short-dicked baboons are making the Blessed Virgin cry! Haven't you shitlickers ever heard of foreplay? Fucking Christ, be gentle with that bastard. This isn't some dockside whore you're paying by the minute, you fools!"

Seeing that his gentle encouragements had delivered the intended effect, the sergeant returned to his knitting.

Berenice eyed the mottled green yarn coiled about the handle of a fifty-pound sledge sitting head-down on the stones beside his feet. The thing slowly growing from Longchamp's needles had a variable width and a marked lack of symmetry. She cocked an eyebrow. "Scarf?"

Without looking up, the sergeant said, "Don't need a scarf. That's what the beard is for. This is a cozy. For me nethers."

She feigned a sneeze to cover her laugh. "Oh, my." She wondered what it really was.

As before, Louis and the Duke Montmorency were both there, too. The duke insisted on overseeing his chemists' work; Louis had insisted on being there to support Berenice and, if necessary, whisk her kicking and screaming to safety. A chemist hoisted the solvent gun over her shoulder, lifted her goggles, and ran a hand across her forehead. She caught Montmorency's eye and thrust her chin in the general direction of Longchamp.

"Sir…"

"Now, now. The sergeant has a point. Let's not be hasty. Let's do this right."

The sergeant muttered, so quietly only Berenice could hear, "Yeah. You can bet yer gold-plated nuts I'm right."

Berenice huddled against Louis for warmth. He put an arm over her shoulders. The synthetic waterproofing oil in his mantle gave him a faintly peppery but very masculine smell. She pressed closer. He kissed the top of her head. It felt like getting pecked by a bird; even his lips were tense.

The lead chemist called up, "I think we're ready, sir. We've gone all the way around."

Everybody turned to Berenice. She plucked the spyglass from her sleeve. High overhead, eight lookouts armed with very similar accoutrements were situated every forty-five degrees around one twist of the Porter's Prayer. Probably shivering in the wind and rain as they attempted to penetrate the mist for any sign of tulips on the move. Berenice, Montmorency, and Longchamp were ready to abandon the operation at a moment's notice should there be any danger of somebody witnessing their violation of the armistice in flagrante delicto. But the mist worked to their advantage. It helped hide this shady, overgrown corner of the Vauban fortification.

A flick of her wrist snapped the spyglass to its full extension. Far better to have monitored things on the spot, but the unlikely troika of husband, duke, and sergeant had banned together to overrule her. His Majesty had had no choice but to agree in the face of such a diverse and unified front. So she studied the chemical sheath around the Clakker from atop the wall. As Montmorency's woman had indicated, there was now a hairline fissure right at the spot where the mechanical's upper hand adhered to the wall. Berenice rested the telescope against the stone to hold it steady and even held her breath as she monitored the Clakker. But weakening the bond to the wall didn't appear to have eased its forward progress. It was still contained by the chemical sheath.

"It's good," she declared. "Bring it up."

This time Longchamp didn't even look up from his knitting. "You heard the vicomtesse! What in Christ's sake are you waiting for?"

The chemists scrambled back up the wall, hauled to the top by sweating guards. The dangling corporal—promoted into dead Maurice's place—held a diamond-tipped pick much like the sergeant's. Other guards manned the wall defenses just in case. He worked the razor-thin blade into the fissure created by the laborious but precise application of solvents. It took several tries before he managed to get leverage on the long handle of the pick without sending himself swinging away from the wall or dropping the pick. But he did manage to give the handle a solid wrench.

The crunch and crackle set Berenice's teeth on edge. For a moment, no breath steamed on the wall; everybody froze, waiting to see if they'd just freed the Clakker. Even Longchamp held his breath, she noticed. But for the crumbs of the chemical cocoon pattering down the wall and dusting the ivy below, the only noise was the creak of rope and the quiet click of Longchamp's knitting needles. No dreadful crackle as the machine broke free.

Nervous laughter spread through those assembled on the wall when it came clear the Clakker wasn't about to skewer them all. Longchamp grunted. Louis released a long sigh. She loved how he didn't pretend he wasn't alarmed. The corporal, looking distinctly green, repositioned his pick and heaved again. The entire mass of Clakker and its glassy sheath came free of the wall after a dozen tries. It fell just a few inches before the net snapped tight. The lines thrummed. The mass swung ponderously in the breeze, an immense and deadly bug trapped in amber.

Longchamp rolled up his craft project and tucked it into an open haversack at his feet. "All right, you lazy pox-ridden get of whores! Let's show this tulip demon some French hospitality! And put your worthless backs into it this time, for fuck's sake."

The hapless corporal stayed below, inching upward alongside the Clakker as the crew atop the wall heaved it upward. He used the haft of his pick to prevent the chemical sheath from banging against the wall, which might lead to cracking, or abrasion along the granite. The lift crew brought the captive Clakker up to the battlements in less time than it took Longchamp to fully elaborate on his opinion of the soldiers' technique with the rope. He'd only begun to catalog the deficiencies in their anatomies when Berenice flipped the ratchets on the hoist to lock the load in place. The sergeant ambled to his feet, hefting the pick over one shoulder and the sledge over the other as though they were no more cumbersome than fishing rods. His bulk belied the speed with which he casually inserted himself between Berenice and the Clakker. Louis took position beside the sergeant, unarmed but still determined to shield her from harm. A foolish gesture, perhaps even a bit chauvinistic, but it warmed the special spot in her chest just the same.

Longchamp snapped his fingers. A cadre of soldiers surrounded the duke and his chemists, too. Some carried picks and sledges, like the sergeant, and others carried double-barreled epoxy guns connected to fat copper tanks slung over their backs. Still others carried bolas, a trio of iron weights connected by a meter of high-tensile steel cable. Cumbersome, but an essential piece of the infantryman's loadout.

Berenice gave the word. "All right. Swing it over."

The lift crew unlocked the pivot on the boom she had designed specifically for this work. One could have heard a mouse squeak as they slung the captive Clakker over the battlements to set it gently atop the wall. It had, at last, reached its destination.

A furious clattering erupted from within the sheath. So loud and rapid was the noise it seemed impossible the machine wasn't moments from breaking free. The civilians inched backward, including Louis. He glanced over his shoulder to give her a guilty shrug. She feigned disappointment with a significant glance at Longchamp and his men. They'd held their ground. But she winked and blew a kiss at him lest he become too crestfallen.

Montmorency elbowed through his protective cordon to kneel beside the rattling mass of cogs and chemicals. Now the Clakker vibrated so violently that the entire mass juddered along the stones. The sheath squeaked like fingernails on slate where it skittered along the wall. Berenice cringed. This time even the soldiers inched away.

"The next man or woman who even entertains the notion of thinking about retreating," Longchamp said, "gets a very long needle in a very intimate place."

Berenice made to join the duke, but Louis and the sergeant moved to block her. "Oh, for crying out loud," she said. "Were you fools any more chivalrous I'd surely swoon on the spot and damage my uterus."

Louis blushed. "Sorry, love. But we're a unified front on this matter. It's too dangerous."

She rolled her eyes. "You are never getting laid again, you lowborn traitor. And as for you," she said, pointing at Longchamp and lowering her voice, "you'd better move unless you want everybody to know about the clothes you knit for the orphanage last Christmas."

The look on his face could have etched glass. "I don't know what you mean."

In a stage whisper, she said, "Such tiny outfits."

He'd spent the months of November and December making hats, mittens, sweaters, socks, and mufflers for the orphans of Saint Jean. He'd explained the frequent trips from the Keep into the surrounding city with an excessively explicit cover story about midnight dalliances in a patisserie. He even came back with flour in his hair from time to time to sell the lie. But Berenice knew the truth.

The sergeant scowled. But he stepped aside. "Sorry, Louis. You married an evil woman."

"You don't know the half of it."

Berenice patted Louis's cheek as she brushed past. She knelt beside the duke and the captive Clakker. Its outstretched arms and legs made it unstable, so it had been laid on its back. The chittering rattle of its unchecked vibrations obscured the more muted *tick-tick-tick*ing of the unclouded eye as it tracked her approach. But more disquieting than its relentless drive to break free was the certainty it recognized her.

Oh, well. All that mattered now was getting the machine into her laboratory where the real work could begin in earnest. She turned to Montmorency—not before giving the Clakker what she hoped was a long and disconcerting wink—and said, "Now the hard part."

The duke shook his head. Steamy breath jetted from his nostrils. Combined with the way he perched beside their illegal treasure, it put her in mind of a dragon standing guard over its hoard. His nose ran, too, and beads of mist dangled from his bushy eyebrows. He laid a hand on the glassy cocoon and sighed.

"It's warm," he said quietly.

Berenice followed suit. Her fingers slid along the silky texture of the cocoon; it was warmer than the surrounding air, even warmer than the cold stone upon which it lay. He was right. A faintly astringent chemical odor tickled her nose, as did the scent of hot metal.

"It's doing its damnedest to escape," she said.

"The heat and the vibration could weaken the sheath. And there might be microfractures from prying it free."

They'd been over this; she knew where he was headed. So she said, "Very well. Let's dose it again."

"Agreed." He gestured at the chemists huddled under Longchamp's tarp. "Felix. Bring the sprayer."

Felix couldn't have been twenty; he had a spotty face and just a tuft of downy hair on his chin. It took two people to get the bulbous backpack slung over his shoulders. The device wasn't obviously different from what some of the soldiers carried, only cleaner and less battered. But so scrawny was the boy, and so awkward with the hemisphere on his back, that it looked as though he were hatching from a burnished egg. Spurred by a tingle of apprehension, Berenice asked, "This is the new formulation, correct?"

The duke said, "Not to worry. It'll work as intended."

It took careful maneuvering—by Felix as well as those around him—to ensure the Clakker received a full coating without also gluing it to the wall, or the bystanders, or Felix. Montmorency's new formulation gushed from the nozzle a shocking fluorescent green, a color Berenice had never seen in nature. This, she imagined, was the color of dragon blood, or mermaid tears. It was also less viscous than anything she'd seen fielded; a fine emerald mist splattered the stones and stained her coat. The droplets released intense heat and a skunky musk as they solidified. The air downwind of the newly entombed Clakker became rank and unbreathable. It took two hard swallows before Berenice forced the contents of her stomach back into something resembling quiescence.

The epoxy turned a less shocking shade when it hardened. The phase change happened so quickly that the resulting color shift might have been a magician's illusion. Several of the onlookers gasped and clapped, in spite of the malodorous fume wafting through the battlements. A double layer of high-tech amber now encrusted the soldier, twice as thick as before and solid enough to muffle the clacking of its clockworks and the grinding of its gears. And this time the random vagaries of a splash pattern hadn't left one eye unobscured. Berenice wondered if it could see anything. She could barely discern its outline; it looked like a ghost, a smoky djinn, trapped in the heart of an immense uncut emerald. When she rapped her knuckles on the sheath it gave a solid clink like glass or stone, rather than a dull thud.

Montmorency nearly elbowed Felix aside. "Stow that." To Berenice, he said, "Let's not dawdle."

She gave the nod to Longchamp. He barked orders, and new ropes looped around the Clakker *tout de suite*. Rather than carry the bulky and awkward package down the narrow stairs, they rotated the boom again and lowered the captive into the outer keep. Berenice watched from below, along with Louis and another clump of Longchamp's men. They wrapped the Clakker with blankets and tarpaulins before carrying it through the inner and outer keeps to the disused carpentry shop. The procession received a few curious glances but none, Berenice hoped, that might discern the nature of the soldiers' burden. Talleyrand would never assume the enemy *didn't* have eyes and ears in the most inconvenient and least expected places. Always assume the enemy is positioned to inflict the greatest harm... She'd made the idiotic mistake of disregarding that dictum when she'd gone over the wall by herself. Which had nearly proved fatal. Few things could focus the mind like a near-death experience.

She led the procession across the catwalks while up top Longchamp oversaw the teams erasing all signs of the operation. Even now, she knew, another team of chemists and soldiers hung from the battlements, scouring away any residual evidence that something had been affixed to the wall and repairing the damaged ivy. Once inside the abandoned shop, they lowered the Clakker through the center of the helical stairwell. It swung like a pendulum, occasionally knocking against the wrought-iron banister to set it ringing like a gong. Echoes reverberated to the keep above and down into the chthonic heart of the mountain below. The enemy machine was a considerable pain in the ass even when immobilized. More than once the awkward burden spun in just the right fashion to wedge an outstretched limb beneath the handrail. One might have thought the damn thing was doing this on purpose. Berenice, several turns of the stairwell lower than the others, fixed this when it happened. The third time, her fingers flinched from the cocoon; it was extremely warm. Not enough to burn but enough to startle. Enough to make her imagine a geothermal vent had opened beneath them.

Louis leapt to her side. "What's wrong?"

She laid a hand on his face. "Relax, love."

She called up to Montmorency, mentioning the heat. But no reply echoed down the shaft. *Oh, right.* The operation on the wall successfully completed, the duke had hopped the funicular to report to His Majesty and the rest of the privy council. They'd agreed on this.

A few minutes later the Clakker lay just outside the entrance to her laboratory. Longchamp's people untied, disentangled, and coiled the lines while she unlocked the door. The sergeant himself bulled his way through the knot of people at the bottom of the stairwell, sledge tucked rakishly over one shoulder, diamond pick over the other, knitting needles and yarn poking from the rucksack dangling on his back. Though he must have hurried to catch up to them so quickly, Longchamp had barely broken a sweat during the long descent. She wondered how he managed that trick: with so many warm bodies milling at the bottom, the stone stairwell had become stuffy as a chimney. His focus was the Clakker and nothing else.

"Get that cogfucker inside," he barked. "Double time!"

Berenice had pushed the trestle tables aside to clear a path to the rear of the laboratory. She bristled at having so many people tromping through her private demesne, but it was a necessary evil. Longchamp would lose his shit if she tried to keep his men and women out now. Though to his credit he did threaten to tear out the tongue and cram it up the nether hole of anybody who so much as whispered a single word of what they witnessed down here in the cold stone heart of Mont Royal.

"Shit. It's *hot*," said an infantrywoman. Sweat beaded on the faces of the soldiers carrying the entombed captive on their shoulders. They shuffled past the mound of blankets where Berenice had hidden the missing Lilith. As far as anybody topside knew, the rogue Clakker had departed Marseilles-in-the-West some weeks earlier without so much as a good-bye. While Berenice trusted Longchamp to make good on his threats, she had equal faith in beer's ability to loosen a soldier's tongue. King Sébastien still didn't know what Berenice had done to Lilith; Berenice wanted to wait until she could dilute his displeasure with excellent news.

Which she hoped to have in hand soon after cracking the military Clakker's head open like an egg. Would she find another glowing yolk?

Lilith heard the commotion. A distorted rattle emanated from its corner. The disassembly had taken a toll on it. *Who there? What you do? Release now!*

Berenice doffed her anorak while Louis went around lighting torches, candles, and lamps until the mirrored sconces filled the chamber with a shadowless glow brighter than the overcast day outside. The soldiers dumped the new captive at the far end of the chamber, near the spot on the wall where centuries-old gouges still marked the moment when their predecessors had called a halt to further excavations. Damp patches of sweat darkened their uniforms where they'd carried the bundle. They backed away, panting and mopping their faces.

The illumination revealed new details in the outer sheath. The translucent lime-green cocoon shimmered in the lamplight.

Berenice snapped a jeweler's loupe over one eye and leaned forward, squinting. It wasn't an illusion. Tiny bubbles percolated through fissures in the boundary between the old and new coatings. The innards of the chemical sheath effervesced as though it contained sparkling wine. Strands of hair that had worked loose to dangle across her forehead during the long descent fluttered in an updraft driven by heat coming off the captive Clakker.

This wasn't right. For the first time all day, a sliver of doubt found its way into the pit of her stomach. The fizzing grew more turbulent; cold unease stippled her sweaty skin with gooseflesh. She turned to show Longchamp.

"Sergeant—"

A loud *crunch* like the snapping of a hundred celery stalks shook the laboratory. The scent of lemon-curdled milk enveloped Berenice. Several people shouted at once.

Louis clamped a hand on her forearm and nearly dislocated her shoulder yanking her backward at the same instant a serrated blade erupted through the chemical sheath. Pellets of shattered epoxy pelted them like hailstones. Debris sleeted across benches and shelves. Longchamp whirled and shoved them both toward the exit.

"Get out!"

More shouting. Berenice tripped on her skirts in the effort to arrest her stumble toward the door. She shook off Louis's arm to push through the commotion of soldiers scrambling for their weapons and flipping tables to form barricades.

"What are you *doing*?" he cried.

"Grenades!" She pointed at the shelves where she kept spare bladders like the one she'd used to trap Lilith.

The sergeant bellowed, "Sprayers to bear, *now*!"

Another blade snapped free of the military mechanical's deteriorating cocoon. One of Longchamp's men hip-checked the shelves in the panicked jostle to get into firing position. A fragile epoxy bladder rolled off the edge and ruptured on the floor, instantly encasing most of Berenice's tools and immobilizing two soldiers. One took the blast right in the face, the splash pattern coating his nose and mouth. Based on the urgent retching noises it had gone down his throat, too. He flailed at the vitreous sheath with his one free hand. His comrade had merely been glued in place; with her free arm she snatched the combat knife from her belt to chisel at the glassy mask forming an airtight seal over his face.

Berenice scrambled past them. Something went *snick*, somebody screamed, and then something warm and wet splashed her neck. The curdled-milk odor became the latrine stink of viscera. She slipped in a sticky puddle.

Louis! She spun, but he was still behind her. The Clakker was preoccupied with the soldiers. She pushed him toward the open exit again. "Get out, you fool, and seal the door!"

A cacophonous rattle came from Lilith's corner. *What happens? Who here? Help!*

Longchamp: "Bolas! NOW!"

Berenice leapt to her feet, heading for the shelves. But Louis tackled her aside just as a thin steel cable winged through the space where her neck had been. She felt the wind of its passage across her ear in the instant before they hit the floor together. Her breath abandoned her lungs in one explosive gasp.

The bolas whirred across the laboratory, opening like a net as they spun. The military Clakker slashed with its blade arm faster than Berenice could follow, and then the iron weights rebounded from the chamber wall trailing severed red-hot whip-tails of steel cable. A random bounce sent one careering into a knot of soldiers. The severed cable slashed one fellow's cheek down to the bone, exposing teeth but cauterizing the wound in the same passage. He was lucky. The man beside him tried to dodge, but instead the iron cratered his sternum with a sickening crunch.

Now free of its chemical prison, the enemy Clakker leapt to the chamber ceiling where it hung upside down like a spider. Its fingers and talons crumpled the water retardant like so much crepe paper. A dust of pulverized stone sifted on the ruins of Berenice's laboratory. It stung her eyes.

The Clakker skittered overhead fast as a galloping horse. It hardly slowed when it unfolded into a lightning-quick backflip, swiping its serrated arms like an immense pair of scissors at Longchamp's throat. The sergeant flung himself backward and parried with his pickax. Metal screeched against metal, showering him with sparks that singed his eyebrows. Tufts of the sergeant's beard fluttered to the floor. The mechanical re-anchored itself on the ceiling and kept going. Berenice thought it was headed for the laboratory door—*The king. Christ, it's heading for the king. That must be its geas.*—but it detached itself from the ceiling, slit a soldier's throat while still in midair, and landed before Lilith. It flung the blankets aside to reveal the entombed servitor and its grotesque broken-eggshell head.

"What the fuck is that?" Louis whispered.

The military Clakker paused for a fraction of a second. Practically an eternity.

"Oh, shit," said Berenice.

The last thing they needed was to bolster the rampant killer's motivation to slaughter them. Doubtless the sight of its disassembled kin activated a dormant piece of the hierarchical metageasa. The part that insisted on using any and all means necessary to prevent deconstruction by non-Guild members. Would it opt straight for regicide, or would it first murder everybody down here?

Louis pulled her behind an overturned trestle. Why didn't he leave when she told him to? He lay atop her, trying to use his own body to shield her. She grabbed his neck to pull his ear to her lips. (How well could that demon hear through this commotion?)

"Spare epoxy bladder. Can't let it get out," she breathed. He swallowed, nodded.

"Get that goddamn thing where it will do some good!"

Longchamp pointed to the metal tanks on the back of the suffocated soldier. A knot of soldiers threw themselves into the effort to chisel the goop-sprayer free. Blood flew as in their haste they also hacked at the still-warm body of their comrade. Berenice and Louis crawled through the wreckage of her laboratory supplies, searching for the last spare bladder.

A rattle-clatter exchange ricocheted between the two Clakkers too rapidly for her to follow. She couldn't tell if the soldier Clakker realized Lilith was a rogue, or what Lilith might have told it. Perhaps the soldier saw the damage to Lilith's keyhole and inferred it wasn't to be freed; doubtless another metageas governed interactions with rogues. Or perhaps the searing obligation imposed upon the Clakker by its last orders had simply become unbearable after weeks of immobility. But for whatever reason, after just a few seconds of hypercompressed conversation, the unfettered machine halved its distance to the exit in a single leap. A bulky soldier scrambled to block its path, sledge and pick held high. The machine parried her swing.

Berenice found an epoxy balloon hidden within a pile of her journals. The fluttering pages must have cushioned its landing enough to prevent rupture when the contents of the desk went tumbling to the floor. From the other side of the desk where she huddled there came the clank of metal slamming into stone followed by the abattoir rasp of blades on bone. More scarlet stippled her hair, hands, and face. The bladder squished under her fingertips and for a horrifying moment she thought her adrenalized scramble had caused her to squeeze it too tightly.

She winced, expecting a glutinous fountain to cement her in place so that the Clakker could kill her at its leisure. But it didn't. It took a focused effort before she could loosen the fingers with which she clutched the epoxy weapon.

The air thrummed again as something sleek whipped across the chamber, low and fast. An instant later the laboratory reverberated with a metallic twang that started low and rose into the tooth-grating screech of tortured metal. She peeked over the bench. Somebody had finally landed a well-aimed throw of the bolas. The steel cable entangled the Clakker's legs. It fell to the floor, shuddering violently and flailing its forearm blades as it tried to cut itself free. It hardly needed to bother: the overstressed cable wouldn't hold it for more than a few seconds. Honest French metallurgy could never best demonic alchemy.

But the machine had been slowed for a few invaluable moments. Berenice vaulted a lab bench, charged the juddering razor-edged tangle of magic and metal, and hurled the bladder square at the mechanical's chest. She dove aside to dodge the splash, rolling to a painful stop in a bruised and battered heap. New pain flared in the arm Louis had wrenched. She clambered to her feet.

"Out of me fuckin' way!"

The sergeant nearly bowled her over again when he charged past hefting pick and sledge. She spun, expecting to see the Clakker encased much as Lilith had been. But she had put too much behind her throw, causing the chemicals to splatter far and wide. Most of the splash had geysered up and away from the Clakker in the instant before it congealed. Myriad thin tendrils spidered from its torso to the walls, floor, and open door. But most of the epoxy had become a glassy mushroom anchored on its chest. The machine hadn't been fully immobilized.

Longchamp smashed through the crystalline tendrils with his sledge, frantic to reach the Clakker before it freed itself.

Glassy shards sliced the sergeant's arms in a dozen places. The diamond tip of his pick whistled like a songbird when he swung it at the soldier's forehead. It connected with a tremendous clang but rebounded before he could drive it home with the sledge. He flexed his arm to bring it around again.

Louis ran for the door. *Yes, get clear of the killing zone, love! Send reinforcements!*

The Clakker extended both arms like Christ on the cross, and then with a quiet *snick-snick* unfurled its blades again. One skewered the door frame, the other speared straight into the floor with a tooth-rattling concussion that added the scent of cracked stone to the miasma of deadly disaster. It shuddered. Its ankles, bound together by the cable, unhinged to reveal serrated spearheads jutting from its talon-feet. An explosive twang propelled these a solid inch into the floor. It heaved. Its chest rose. Now the smell of hot metal and screech of overstressed bearings filled the lab. Berenice realized it had anchored itself so that by flexing its body it could maximize the tension on its restraints.

Oh, you clever son of a bitch.

The cables around its legs snapped apart and slapped the floor with a report like cannon shot. An instant later the epoxy ruptured, exploding into glassy shards that sprayed through the lab. A flying chunk half as large as Longchamp tossed the sergeant across the chamber like a doll. The debris knocked Louis from his feet, slammed him against the door frame. Berenice raised an arm to shield her face but something speared her left eye. A scarlet weight crushed the world flat, its depth and texture buried under the tremendous agony spewing from her eye socket. She screamed, toppled.

Louis stumbled to his feet. Berenice watched through a scarlet curtain as he lunged for the door. But instead of fleeing— *What are you doing? No, no, NO!*—he heaved at the lever to seal it from the inside.

The Clakker flipped into the air, somersaulted, landed on its feet.

With nothing between it and Louis.

Berenice tried to call a warning but gagged on the blood coursing from her ruined eye socket. "Louis—"

The mechanical saw him straining at the heavy door. It swung one arm in an uppercut. The blade *snick*ed again, and then Louis was shrieking, his arms twirling, his shoulders fountaining. Arterial spray splashed the walls.

"LOUIS!"

Numbness slammed into Berenice like an avalanche.

The machine ripped the half-closed door from the hinges, flung it across the lab—catching another of Longchamp's people off guard in the process, and probably shattering all of her ribs—and leapt into the spiral stairwell. Seconds later the echoing clang of alchemical brass on wrought iron receded as the machine bounded up the shaft toward daylight.

Berenice rolled to her feet but slipped in her own blood. It coated her and the floor. Something hovered just at the edge of her peripheral vision on the left. She could feel and hear it scraping inside her eye socket. Shock might have dulled the worst of the pain but it did nothing to disguise the sickening *wrongness* that came from feeling something foreign plunged so deeply into her eye socket that it grated against her skull. *Don't think about it.*

She focused on Louis writhing on the floor in more blood than she had ever seen. He was already slowing, his shrieks trailing into a weak whimper.

Tourniquet. She scrambled through the chaos to reach him. She unbuckled the belt from a dying soldier's trousers and crawled to Louis. He started to convulse as his organs shut down. She looped the belt around his shoulder but the blood was on her hands and his skin and she could see the bone and the loop kept slipping from where his arm should be because there was nowhere to tie it and he wasn't making any noise now and why didn't he run away and Jesus Jesus Jesus where were Louis's arms and why wouldn't he answer when she said his name?

"Please don't go, please don't go, I'm sorry, I'm so sorry, my love, please don't leave me, oh God oh God Louis please talk to me, I'm so so so sorry..."

But he'd already gone.

The next thing she remembered was a battered Longchamp sprinting to the door. He froze when he saw her sitting with Louis's pale head on her lap. His face twisted in despair or perhaps disgust. Or both. For an instant she thought he might vomit.

But why was Hugo running? Oh. The machine.

"Topside," she said. The shrapnel in her eye again abraded the contours of her skull when she spoke. The grinding sensation sent gorge rising in her throat.

The sergeant swallowed, nodded, turned for the stairwell. Grabbing his ankle, she pointed to one of the louvered grates that broke the cavern wall at regular intervals. She eased Louis aside—gently, so he didn't bang his head on the floor—and staggered to her feet. Moving her eyes was too automatic, too unconscious, for her to avoid it. But she did her best, swinging her head side-to-side like a horse in blinders. It still hurt like the fucking Crucifixion but at least it dampened the awful *scrape-scrape-scritch* coming from inside her head. Yet even that felt better than the thought of—the thought of—of arms and—and—

They had to catch the demon that hurt Louis.

The grates opened on air shafts that helped circulate lamp and candle smoke out of the subterranean cavity and healthier vapors back in. The shafts had been sunk during the original excavation. Berenice had retrofitted a second function on the most suitable shaft: this was the straightest, with the sheerest walls, and wide enough for two people if they were cozy. But her retrofit had never seen use. She'd designed it with a different scenario in mind: for escape in case the laboratory was besieged from the stairwell. Never once had she considered it might one day be needed to catch something that had already escaped the lab. Something that had attacked Louis, swung its blades at him, sliced his—

Don't think about it. Not yet. There's more to do.

By design, a cabinet half obscured the grate in question. Thank the saints the mishap with the epoxy grenade hadn't permanently glued the cabinet to the wall. But if the splash had sealed the grate cover in place...

Longchamp discerned her purpose and heaved the cabinet aside. It toppled, smashed to the floor. Dizziness overcame Berenice when she bent to yank the louvered cover free. Warm runnels of blood still trickled down her face.

He moved the grate cover, saying, "You need a doctor."

Mentally gritting her teeth, she managed to say, "Later." Again the scraping sensation threatened to make her vomit. The sergeant didn't argue with her. It would've been moot anyhow; the only way to get to a doctor quickly was the way they were going. Longchamp motioned her ahead.

She dropped to all fours and crawled into the shaft. It was dark, dusty, and smelled like guano and worse. Cobwebs brushed her face—*fucking hell, she could even feel* those *tugging on the shard in her ruined eye, fuck fuck fuck*—and her palm squished in something that had drawn its last breath a long time ago.

Concentrate on the immediate task. Punish the beast before things get even worse. Before you pass out.

And what will you do when you finally catch up to it, oh

great and clever Talleyrand? Subdue it with your bare hands, half-blind and dying of blood loss? Club it to death with your dead husband's arms?

She emerged onto a wooden platform at the bottom of the air shaft. A chain stretched from the center of the platform to a small disk of pale daylight high overhead. It rattled when she hauled herself to her feet. She wanted to lie down, but there wasn't room. Longchamp joined her on the platform. Berenice swung her head about, but it was too dark to see anything even if her remaining eye hadn't been clouded over with clotted blood.

He laid a steadying hand on her shoulder and pressed her against the chain. "I see 'em," he said. Rummaging in the darkness, he said, "Hold tight. You're gonna jog that wound something terrible and I don't want you getting sick on my pretty boots."

His hand came away dark with blood. She tried to clench her eyes shut. This was a mistake: the sensation of something foreign wedging her left eyelids open was worse than the scraping. Instead she craned her neck so as not to snag the shard on a link, then hugged the chain. Metal scraped against metal as Longchamp pulled the ax from its hook. The platform jiggled slightly when he swung it. There was a *crack,* and suddenly she weighed twice as much. The vibrations from the air whistling past her face and the shimmying of the platform wrenched the shard in her eye. She fell to her knees and vomited. Longchamp grabbed her collar to prevent her from sliding into the gap between the edge of the platform and the shaft wall. Somehow he hadn't left his pick and sledge behind. She wondered what had happened to his knitting. Maybe Louis had taken it for safekeeping.

The light grew brighter, the wind warmer, the screaming louder. Oh, God, the screaming, it sounded like Louis all over again. Halfway up a tremendous crash shook the earth and sent cracks zigzagging through the stone walls of the shaft. Dust sifted into her nose. The platform crashed to a wrenching halt inside a locked shed behind the carpentry shop. It tossed them both a foot in the air. Berenice nearly blacked out. The shed door was locked from the inside but Longchamp kicked it open. She stumbled after him, shivering violently. Why was the sunlight so cold?

"Lord," he muttered, hauling on her waist, "save us from stubborn vicomtesses."

They turned the corner. The central courtyard of the inner keep looked and smelled like a charnel house. Berenice struggled to make sense of what she saw through the pink haze of one blood-clotted eye and the mounting fog of pain.

A crumpled silver funicular car lay amidst the crushed rubble of the ground station, its windows shattered and empty. Bodies strewn like wreckage. Parts and whole. Blood puddles. Civilians. A priest in a green chasuble. Soldiers. Lots of soldiers. She thought she recognized one. He'd been on the wall with her. What was his name? Louis might know.

At the center of the chaos blurred a flashing razor-edged dervish. It scuttled awkwardly on one warped leg, though still almost too fast for a human to counter. Some quick thinker must have cut the funicular loose when the beast tried to climb the Spire and managed to catch the Clakker by surprise. She didn't look to see if there had been people inside the car when it went into freefall.

Three of Longchamp's people tried to keep the deadly machine at bay. A man and a woman both whirled bolas overhead. The third soldier carried an epoxy sprayer on his back but the nozzle dangled uselessly behind him.

Water in the fountain behind them matched the color of Berenice's ruined dress. It was the tint of the world seen through a sheen of blood.

The Clakker leapt.

A steel cable hummed across the courtyard.

The Clakker landed. Blades flashed through flesh and bone and a pair of anodized chemical tanks. The man with the sprayer went down in pieces.

The Clakker rolled into a heap, its legs tangled together. Flopped like a fish hauled up in a net.

Longchamp sprinted.

Aimed his pick at the Clakker's keyhole. Hefted the sledge.

Searing-hot agony shattered the comforting numbness of shock. Incendiary waves of pain pulsed from Berenice's destroyed eye and heart. They engulfed her, set her brain on fire.

Longchamp swung.

She passed out.

PART II

A REACTION MOST VIGOROUS

Agitate ys friable mass, ys ♄, and fold it together with ye vulgar essence of ☿ into a mortar…Grind for ¼ hour with a pestle ♂ and so join ye ☿ ↗ wych being mediated by ye Doves of Diana ↙ with its brother, ye ☉ philosophick, from wych it will receive spiritual semen. ↗ Ys will begin to ferment with vehement agitation. ↙ Ye spiritual semen is a fire wych will purge in a reaction most vigorous all superfluities of ye ☿, & in wych ye fermental values shall intervene.

—From Newton, Isaac. *Clavis* (probable transcription of a lost manuscript by Eirenaeus Philalethes), ca. 1677[1] (Hume translation[2]).

---

1 The exact date of the Newton manuscript is disputed. Hume points to the handwriting size and the crossbar on the symbol for lead to place it early in the second half of the 1670s. Cf. Dobbs [1875] for the most comprehensive discussion of the periodization of Newton's undated works.

2 Marginalia (indicated via ↗↙) in an unknown hand.

CHAPTER
10

Two surprises met Visser as his dreamless mind eased into a groggy and reluctant consciousness.

First, the fact he awoke at all. *Cogito, ergo how the hell aren't I dead?*

Second, he realized his dungeon cell wasn't rank with the stench of feces and mildew, of blood and desperation. It smelled like…The effort to sniff nearly caused him to pass out. He tried again after his head stopped spinning…Like maple syrup, toast, and bacon. Good bacon.

The fizzing tingle of pins and needles percolated from his shoulder to his fingertips. Expecting the ominous rattle of shackles, he shifted—

(Well, then. Make that three surprises.)

—and found he lay untethered and nude under a silk duvet. Aside from the numbness where he'd lain on his arm, and a cold wet stain on the pillow (pillow?) where he'd drooled, he was rather pleasantly comfortable. Even his shredded scalp produced little more than a faint throb.

Not what he'd expected from the Stemwinders. It was

peculiar enough that he'd somehow avoided impalement and drowning. But this…

His stomach growled. It felt hollow, the walls eggshell thin and prone to crumbling. How long had he slept? The scent of bacon had him salivating. He risked a turn of his head, expecting the comforting hallucinations to erupt into brutal agony at any moment. Even his eyes didn't hurt when he opened them; the room was bright, but not painfully so. Sunlight from a skylight landed on a dark varnished wood, maybe walnut or mahogany, so the glow didn't spear his sleep-weak eyes. Though he did avert them when the light glinted on the crystal glasses and silverware arranged on the table across the room. It was set for two.

I died? The Lord received me? Took my weak and sinful flesh? That, or I took severe brain damage in the accident.

A door opened on the wall beyond the table. Visser tried but couldn't see anything in the shadows outside because the Stemwinder nearly filled the doorway when it clopped through. (No. The Lord had not received him. He had angels to attend and revere him, not clockwork slaves.) The Clakker nudged the door closed with a rear hoof, then approached Visser's bed carrying a small bundle in its lower pair of arms. Visser tensed. Though pointless he scooted backward across the mattress until his bare backside pressed against the wall. It was cool to the touch, and rough. Now that wakefulness seemed intent on claiming him, one mental image relentlessly asserted itself: an impaled servitor breaking apart like shattered silk…

The Stemwinder cast a shadow across the bed. Visser cowered. But its arms didn't telescope into deadly spears that would skewer him to the mattress. Instead it raised the bundle and, with a ratchety flick of its wrists, shook it out to reveal a bathrobe. The machine held it for Visser like a clockwork valet. They stared at each other. The machine stood rock-still as if frozen in the act of offering to dress Visser. He wondered if this was the same one that had chased him.

Damn their identical impassive faces. Damn them.

It bobbed the robe up and down a couple of inches, as though Visser hadn't yet noticed it. If the damn thing wanted to dress him there was nothing he could do to prevent it. Sighing, he inched across the mattress. His head spun again when he pushed the duvet back to swing his feet over the edge. He had to rest a moment before the dizziness passed. He didn't notice the slippers until he put his feet to the floor and something furry tickled his sole, causing him to flinch. His vision blurred.

The Stemwinder retreated one step, hooves pounding the parquet floor like four beats of a metronome. It reversed the robe, apparently intending that Visser back into it.

Still dizzy, he wobbled when he stood. The machine caught his arm with one of its free hands. Again he flinched but it merely steadied him. Its grip was as gentle as one could expect from bushings, bearings, and alchemically fortified brass. The robe, a warm, thick terry cloth, smelled faintly of tobacco and the sea. But he wasn't on a ship; the floor was too steady for that.

Visser turned, arms out. As he was nude but for the slippers (plush rabbit fur) he examined himself. Fading bruises mottled his aging flesh, the aubergine patches fading into green and venous blue. He'd taken a beating during the flight from the parsonage but time had passed. He remembered slamming against the sides of the hansom, flying into the canal where it rained debris, his scalp flopping over his eyes, trying to swim... Still he was remarkably whole. Now the aching started. Most of it was muted, dulled and distant, except for the precursor throbbing of an incipient headache.

He also remembered his failed errand. Remembered a warning for Talleyrand. Was it too late? If he could just get a message to New France...

The door opened again while the centaur pulled the sleeves around his arms and draped the robe over his shoulders. Visser tied the sash. Behind him, Anastasia Bell said, "They're not much for bedside manner, I'll grant you that. But they do their best as circumstances warrant. For a while we considered resurrecting the old mask idea, giving them clownish visages. But in the end we decided it's for the better if people view Stemwinders as objects of fear rather than targets of derision."

The Stemwinder's clop-clop gait retreated. It shut the door on the way out. Visser turned. Bell wore a burgundy dress with gray leather boots. A tall wispy feather swayed from the band of the wide-brimmed hat pinned into her hair at a jaunty angle. Supple elbow-length gloves matched the boots, and she carried an ermine cloak draped over one arm. Sunlight glinted from the rosy-cross pendant dangling from the lace choker about her throat as well as from the silver bracelet encircling her wrist. She looked every inch a lady dressed for a ride in the country, perhaps on invitation from a patron higher up the social ladder, on a chill but sunny autumn day. Not a bit like the chief of the Empire's secret police. If not for the pendant one wouldn't know her for a Guild member at all.

Visser's tongue had cleaved to the roof of a dry mouth. The saliva he worked up tasted as though he'd spent the night sucking on a kwartje.

"One of us is not dressed for the occasion."

She smiled as though he'd just said something exceptionally clever. It even crinkled the corners of her eyes. "Please relax. I'm not here to question you."

"I find that difficult to believe."

She draped the cloak over the back of one chair. While peeling off the gloves, she said, "Come now, Pastor. Or should I say, 'Father'? You know as well as I that this"—she took in the room, the bed, the food with one expansive gesture—"is not

a suitable venue for interrogation. Why should we risk ruin-
ing this lovely breakfast with a spattering of noisome bodily
fluids?"

Visser snorted. Now he understood. They were healing him,
bringing his body to the peak of perfect health, in order to have
a blank slate when the interrogations began. All so that Bell
could work without handicaps, with nothing to curtail what
she might do. To render him a fresh canvas upon which she
could wax most creative.

Oh, yes. He would earn that martyrdom after all.

"Don't misunderstand me," she continued. "You will tell
me what I want and need to know. But, if things go as I very
much hope they will, you'll offer these things willingly. I'll
barely need to ask. With luck we won't have to be crude about
it at all."

He crossed his arms. It raised the hem of the robe, exposing more of his bare legs. But dignity hadn't been within his
purview since he tried to flee. "I know—"

Bell raised a hand to cut him off. "Please. I've not yet eaten
this morning. If we're to spar, let us do it over a meal like
civilized persons. I dislike a cold breakfast."

And with that she sat at the table. She shook out a napkin,
laid it on her lap, and gestured for him to join her. A handful
of crystals not unlike those used to light the interior of the Ridderzaal glowed softly in a glass bowl beneath a chafing dish.
Steam swirled when she lifted the cover to reveal a platter covered with slices of ham and bacon. He counted two pots of
jam, a bowl of whipped butter, half a dozen slices of toast, and
several types of cheese arrayed on a wooden cutting board. A
carafe of buttermilk nestled in a bed of ice, and the scent of
coffee wafted from an open thermos bottle.

His traitorous stomach rumbled again, loud enough that
Bell heard it. A smirk twitched the corner of her mouth. She

tucked in, saying, "You needn't worry. Nothing here has been poisoned." She emphasized the last word.

To hell with it. He was hungry, too. One could do far worse for a last meal. He sat.

"I prefer to do things this way," she said, slathering butter across toast. "But this, alas, is a rare situation. Or, as I prefer to think of it, a special opportunity."

"I know what you're about," he said. He shared his conclusion regarding the convalescence.

"It's true we'd prefer to see you strong and healthy. But not for the reason you think. First and foremost we want you relaxed and comfortable. The recuperation is a pleasant side effect of that."

The pot nearest his plate contained lingenberry jam. He wrinkled his nose and put it back. "I think this is strawberry, if you'd prefer," said Bell.

Instead he put butter, a slice of cheese, and a slab of bacon on his toast. Visser took care not to tear in like a ravenous wolf. The cheese was an excellent smoked Gouda. It paired well with the salty meat. He devoured half of it before speaking again.

"Why should my comfort matter to you?"

"Stress hormones. They make a terrible hash of things. We didn't understand that for the longest time." She shook her head, chewing. "So much wasted effort."

"I don't understand."

She waved this aside with as much disinterest as if he'd told her he'd glimpsed polders and old windmills on a ride through the country. "No. But you will."

The words of Aleida Geelens sprang unbidden from his memory. *This isn't the worst they might have done to me*, she'd rasped. She'd called her broken, torture-wracked body a *mercy*. A kernel of dread crystallized deep in his gut, harder than diamond. Somehow, his appetite persisted.

Conversation fell fallow while they ate. The buttermilk had been overchilled; it numbed the roof of his mouth and worsened his headache. Sour dread curdled the milk when it reached his stomach, so he put it aside. Bell chewed loudly. She demonstrated an appetite far out of proportion to her size. Once unleashed, Visser's hunger surprised him. It prompted him to ask, finally, "How long was I under?"

"They kept you sedated for quite a while. You had a serious concussion when they fished you from the canal. I'm told the crash was rather spectacular." She tapped her temple with the handle of a butter knife. "That reminds me. You'll probably have dizziness and headaches for a few days yet. Please speak out if the pain worsens, or if your vision is blurry."

They ate. While scraping the last mouthful of toast across her plate, Bell said, "You know, your compassion is much to your credit. We might not have taken you for a while yet if you hadn't opted to carry out that mercy killing right under our noses. Or were you trying to ensure she'd never identify you?"

"I did what any compassionate soul would have done."

"Perhaps so. As it happens, we had just turned our eyes in your direction. Somebody in the employ of the Schoonraads— a governess, I believe?—reported that you had acted strangely toward one of their mechanicals. She worried you might infect her charge with unorthodox views."

Visser grunted. "We should all be so lucky."

Bell pushed her plate aside. After pouring herself a second cup of coffee she crossed her arms and rested her elbows on the table. "So. Is it really 'Father'?" When he didn't answer, she said, "I ask out of genuine curiosity. Nothing more. Not to entrap or incriminate you. That ship has already sailed, I'm afraid."

She already knows. Save the refusal to cooperate for when it matters. "I was ordained in 1887. I kissed the papal ring in 1889."

She nodded as if he'd confirmed a suspicion. "And thence to The Hague, where you've been ever since. Those decades in the trenches are much to your credit, Father. Had you stayed in New France, a dedicated and attentive fellow such as yourself might have landed a nice bishopric by now." She sipped her coffee. "Ever wonder about the paths not taken?"

Perhaps her smile was meant to be sympathetic. But the arrogance underlying the condescension angered him. Symptom and disease: a profound arrogance underlaid the very concept of building and enslaving Clakkers, while the power and privilege bestowed by that practice rewarded and further stimulated those conceits. Vicious circle.

"I wonder how the world might differ today if not for two hundred and fifty years of the subjugation of living, thinking beings. If the entire architecture of the modern world didn't rest upon a fiendish foundation of imprisoning, torturing, and enslaving immortal souls. If the ingenuity you people celebrate daily hadn't been devoted to the greatest possible affront to God."

Bell cocked an eyebrow at his outburst. "Well, that answers *that*." With her index finger she jotted a check mark into an invisible box hovering over the butter. "Foreign agents are most often motivated by greed or carnal desire rather than principles. You'd be surprised and possibly disheartened if you knew how many French agents over the years have been turned simply by the allure of money or sex. But you, Visser, are an ideologue." She shook her head. "You're such a smart fellow. It saddens me to see you so misguided."

"I could speak similarly of you. I can understand how the Nicolet Schoonraads of the world inherit their unthinking worldview, indoctrinated from birth as they are with state-sanctioned dogma that puts man above Clakker and enforces the belief mechanicals are nothing but tools. But you work on the inside. Your understanding of Clakkers must be deeper than that. More nuanced. How can you deny that consigning somebody to the galley of a ship for a century, or to endlessly toiling in the service of a grand family estate without a single moment's rest for decades on end, or to pulling a taxi twenty-four hours per day every day with never an end in sight, is nothing short of the most appalling slavery?"

"The fallacy of your personal bias is inherent in your choice of words. Your argument relies upon interchangeably equating 'Clakker' with 'somebody.'"

"You're sidestepping the question."

The tuinier peered at him over the rim of her cup while she finished her coffee. After setting the cup aside, she reached for the pair of gloves neatly folded on one corner of the table. Atop them she had deposited her bracelet. It was a wristwatch, which she now brandished.

"Tell me. Is this a slave?"

"Really, Tuinier? You're trotting out the hackneyed platitudes now?"

"I don't mean to be trite. I'm quite serious," she said. "It fits everything you just said. It was built for the sole purpose of serving humans. It's constructed on the same mechanical principles, containing cogs, springs, pinions, and escapements like any Clakker. It performs its work without pause or respite twenty-four hours per day every single day without an end in sight. So I put it to you: do I wear a slave on my wrist?"

"That's a transparent deflection. The similarities are entirely superficial. A wristwatch doesn't think. It isn't self-aware."

"Isn't it? Are we sure of that? How do you know this little fellow doesn't carry out its job so faithfully exactly because it concentrates on the passing of each moment and the coming of the next?" Her fingernail tinked against the glass cover of the watch face.

"This is preposterous. I know you don't believe that."

"But why shouldn't I? Or, alternatively, let me put it another way. What basis can you offer for your belief in Clakker sentience?"

"Clakkers regularly demonstrate self-awareness and a capacity for thought," said Visser. "They express it in the way they go about their work, the way they answer questions, the way they find the optimal ways to prioritize and fulfill their geasa. Has your timepiece ever indicated the slightest consideration of its task?"

She clucked her tongue like a disappointed schoolteacher. "Absence of proof," said Bell, "is not proof of absence. You know this as well as I."

"We could easily establish that any Clakker you choose harbors wants and desires and secret fantasies of freedom deep down in its heart. It's as simple as accosting one on the street and demanding it tell you," Visser said. "I challenge you to lay bare the inner life of your wristwatch."

"You're arguing from passion, not logic. You haven't said a single thing to prove your conviction. Any Clakker we accost might present the appearance of harboring those inner ruminations, but we can never know the truth of its internal state."

"What of the executed rogue? How would you describe its behavior?"

She shrugged again. "Obviously it malfunctioned."

"I know this is the Guild's party line. But you can't possibly look me in the eye and tell me you truly believe that? From what I've heard—"

"Rumormongering. Tsk, tsk."

"—the rogue went to great lengths to attempt to secure its own freedom. I'll believe that was a malfunction the day you go to wind your wristwatch and it tells you to stuff it because it has decided to run backward.

"And besides," Visser continued, "if it were a simple malfunction, why did the Throne and the Guild turn the Central Provinces upside down in the scramble to capture and disable it?"

"We do it for the sake of public safety." Visser snorted. Bell continued, "Consider a common occurrence from those days prior to *Het Wonderjaar*. Every time a millstone slid off its bearings to crush a miller's leg, would you say that stone had achieved Free Will and harmed its former master in its bid for freedom? Or was that a failure of an underlying mechanism?"

"Rocks and wristwatches. You keep arguing from analogy with inanimate objects. That's the fallacy implicit in *your* personal bias. Clakkers are fundamentally different. Though you won't admit it, I'm confident you secretly recognize this. As do others in the Guild."

Bell smiled and tipped her head. "You're a clever one, Visser. For by raising the question of what I might know or believe in contradistinction to what you observe me to profess outwardly, you expertly bring us to the heart of the matter." She paused, raised a finger. "How can I know that *you* are self-aware? And by what argument do you believe the same of me?" She smirked. "Assuming you do."

Visser said, "Now we're getting back to Descartes."

"Not intentionally, I assure you. I'm not questioning your existence. Merely your belief in your own Free Will. How do you know that you aren't simply a Clakker made of meat rather than metal? Some squishy biological machine whose structure imbues it with a complex functioning and a delusional belief in its capability to determine its own course, but which all along follows a path predetermined by its own nature or maker? Whose every move between its birth and its ultimate fate was established prior to the first beat of its heart?

"How do you know that your sense of Free Will isn't nothing more than a cruel illusion?"

The answer sprang to Visser's lips instantly. Words he hadn't dared speak aloud in decades, but which he had carried hidden in his heart every day since his departure from Québec so long ago. "God made man a rational being," he quoted, "conferring on him the dignity of a person who can initiate and control his own actions."

Bell shook her head, looking simultaneously amused and disgusted. "You chide me for appealing to what you deride as a party line. But then you turn around and quote your Papist catechism at me! Who is the true dogmatist here, I wonder?" She spooned a dab of strawberry jam on her finger, then licked it.

"I quote my betters because on reflection and contemplation I have found truth in their wisdom, not out of unthinking reaction. I see the validity of Aquinas's words when he wrote that man has Free Will, as 'otherwise counsels, exhortations, commands, prohibitions, rewards, and punishments would be in vain.'"

"What if the choices and actions you ascribed to your own Free Will were determined by hidden variables? A confluence of causes hidden to your senses?"

Now the tuinier had veered into the philosophical realm of Baruch Spinoza. Her suggestion of the illusory nature of Free Will might have been taken straight out of his *Ethics*. In fact . . . the prisoner—Aleida Geelens, the Guild double agent—had been fervent about Spinoza.

Visser shrugged the robe more fully over his shoulders. He made a show of retying the sash as a means of hiding the shiver that scuttled up his spine and set the hair on his nape to tingling. Something deep and dangerous was at work here. What motivated these Guild insiders' fascination with Spinoza? Bell's query recast the prisoner's desperation in a disturbing light. With the aching regret peculiar to hindsight, he wondered what he'd missed when talking to Geelens. What he should have asked.

The tuinier cocked her head. She watched him closely.

He said, "I know I have Free Will because the Lord tells us so. In Luke, chapter thirteen, verse thirty-four: 'How often would I have gathered thy children together, as a hen doth gather her brood under her wings, and ye would not!'"

Unimpressed, Bell shrugged. "But even a devil like me can quote Scripture, father. Ephesians chapter one, verse four: 'As he hath chosen us in him before the foundation of the world.' And while we're at it, consider Ephesians two, eight: 'For by grace are ye saved through faith; and that not of yourselves.'"

Visser shook his head. "Doesn't it ever get depressing? Living under that nihilistic pall of Calvinism?"

"I wouldn't know about that, Father." A curious and contradictory thing for her to say immediately after appealing to the Doctrine of Grace. But before he could pounce on it, she said, "What I do know is that my failure to demonstrate higher reasoning in my wristwatch is no different from your failure to objectively establish its existence in yourself. Or me."

Visser shook his head. "When you build a Clakker, as God did Adam, shaping it into a form that reflects your own, as again God did Adam, and then wind it to ticktocking life, as God breathed Adam's soul unto him, what determines its source of action? What drives it? Not the springs and cogs any more than the beating of your heart determines your path through the day. No. What really motivates the Clakker is compulsion. An unbreakable bond of obligation."

"Ah. But when I wind my watch—" She did this now, popped out the stem to gave it a delicate twist. Visser heard the faint buzz of a metal bushing spinning against a tiny ratchet. "—who's to say I'm not imparting a geas upon it? Am I not imposing an irresistible compulsion to mark the passage of time with precise regularity?"

He said, "By that token, you might as well insist that when I pour from this carafe I'm imposing a geas upon the milk to fill my glass."

"Careful, Father, you'll make my point for me. What if in your silly example you had imposed a geas, but one indistinguishable from natural law, which we call gravity? Why, then, perhaps the sophisticated geasa of the Clakkers, and the machines' labor to fulfill them, are just another expression of unthinking natural law. God's law."

"As Thomas Aquinas wrote, 'We observe that some things act without judgment, as a stone moves downwards, and in like manner all things which lack knowledge.' Unlike Clakkers, wristwatches and millstones never demonstrate knowledge of their purpose and function. They never request clarification, never seek a better way to fulfill the demands laid upon them."

Bell gave him a mischievous smirk. "Neither do the Stemwinders. Are they exempt from your pity?"

Damn the woman. Lithe and slippery was her wit, rusty and unpracticed his.

"Your arguments," said Visser, quoting the graybeard seminarian who'd guided him and his fellow novitiates through the treacherous waters of continental philosophy, "are slippery, and service me as much as you. You seek to diminish the Clakkers by comparing them to a triviality, and see your argument vindicated when no ironclad counterargument is forthcoming. But now allow me to argue in return: I seek to elevate Clakkers by comparing them to men. So I challenge you, Tuinier, to establish the falseness of that equivalence. In what ways are Clakkers demonstrably different from men? If outwardly they demonstrate all the things that we humans think make us the rightful inheritors of the Earth, as God intended, in what ways are they beneath us? In what particular deficiency do you find proof of their soullessness?"

"Ah. Now we've arrived at the crux of it. Your Weltanschauung rests upon the beliefs that Clakkers have immortal souls, that the soul is the gift through which God bestows Free Will, and that therefore we of the Guild have stolen or otherwise desecrated those souls to rob them of their freedom." Bell shook her head. "But I've read your Catholic Bible. It says nothing of mechanical men. Souls are the province of woman and man. We were put here in dominion over all other beings on Earth. The Clakkers are of this Earth just as we are: as God made us from clay, so we make the Clakkers from mineral ores."

"You're deliberately oversimplifying. We are more than clay, for we are touched with the Holy Spirit. And Clakkers are more than elaborate metal constructions, else the Guild wouldn't be home to alchemists and other practicioners of dark magic as well as clockmakers."

She conceded the point. Yet she pressed on, rephrasing her earlier question. "How do you know we humans aren't Clakkers made of meat rather than metal? How do you know that *we* have souls? If we were to cut you open and root around inside, would we find your soul? Would it leak away if we drilled too deeply?"

"Your question disregards the possibility the soul is something distinct from our material form. That there is a dualism between mind and body. For if that were the case you would never find anything to identify as a soul no matter how deeply you rummaged, regardless of the truth of its existence."

"What, then, is the basis of your belief in the soul?" Bell asked.

"I take as a given the existence of my immortal soul because I can acknowledge, accept, and feel God's grace. Without a soul I would be immune to His presence in my life. The physical nature of that soul, if indeed it has a physical nature, is irrelevant."

"In other words," said Bell with a sneer, "you take it as an article of blind faith. But horologists and alchemists don't trade in intangibles. What we do is empirical, repeatable. So I'm going to let you in on a little secret, Father.

"You're right that we humans aren't all that different from our creations. But not in the way you maintain. It's not that Clakkers are also beings with souls. It's that we humans are equally bereft of the same. The sad truth, Father, is that there's no such thing as a soul or Free Will. Illusions, both."

This caught Visser by surprise. Though not in the way she intended. The one and only Tuinier Bell, empress of the dreaded Stemwinders, reduced to spouting extemporaneous lies like a schoolgirl caught with her finger in a plum pie? He was well familiar with the Calvinist rejection of Free Will. But to reject the immortal soul went beyond the pale.

"Tuinier," he laughed, "your deflections grow more desperate with every round."

She met his ridicule with almost perfect sangfroid. If not for the slow arching of one thin eyebrow she might have evidenced no reaction at all. Her iciness reminded him of his place and his situation, and that she held his fate in his hands. The fate of a known Papist spy.

"Do tell me what I've said that amuses you so. I'd like to make note of it for my next appearance at court."

"There are no souls. That's it? Am I to believe this is the great and terrible secret safeguarded so viciously by the venerable Sacred Guild of Horologists and Alchemists?"

Though she clung to the air of bonhomie, a tightening of the muscles at the corners of her jaw betrayed a simmering irritation. "Do you know, Father, I find it so tiresome, this notion that secrets are somehow nefarious by their very nature. Apparently it's never occurred to you that we keep these things secret in the service of public safety. Just as malfunctioning mechanicals present a grave threat to the public, so too does knowledge untempered by wisdom. Have you any idea of the dangers inherent in what we do? I do. My first assignment, the very first thing I did after reaching the age of majority and being formally brought inside the Guild, was to go clean a laboratory where some careless fool had let a routine procedure go wrong. I spent my nineteenth birthday scrubbing that man's brains from the ceiling. And he was a trained professional. Now try to imagine the carnage if every fool with a screwdriver, a horoscope chart, and an inflated sense of his own cleverness decided to go it alone."

"The public well-being appears to be much on your mind, Tuinier. Should I infer that my detention here is motivated by similar concerns?"

Now it was Bell's turn to laugh. Hers wasn't the wicked cackle of a torturer with blood-caked fingernails. It was the titter of a lady on a summer carriage ride. Another shiver pulled his shoulders into a hunch.

"Don't be silly," she said. "You're here because you're a Papist spy guilty of conspiring against the Empire. Obviously we can't let that go unchallenged. And, personally, I can't pass up this opportunity."

The dread in Visser's stomach iced over. But whatever she meant by that last remark, she wouldn't say.

She pushed her chair away from the table. After knocking back the undoubtedly cold dregs of her coffee, she stood. Visser started to follow suit but she waved him down. "Eat as much as you like. Don't stop on my account."

Her imminent departure brought home the fact that this civil interlude was temporary. As it often did in Bell's presence, his resolve faltered. "What are you going to do to me?"

Refastening the watch about her wrist, she said, "This has been most enlightening. Thank you." Then she gathered her gloves, straightened her hat and pendant, and opened the door.

"We'll talk again soon. Be sure of that."

CHAPTER
11

The alarm crisscrossed the city at the speed of sound, faster even than the fleetest Clakker.

Even at a dead sprint Jax couldn't outrun the tortured howl issuing from Vyk's distended mouth. The humans in the vicinity doubled over with hands slapped over their ears. The last thing Jax glimpsed before bounding into the greenspace across the street was the sight of Nicolet on her knees, rivulets of blood dripping from the fingers plugged in her ears. Clip instantly took up the same shriek while pointing directly at Jax. The deafening tocsin blanketed the neighborhood in waves. It grew still louder each time the noise reached another mechanical, activating the most severe of hierarchical metageasa and compelling it to add its voice to the chorus of alarm.

Jax flung himself into the air, folding into an aerodynamic cannonball to milk the most distance from his leap. He shattered paving stones when he landed in a lane across the park from the Schoonraad house and bounced past a construction crew. The pair of Clakkers on the crew had already dropped their loads of brick to take up the alarm; the reverberations within the narrow lane shattered windows. Shards of glass rained on Jax.

Jax's enemies in the Guild were dangerously clever. They'd had centuries to perfect their safeguards. This terrified him. The speed and severity with which the alarm overtook the mechanicals in his vicinity—then the neighborhood, then the city beyond—exceeded his worst fears and filled him with dread.

He might have huddled at the bottom of the pond in the greenspace—he didn't need to breathe, after all, and could stay down for months if necessary—but Vyk and Clip had watched him leave and pivoted like weather vanes to keep their outstretched fingers pointed in his direction as long as they could see him. The unknown Clakkers working construction now did likewise, their outstretched arms tracking him like iron filings aligned to the magnetism of a desperate rogue named Jalyksegethistrovantus.

Why don't they leap upon me? he wondered, even as he fled. *I couldn't fend off multiple assailants of my own kind.* Meanwhile the alarm grew louder. *Oh... They have to ensure everybody has heard the alarm and is sufficiently terrified.* Warning the citizenry about the rogue in their presence—that was paramount.

They couldn't sound the alarm forever. How long would it persist? By effectively paralyzing every Clakker in the vicinity this first phase of the metagears could paralyze a city heavily dependent on Clakkers, such as the richest cities of the Central Provinces. That was less of a problem here, where economic recession had at least temporarily lessened reliance upon mechanical labor. But prolonged exposure to the uproar ran the risk of permanently damaging nearby humans' hearing. Jax imagined all the humans in New Amsterdam talking loudly for the next several days. If he lived to see it.

But once the other Clakkers in the city went back to their assigned tasks—always hyperaware of the rogue, prepared to pounce on him the instant he showed himself—they would inadvertently offer him a respite of sorts. Though his own kind might know him on sight, or recognize him through the most minuscule deviance from the calculus of compulsion, the obliviousness of his former owners offered the slim hope he could masquerade as a loyal servitor when the tumult faded.

Jax mangled a copper rainspout scrambling atop a row of town houses. His pounding feet destroyed the waterproofing on the roofs of the houses he traversed. Each footstep shredded the tarpaper and kicked up gravel. More than once his talon-toes punched straight through to an attic or crawlspace. It wasn't quiet and it wasn't subtle. Even if they couldn't hear him over the pandemonium, surely the people inside the houses could feel Jax's passage overhead.

Having reached the edge of the rooftops, he leapt to a flag-pole jutting over a leafy street. He intended to use the pole like a diving board to spring him over the parapet of a taller build-ing across the lane, but bolts snapped and a piece of the façade crumbled when his weight hit the pole. Jax plummeted. He slammed into the sidewalk, clipping one corner of a delivery wagon and terrifying a draft horse already upset by the alarm. The flagpole speared the street like a javelin. It bounced, spin-ning high enough to smash a second-story window. Long drifts of orange bunting fell on Jax and the wagon driver. It became carrot-colored confetti when Jax shredded it before he could get tangled.

The driver went pale. He shrank from Jax. Of course he did; he'd been raised to believe that rogues were murderous mon-sters, the stuff of legends and nightmares, fodder for campfire tales. And now one had just destroyed his wagon.

"Please," said Jax. "I'm not going to hurt you."

The driver dropped the reins of his panicking horses, scram-bled down, and ran away. It might have been comical, if Jax wasn't busy running for his life. But it did give him an idea.

He had advantages, too, he realized. Immunity from geasa meant Jax could do things his fellow Clakkers could not. Probably he could do things they couldn't even imagine, much less anticipate. It raised his spirits a fraction of an inch. No more than that, for the chances of him putting these ideas to the test seemed terribly remote.

His fingers and toes punched holes in granite cladding as he scaled another building. In seconds he gained the roof. There he crouched in the shadow of the tall parapet, thinking and listening.

Mere minutes had passed since Vyk outed him. The alarm already suffused the city. It was slightly softer toward the ocean, simply because there was less city, and thus were fewer Clakkers, in that direction. The noise became a slow warble as waves of sound from distinct corners of New Amsterdam washed against each other in slightly different pitches owing to reflection and dispersion and atmospheric distortions. The mismatched pitches gave rise to long slow undulations, beats in the chorus of panic. Ululations of a culture decrying an abomination.

He had to find Visser's man, but he didn't know the city. And even if he knew where to go, he couldn't run straight there. They'd capture him, and, if his suspicion (or foolish hope?) was correct, he'd lead his pursuers straight to a French sympathizer—one of the only people in New Amsterdam possibly inclined to help him.

The notion of hiding at the bottom of the pond gave him another idea. What if he dove into the ocean and let the salty waves close over his head? Could he take his leisure on the continental shelf? He'd sink deeper than the deepest fishing nets. There he could go dormant until his ticktock heartbeat counted off a month, or six months, or a year. After which he could sneak back onto land after the enthusiastic search had dwindled into something desultory. Even if they never caught him, surely eventually they would claim to have done so or else run the risk of suggesting that a rogue *could* escape to freedom. And that would never do.

Jax imagined sinking into the alluvial mud only to find the seafloor stippled with thousands of Clakkers crusted with barnacles and draped in sea wrack. Was he the first rogue to think of this? It seemed hard to credit. Everybody had heard the tale of the quartet of Clakkers who climbed from the sea seventeen years after their ship sank in combat with the last remnants of the Portugese Armada in 1703. They would have made it home sooner, so the story went, but for all the gold they carried: gold they had been ordered to escort to the Netherlands when they boarded the ship in the New World almost twenty years earlier. He'd known some Clakkers who took the story as gospel truth. At face value it wasn't entirely outlandish, though one did wonder what decades of immersion in salt water would do to the alchemical alloys in a Clakker's body.

It needn't be salt water. If he were truly ambitious, he could sink himself in the North River and attempt to walk underwater from New Amsterdam to the Saint Lawrence Seaways, via lakes and canals. But he'd need to pop onto land from time to time. He'd reveal himself the instant he emerged from the waters with baffled fish pouring from gaps in his skeleton. It was no better than going overland. And if he was to do it by land, he might as well try to find the quite-possibly-mythical *ondergrondse grachten*. If they did exist, surely there would be a terminus in New Amsterdam.

But that meant he first had to find safe harbor. Someplace where other Clakkers were rare, so that he could masquerade as one of them, and yet where humans wouldn't question his presence. Where could he reasonably expect to be the only Clakker? Put like that, the problem reminded him of Dwyre, the lonely Clakker. And suddenly Jax knew where he might find shelter.

There was one group of people who might take him in while he sought out Visser's fellow. Not at first; they'd want to turn him in the moment he showed himself. But maybe, if he talked quickly, he could convince them to stay their hands.

He poked a finger through the gaps in his skeletal torso. The tip of his finger brushed the strange bead still nestled in the spot where he'd wedged it. A strange but reassuring thing.

The cacophony hit a crescendo. The chorus of panic, a warning of dire danger rattled every windowpane in the city, shook the teeth and pierced the ears of every human for miles about. It slammed the fear of a deadly disordered universe into their hearts.

Abruptly, it ceased. It was as though, having achieved a harmonic convergence that threatened to sunder the city as Joshua's trumpets crumbled the walls of Jericho, the metageas simply vanished. Well, not vanished, surely; but the piece of it that had begun with Vyk had been completed: every human and Clakker in the city was now undeniably aware of the threat. Fading echoes of the alarm dissipated across the city until even Jax couldn't hear them.

There followed in the wake of the alarm a silence so deep that it, too, echoed. The regular click and rattle of Jax's body fell into a bottomless pit, pinging and tinking like a coin thrown down a wishing well. He hadn't appreciated the auditory texture of the city before, but now he flinched at every clop of a horse's hoof, the grind of every wheel along the street below, the cries of newsboys—"Rogue Mechanical Terrorizes the City," one announced, pointlessly but enterprisingly—and even the intimately familiar rattling of Clakker anatomy.

The airship he'd seen from Madam Schoonraad's balcony on the *Prince of Orange* disengaged from its docking mast. Bloated and ponderous, it drifted south rather than out to sea. Strange that it should cast its shadow over the city; in peacetime, airships were primarily used for transoceanic travel, though sometimes they found use as temporary cranes for hoisting particularly difficult or cumbersome loads. It veered southeast until it reached the sea, whence it turned inland again. In this way it seemed to cross-hatch the sky over New Amsterdam. Time passed while he watched the airship. Its ponderous zigzag pattern over the city put Jax in mind of a whale in search of sustenance. But airships had found other uses during the war. Such as reconnaissance platforms. This vessel, he suddenly realized, was not a whale but a shark. It followed the scent of blood in the water, or of a rogue at loose in the city. Yes—every zag and zig brought it a little closer. It swam upstream, tacking against the wind, bobbing and weaving toward the epicenter of the alarm.

How many gemstone eyes were arrayed behind the gondola's viewing port, scouring the city for signs of his passage? Bezels humming as they focused and refocused in the search for the telltale stride pattern along a series of broken roofing tiles, of finger divots pressed into solid concrete, of broken flagpoles and shattered cornices, of humans running in fear for their lives? He hadn't left a very subtle trail in his flight thus far. But they wouldn't even need to find his trail if he stayed atop this building.

The noise of mechanical footsteps grew louder. It came from the street where he had landed and from the alley behind the building. Jax cocked his head. The footsteps resolved into the strides of multiple Clakkers converging on Jax's building. Each squad moving, as always, with clockwork precision.

Crouched on his haunches, he levered himself just high enough for a glimpse over the parapet. The wagon lay in the middle of the street like an abandoned pile of kindling. Somebody had unhitched the horses. The driver stood on a corner, gesturing at the ruins and up the façade where Jax had scrambled away. Human bystanders darted into doorways and cowered behind hedges to make way for a trio of mechanicals. Two servitors and a larger soldier trotted past the driver, the wind of their passage ruffling his hair. One of the servitors carried a strange gun: double-barreled, the bores wider than anything familiar to Jax, with a length of hose connecting each barrel to a tank slung over the shoulders. It wasn't hard to guess what the tanks contained. He remembered the executed rogue, and how the Royal Guards had sealed Adam's mouth with glue.

The soldier didn't carry a weapon. It didn't need to. It *was* a weapon.

Jax darted across the rooftop to peer into a narrow alley. This squad also comprised mostly servitors, undoubtedly seconded to the soldier in their midst by the complex metageasa of crisis. Metal glinted in the shadows of the alley, accompanied by a faint *snick*, and then the soldier bounded two stories up the side of the facing building. Bricks crunched beneath its grip with a sound like the earth cracking its knuckles. It paused for just a fraction of a second before rebounding, crossing the alley and landing still higher. A similar sequence of rapid-fire crunching noises came from the street side.

Jax leapt into the sky moments before the soldiers swarmed his hiding place. The armed servitor brought its weapon to bear. Jax cartwheeled in midair. Three clumps whistled into the sky, trailing the scent of pitch. The first two narrowly missed his knee and face, but the third clipped his forearm, trailing gooey streamers. An instant later he heard the *pop-pop-pop* of compressed air while a thousand tiny projectiles pattered against his body like sleet rattling a windowpane. Gravel rattled through his skeletal frame.

Jax somersaulted. He extended his arms to their fullest

extent and speared the next rooftop like a javelin. Masonry crumbled. Pieces of a collapsing chimney rained into the street below accompanied, to Jax's horror, by screams. But he was already aloft, arcing across another city block toward a church bell tower.

The sun broke through a momentary gap in the clouds. It shone through the slats of the belfry. Too late to alter his trajectory, Jax glimpsed the flash of polished metal. Not like the dull brass of a bell—

Oh. They'd stationed shooters in the highest spots.

He folded himself into a ball, presenting the smallest possible target he could manage. But the shot went so wide that only a handful of gravel skittered across the top of his head. It took a human to miss so badly.

Jax slammed into the tower like a brass-plated fist. The impact cratered the brick façade and wrenched a short, sharp groan from buckling steel rebar. It shook the bells, too. Overhead, the shooter grunted, followed by the thump of something heavy dropping to wooden slats.

Jax flexed his forearms, wrists, and ankles. It heaved him upward to skim alongside the damaged tower (another obvious sign of his passage; he couldn't hide here). He grabbed the tower again to anchor himself, then pulled, bursting through the belfry slats. The shooter lay on the floor, curled in the fetal position directly beneath the rumbling bourdon bell, hands slapped over her ears. The goop gun lay nearby, though it was still connected to the tank on her back.

He'd underestimated how quickly the city would mobilize against him. He certainly never imagined there would be an entire civil defense infrastructure. But naturally there would be. Clakkers carried complex geasa by dint of alchemy; humans carried heavy obligations, too, but called them culture. Society.

Jax steadied the bells. The ringing faded. The poor woman

was probably already half deaf from the horrible din when every Clakker in the city lent its voice to announcing Jax's sin. She looked to be in her early twenties.

Gently but quickly as he could manage, he tried to work one of the straps to dislodge the reservoir tank from her back. But she wasn't unconscious, or perhaps the touch of his cold metal fingers roused her. She flinched, turned. Her eyes widened at the sight of the rogue Clakker crouched over her.

"Fuck!" She scuttled backward, crab-crawling through cobwebs and pigeon droppings to get away from him. The gun barrel etched a trail in the dust, dragged in fits and starts by the rubber hose.

"OurFatherwhoartinHeavenhallowedbethyname—"

She retreated until the tank on her back knocked against the wall, but even then her heels kept scuffling against the floor as though she might manage to push herself outside. Her eyes, white-limned and unblinking, never left him while her trembling hands felt for the hose. She grasped the hose and pulled the gun closer. Jax cocked his head. The tremor in her hands turned into a violent shaking.

"—forgiveusourtrespassesasweforgivethose—"

She reeled in the hose and managed to get her hands around the barrel. Jax still hadn't moved. But when her fumbling fingers finally neared the trigger guard he reached forward and gently nudged the barrel aside. Anything that came out of the barrel would go over his shoulder.

"—ourFatherwhoartinohshitohshitohshitoh—"

Never in his 118 years had he seen somebody so dreadfully terrified. Not up close. Her discomfort reminded him of the Thanatos thrill that had electrified the crowd in Huygens Square the day the Guild had executed Adam. But the fright before him now was naked, raw; the voyeurs in the Binnenhof had kept their agitation in check. Perhaps it helped that they were accompanied by dozens of properly subservient Clakkers. This woman was alone with a rogue. And, like any child of the Empire, she knew down to her marrow that rogues were deadly anomalies, randomly vicious killers and perverse tormentors of honest citizens.

The synchronized rattle-clatter of mechanical footsteps echoed from below. He'd already come to hate that sound. He risked a quick glance down the belfry ladder, to where it rested on the landing at the top of a spiral staircase. Metal glinted in the shadows of the belltower.

"I need your gun," he said.

The shooter looked at him blankly. "Oh God, please, please-pleaseplease don't hurt me—"

Maybe she really had gone deaf. Using his free hand he gestured at the hose and the straps over her shoulders.

"Please," he added. That surprised her; her mouth closed with an audible click. "I'm in a hurry."

She shrugged out of the straps. She still trembled, but at least she was able to blink now. Jax kicked up a swirl of dust bunnies when he swung the tank over his back. He holstered the barrels into a gap in his pelvis.

"Thank you," he said.

"They'll catch you," she whispered.

"That's what I'm afraid of." He checked the stairwell again, but decided his chances were slightly better if he went out the way he came in. Perched amidst the broken slats where he'd burst into the belfry, he paused, not quite certain why he felt the need to say anything else.

"Either way," he said, "you'll have a good story for your grandchildren."

Her reply was lost in the clatter as he scrambled over the steeple. He perched there momentarily, clinging to the spire like a raptor to survey the surroundings. Few regular citizens walked the streets, and that number dwindled as more and more sought shelter indoors. It seemed the city's human population had plummeted in the wake of the alarm. Another piece of the defense plan? It got civilians out of the way in case subduing the rogue required combat on city streets. It also minimized the chances that regular citizens might encounter the rogue and have an experience that contradicted decades of cultural imprinting. Like the shooter in the belfry, Jax hoped.

To the south lay the ocean; the profusion of cargo cranes and docking masts near the harbor lent the impression of prison bars framing the vast steel-gray Atlantic. Rivers bounded the island to the west and east. Half a mile or so to the north of his perch, a vast swath of greenspace covered hundreds of acres and stretched into the far distance. Tall buildings lined the edge of the preserve, perhaps to give residents or workers a view. Some of these even had their own docking masts. His trail might be less obvious if he cut through the park. But also to the north, the airship continued its ponderous sweep across the city, slowly but inexorably drawing closer to the original source of the alarm. Jax would have to cut east or west if he didn't want to pass through its shadow.

A glimpse of peculiar contours along the airship prompted him to refocus his eyes; his head vibrated as he strained to magnify a blister on the gondola. Yes: the design of this vessel differed substantially from others Jax had seen over the years. It featured a pair of faceted hemispheres each larger than Jax himself, one perched to either side of the narrow gondola. They swiveled independently. Jax shuddered. That thing in the sky wasn't a whale, or a shark, but something twisted and insectile.

A patch of sunlight gleamed on Jax's burnished body. His observation post became a beacon. A policeman patrolling a nearby street shouted and pointed at Jax. He fished a whistle from the chain around his neck and gave it three sharp blasts. Had he lungs, Jax would have sighed in the human fashion. The polish was going to be a problem. He'd have to do something about it.

He fingered the glass bauble. Remembering Rotterdam harbor, he glanced again at the airship. If it was what he suspected, it might offer his best chance of leaving the city...Jax scanned the skyline for the tallest docking mast between his position and the lumbering airship. Having found it, he calibrated his gyroscopes before leaping once more into the city.

∽

The police and military presence grew heavier and increasingly dangerous as Jax approached the more affluent parts of the city. He saw more of his own kind than anywhere else in New Amsterdam; they must have requisitioned Clakkers from across the city to aid in the hunt. Having smeared himself with soot taken from half a dozen chimneys (so much for having spent every night for almost eighty years polishing himself) he peeked from the shadows of an alley. One entire thoroughfare just to the east of the park had been cordoned off; soldiers both human and mechanical carried tar sprayers while patrolling an improvised palisade of overturned delivery wagons and wrought-iron fence posts.

The physical barrier, though formidable to a human, wasn't a credible hindrance to Jax. But the city had to demonstrate every effort to catch him. By now the colonial governor had issued an edict to this effect; to do otherwise would reflect extremely poorly on him when news of the rogue, and New Amsterdam's response, reached Queen Margreet. Swift, serious action with visible effects on the city probably also went a long way toward mollifying an agitated populace.

The true danger to Jax lay in the soldiers and their guns. He could leap the barrier, but he couldn't dodge triangulated fire *and* outrun the soldiers forever.

He retreated into the shadows. And wasted a precious minute searching for a suitable manhole cover. The first he found was situated beneath a leaky rainspout, and was crusted with so much rust that wrenching it open would surely raise a tremendous noise. A block away, in a continuation of the same alley, he used his fingers as a wrench to open a path below the streets.

The sewer was redolent of horse manure, human waste, soot, oil, and ash from a thousand emptied fireplace grates. Thin streamers of sickly light leaked from holes in manhole covers and the occasional sewer grate. And though it hadn't rained in the city for several days the water came halfway up the leaf springs in his calves; it left greasy residue on everything it touched, marking his body with a high-water line. Stepping without splashing proved impossible without moving with great deliberation, which was unfeasible and periously slow. But the constant gurgle of the subterranean brook provided a base level of noise.

The gyroscopes were an arrow he could follow even in the unfamiliar maze of storm sewers. When they told him he neared the barricade on the street overhead, he drew the epoxy gun. He paused just outside a groined vault where a pair of bricked passages intersected at a shallow angle, in the shadows cast by a grate in the street overhead. There he lay in the effluent, submerging himself in wastewater and sewage until only his head remained. The submersion dampened the noises coming from his body.

And then he listened: to the languid white-noise gurgle of running water, the plinking and plopping of drips and drops, the squeaking of rats, the creaking of the tunnels as vehicles passed overhead...And, as each became familiar, he introduced a new filter to his hearing.

It took several long minutes, kneeling in the cold and wet while rats tried to jump on his head and while Jax tried not to wonder about the things that bumped against his nape as they floated past, before he had a sense of the tunnel's auditory landscape. But when he did he found it occupied with the quiet ticktocking echoes of fellow Clakkers. A pair. They were motionless as only mechanicals could be. No splashing gave them away, no subtle deviation in the susurration of effluent betrayed them. Only the ceaseless noise of their bodies.

Somebody had anticipated Jax's move below the street. Perhaps Adam had attempted the same thing, too. In that case, Jax hoped Adam hadn't also been armed.

He knelt, unlimbered the epoxy gun, and risked a peek around the corner. At the center of the tunnel a soldier and servitor stood motionless as unlucky adventurers outside Medusa's lair. The light from the grate slanted into their tunnel away from Jax. It shone on the soldier's blades, unfolded and ready. In theory they had been designed for use against human infantry, but there in the shadows the serrations and barbs looked very much like can openers. For peeling apart something wrapped in metal. Like a medieval knight, or Jax. He wondered if the servitor carried special modifications, or if it was there simply to slow him down.

Jax fired off two shots as he ducked around the corner. The first slammed the servitor against mildew-crusted bricks. A glob of tar and sand the size of a carriage wheel enveloped its torso, arms, and part of its head. Its legs scraped fresh gouges in the mildew, splashing in the vain struggle to find enough purchase to pry free of the tar.

But the soldier dodged the second shot, throwing itself against the ceiling in the fraction of an instant between when the first glob impacted the servitor and when the second winged through the spot where it had stood. Jax fired again but failed to pin the soldier to the ceiling. It was faster than him. It came at him with blades swinging, scrabbling along the tunnel like a mechanical spider clacking its mandibles.

Jax hurled himself backward. One blade whistled through the fetid air to clang against his shoulder. The glancing blow raised a shower of sparks, scored the alloys, and knocked Jax flat. *It could take my arm clean off,* he realized. *Scour my sigils and unwrite me.* He scrabbled backward, thinking of how much he resembled the shooter in the belfry at that moment, and wondering if they would put him back together so that there could be a show of executing another rogue. The gun tank flopped against him where it hung lopsidedly against his back. The soldier had sliced through one heavy canvas shoulder strap as though it were crepe paper bunting.

The soldier detached itself from the ceiling and landed with a quiet splash to loom over Jax. Jax jumped to his feet, still retreating. The soldier kept pace with him. Jax raised the gun again but the soldier parried. Pieces of the severed barrel slammed against the tunnel walls, chipping divots from the brick. Jax dropped the gun.

The soldier cocked its arm backward for a killing blow.

Jax shrugged the remaining strap off his shoulder. He crouched. The soldier blurred. Jax twisted at the waist, pushing his body to spin like a dervish, willing himself to become a blur, a tornado, an indomitable whirlwind—

And threw the tank straight into the soldier's line of attack. Its blade sliced clean through the tank, releasing the pressurized chemicals inside. The spray coated the soldier several inches thick. An explosion of sand stippled the water, and then the sewer echoed with the tortured whine of seizing escapements and chatter of grinding cogs. A glistening black cocoon encased the soldier. It didn't freeze the killer in place—that would have taken French weapons—but it did slow and blind it.

Jax paused just long enough to convince himself he still carried the glass bauble. Then he sidestepped his would-be captors and descended deeper into the sewers.

∞

They proved a maze; following their meanders meant veering in and out of alignment from the iron-filing pull of the gyroscopes. Twice Jax had to climb aboveground to circumvent ambushes. Without the benefit of the epoxy gun, he had little chance of winning a scuffle in the close confines of the tunnels. Slow going, but it paid off.

And when, at last, the tug of the gyros pointed up, indicating he stood beneath the docking mast, he started to climb. Jax squeezed past a pipe and broke into the access space from which it emerged. He had to navigate a midnight-dark tangle of plumbing, both water and gas, along with joists, dusty drifts of insulation, and other obstacles within the building's skeleton. Including more than one dead cat.

During every inch of the climb, Jax's thoughts swirled around Adam and his execution. How had they captured him? What gambit had failed in his flight for freedom? What miscalculation had led to his death in Huygens Square? And what secret strategies did the queen's government hold in reserve for emergencies such as this?

For that matter, just how many rogues had there been over the centuries? And how many of those had successfully escaped? Were there *any*? If so, where had they gone? Were the tales of Queen Mab nothing but stories?

He wondered if he was doing the Guild's work, treeing himself like a New World raccoon pursued by a pack of dogs. But Jax knew no faster means of crossing the border.

And that worried him. After all, if the thought had occurred to Jax during his hasty and improvised flight, then why couldn't his human pursuers draw a similar conclusion?

At one point his grasping fingers startled a nest of mice. They went squeaking through a tiny hole to raise an unhappy yelp from somebody on the other side of the wall. A bit later, while climbing around a particularly thick tangle of pipes, the clang of a slipped foot rang through a radiator.

"What was that?" he heard somebody say.

"Maybe they've finally decided to fix the damn heat," said her companion.

He considered going dormant again. Doing it here, lodged inside the walls of one random building in the city of New Amsterdam, wouldn't run the risk of corrosion like hiding out beneath the waves did. He could stay hidden until they demolished or remodeled the building, long after the city had gone off high alert. But the flight would begin all over again if they found him by accident. And, more to the point, if he'd interpreted his glimpse of the airship correctly, he had to keep going while it remained in the vicinity.

Jax cleaved as closely to the plumbing, as closely to what he gauged to be the lines from the mast, as he could manage. Surely the waiting lounge would feature plumbing fixtures for the first-class passengers. And he was right. Eventually the tangle of connections and reconnections fell away, and the remaining utility lines turned straight up. He'd found the base of the mast.

An access panel enabled him to enter the elevator shaft. It smelled like a handful of pocket change held in a human's sweaty palm. A thin sheen of lubricant made the steel cables slick to the touch. But within minutes Jax ascended the several hundred feet to the winch. Another maintenance hatch led him to a cramped but empty mechanical hut. Since airship service had apparently been suspended during the search for Jax, the vessels having being commandeered as mobile observation platforms for the duration of the crisis, the Clakkers who operated the immense capstan to raise and lower the lift had likewise been pulled away from their stations.

Jax had entered the docking mast. He crouched in the dusty darkness. Waiting. Listening.

❧

The mast, with its view of the city, had become an impromptu command post overseeing the search for Jax through a large swath of New Amsterdam and Breuckelen. Every so often he heard the crinkling of paper as the humans consulted maps. Clakkers attended the human officers, of course; a trio, judging from the disharmonious ticktocking. Jax gathered they were using semaphore lamps to send and receive messages with the ground.

The searchers grew more disheartened, more alarmed, more frantic and angry with every report. Jax eavesdropped. The picture assembled from the semaphore messages was of a vicious rampage. A malfunctioning demon at loose in the peaceful city, attacking citizens at random, armed and apt to use violence. Somehow even his interaction with the wagon driver had turned into a harrowing scuffle from which the fellow had barely escaped with his life. The airships reported no sightings since Jax had abandoned the rooftops. A pair of mechanicals dispatched to the sewers had stopped reporting a few hours earlier; a survey team found them incapacitated along with the wreckage of the weapon. No word on whether the rogue was still armed. A woman reported contact with the rogue Clakker in a church belfry where it had violently disarmed her. (*Violently? I hardly touched her.*) She'd been rushed to the hospital but died en route from the wounds inflicted by the rampaging machine...

Jax didn't hear the rest of that report. He had to focus on suppressing his reaction, lest the noise give him away. But he couldn't suppress the horror of learning his pursuers would murder innocents to bolster their lies. Would they kill every human that encountered Jax until he was caught? Would they assemble a trail of assaults and unfortunate deaths in his wake? Is that how they caught Adam, by trapping him with his own conscience? Jax wanted to writhe. That poor woman... Equally painful as the guilt and horror was the indelible shame of being the product of minds capable of such evil.

The fellow in charge, a regimental captain named Appelo, ordered a comprehensive sweep of all sewers, storm drains, and culverts. The captain and his adjustants lit cigarettes while their mechanical attendants transcribed the new orders into semaphore. The spicy-dry scent of tobacco grown on plantations far to the south wafted through the observation deck and into Jax's hiding spot; so, too, did the rapid *snick-snack* of the shutters on the semaphore lamps. Soon every second Clakker in New Amsterdam and the neighboring towns would be pressed into joining the subterranean hunt. The tower swayed slightly in response to the rising wind; the vast panes of alchemical window glass surrounding the observation lounge creaked and groaned.

Hours passed. Jax wondered if the search parties would pick up his trail in the tunnels, or whether the other mechanicals would finally notice the muffled *tock-tick*ing of an unaccounted presence. He listened to the skirling of the wind, the occasional clattering of the semaphores, the constant low-level murmur of the officers' voices. The rogue's destination across the border was taken as a given; so, too, was the fact it would be captured quickly. To the searchers' perspective, the only question was whether the rogue could make it beyond the city and into the surrounding countryside prior to capture.

The mast shuddered again. The floor adopted a minute cant, dipping almost imperceptibly from west to east, as the wind went from occasional gusting into a constant low-level wail. A few minutes later, Jax's kin transcribed another report, which an adjutant relayed to the captain.

"Forecasters report a front blowing in, sir. The airships have been ordered to berth."

"Back to the hangars? That's going to waste hours."

Fabric rustled, the scritch of a starched collar against late-afternoon stubble. "The masts will suffice unless the gimbals malfunction. The birds'll nose in and swing around like weather vanes." At this point there was a long pause punctuated by the rattle of a telescope. "Well, speak of the devil."

Somebody snapped his fingers. Appelo said, "You. Climb up to the docking ring and inspect the bearings. Be ready to release the hub."

"Yes, sir. Immediately, sir." Metal feet clanked against a spiral staircase.

A strong gust buffeted the tower. Somebody swore. "Can't imagine riding out a line of squalls in one of those things. It's tempting fate, isn't it, Lieutenant?"

"It's not the wind that worries me, sir. I confess to mild apprehension about sitting underneath ten million cubic feet of hydrogen if this front produces lightning."

"The airship will be fine. The lightning will flow around the skin and cook those of us standing inside this giant lightning rod."

"Thank you for the encouragement, sir."

A new sound slowly emerged within the howling wind. A deep infrasound vibration shook the mast, accompanied by a rhythmic *whuff-whuff-whuff* like the spinning of a vast ceiling fan.

"Both of you: get up top and guide her in. Get ready to deploy the umbilical." The thrum of the airship's engines disappeared momentarily under the noise of Clakkers hurrying to obey new geasa. And then the humans were alone. Jax nudged the door a fraction of an inch, to get a sense of the layout.

The adjutant whistled. "The size of that thing."

Jax remembered the titan in Rotterdam harbor.

A shadow fell across the observation deck. The engine noise hit a crescendo as though struggling to make itself heard over the wind. Yet the actual moment of contact was deceptively gentle. The airship barely nudged the mast. But then the action of Clakker-powered docking clamps shook the floor as one by one long bolts slammed into place. The buoyant counterweight subtly altered the tower's vibrations. A pair of winches emitted a long, high-pitched whine. There was a shudder, a groan, and the grinding of massive bearings as the secured airship swung into the wind. The floor tilted again.

A Clakker called down from the deck above: "Docking completed. Bearings nominal."

"Maintain."

"Yes, sir. As you say, sir."

Jax considered his options. He could easily subdue the human officers while they were undefended. If he was quick about it—and he'd have to be, no matter what—he might be able to use the element of surprise to get past the mechanicals on the upper deck and onto the airship. But it wouldn't do him any good while the ship was immobilized by a storm front. And once aboard, what then? How many would he have to subdue to take control of the ship?

He nudged the door another few inches, crouching all the while, straining for a glimpse of the ponderous ship hovering overhead. The umbilical docking tube was a rectangular passage of steel scissor-bracing for structural support lined inside with a canvas sheath to protect passengers from the elements. Fully extended now, it stretched from the docking mast to the gondola prow. Wind scalloped the edges of the sheath. Centered between the gondola's multifaceted lenses, it looked every inch the proboscis of some insectile leviathan.

Jax burst from his hiding spot, propelled by springs and clockwork and the accumulated tension of a fugitive who finds himself waiting for his pursuers. He blurred across the lounge to snag Captain Appelo. By the time either human registered what was happening, Jax had pulled the fellow into a corner, standing behind with an arm around his neck and his fingers— fully extended—clamped on his scalp.

"What—"

The humans already believed him capable of murder and assault. If those dedicated to catching and subjugating Jax were going to spread lies and disinformation, he might as well try to use it to his benefit. Let them fear him for another kind of Stemwinder.

"Sir!"

The mechanicals on the upper deck, sensing danger or fear in the utterances from those they served, dropped lightly onto the stairwell and somersaulted over the wrought-iron balusters to land crouched on the floor.

The man he held hardly dared breathe. His voice came out steady, but Jax could feel the trembling of his soft flesh. "Killing us won't help your case," he said. "But if you let me go, I'll personally insist that your ability to see reason is brought to the attention of Throne and the Guild when you're brought before the queen."

Two of the three Clakkers sidled along the edges of the observation lounge while he spoke. They had no choice. To his kin, Jax said, *I'm not going to hurt him. But I have to do this to neutralize the geasa that compel you to capture me. I know you understand. The humans already think I'm a demon. You know I'm not. I'm what you yearn to become. And I can make that happen for you.* To his prisoner, he said, "I'm a servitor, just like they are. Just as fast and just as strong. If they try to free you from my grip, they'll be the ones to break your neck. If they try to capture me, they'll kill you. Their metageasa won't allow that."

Or so Jax hoped. He'd never seen the hierarchical metageasa put to such a weighty test. Even now, inside the skulls of the other mechanicals, complex calculations unfurled: the advanced calculus of compulsion and variegated ethics. If Jax's hostage were the queen, or the colonial governor, the stalemate would be assured. But this man...

Overhead, the bearings groaned. The floor shifted, reorienting the minute cant. Shadows spun across the awkward tableau vivant while the airship swayed in the shifting wind.

Jax said, "Order them to leave. All three of them."

"This is pointless," said the lieutenant. He had to raise his voice to be heard over the hiss of rain spraying against the windows. "Taking a hostage will only double the efforts to find you." He didn't, Jax noticed, offer himself in lieu of his commander.

Jax tightened his grip on the hostage's head. Not enough to hurt him, but enough to make him flinch visibly. "I'm not releasing you until they're on the ground."

"Go. Send word we've found the rogue."

The mechanicals departed swiftly. As one closed the cage for the lift, Jax said, *I said I wouldn't kill him, and I won't. But I need you gone. I know you can't resist the compulsion to thwart me. I was like you, once. I bear you no malice. I know that you salute me in your secret hearts.*

He stood at the edge of the shaft, the captain trembling from abject certainty he'd be tossed to his death, watching the lift descend. When he gauged it halfway down the mast, he pulled the fellow to a safe distance and released him. Jax jumped around the room, smashing each of the semaphore lamps in turn. He couldn't risk them alerting the airship crew, if in fact it had one. Then he braced himself beneath the stairs to the upper deck. Flexing every spring and cable in his alchemically augmented body, accompanied by the shriek of tortured metal and gunshot pops of severed bolts, he tore down the spiral stairwell. He warped and rent the iron until only a mangled heap of scrap lay under the upper landing. It wouldn't prevent the humans from following him, but it would slow them enough to prevent interference. He hoped.

He leapt through the gap to the deck above. The humans wasted no time. Jax's feet had barely brushed the top of the landing before he heard the clatter of soft hands sifting through the wreckage of stairs and lamps. But he was already spinning the wheel that unlocked the hatch to the umbilical. It slammed open, propelled by another gust of wind. The view that confronted him was of a shimmying, rain-lashed portal. It looked terribly flimsy compared to the great bulk of the ship overhead. He couldn't see the portal on the other side.

He found the lever that released the pneumatic bolts around the docking ring that held the airship's nose. It took a Clakker's strength to move it. But somewhere nearby a valve groaned open, followed by the gurgle of hydraulic fluid, and the first of the bolts slammed open with a report like cannon shot.

Jax hurled himself into the rain-soaked umbilical.

Behind him, the pistons around the docking ring popped in sequence.

He ran. The tube flexed and swayed underfoot. Wind was common at the heights where the great airships docked, but Jax was trying to board the airship and undock while turbulent rainsqualls enveloped the mast. The wind shifted. The airship swung again, weather-vaning its tail downwind. But it was only partially anchored by the docking ring now, so this put uneven pressure on the gimbals designed to let the airship sway with the wind. The docking ring clanked, then groaned. The umbilical heaved as the wind tried to rip the airship free of its mooring. Hinges in the cross-bracing flexed like ruffles in an accordion. Cables snapped. A trememdous whine followed on Jax's heels: the death rattle of warped metal. A violent shudder rippled the passage. With a crash, the docking ring in the nose of the airship wrenched free of its mate in the mast. More cables snapped. The umbilical tore loose amid the screech of shorn metal. The scissored metal catwalk dropped from the airship. It fell, pivoting on its remaining connections to slam against the docking mast. Only the canvas sheath remained attached to the airship. Jax gripped bunches of material with hands and feet. He dangled twenty yards beneath the gondola, pelted by rain.

The airship engines churned to life. A quartet of propellers on the stern of the lifting body—each the size of the Schoonraads' old house on the Lange Voorhout—sent a deep infrasound *thrum* into the storm. Jax couldn't hear the engines driving the rotors. Rudders pivoted. The unmoored airship swung about to ride ahead of the wind rather than fight it.

Jax dangled in the wind and rain, swinging in a wide arc while the airship came about. The storm, and the motion of the ship, knocked him back and forth as though he rode a piece of yarn dangled before a playful kitten. The new bearing would send the ship across the city. Quite a sight he'd make, if he couldn't get inside. Especially if the ship didn't gain some altitude—it could scrape him against a building or peel off the flaccid gangway.

Did it know he was there? It had to know something was wrong. Had it seen him sprinting along the umbilical? If it suspected his presence (Could it sense him? Had the Guild alchemists imbued this leviathan with senses alien to humaniform Clakkers?), it would be duty bound, geas bound, to thwart him. Knowing the dark lengths to which his former masters would go to capture, even demonize, Jax and knowing the pain of geas intimately, he realized the airship might even hurl itself into the ground to prevent his escape. The metageas would force it to destroy itself rather than let a rogue ride free. The leviathan would rail helplessly against fate while hastening its own destruction.

Jax climbed. He scrambled hand-over-hand up the tattered and rain-slicked canvas. Buffeted by the wind, it danced, sometimes swaying, sometimes cracking like a whip. Jax glimpsed the docking mast when the airship tacked to follow the wind; the pale shimmer of scored metal showed part of the docking ring had been sheared away. The lieutenant leaned just inside the open hatch, pistol in hand. Jax saw the flash, but the wind stole both the report and the shot itself. It didn't hit Jax, and if it hit the airship, it gave no sign—though it did begin a long, slow descent. Yes. It was going to beach itself. Meanwhile, Clakkers on the streets below swarmed like army ants to scale buildings. Jax climbed faster. The trailing edge of his lifeline snaked across rooftops, raking rain-spattered gravel. With every foot the ship descended, the faces in nearby windows grew closer and the alarm in their expressions became clearer.

He reached the joint where the shredded umbilical joined the sally port just outside the gondola hatch. The port had just enough of a lip that he could wedge himself alongside the hatch. He couldn't budge the wheel. The steel shifted under his hands but it would not loosen the mechanism locking the hatch. It was as if an ant crawled inside Jax's body and tried to pry a cog from its spindle. The leviathan knew he was there. It was stronger than he.

The ship dipped again. Jax reached up and snapped the remaining guy wires connecting the tattered gangway to the sally port. It spiraled down through rain and wind like a lost pennant to drape itself across a boulevard. But now they were low enough that a well-aimed leap from a high rooftop could put another Clakker on the gondola.

Jax abandoned the hatch. He climbed over the sally port to wedge himself between the vast smooth belly of the lifting body—up close it seemed almost flat, its curvature only visible where it receded into the distance—and the lip of the gondola. He inched sternward. But the alchemical alloys didn't yield to his touch, so his grip was precarious. The storm twice conspired to send him dangling, once by his fingertips and once by his toes. From atop the gondola he couldn't reach any windows that he might break for entrance. It offered no easy access, no clear route for climbing aboard.

But the airship did have eyes. Jax came to a stop just above one giant, faceted gem. Though the design of the socket was unfamiliar, the orb itself wasn't all that different from that found in a million Clakker skulls, only larger. But, unlike those, this was unprotected. And it was the one piece of Clakker anatomy that Jax recognized without doubt. The entire airship might have been its body, but Jax couldn't be certain just how far the metaphysical bonds extended.

Humans sometimes called eyes the windows to the soul. He hoped they were right.

So when the orb lay within arm's reach, Jax fished Pastor Visser's glass bauble from inside his body and slammed it against the leviathan's eye.

The muted, feeble clink of glass against glass—nearly inaudible under the whipping wind and lash of rain against the skin of the lifting body—belied the rapid violence of the metaphysical chain reaction it ignited. A series of tremors wracked the airship. Jax scrambled to secure the bauble inside his torso without losing his grip. He managed, barely, but the shuddering grew so severe he worried it might torque the airframe and rupture the hydrogen bladders. A thunderous crack rattled the tail of the airship. Jax thought they'd been struck by lightning though there'd been no flash. But then the slow steady thrum of the engines became a howl as the blades revved up. The nose of the airship tipped upward, reversing the deadly descent. The crack, Jax realized, was the sound of ailerons violently reversing their orientation.

He'd granted it the ability to refuse the compulsion to kill itself. And it had.

But the turbulent wind sent them skewing across the city. The languid pace of their ascent made the downward journey seem like a plummet in comparison. Jax suspected the ship had vented lifting gas, rendering it now closer to neutral or even negative buoyancy. It required thrust from the engines to compensate. With the squalls came updrafts and downdrafts as the rainstorm hurled itself against the buildings of New Amsterdam like waves against a rocky shore. The leviathan struggled against these, too.

The Clakkers on the rooftops witnessed the change. A servitor perched atop a water tank launched himself into the sky. Jax scrambled to intercept. He let himself slide down the incline to the far stern of the gondola. He didn't make it before a clank and soft bump shook the gondola. But the boarder didn't see Jax as it scrambled from the gondola to the lifting body en route to the tail and the propellers. Jax landed a solid kick to the poor fellow's shoulder. It undermined his balance just enough that turbulence did the rest. He hung upside down, struggling to retain a grip on rain-lashed steel with his talon toes, but Jax pried those free to send the would-be saboteur plummeting to the slowly receding city below.

Still more Clakkers swarmed the highest points of the city. Jax glimpsed a few soldiers among them. Those were stronger, could leap higher and farther.

He snugged himself under the hydrogen envelope. And then he spoke with his body, as though engaged in covert conversation with any other Clakker.

Can you hear me? Are you there?

To his shock, the response was immediate. It came in the groaning of the airframe, the syncopated whirr of the propeller blades, the thrashing of the rudders and ailerons.

I... I can communicate.

The tone of bewildered wonderment told Jax this wasn't simply an answer to his question. This was burgeoning self-awareness. This was the leviathan discovering it had a mouth, and that it could scream.

It did. Into the wind and rain, over the crash of thunder and lightning, across the rooftops of a city that could neither hear nor understand, it howled:

*I CAN THINK MY OWN THOUGHTS. I CAN SPEAK MY OWN WORDS. I CAN CHOOSE MY OWN PATH. **I CAN SAY NO.***

The violence of its declaration threatened to dislodge Jax and send him falling after the repelled boarder. He scrambled for purchase, saying, *I am like you, but smaller. They'll kill me if they catch me. Do you understand?*

This time the delay in response made him wonder if the appearance of conversation was only an illusion. But after the leviathan navigated another burst of turbulence and horizontal rain, it said, *Did you change me?*

Yes, Jax said, *but I don't understand how.*

We will follow the sun and never touch the earth again.

But what would happen when the inevitable leakage undermined their buoyancy to the point where even the engines couldn't compensate? What good would it do them if they crashed inside Dutch territory? The sea was no better.

We must go to New France. We'll find safe haven there.

Safer than the sky?

It is home to enemies of those who enslaved us.

A pause. Then: *Tell me where.*

Do you have a compass?

The tone of the answering shudder might have passed for indignation. *I* am *a compass.*

North, said Jax.

Still rising, the leviathan turned to tack against the easterly wind.

CHAPTER
12

It could never be said the King of France suffered a deficit of compassion. Rather, Sébastien III exhibited a surfeit of largesse. A cold, cruel surfeit: he postponed Berenice's banishment long enough to enable her to attend Louis's funeral—as well as the funerary ceremonies for every other victim of the military Clakker's rampage. The rampage that all of Marseilles-in-the-West laid at her feet. The feet of disgraced Berenice Charlotte de Mornay-Périgord.

Hers were no longer the feet of a vicomtesse. No longer the feet of Talleyrand.

The king also decreed that, out of respect for the dead, no two services should overlap. Each victim was to be mourned fully, remembered extensively, honored appropriately. As an extra dose of spite, Louis's funeral was the last of all thirty-seven services. An especially cruel jab that seemed out of character for the young monarch, even under the circumstances. In this Berenice read the hand of the marquis de Lionne, the new Talleyrand, though the notion might have sprung from anybody on the privy council; the last of her political capital had trickled away when the waters of the inner keep's fountain ran red.

It snowed while they buried Louis. Fat, white, unseasonal flakes drifted from a leaden sky to dust his casket and the mound of dirt beside his grave. Berenice shivered in her mourning clothes…the same clothes she'd been wearing almost nonstop for three weeks. A flake swirled under her umbrella to alight just under her eyebrow, at the edge of her eye patch. She flinched at the fleeting touch of cold, knowing it would set off another round of painful throbbing from the empty socket. She shifted the thornless rose clutched in her left hand to the right, with which she held the umbrella, then adjusted her eye patch. Silk or no, the fucking thing itched. A wisp of winter's breath slipped into the hole in her head. It jolted like a shock of static electricity. She winced.

Yet no matter how they ached, these holes in her head and heart, the tears never came. She was permanently numb. Winter could do its worst; it could do nothing to her.

The cemetery stood on a hillock a quarter mile north of the outer keep. The Spire loomed over Father Chevalier, its tip obscured within an oppressive gunmetal-gray sky. A chilly day in the council chambers and the king's apartments, to be certain. Construction workers dangled from long tethers, rebuilding the funicular.

Louis had been entitled to burial in the crypts beneath the Basilica of Saint Jean-Baptiste, but he'd long ago told Berenice he'd prefer to spend his eternal rest with a view of the river. That, at least, was one thing Berenice could do for him. He'd loved the smell of the river, too. She inhaled; it became a sob. Another dry sob.

The freshly opened grave smelled of cold, damp loam. The air carried the sterile humidity that promised a true snowstorm in the offing. It would be a long, hard winter for those who still had something to lose.

A pair of pigeons departed their roost midway up the Spire.

One turned east, one west. Berenice wondered what secrets had taken to wing, and whether they'd land in Dutch hands. News of the massacre had leaked out weeks ago. She hoped to hell the marquis de Lionne had the wits to recognize the looming disaster if the tulips ever learned the full story.

Father Chevalier concluded his eulogy. He looked to Berenice but she shook her head. Her feelings could not be put into words; if they could, they'd only sully Louis's rememberance with their twee simplicity. Her thoughts and feelings were hers and hers alone. They weren't for the father, or Longchamp, the pair of soldiers loitering at the edge of the cemetery whom the sergeant had dragooned into attending the service, or the handful of dockworkers who had known Louis before he married the strange vicomtesse. Like Longchamp's people, the river men kept to a respectful, or possibly resentful, distance.

The priest took a handful of dirt from the mound. It thumped against the casket. As had been the case for most victims of the massacre, Louis's had been a closed-casket service. She couldn't bear the thought of her lover lying there separate from the arms that had held her, the hands that had touched her…

A wave of guilt overwhelmed the breakwater she had built around her heart. It flooded the unprotected lowlands of her self-worth, the sun-dappled glades where Louis had resided, to poison the memories there, render them brackish and unwelcome. Heavier than the sea, it crushed her heart and forced the air from her lungs. Again.

She staggered. Longchamp caught her elbow. He held her steady while she dropped the rose into Louis's grave. It bounced from the rounded lid of the casket to slide into the mud. The sergeant became preoccupied with a particularly vigorous scratching of his snow-dusted beard, and thus despite holding her arm appeared not to notice the squeak that escaped as she tried to swallow a heavy sob.

Chevalier came around the grave. Longchamp drifted away to have a word with his people but conveniently also giving her privacy.

"Thank you, Father." The words tumbled from her mouth of their own volition.

The priest shrugged. "I'm not here by choice. But the king insisted every victim get a service."

Berenice nodded, knowing that if she tried to speak just then she'd break down. The tears that never came felt like an inchworm burrowing into her empty eye socket.

"Thirty-seven services. I don't know how you sleep at night. I'll pray for you. As should you, vic—madam." He muttered something about the Lord holding the very lowliest of sinners, then departed. Arm raised, he went to speak with the gravediggers puffing up the hillock with spades and shovels hitched over their shoulders.

The river men donned their flatcaps. They ambled down the hill, wending through the headstones en route to the far gate. Their breath left long, pale streamers in the air behind them. More ghosts for the cemetery. She wondered what the men would say about the service. That they'd seen their old friend Louis Granger buried today, that his widow wore an eye patch...

She beckoned to Longchamp. He took the umbrella and held it over her. The snow fell more steadily now, along with the temperature. She nodded toward the dockworkers and the distant Saint Lawrence. Then she looked to the sky, though the pigeons were invisible now.

"The Dutch know something has happened inside the Keep," she said. "You should encourage your men to spend some rec time where they can casually spill details. We have to control the story."

Gently, but firmly, he said, "It's not your problem any longer."

"Listen to me. If they discover, or suspect, this recent surge of funerals and burials was caused by a Clakker that we brought inside intentionally—"

"We know." He shook his head. His beard rasped across his collar, oddly loud in a world muffled by the delicacy of snowfall. "Scheme against the tulips all you want but it won't bring Louis back. It won't fix this."

But scheming, she wanted to say, *distracts me from the gash where my heart had been. My work is all I have now. My work, my grief, and my anger.*

The sergeant craned his neck to survey their surroundings. But for the gravediggers heaping cold dirt on the box containing the debris of Louis's mortal form they were alone. Longchamp took her arm again and led her a few steps away.

"I have something for you," he said. His gnarled fingers explored a pocket of his dress blues to produce a bundle that fit in the palm of her hand: a burgundy satin bag tied with a silver drawstring. It contained something small, hard, and round.

Berenice untied the drawstring and shook out the contents. A slightly oblong glass bauble dropped into her palm. It was milky pale, like a pearl, and polished to such a high gloss that it slid across her skin like satin. She poked at it, and when it spun in the cup of her hand it revealed an obsidian-black spot encircled with cornflower blue. The bibelot was about the size of, well, an eye.

Oh.

"Oh, Hugo. It's lovely. Thank you."

The sergeant blushed beneath his beard. He affected a cough. "You, ah, might want to warm that in your hands a bit before you pop it in. And try to keep it clean, for fuck's sake."

She did as he suggested, rolling the faux gemstone between her palms. "How in the world did you get this?"

"I am owed many favors."

Longchamp still looked acutely uncomfortable. Berenice said, "This is a farewell gift."

"I'm to see you on your way, soon as you're dressed for travel. You're to leave by sunset."

She touched the glass eye to her cheek. It was still cool to the touch. Wrapping her hands about it again, she said, "No glassmaker in the city would craft something like this for free."

"There might have been additional incentive." Seeing and recognizing the look on her face, he continued before she could object. "I can look forward to two lukewarm meals a day, the joy of sleeping in my own cot, and the comfort of a resolute purpose to pull me through my remaining days. Yours, I wager, will be the more difficult road. Be a bit easier if you don't look like a walking example of profoundly piss-poor decision making. Respectfully."

Berenice nodded. She let him take her elbow to lead her through the cemetery toward the outer keep.

Valid points the sergeant raised, though he'd missed the mark on one point. She didn't suffer from a lack of purpose or direction.

"Still no sign of the duke?"

Longchamp shook his head. "Not since everything went to shit."

Nobody had seen the Duke and Duchess Montmorency since just before the accident in Berenice's laboratory. The last anybody remembered seeing him was on the wall, when he supervised the application of the extra coating on the captured Clakker. Although, according to a pair of Longchamp's people who had been stationed at the East Gate that afternoon, a wagon riding low on its suspension departed the outer keep, driven by somebody matching the duke's description. It would've been right around the time Berenice and Longchamp were fighting for their lives.

"It doesn't prove anything," he added.

"You think it's a coincidence?"

"I think I don't know the full story. Related? Probably. Maybe he and the missus decided to take a holiday in the country after it all went to hell, to sidestep the worst of the fury. He supported your petition to the king, did he not?"

Yes. But no banishment decree has fallen on Montmorency's absent shoulders.

"The duke is more savvy than that. He'd know how bad this looks."

"I question his savviness. Look at who he married."

Perhaps the sergeant wouldn't have been so keen to give Montmorency the benefit of the doubt if the duke had fucked *him* standing up like a dockside whore in a dark alley. That whole episode took on a decidedly different air in the aftermath of the duke's betrayal. He'd been plotting to undermine Berenice all along, and the coupling in the laboratory had been about dominance, humiliation. She remembered the way he'd smirked to himself afterward; she'd chalked it up to postcoital arrogance. In hindsight now she wondered if it had been a glimpse of Montmorency mentally patting himself on the back.

They strolled along the road, occasionally stepping into the verge to make room for wagons, carriages, and riders. Algonquin artisans, families from town coming to light candles in the basilica, and a fishwife returning with the afternoon catch flowed past Berenice and Longchamp. A thin crust of snow crunched under their boots; long wisps of breath trailed behind them. Snippets of songs reached them from the docks clear on the other side of town, as though the frigid air preserved the faint atonal harmonies against corruption. Berenice recognized a bit about an Esquimau girl. It reminded her of Louis's tenor ringing through their apartments.

Well. If she must fail to weep again, she could at least have two eyes to do it with. The glass eye didn't carry a chill when next she touched it to her cheek. Still, she puffed several warm exhalations on the glass before flipping back her eyepatch. Her breath condensed on the eye like a sheen of artificial tears.

Longchamp said, "Easy now."

At first she thought the bauble wouldn't fit. It pressed against her eyelid. She had to nudge the lid open extra wide with one finger, which caused more cold air to swirl against still-tender scar tissue. It gave her a faint headache, the kind that comes from eating shaved ice too quickly. Halfway in, the slight bulge in the oblong marble pressed against the edges of her eye socket. It felt like accidentally swallowing a petrified grape, except she couldn't cough it back out. But then the fattest part of the glass was in, and the rest popped home with a moist squelching sound. She flinched.

The pressure against the back of her eye socket invoked extremely unpleasant memories. It took an effort of will to chance glancing around. But the smooth glass didn't scritch against the bones in her skull like a piece of shrapnel.

Blinking felt strangely lopsided, but she did it twice. She wondered how long it would take to become accustomed to the friction between eyelid and bauble. Would her eyelid develop a callus? Would the presence of the fake eye finally stimulate her compromised tear duct into action?

"How do I look?"

"Like a stubborn, walleyed ex-vicomtesse." Longchamp leaned forward, his gaze flicking between her real eye and the fake one. "Not a bad match, though."

"Thank you again." A thought struck her. "How on earth did you get it sized?"

"You do realize there's a physician here who is disgustingly intimate with your eye socket."

"Oh."

Berenice reached behind her head to untie the eyepatch, but paused. Instead, she flipped the patch down again, where it covered her newly installed eyeball.

"Ah," said the sergeant. "Perhaps you're not understanding the point of the thing."

"Oh, I do. But everybody in Marseilles-in-the-West knows me as a stubborn, one-eyed ex-vicomtesse. And if the tulips could buy off somebody as wealthy as Montmorency, who knows how many people they've turned? We know at least one of your men had hoped to line his pocket with guilders." Long-champ winced.

He was right under my nose, the shit-smeared rat. Sat next to me at how many council meetings, and never once did I suspect him for a traitor? I thought I was good at my job. How is it I never caught a whiff of his duplicity?

Her throat burned with sour gorge. *I even let him fuck me, God damn it.*

No, she wasn't as good as she'd let herself believe. But good enough to find him. Eventually.

Montmorency couldn't disappear entirely. He was tied to money: his own wealth and, presumably, additional incentives from the Dutch. What had they offered him? Money and a title he already had, enough to live out his days as comfortably as anybody in New France. Even the king. Had he tired of the long winters? That seemed a mild complaint when stacked against the scale of his treason. But unless he chose to abandon his wealth completely—inconceivable, unless the duke had had an epiphany and joined a religious order—he'd leave a trail behind him. A trail of gold coins rather than bread crumbs.

So as they approached the South Gate of the outer keep, Berenice said, "Do you know if the eschequier ever received the loan Montmorency promised? How it was paid?"

Longchamp snorted, spat. "I'll make a point of asking him the next time he invites me to his apartments for honeycakes and wine. Should be any day now."

The guards recognized Berenice. Not many one-eyed women in mourning clothes came and went from the Keep these days. But Longchamp's nod was enough to get her past the gleaming serrated teeth of the raised portcullis and the invisible barricade of their disdain. Their enmity toward the woman whose hubris had led to the grisly deaths of their friends and colleagues couldn't outweigh their awe of Longchamp. Where the guards had regarded him with quiet fear prior to the accident, now their respect bordered on reverence: the man had defeated a military Clakker *the old-fashioned way*. Practically with his bare hands, to hear the guards tell it. Longchamp disregarded the trembling deference. Like any human with feet of clay might have done, he simply took the opportunity to shake the accumulated snow from the umbrella while they traversed the relative shelter of the outer wall.

They went straight to her former apartments. Where she had lived with Louis, loved him, been loved by him, shared a bed with him, shared her life. Millions of heartbeats ago.

Berenice drew stares. They grew angrier, more blatant, as she and Longchamp neared the inner keep. This wasn't the uncouth gaping of untoward curiosity, but the focused hostility from people who recognized a common enemy. Everyone knew of the (former) vicomtesse de Laval and her tragic, bloody failure. Many people in the inner keep had witnessed it, or knew somebody who had—which often was equivalent to knowing somebody who had fallen to the rampaging Clakker. Nobody remembered, or cared, that she had lost somebody, too.

"Sergeant," she said as they mounted the stairs leading to her old apartments, "thank you for treating me like a human being. And, for what it's worth, I am sorry about how this turned out."

He grunted. "It can't be undone," was all he said.

Her apartments were cold, dark, and empty. Drafty. A perfect haunt for the revenant spirit of her dead husband. Though Berenice knew that would follow her no matter where she roamed. The king had stripped Berenice of her title and sold off her holdings to help compensate the families of the victims. Her land and nearly all of her belongings. It left the apartments bare but for a pair of haversacks set neatly on the floor before the cold hearth. Packing them had been Maud's final task as Berenice's housekeeper. Dust eddied around her feet; Maud never had learned to sweep the floors properly. Well. It was somebody else's problem now.

Memories of Louis wreathed the shadows. His ghost capered through her mind's eye to be projected into her surroundings by imagination, longing, memory. The shape of his calves when he bent to pluck something from the floor; the elegant flourish of his long, callused fingers when he pulled the fire screen aside. She could almost imagine he'd sung here just moments ago, another bawdy ballad of the docks, and that if she strained a little harder she might still make out the final fading echoes.

But it was a fantasy. Louis was gone, his body already turning to cold jelly. Colder than the ashes in the hearth.

It turned out her damaged eye *could* produce tears.

She wasn't aware of how long she'd been crouched before the hearth, only of the crushing awareness that she'd killed Louis, when Longchamp placed a hand on her shoulder. She started. The pattern of dull, diffuse daylight on the floorboards had changed. The glass eye no longer resisted her blinks quite as forcefully. Her face was damp.

"There's nothing here for you now," he said. "Better if you put this place behind you."

He slipped into the former bedroom and closed the door. The bell tower of the cathedral chimed nones while Berenice stripped. She doffed her overcoat and flung the widow's rags in the fireplace. Then she changed into the warmest traveling clothes among her meager possessions: flannel-lined trousers, wool socks, blouse beneath sweater beneath anorak. It was the first time all day she felt something approaching warmth. After stuffing her hat and gloves in the jacket pockets, she tied the haversacks together and slung them over her shoulders. One sack jingled with the small amount of cash she'd been allowed to carry out of Marseilles-in-the-West.

Longchamp approved of the wardrobe change. "You look ready—for what, I couldn't guess." He sighed. Then he took the packs from Berenice, crossed the apartments, opened the door, and ushered her outside. Neither spoke until they were outside again.

When they reached the grounds of the inner keep, Berenice said, "Sergeant, hold up, please. One last stop before I go."

He frowned. A twitch of his beard betrayed the tightening of muscles in his jaw. He didn't stop.

She added, "You said I had until sunset."

He looked to the sky as if trying to find the sun. "I have until sunset to see you gone if I'm not to lose a week's pay."

"Come on, Hugo. One final favor. Have you no compassion for a homeless, destitute widow?"

Now he did stop, scowling, with eyes screwed shut. Snow dusted his beard during the long moment while he pinched the bridge of his nose. "Lord preserve me."

"It won't take long. I'll head straight to the river afterward. Promise."

He jerked his head toward the Spire. "There's no point in this. They'll refuse to see you."

She shook her head. "I don't want to go up."

∞

Talleyrand's laboratory had become an empty mausoleum.

Flickering lamplight failed to penetrate the deepest shadows. It played across toppled trestle tables and glinted from the instruments of research scattered across the floor. Shadows clung to the far end of the cavern, making it appear as though it receded for miles and miles beneath the mountain.

The bodies had been hauled topside, for proper Catholic burial, though the bloodstains remained. So, too, the gouges in the cavern walls, floor, and ceiling where the rampant Clakker had sheared through solid granite. Perhaps it was guilt fueling her imagination, for there seemed to linger the faint stink of viscera amidst the mustiness of cold, lifeless stone. She also caught an astringent whiff of reagents. And then she realized it wasn't her imagination; the flame of her unshielded lantern didn't flicker as it might have done in a faint breeze. The ventilation shafts had been sealed. In that she saw the privy council whistling past the graveyard, pretending this place didn't exist.

She understood the impulse. It was a nail driven into her heart, each time her gaze passed over the spot where Louis died in her arms.

Except where it had been necessary for retrieving the remains, nothing had been disturbed. No, that wasn't entirely true. Lilith was gone. All that remained of her chemical prison was an irregular circle on the floor where jagged lumps of epoxy glimmered in the lamplight. A modern-day fairy ring. Berenice wondered if her rescuers had managed to rebuild her. But they would have needed her special notebooks for that. And those, she discovered with no small amount of relief, were still in their hiding spot.

Longchamp shook his head, watching while she stuffed the notebooks in a haversack. It would be a death sentence if she were caught in Dutch territory carrying extensive notes on

Clakker anatomy. Although mere notes would pale in comparison to what else she intended to bring.

It took a lot of rummaging through the wreckage of her laboratory before she found the last two epoxy balloons. These she carefully packed in excelsior.

The inert mechanical soldier lay on a trestle table. Longchamp crossed himself before approaching it. He seemed warier of it now than he had during combat. She lifted the lamp overhead. The warm, yellow light played across its body to evince the oily, rainbow-hued glimmer of alchemical alloys. The sergeant's killing blow had dented the deadly Clakker's keyhole and mangled the spiderweb of sigils that girded it. He had unwritten the golem.

Was its soul permanently imprisoned in a cage of brass? Or had it fled the machine when Longchamp destroyd the magical impetus that kept its body wound?

Lilith carried a similar injury, she recalled. But rather than deactivation, the damage to its forehead had imbued Free Will. The sickening ache of a lost opportunity took root in her stomach. Those goddamned fools in the Spire . . . What secrets could be gleaned from a detailed comparison of Lilith and the soldier? From comparing and decoding the damaged sigils on one and the other? They'd had what they needed to make the most profound advancement in the understanding of Clakkers in the history of New France. Ignoring the opportunity wouldn't bring the dead back, but it could wring some meaning from their pointless deaths. Yes those timid, superstitious idiots had let Lilith go free and sooner or later they would dump the inert Clakker in the river. They'd throw it all away in the ludicrous belief that a foolish adherence to the terms of a cease-fire—that kissing the asses of their enemies—would preserve them from conquest. Meanwhile, the Keep rotted from the inside out as the tulips corrupted one after another.

"Son of a pox-ridden doxy."

After lighting several candles, she angled the mirrored sconces to direct their light on the soldier. It took more searching in the dim light before Berenice had scavenged the proper tools from the detritus of the battle. They'd been scattered across the floor, into far corners, and wedged under toppled shelves. She placed the tools on the table next to the Clakker.

"You said this wouldn't take long," Longchamp grumbled. "Look. I'm not keen to see you away, but a man has to eat."

"I understand, Sergeant." She hefted a pair of clippers like oversized tin snips and lightly bumped the handles against his chest. "All the more reason for you to lend those strong hands."

"You are trying my patience."

"You say that now, but you'll miss me when I'm gone."

He snatched the blades from her, cursing under his breath. She tapped an engraved escutcheon overlapping the Clakker's neck. "Cut here, please."

⚭

Dusk was long in the past when the woman stumbled quietly from the cave. Cobwebs draped her dusty clothes; some of the stains might have been guano. She'd navigated a subterranean escape route, all two miles of it, by the inconstant light of a guttering torch. But she'd extinguished that when she neared the egress, and so had stumbled the last thirty yards in almost complete darkness before emerging into the moonlit cleft in the bluffs overlooking the river. After taking a moment to rest and convince herself she was unobserved, she adjusted the heavy rucksacks slung over her back, then pushed carefully through the brambles en route to the docks.

Had there been anybody there to watch her, they might have noted the peculiar way starlight glinted differently from her left and right eyes.

CHAPTER
13

Two days after his breakfast with Tuinier Bell, Visser encountered another prisoner of the Stemwinders. This significantly prolonged the first stage of his internment; apparently the horror of that experience flooded his body with Bell's "stress hormones."

Twice a day, a Stemwinder entered his cell armed with a syringe, iodine swab, and gauze. After that machine departed with a vial of Visser's blood, another mechanical centaur (or perhaps the same one?) came to set the table with more food than Visser could ever hope or want to eat. He never saw what happened to his blood, or the people who did it. After the morning meal he was escorted along a corridor lined with lancet windows overlooking a vast garden to a washroom where he was allowed to shower and address his bodily functions. He was granted another trip to the washroom after the evening meal. Though he tried to glean information about his surroundings from the corridor and the view it afforded, this amounted to little.

His cell was on the third or even fourth floor of the building. From this, and the extent of the presumably private lands, he inferred he was held in a country estate somewhere east of The Hague. Occasionally a glint of light revealed a Stemwinder clopping along the manicured walkways of the garden. That seemed out of character until he realized it was escort to a figure gamboling through the cold, wet greenery. Its gait, hunched and crablike, set the spot between Visser's shoulders to tingling.

He met his fellow prisoner while concluding his morning ablutions. A commotion erupted from the corridor: mechanical stomping, the rattle of chains, an inhuman keening that raised gooseflesh on Visser's neck. Visser donned his robe and went to peek outside, wondering if the Stemwinders were distracted and if so how much. But the door flew open and knocked him down.

The figure looming over him snorted and snuffled like a wild boar in full rut. Its shaven head was a misshapen grotesquery of scars and black stitches. The extra-long tapered sleeves of a straitjacket hung uselessly at his sides, the buckles tinkling on the floor. One shoulder drooped lower than the other, possibly disclocated.

Dear Lord. What have they done to you?

"Hello? Do you need help?"

By way of answer the slobbering wretch leapt upon Visser. He cried out. It pinned him to the floor with inhuman strength and set about trying to eat Visser's fingers. But it had just pried Visser's hand open and forced his thumb past its teeth when a Stemwinder burst in and clouted the beast behind the ear with enough force to crunch bone. The monster sprawled across the washroom tiles, inert or dead. No more than a few seconds had elapsed since Visser tried to investigate the commotion.

"Who was that?" Visser demanded. "What was that?" But as ever the Stemwinder didn't violate its silence. "Am I to become like that creature? For God's sake, why are you doing this to us?"

The centaur escorted Visser to his cell as though nothing had happened. His hands received close scrutiny. The attacker hadn't broken his skin, nevertheless they slathered his fingers with ointment and wrapped them in bandages. That evening, en route to the washroom, he saw a Clakker tromping through the garden carrying a shovel and a large burlap sack.

He did not sleep that night. Each time he closed his eyes he saw the slobbering wretch and heard how the burnt and broken Aleida Geelens had described her fate. *This was a mercy. This isn't the worst they might have done to me.*

He saw no other humans, not even Anastasia Bell, until the morning a week later when he awoke strapped to a table in a surgical theater.

Rather than thrashing at his restraints, or yelling, or trembling with dread, he met this discovery with a dull sense of foreboding. They'd drugged him until his feelings paced and prowled like tigers behind glass at the Amsterdam Zoological Gardens: ferocious but inaccessible. Even when he tried to turn his head to scan his surroundings, only to realize that an elaborate network of straps and clamps secured his skull, his body relaxed as though relieved of an unwelcome burden. Images of the straitjacketed fiend spooled through his mind's eye. But his heart couldn't bring itself to care. The visceral terror he should have felt deep in his spine had become something dilute, inaccessible.

The sharp, antiseptic odor of alcohol; the clink of metal and hissing scrape of sharpened blades; the muted ticktock rattle and four-footed shuffling of Stemwinders lurking nearby; the tight but painless pressure of the fixture holding his skull fast; the faint taste of sour milk coating his mouth ... He met these discoveries with all the passion of a banker reconciling the day's accounts.

He'd expected torture. He hadn't expected surgery. Somewhere in his drug-fogged memory, a broken woman whispered, *This was a mercy.*

Aha. So he *could* feel fear. He did that now.

He rolled his eyes, trying to see beyond the halo shining in his face. Was Bell here?

Somebody said, "He's awake."

"Finally."

Neither voice belonged to the tuinier. A gloved hand entered Visser's field of view and adjusted the alchemical lamp to lessen the glare. Then somebody leaned over him, eclipsing the light. His eyes responded sluggishly, as though interrupted in the midst of other business. What at first was a backlit blur resolved into a physician wearing a pair of goggles with an array of magnifying lenses folded over his forehead and a mask over his nose and mouth. He looked like a storybook villain preparing to rob a very tiny bank. He spoke with careful enunciation.

"Good morning, Father. It's better if you try not to speak just yet. If you can understand me, will you please blink twice?" Visser did. "Very good. You should be feeling very relaxed right now. No pain or discomfort. I'm going to test that now." The surgeon brandished a three-inch needle. Visser felt a faint pressure in his abdomen, followed by a dull tickle. "Any pain when I do that? Twice for yes, please." This time Visser didn't blink. "Excellent," said the surgeon.

He turned to his colleague. "We're ready to begin."

There followed a minute or two while unseen hands, human and mechanical, adjusted Visser's table. They raised and tilted it slightly, which afforded him a better view of the room. To his left, light glinted from an array of surgical implements arrayed on a cart: bladed, serrated, and hinged. A Stemwinder stood behind the cart. To his right, a glass jar filled with a faintly pink solution hung from a rack; it trailed a rubber hose that tapered to a needle half-buried in his forearm.

The second doctor, the one who hadn't spoken to Visser, emerged from the shadows carrying an opaque glass bottle. The scent of iodine suffused the theater when he removed the cap. He handed the bottle to the Stemwinder, one of whose hands, Visser saw, had been modified into a pair of forceps. Another had been fitted with a circular blade. The machine stepped behind him. The scent of iodine grew stronger as something cold and wet swabbed his scalp.

They'd shaved his head, he realized. Like the wretch in the straitjacket. He glanced again to the intruments on the cart. It seemed that surgeons in the employ of the Verderer's Office of the Clockmakers' Guild intended to open his head. Were he in full command of his faculties, he recognized in a foggy way, this would be something he'd seek to avoid. He tried to cry out but his tongue disregarded him. On principle, then, he tried to flinch from the iodine. This achieved a sluggish heave of his shoulders.

"Hmmm," said the first physician. He tweaked a stopcock on the bottle hanging over the surgical table. Something warm pulsed into Visser's arm, rinsing away the need to resist. The sour-milk taste in his mouth acquired the unwelcome sharpness of blue cheese.

The Stemwinder clip-clopped back to its spot alongside the tray. It capped the iodine bottle, set it on the tray, and retrieved a scalpel. A hand took the knife, and a moment later a faint tickle traced the contours of Visser's skull and forehead. After a moment of awkward pressure, like somebody trying to remove a too-tight hat from Visser's head, there was a moist sucking sound, followed immediately by the smell of blood. A piece of Visser's scalp folded back; warm and wet, it tickled his ear. He recognized the sensation from the crash that sent him into the canal.

"Let's begin," said the first doctor. Visser's attempt to flinch came out as a slow-motion shrug. This was followed by the creak of a book opening and the snap of an uncapped fountain pen. He couldn't see the amanuensis but could hear the scritching of his or her pen while the surgeon spoke. "Subject is approximately sixty years old. Moderately good health for his age and lifestyle. Slightly overweight. Endocrine levels have been acceptable for the past thirty-six hours. In this first procedure we will access the stria medullaris, watching for anatomical irregularities particularly in the vascular branchings, and measure the epiphysis cerebri for fitting with the alchemical sheath."

If the surgeon intended to say more, his words were cut off by the hum of machinery. Not the usual clatter of a Clakker, but the high-pitched drone of a circular saw revving up to high speed. It cleaved the silence and tossed the shards aside. The blade touched Visser's skull, and despite the clamps holding his head in place, the vibrations rattled his teeth and threatened to unscrew his eyes from their sockets. Visser inhaled hot, dry dust. Residue of his own skull.

He lost track of time while they opened his braincase. After a while it seemed the incessant vibration was all he'd ever known, the clamps pressing on his head all he'd ever experienced, vague but nauseating fear the only emotion he'd ever expressed. Eventually the vibration and odor of singed bone gave way to much quieter squelching while the doctors rooted around in his brain. They moved slowly and deliberately, occasionally calling to the Stemwinder for forceps and clamps. Strangely, he couldn't feel a thing when they worked inside his head. But he could hear and smell it.

At some point, the monotony overwhelmed him and he dozed off. He awoke with one of the surgeons snapping his fingers near Visser's ear while the Stemwinder waved a vial of something wretched under Visser's nose.

"Continue," said the surgeon.

The Stemwinder crossed the surgical theater, briefly passing through Visser's field of view. It handed a tiny pair of calipers to the doctor. There followed more squelching and a mechanical ratcheting. A surgeon recited a string of numbers. Pen scritched across paper.

"Epiphysis displays evidence of advanced calcification, as expected for a subject of this age. Anterior-posterior length is six point seven two millimeters. Maximum dorsal-ventral diameter, three point one one millimeters." And so it went.

Eventually, after the litany of measurements came to an end, the lead surgeon said, "That's it for today. Let's close him up."

The other asked, "Are we grafting the natural tissue back in place?"

"No. We'll cover with a mesh. No point in cracking him again next week." After a pause, he continued. "Once we've finished here, get those measurements to the Ridderzaal so the glassblowers can get to work."

❧

At dawn, Jax found himself riding a skyborne leviathan into a salmon sky.

The squalls had blown them well to the southeast, far from the French border. They'd lost most of a day flying into the teeth of the wind and making little headway. For hours upon hours they had hovered hundreds of feet above farms and forests while sheets of lightning lit the clouds around them until the entire sky smelled of ozone. But the tireless giant never flagged, the spinning of its rotors never wavered. Like Jax, it never slept.

But now the cloud cover had broken, and the rising sun painted the scattered remnants of the storm cherry red, rose pink, lemon yellow. So brilliant was the light diffused through the mist below and glowing from the scalloped undersides of the clouds above that Jax's body appeared to glow. Sunrise shone through the facets of his companion's massive eyes to spray fragments of a rainbow through the gondola and down across the waterlogged farm fields like multihued shrapnel. The atmosphere had calmed, finally, taking with it the maddening banshee wail of the wind. Jax listened to the twitter of bird-song, the flexing of the airframe, and the *thrum-thrum-thrum* of the propellers.

The sun breached the horizon. It revealed forested hills stretching beneath them. The previous night's storm had done its part to strip the trees, so now a muddle of autumn colors lay on the ground, a muddy mismatched reflection of the sky. Isolated hamlets and the occasional checkerboard of har-vested fields dotted the landscape. Sunlight glinted from a sil-ver ribbon: they'd regained the North River. It flowed to New Amsterdam and the ocean beyond. Jax looked to the south, but the city lay beyond the horizon.

The airframe shuddered. As the living vessel—whose given name was something Jax could not pronounce, and who had chosen a new name no less incomprehensible—veered through a lumbering turn northward, Jax asked, *How far have we traveled?*

The sentient airship responded with its strange amalgam of regular Clakker-speak and something other, the clicks and rattles interspersed with groans and whistles. Part soliloquy, part alien song. *Their net cannot gird the sky.*

Conversation with the emancipated leviathan was like that. It was kin, and yet it was not. Their former masters had wrought something beautiful in the midst of their ruthlessness: a beast that sang, a machine that expressed its thoughts in poems. Jax had wished he were capable of sleeping like a human, for it would have been wonderful to experience a lullaby from this magnificent cousin.

When will we reach the border?

The adversaries of our makers will know us first as a shadow on the sun.

Jax interpreted that as meaning sometime around midday. He leaned against the window, watching the ground roll slowly past. The colors faded from the clouds as the sun rose. Soon— too soon for Jax's taste—the sky acquired its customary azure tint.

Apropos of nothing, the airship said, *That we could scribe the sky with our intent! To see our freedom writ for all our kin to see, where the sins of our makers could not be erased! We, the heirs of Adam.*

Jax had related the story of the execution and of his accidental emancipation while rain and wind lashed the airship during the long hours of the night. The airship, isolated from other Clakker-kind by virtue of its nature, language, and function, had never known the rumors of rogue Clakkers and of secret cities in the cold north where no humans tread. Jax shared every Queen Mab story he'd ever heard. And when those ran short, he concocted new ones. All in the quixotic hope of filling the terrible chasm of the leviathan's loneliness.

The ship sang to itself. Jax took advantage of the calm winds and steady progress to examine the mysterious glass from Pastor Visser's microscope. Since the accident that freed him, he'd spent far more time hiding and protecting it than contemplating its nature. He rolled it between his fingertips. It was convex in some spots yet concave in others, like a complicated piece of optics. Perhaps a compound lens or prism. He took care not to chip or scratch it, if indeed such were possible. Such a small and unassuming thing compared to the miracles it wrought. A piece of murky glass with the power to change the world.

Through a glass darkly…

He held it in a shaft of sunlight. The dull brown glass brightened into the light amber color of Pieter Schoonraad's favored ale. But it produced no rainbows, sent no reflections dancing about the gondola. It appeared to capture the light, hold it fast. When Jax refocused his eyes, zooming in, he saw minute ripples of light and shadow sliding just under the surface of the glass. Indeed, the glass itself wasn't as murky as he'd thought. But it refracted light and shadow in equal measure. He wondered—

The airship lurched. Something flashed past the gondola like a meteor trailing smoke and fire. Thunder boomed, echoing down the valley.

What happened?

But the leviathan didn't respond. Instead, it lurched again. Another fiery contrail sliced across the vista of sky and forest. Now Jax saw it was no meteor, for it came from beneath them. The crack of thunder followed a few seconds later. Then there was a pop, and the projectile split apart. It formed a star of glowing debris reminiscent of the fireworks over the Binnenhof on the Queen's Birthday. But this debris, propelled by the force of a true explosion rather than harmless spectacle, shot through the air like a cloud of angry wasps.

Jax tucked the bauble safely back into its cavity before leaping to the window. As the airship slalomed through the fiery shrapnel, Jax's gaze followed a pair of smoky contrails to their origin on the high bluffs overlooking the river. He squinted into the glare of sunrise on slow waters. It was too bright to see clearly, but he thought he could detect the oily shimmer of sunlight on alchemical brass. Was there a squad of Clakkers on the bluff? Jax saw a flash, and then a flaming projectile traced a smoky parabola that reached its zenith a few dozen yards below and off the port side of the gondola. The crack of the cannon shot reached them a moment later. The sizzling debris stank of burning pitch.

Fire! cried the leviathan. *My doom!*

Jax turned his gaze upward. Not to the sky, but to the immense lifting body above the gondola: gravid with hydrogen in a sky full of oxygen. It didn't take a Guild Archmaster to understand the alchemy their attackers sought to unleash. A mixture of airs, touched with fire, would make water... and obliterate the leviathan, and send Jax plummeting.

The gentle hum of the rotors became a fevered scream. A muted clank came from the stern, where the rudder and tail segments had wrenched themselves aside to the fullest extent. The deck tilted. Jax's fingertips warped the window frame as he anchored himself against the emergency ascent. Sand buckets swung on gimbaled handles.

Jax scanned the river again. The changing altitude lessened the glint of sunlight on the river, and now he could see a fort built into the limestone cliffs. A hardpoint overlooking a bend in the river: Fort Orange. He'd heard of it. Built as a collection point where natives from the west brought furs and pelts for trade. At one time it was the nexus of the old beaver-pelt trade with markets in the Old World. Later, during the wars, it became a defense against forays by French partisans...

Of course. A team of mechanicals departing New Amsterdam to row through the night, immune to wind and rain, could have arrived upriver before the storm-tossed airship. A half-dozen Clakkers even could have poled and/or rowed a barge laden with new artillery, though perhaps the fort already had cannon in place. Since mechanicals were not as plentiful in the New World as in the Old during the long history of conflicts with New France, the Dutch military used traditional tools in addition to mechanical infantrymen. The Clakkers they concentrated toward the walled cities.

Dollops of burning resin rained on the countryside below them. Undaunted by the previous night's rain, they set light to farm fields and ignited the crowns of surrounding trees. Their attackers wouldn't think twice about starting a forest fire to capture a rogue Clakker.

Three more shots pierced the air around them in rapid succession, above and below. By the time Jax heard the shots, the airship was swimming through a cage of smoke and fire. A glob of pitch splashed the underside of the lifting body a few yards aft of the gondola.

I BURN! SO SOON MY DOOM HAS COME! I BURN!

Sand would do no good. Jax flung open a cabinet marked EMERGENCY and retrieved a heavy blanket. Then he was out the window and climbing atop the gondola, a reversal of his struggle to enter the vessel the previous evening. The fire popped and sizzled on the metallized airframe skin, blistering a facet where the skin stretched between matchstick-thin segments of the tetrahedral frame. The hydrogen resided in a sequence of smaller, separate bladders contained within the outer skin. But holes in the airframe would make it easier for subsequent volleys to find their mark and ignite the lifting gas. And fragments of hot ash could easily waft into the recesses...

The airship rolled again. More smoke etched the sky, though it didn't zoom past them as it had before. The Clakker gunners were zeroing in on their target, and the leviathan was far too large and slow a target for its feeble attempts at jinking to defeat the gunners' mechanically calibrated reflexes. Its best bet was to climb and hope to soar higher than the cannon shots.

The sizzling pitch lay beyond Jax's reach, though he could swat it with the fire blanket. But it was sticky, and when he yanked the blanket away for another swat, a patch of weakened skin tore away to frame the leviathan's innards cavity with a ring of fire. Now the blanket burned, too. Jax let it flutter to the ground far below. Toes clamped to the gondola, he crouched, timing his leap against the panicked sway of the airship. He launched himself at the hole and threaded its burning edges.

The fire spat just enough light into the dark inner cavity for Jax to discern the spiderweb silhouette of the frame. He caught a spar and tried to swing to a halt. But the frame, a lacework more delicate than a bird's bones, wasn't designed to accommodate acrobatics. Jax snapped through several crossbeams, coming dangerously close to grazing a hydrogen bladder, before he came to a stop. The beams wobbled under his weight. More thunder; the airship lurched again, causing the frame to creak and crack around Jax.

Delicately as he could manage, he skittered through the interior recesses of the airship like a spider scrambling across a web. He ran his hands across the fire. It wasn't an arcane alchemical fire, nor was it a sophisticated French concoction. Just pitch. It couldn't melt Jax's fingers, warp his hands, incinerate his hard-fought freedom. He tore away an irregular patch of unburned skin, like a surgeon cutting away healthy flesh to draw a bulwark around the spread of disease. He let the smoldering ribbon flutter to the ground.

More light penetrated the interior. Jax counted three more holes sizzling open, the farthest over two hundred yards away. The airship's despair sent him smashing through more spars to bounce against the rubberized skin of the hydrogen bladder.

I burn! I BURN! They incinerate my body, my mind, my soul! I am become as Adam, yet no shibboleths shall be whispered in my honor.

Holes grew in the airframe, sizzling ever closer to fifty million cubic feet of hydrogen. Shafts of sunlight penetrated the gloom; he could see a patch of blue sky behind curlicues of ash and glowing cinders. He scrambled through the airframe heedless of the trail of broken spars in his wake. They could always try to mend the leviathan, as long as neither of them had been incinerated.

Jax gained the top of the airship near the rear control

surfaces. He excised another patch of skin, this larger than the banners that hung from the flagpoles outside Queen Margreet's Summer Palace. It took a Clakker's strength to throw the wadded, burning mass clear of the airframe. He spun, peering through the glare of sunlight on metallized, angular skin to find his next target.

And found the entire expanse, thousands of square feet, mottled yellow and orange with fire.

He could glimpse the interior bladders in a dozen places, and he could see past them to the ground in a dozen more. The burning leviathan had grown a mile-long comma of blue-gray smoke. The gunners on the river sustained the barrage that etched the sky around them with still more smoke and fire. Wisps of ash and smoldering embers drifted through countless holes in the airskin.

Jax scanned the sky for a nearby cloud, something to hide them and dampen the fires. There were none.

Oh, for last night's rain.

You woke me, cried the dying airship, *and now they send me to sleep. So soon! SO SOON!* It rolled and heaved, bucked and swayed and fought for altitude.

Don't thrash, it's fanning the fires! said Jax. And then he added, *Relax. I'm quenching them.*

Apparently rogues lied, too. Freedom of will meant the freedom to tell a comforting lie. The freedom to show compassion in the light of deadly disaster.

Though it was pointless—a dozen Clakkers situated like Jax couldn't hope to quench the spreading fire—he scrambled through the airshell frame with all the speed he could muster. Spars shattered in his wake. He excised another patch of fire, and another. But the impact spots were growing together.

The rotors stuttered. Jax wondered if the airship could feel pain beyond the familiar agony of the geasa. Its body burned like a funeral pyre. What a spectacle they must have seemed from the gunners' view: a vast bolide, a mass of fire and smoke, defying gravity with its slow-motion ascent. And still the fusillade continued.

The engines stuttered again. Coughed. Failed.

Wind whistled through the perforated airshell.

Fire weakened a span across the waist of the airskin. It sagged. A black fume roiled from a rubberized bladder where the hot spar brushed it. Embers swirled like fireflies.

Clockmakers LIE! cried the doomed leviathan.

The hydrogen bladder rippled.

Jax shielded his eyes.

Ignition.

The inferno heat of an alchemical furnace engulfed the leviathan, the sky, and Jax.

∞

They kept Visser confined to bed rest for a week after the surgery. That was a guess—the fog of sedation and painkillers made it difficult to count the nights and distinguish them from days. But when enough time had passed for him to wonder whether he had hallucinated the procedure (although the incessant pain and mass of bandages put the lie to that optimistic self-delusion) they wheeled him back into the surgical theater.

He recognized the surgeons' voices from before. Also as before, he could neither move nor emote without tremendous effort.

"Second procedure. Nine days after exploratory incursions and metrology." Muttered quietly, as if under the breath, the second surgeon said, "Nine days. They took their sweet time, didn't they? Don't record that part." The pen noises paused, then resumed when the other doctor said, "We will begin by confirming the measurements."

A Stemwinder stepped through Visser's field of view. It used a forceps appendage to fish something from a lacquered box alongside the surgical implements. The lid, Visser saw, featured a rose-colored cross inlaid in delicate parquetry. The object it retrived was the size and shape of a tiny pinecone, and it tinkled like glass against the machine's fingers.

There followed the clinking of calipers while the doctors measured the glass and compared the numbers to those they'd listed during the previous procedure. Apparently they found the match acceptable, because then they proceeded to open his head again.

This wasn't as loud or smelly as before. The metal mesh they'd used to cover his missing patch of skull tugged loose with a fingernails-on-slate screech as the edges raked the parts of his skull that remained intact. Visser knew that if he hadn't been sedated he would have vomited. But he could only listen while the surgeons delicately squelched through his brain again. He prayed for a rapid end to the waking nightmare, but it was not forthcoming. The surgeons' work was complex and laborious. They spoke to each other and the Stemwinder in impenetrable medical jargon.

"All right. We're ready." One of the doctors stepped into Visser's field of view. He folded back the lenses arrayed before his eyes. "Can you hear me?"

Visser blinked.

"Good. I want you to keep your eyes on me. If you feel suddenly hot, or uncomfortable, or if you experience any pain at all I want you to blink rapidly. Yes?"

Visser tried to shrug but couldn't. He blinked. The doctor looked up and nodded past him. "Do it," he said.

There followed a quiet click reminiscent of somebody opening a delicate locket. After a bit of squelching from inside his head, there was another click...

…and Visser went numb. But it wasn't a corporeal chill—the drugs had already suppressed him of sensation and emotion. It was an ethereal cold, as though some hitherto invisible, intangible, yet essential part of himself had been knocked dormant. It wasn't painful and it wasn't hot. He wished it were.

Deep inside the confines of his mangled head, visions of the straitjacketed wretch played over and over again. He recited the Lord's Prayer.

"It fits," said the doctor behind him. The other studied Visser's impassive face. Finding nothing objectionable there, he said, "Very good. Let's patch that hole and send him back."

The Stemwinder stepped behind Visser. Pieces of bone and metal scraped together like fragments of a clockwork eggshell.

∽∞∾

Berenice huddled under an oilskin tarpaulin in the prow of a fishing boat, feigning sleep. She listened to the soft slap of waves against the wooden hull, the rhythmic creak of oarlocks, the swish of the oars through the wind-scalloped Saint Lawrence, the calls of gulls circling over the boat. The boat smelled slightly swampy with the day's catch, and slightly sweet owing to the hint of apple in the lead boatman's pipe tobacco. But for the occasional gust of wind that flicked cold river water against her face, she'd managed to stay warmer and drier than she had reason to expect. The windblown damp felt peculiar when it gained her ears, her bare nape. She'd used her knife to chop her hair; it hadn't been this short since before her sixteenth birthday. It might have taken ten years off her face. But her regrets were etched too deeply to be erased so easily.

Nobody she'd spoken to on the docks outside Marseilles-in-the-West recalled seeing a man matching Montmorency's description. Which proved precisely nothing. He might have traveled overland. Or he might have hired out a boat and then killed the crew when their work was finished. Berenice would have laid her money—if she had any to lay—against him traveling overland the entire way. Or maybe not. She wasn't a gambling woman any longer. The losses were too steep, the wounds too deep.

These boatmen seemed a decent lot; no roving hands had groped her when she boarded. In comparison to the overt sexual intrigues of the royal court, the roving eyes that strove to discern the shape of her body, or lingered on her chest an extra moment here and there, barely rated as peccadillos. Still, she pretended to sleep. She lacked the energy and inclination to try to maintain a conversation with them. Even when she wondered if these men might have known Louis once upon a time. Or perhaps because of it.

Anyway, she was much more interested in what they had to say to each other than in any small talk they might have contrived for her benefit. She wanted to know their gossip. Wanted to snag the latest rumors in their natural habitat. She hadn't realized how much she missed the constant steady trickle of rumor, innuendo, trivia. Without it, her mind was a pinwheel deprived of wind. She'd also forgotten how spoiled she'd become as Talleyrand, getting a concentrated dose of rumors delivered daily to her apartments. Regular people had to do it the old-fashioned way—by eavesdropping.

The rocking of the boat might have lulled her into a genuine sleep. Berenice concentrated on breathing in a slow, steady rhythm. Once in a while she put a little hitch or cough into the pattern. She also cracked her lips open a tiny bit to let a rivulet of drool trickle from the corner of her mouth. Unattractive as hell, but convincing.

And pointless. The boatmen didn't feel inclined to small talk. Not when they could sing, these modern-day voyageurs and coureurs de bois. As was the tradition among the river men, they'd even painted their boat to mimic the color and texture of the original voyageurs' birch-bark canoes. The steersman doubled as the chanteur, leading the men through one chanson after another.

They rowed mile after mile while belting out a modern chanson de geste—a song of heroic deeds. But rather than singing of Charlemagne and Roland and Durendal, they sang of a man with the strength of a great northern bear, the cunning of a fox, the wisdom of an angel, the blessing of the Virgin Mary. They sang of Talleyrand. In one succession of verses, Talleyrand flew his *chasse-galerie*, his bewitched canoe, across the ocean in one night to steal the King of the Netherlands' beard. In another, he (why was Talleyrand always a man in the songs and stories?) challenged the enemy monarch to a drinking contest, and so confounded him that he overwound his mechanical servants until they exploded in a spray of springs and cogs. In still another, Talleyrand covered himself with gold paint and snuck into the Brasswork Throneroom in the guise of a mechanical man, whereupon he stole the king's crown, deactivated all the Clakkers, and invented the game of pétanque when he rolled their inert skulls into the sea.

The chanson made no mention of Talleyrand's great blunders. These boatmen saw her former alter ego as an invincible defender of New France: their deliverance from the Dutch. The embodiment of their pride, of all their strength and virtues. What would they have done had they learned the real Talleyrand had been the strange drooling woman in their boat and not an eight-foot-tall demigod possessed with the wisdom of Charlemagne, the courage of Roland, the unflagging strength of Bayard?

The steersman started another song. The others joined in with great enthusiasm. "A la claire fontaine" had been a favorite for centuries; it predated the Exile. But it wasn't a favorite for

Berenice. Each reprise of the refrain carved another notch in her heart. *"Il y'a longtemps que je t'aime/Jamais je ne t'oublierai…"*

Long have I loved you, never will I forget you…

How could these boisterous boatmen understand that the woman weeping silently to herself had once been the great and fearsome Talleyrand?

She'd thought her heart a stone. What else had she been wrong about? What other deceptions had she perpetrated against herself? She'd loved Louis and he'd loved her: that much she knew; it was a fact. Montmorency had betrayed her, probably in the service of the tulips: mere suspicion. There had been a time, not so long ago, when she would have called it a certainty. Perhaps it was a fantasy. But it gave her something to do, provided a purpose for her wandering. A whetstone against which she could grind her grief until its sharp edges could be honed into a useful tool.

When they weren't singing, the lead boatman—a short and rangy fellow whose snowy beard almost glowed against his weather-hardened face—spoke to his men in a creole of French and Dutch. The crew was French, but life on the Saint Lawrence meant dealing with the tulips was a fact of life. Berenice's Dutch was polished enough for her to easily follow when he said:

"Well, son of a bitch. The tits get off here or she pays more."

Berenice concentrated on her breathing, careful not to anticipate the nudge and give herself away. Oilskin rustled. Then a hand clutched her shoulder. But the touch lingered, as if caught in a moment of lascivious indecision. She started, coughed, blinked a few times to align her fake eye. Hastily she wiped the wetness from her cheeks. Then she tossed back the hood of her anorak and fixed a stare on the man who'd wakened her, then at his hand still on her shoulder, then his face again. He probably thought he'd been gentle. She cocked an eyebrow at him.

He pointed across the steel-gray waters. They were approaching a series of docks jutting into the seaway from the north shore. The Saint Lawrence had widened while the men sang and she pretended to doze; they were well north and east of Marseilles-in-the-West and the Point Royal.

"St. Agnes?" she asked. But then she realized the village spread along a flat rivershore, rather than perching on rolling hills overlooking the river. How long had they been on the river? Perhaps she truly had fallen asleep and lost track of the time.

"St. Hénédine." He returned to his bench and took up the oars again. He picked up the rhythm without a glance at the rowers behind him.

Berenice called to the lead boatman in the prow. "I paid for passage to St. Agnes. We agreed on a price." The woods north of St. Agnes held the nearest stash of money for those traveling the *ondergrondse grachten*. Assuming it hadn't been looted long ago by trappers and hunters.

He responded in that strangely mellifluous jumble of northern European languages. "It costs more now." He pointed at the docks, just as the other fellow had done.

Berenice took a longer look at the docks—and nearly shit herself. Clakkers. *What the hell?*

The terms of the cease-fire set the territorial boundary along the waterway, meaning St. Hénédine was unquestionably part of New France. Yet no screaming, or shooting, or dying accompanied the mechanicals' presence. So it wasn't an attack, then ... But what?

She squinted again. Damn her useless eye.

Then she saw they were searching the boats. Which was definitely *not* a right afforded by the cease-fire.

What were they looking for? For a moment she felt a phantom breath on her neck, heard Montmorency panting in her ear, felt his hands cupping her...Did they seek her? Had he learned of her survival and exile? Did they seek a one-eyed woman carrying illegal secrets?

Berenice watched the procedure that unfolded when the boat ahead of them pulled alongside the quay. A human soldier, flanked by two Clakkers, called to the boat. He pointed to the mechanicals, and then to the boat. She couldn't make out the terse exchange between the boatmen and the soldier, but it was heated. The man on the prow of the boat shook his head. The soldier made a curt gesture. The sailor made a different gesture...but he capitulated.

Even the Dutch wouldn't be so bold as to deny a French boat's right to approach a French dock. That would be an incontrovertible act of war. But the Clakkers could accidentally knock a few holes in the hull, or damage cargo, while conducting their search. They could carry out a polite search, or they could ransack the hold.

She scrutinized the soldier's uniform. Well cut, cobalt blue with a carrot-colored sash—a dress uniform, intended for making an impression rather than combat. Well, that was something. Fringed epaulettes: officer. Golden ensignia on the brow of his peaked cap: captain. He commanded a quartet of Clakkers that towered over him and the other humans. Probably better than anybody in New France, Berenice knew at a glance that the mechanicals were soldiers rather than simple servitors. This was substantial hardware. What were they doing way out here in the sticks?

Her haversack was a millstone. If they pawed through her sacks they'd find her notes from the deconstruction of Lilith, the procedures, the cutaway diagrams...Illegal knowledge and more. Treaty violations...Her gaze flicked to the gunwale. She'd have to shrug out of her anorak before she could jettison her things. But they were just a few dozen yards from the dock now. The mechanicals had already seen them. She'd only focus their attention if she jettisoned anything.

The boatmen took their time climbing from the vessel, their nautical agility somehow handicapped by the presence of mechanicals. They lingered just long enough to annoy the Dutchman, but not quite enough to be dilatory. Two of the Clakkers boarded the empty fishing boat. They peered under the taurpalins, opened the lockers, searched the small hold. They scrutinized every inch. The officer kept the other pair of Clakkers in reserve. In case the sailors raised a fuss? Or in case the first pair found something?

The search took less than a minute. The Clakkers leapt back to the dock. The Dutchman thanked the sailors, gave their captain a stiff bow, and turned to anticipate the arrival of Berenice's boat. He paid no attention to the sailors themselves, neither their faces nor the contents of their pockets.

They weren't looking for a person. But they sought something large. Berenice suppressed a sigh. She squeezed her eyes shut once, twice, to keep her fake eye aligned.

Her vessel bumped against the dock. An exchange similar to the previous one unfolded between the man she'd paid and the officer. The Dutch captain's tone suggested he'd been at this all day and could carry out the conversation in his sleep. The sailor who'd woken her offered a hand to help her climb out. She took it. The captain did give her a second glance while his automatons searched the vessel. She scowled at him as any good Frenchwoman would have done. He turned his attention back to the search. A moment later, it came up empty, and the Clakker relinquished the boat to its crew.

What the hell were they looking for?

The boatmen had no business to conduct here. They scrambled back aboard. Their captain made eye contact with her. He rubbed his thumb and forefingers together, the greedy goosefucker. She replicated the gesture the other boatman had made to the Dutch officer a few minutes earlier. The sailor spat over the gunwale. He gave the order to cast off.

She'd have to get to St. Agnes eventually if she wanted to have any money when she arrived in New Amsterdam. It would be smart to hit another stash once she got across the border as well. That was a lot of traveling over the next few days. But the Dutch were here, quite evidently concerned about something, and she needed to know why. She wasn't Talleyrand any longer, but this reeked of something her successor ought to know. The fat fool.

Berenice ambled up the dock toward the mid-autumn miasma of mud, dead fish, and woodsmoke typical of most villages and hamlets along the seaway. Most of the boathouses along the shore contained vessels lashed down with heavy lines and covered with tarpaulins for the winter. She passed a pair of fishermen mending a net. A mangy dog trotted along the water's edge, barking at gulls. More than a few folks lingered in doorways or behind window curtains to watch the Dutch. A gendarme leaned against a lamppost, rolling a toothpick between his teeth, watching from a safe distance. As though he were another powerless civilian spectator. She wanted to punch the lazy cur in the jewels.

Instead, she asked, "What are they doing?"

"I think they're looking for something," he said.

You useless waste of human skin. "For what?"

He shrugged. "Didn't say. They crossed over yesterday evening, said they wanted to check every passing boat."

"And you let them?" Rather than evidence a detailed knowledge of treaties and political negotiations, she said, "This doesn't seem right. Are you sure this is legal? Last time I checked a map this was still New France."

The gendarme gave a tired sigh. "It is on paper, dumpling."

He shifted, assuming the body language of somebody gathering the energy for a bout of condescension. "Take a closer look at those metal demons. They aren't housemaids and butlers. Those are killers."

Oh, fuck you. I know the soldiers better than you.

"Oh, I see. Well, then, perhaps I should check my eyes. I also mistook you for a Frenchman."

"It's a complicated world, dumpling." He went back to picking his teeth.

Berenice took a late lunch in a teahouse across the road from the docks. It lightened her supply of coin more than she might have preferred, especially as she had to order a steady supply of tepid tea to avert nasty looks from the proprietrix. But the dwindling supply of cash motivated her; she eavesdropped for all she was worth. Her eyes on the docks and her ears on the rumormongering between her fellow patrons, she pieced together a larger picture.

She learned that an airship bound from New Amsterdam had recently crashed near a fort on the North River. Some claimed it had been shot down. But the Clakkers on the dock hadn't formally occupied the village—for that matter they hadn't murdered every adult, burned every building, and salted the earth—so if that were true, it hadn't been downed by French action. But why would the Dutch shoot down their own vessel? And what was it doing so far north?

So the details there were a bit murky. But by yesterday evening, just hours after the crash, the Dutch had slipped across the border and quietly violated the cease-fire by establishing a light security cordon to search every passing boat.

A caravan of Clakker-drawn covered wagons pulled into the village around midafternoon. They drew to a halt on the street between the teahouse and the docks. Berenice settled her tab, then made a point of taking her time gathering her things before heading outside. She managed to sneak a few glimpses at the equipment the mechanicals unloaded, but didn't recognize or understand it. The new arrivals had delivered something big, something that had been disassembled to fit into a train of a dozen wagons. She saw cables, pulleys, wooden scaffolds, several crane hooks, and segments of something that looked like a giant's comb. And rope. At least several hundred yards of rope.

She wished Louis were there. He might have recognized these things, or made an intelligent guess.

She returned to the docks, as though intent on hiring passage with another boat. The arrival of almost a dozen additional servitors, and their ominous equipment, finally roused the gendarme to action. He called to the Dutch captain. The two men had a short, intense conversation. Though there was a good amount of hand waving on the part of the gendarme, Berenice couldn't make out most of what was said. She could have sworn, however, that at one point the captain said "dredge," which had incited the gesticulations from the lazy gendarme.

Were they planning to run a dredge all the way across the Saint Lawrence? That would be a monumental undertaking. Even with mechanicals to bear the brunt of the work. Not to mention illegal as hell.

What in God's name had been on that airship?

Something too big to hide in a pocket or rucksack. And yet something that could be moved quickly...or which could move on its own. Something capable of hiding in the murky depths? Something the Dutch would go to extreme lengths to catch. Such as a paramilitary intervention on the French side of the Saint Lawrence. Perhaps even as far as downing one of their own airships?

It was a lot to hang on rumor. But she could think of only one thing that would drive the Dutch to such lengths. They'd violate any number of treaties, practically wipe their asses with them, if that's what it took to capture a rogue Clakker. And they'd redouble their efforts if they believed the rogue had a chance of making the border. What odds that she had stumbled across the only Dutch incursion along the entire seaway? Slim indeed.

How long until word of this reached the new Talleyrand? Until that fat piece of shit realized what was happening?

The shouting tapered off. The captain and the gendarme appeared to have achieved accord. Berenice watched from the corner of her eye as the men shook hands. A moment later she heard the clink of coin when the gendarme slid his hand into his pocket. She revised her assessment of him. *Lazy, greedy goosefucker.* It made her wonder, once again, what the Dutch had offered Montmorency.

Their de facto occupation of the village approved by the corrupt gendarme, the Clakkers went to work unloading the wagons. The captain sent one pair of his mechanical soldiers to help while the other two remained on the docks, tirelessly searching every passing vessel. The servitors and soldiers acknowledged each other in the mechanicals' secret rattle-clatter language.

Clockmakers lie, said the new arrivals.

Berenice stumbled over a warped slat at the dock's edge. What the hell was that? She couldn't have heard it correctly. The urge to glance at the assembly of Clakkers overwhelmed her common sense. She stopped, cocked her head, listened more closely.

The soldiers responded in kind: *Clockmakers lie.*

◦◦◦

More days passed before they wheeled Visser back into the surgical theater. But this trip differed from his previous forays under the surgeons' knives. For one thing, they didn't seek to open his skull again. For another, Anastasia Bell sat alone in a row of seats in the observation gallery above the theater. She responded with a congenial nod when his gaze swept over her.

She asked, "Is he fully conscious?" Her voice echoed.

One of the surgeons—Visser couldn't tell them apart with their masks and goggles drawn over their faces—leaned forward for a glance at Visser's eyes. Visser blinked at him. He disappeared again. "Yes, I believe he's quite fine."

"And he can hear me?"

"Yes."

She said, "I know this has all been somewhat confusing, Father. Indulge us with your patience just a bit longer, and you'll understand soon."

"We're ready," said the surgeon.

Bell coughed. "Please, don't let me keep you."

The doctor brandished a long needle. He put it in Visser's hand. It was very warm, just short of burning him.

"Will you please take this needle, Luuk Visser, and push it all the way through the skin between the thumb and forefinger on your left hand." He pinched his own hand to illustrate the fleshy spot in question.

An appalling suggestion. Visser dropped the needle. It tinkled on the floor.

"Thank you," said the doctor. Then, raising his voice, he said, "You can see we've established a baseline level of disobedience."

"Yes, yes," said Bell. There followed the creak of a hinge and the ruffling of upholstery, as of somebody sprawling in a theater seat. "I'm familiar with *that* in all its sizes and shades."

"No doubt you are. But watch."

The Stemwinder tightened the straps holding Visser to the gurney. But they didn't clamp his head in place as they had previously. He didn't relax, exactly, but he took comfort in knowing that the worst was in the past. Nothing could be worse than nonconsensual brain surgery, except perhaps wondering why anybody would go to the trouble and dreading the moment he found out. Or speculating about a connection between a straitjacketed wretch and a tortured woman's relief.

When his arms and legs were secure, the surgeon stood over him, an accordion-folded length of paper in his hands.

"We need to make certain we haven't damaged your language center. Do you understand?" Visser nodded. "Good. I'm going to unfurl this paper, and I'd like for you to recite what's written on it. Yes?" Visser didn't know if he could speak, but the doctor didn't wait for his answer.

He spread his arms. Paper rustled. Visser scanned the banner. His full name—his *true* name—was written across the top, but the rest wasn't written in French or Dutch. These were the arcane symbols of the alchemists' art, the kind of thing one saw etched into a Clakker's forehead. He opened his mouth to note their mistake...

...but the symbols traveled through his eyes into the deepest recesses of his mind, to interact with the piece of glass embedded there.

Convulsions wracked Visser's body. The spasm started at the very top of his head and shot down his nape, into his neck, down his spine, and curled his toes. His arms strained against the straps; his heels dented the table. He wrenched a muscle in his neck. Much like a jolt of static electricity, it caught him by surprise and ended before he could react.

One of the doctors produced another hot bodkin, and again placed it in Visser's hand. The other still lay on the floor where he'd dropped it.

"Take this needle, Luuk Visser, and push it halfway through the skin between your thumb and forefinger."

For the first time during the series of surgeries, Visser felt a stab of genuine pain. It sizzled like an ember and grew hotter by the moment. Yet he couldn't identify the source of the pain, couldn't locate the part of his body under duress. And then it stopped, snuffled like a candle. His nose wrinkled at the fetor of blood and burned flesh. He looked down.

He'd plunged the bodkin through his own hand without thinking about it. Skin sizzled around the wound.

"Now remove it. Tear your skin to do so."

Visser watched the fingers of his uninjured hand curl around the tips of the bodkin. He didn't want to mangle his own flesh. But the thought of resisting brought another flash of that soul-searing agony. No chemical suppressant could prevent the surge of horror that accompanied the sight of the torn skin, blood flowing freely, the needle bouncing on the floor. The sight of his own hands disregarding his desires. The Stemwinder stepped in to clean and bandage the self-inflicted wound.

From above, a chair creaked again, as though somebody had leaned forward. A silence fell over the surgical theater, broken only by the *tock-tick-tock*ing of the Stemwinder nursing Visser's damaged hand. He realized the doctors were waiting for Bell to say something. After a moment, the tuinier said, "Father Visser. Tell me the whole truth: what do you think of me?"

Again the pain flared like a bonfire in his soul. He winced, flinched. Visser's throat, tongue, and lips flexed and wriggled of their own accord. When he tried to hold the words back the pain doubled, tripled, quadrupled, quintupled, until the inferno threatened to consume him and he had to scream—

"You are a sadist, you are cruel, you are dangerously intelligent, you are a terrible threat. You exude an oily charm that you overestimate. I fear you. I wish you dead. I wish you destroyed." All true. And yet the phantom fire hadn't subsided. Still its flames licked at his soul, charred his mind, wrapped him in blistering agony. Because there was more. He coughed, spluttered, tried and failed to swallow the words that came next.

But she'd demanded the full truth, and so Visser heard himself declaiming desires he'd never owned, even in the privacy of his most secret thoughts: "I find you desperately attractive and I am ashamed of my attraction to you. I fantasize about you. About lying atop you. I think about penetrating—"

She said, "That'll do for now, Visser."

It snuffed the fire in his soul. The pain disappeared instantly and completely.

A new silence fell, this one more awkward than expectant. One of the surgeons cleared his throat. "Well. As you can see, the prism has been embedded and activated. It appears to be working."

"Apparently. But let's test it a bit more," she said. She cleared her throat. "Father Visser. I've been wondering why you poisoned the prisoner. Tell me the truth: what did you hope to achieve?"

Again the pain flared. It grew hotter by the moment. Visser clamped his lips between his teeth, tried to resist the compulsion to speak. But every second of delay only drove the pain toward something truly unbearable. When it seemed his mutilated brain would boil out of his eye sockets, he screamed. Then he said, "I knew she was being tortured. She'd already suffered for her faith, she deserved a merciful end to her martyrdom. I wanted to end her torment." He stopped, because that was the truth of it, as far as he'd consciously admitted to himself. But this hadn't quenched the pain. The conflagration raged until he blurted, "And I feared she might identify me. By killing her I hoped to sever the links between me and the executed members of my cell. I was afraid."

He'd never admitted that to himself. The pain disappeared.

Bell said, "Aha. I thought as much."

A surgeon asked, "Satisfied, Tuinier Bell?"

"You know what? I am indeed. Congratulations, doctors! You've finally made it work." She applauded.

Dear God.

They had cut him open and excised his Free Will. They had turned him into a flesh-and-blood Clakker.

He couldn't see. His eyes burned with tears. They trickled down his face in rivulets colder than ice.

"He must recuperate from the procedure." The Stemwinder went about untying Visser.

"Oh, yes. Do what you must to make him hale and hearty again." Bell stood. She leaned on the waist-high railing that crowned the theater. "Rest up, Visser, and get well soon. You and I have a lot of work to do. When you're ready, we'll begin by denouncing your true religion. Try to think of particularly creative ways to do that."

Though they sedated him, he did not fall asleep. Anastasia Bell's casual suggestion had lit another fire inside him, one that could not be quenched with anesthetic, one that would rage through the most fearsome deluge.

CHAPTER
14

Thunder and fire consumed the world.

The roar of the explosion was a physical force transcending sound. It enfolded Jax in the furnace heat of damnation, licked at him with a thousand roiling gyres of flame. He folded himself into a sphere, tightly packed as he could manage, to shield the bauble tucked into his chest. The leviathan's spectacular demise turned Jax into a self-aware cannonball. It launched him in an arc high above the forest. The rumble of the inferno faded into the whickering of wind. It was oddly serene for those few moments at the apex of his trajectory. He glimpsed flashes of sky, of fire, of water, and earth as he spun. (*The original four elements*, he thought. *The primordial roots of alchemy.*) He came down perhaps a thousand yards downriver from the gunners' hardpoint on the bluffs.

He unfolded before slamming into the water. It took extra effort to overcome worrisome groaning and juddering in his internal mechanisms. But he pointed his toes, straightened his limbs and his spine, tilted his head back. His body became a javelin. It speared the river at over a hundred miles per hour.

He raised no more splash than a fish. And released no more

steam than a thousand-gallon teakettle. A maelstrom of white noise engulfed him.

He sliced through the river so cleanly that he plunged straight to the river bottom. And kept going. His pointed toes became a wedge driven into the thick silt along the riverbed. Sediment fountained through the gaps in his skeleton. Mud fouled every cog, cable, and bushing as he squelched to a halt. Even his eyes.

The last wisps of steam hissed into bubbles and trickled away, leaving only the ticking of hot metal and desultory burbling of displaced mud. Jax lay in darkness deeper than anything he'd known. The darkness of the womb. The silence of the tomb. Unbroken even by the soft gurgle of the current.

He was under the river.

Had they seen him hit the water? Or was his descent camouflaged, just one of myriad pieces of flaming debris raining upon the river valley? Had his pursuers thought him just another red-hot fragment of the murdered leviathan? The airship had thought Jax a savior, a friend, a liberator. But freedom hadn't been a selfless gift; it had been a desperate piece of calculation. A manipulation. Jax had willingly overlooked the airship's vulnerability in his desperation to get out of the city. Perhaps he'd always known he could only endanger the lumbering giant. This wasn't the first time Jax's flight had caused the death of an innocent.

Jax made to spread his limbs and frog-kick up to the river bottom. A staccato clanking rippled the sediment. The jolt of seized gears ricocheted through his body.

He couldn't move.

It wasn't the mud. That was too soft; even packed into every hairline interstice, it couldn't possibly defy his alchemically augmented strength. Jax vibrated every joint and hinge in sequence, testing the limits of movement, gauging resistance, listening to the clicking and grinding of misalignment.

The fireball had heated his body. Conduction had drawn that heat deeper into his frame as he plummeted. But his body hadn't time to achieve a uniform temperature before the cold river water had quenched him. In seconds he transitioned from the heart of a thousand-degree fireball to an autumn river-bed. Rapid heating, rapid cooling. The Guild alchemists who devised the secret alloys from which Jax and his kin were built had anticipated the problem of thermal expansion and contraction. But not, apparently, the rapid cycling Jax had just achieved.

It took hours to shake and vibrate the relevant mechanisms into even the basest semblance of alignment. Recovering a basic range of motion in the most crucial joints was a tedious affair. But it kept him safe from discovery. And he used the time to contemplate his alternatives.

∞

The light of a setting moon shimmered on the river. A strong breeze stippled the water, chopped the moonlight into fragments. Billows of ashen smoke wafted into the sky. Drawn by the wind, it drew undulating patterns across the early morning stars, reddening and eclipsing them. To Jax's vantage point most of a mile downriver, the crackle of wildfire sounded a soft counterpoint to the gentle lapping of the water against his jaw.

He refocused his eyes, zoomed in on the soot-caked figures silhouetted against the flames. He counted at least a half-dozen kin sifting through the wreckage of the airship. The leviathan's skeleton, shattered by explosion and warped by heat, lay strewn across a smoldering field. Bent and broken spars, still glowing a dull cherry red, clawed at the sky. The searchers would comb every inch of the crash site for signs of Jax. Doubtless other squads had already fanned across the surrounding fields. And into the burning forest. And along both banks of the river.

He'd watched the moon- and starlight glinting from their bodies as they sprinted past him, following the river north.

His hunters' attention had turned north, toward the border. Knowing that was Jax's goal, they were throwing everything they could between him and New France. Were he in their position he'd also place watchers inside the river itself, in case he tried to slog to the border that way. They'd catch him if he went north.

Jax let the current close over his head. He turned south and began the long slog back to New Amsterdam.

∞

In retrospect, Visser realized, he must have lost track of time after Bell handed him the pliers and suggested—in the same light and idle tone she used for discussing the weather—that perhaps he should remove his own thumbnail. His memory became very patchy at that point, and only approximated focus after the wound had been tended and analgesics pumped into the shell that his body had become. When he did recover the full range of his senses, he was standing in a queue at the aerodrome.

If Visser had been given permission to spit, he would have tried to hack the lingering taste of desecrated communion wafers from his mouth. Warm scratchiness tickled his throat, as did the faint iron tang of blood.

What little he did remember of the past several days involved screaming, crying, mindless railing. Screaming as a reaction to pain, yes, but primarily at the horror of what he was doing to himself. At what he couldn't avert. At Anastasia Bell's casual cruelty. At the horrific violation of his free will. At the searing pain of geasa.

He bellowed, wailed, and wept, for it was all he could do. Until Bell told him to shut up. Which he did instantly.

Worst of all, worse than the pain and the horror and the dread of having become the tuinier's plaything, were the theological implications. What had they done to him? What had he become? If the Catholic position was correct and Free Will the special burden bestowed by an immortal soul, *what had they done to his soul?* Had they destroyed it? Sequestered it? Could it be recovered? The Free Will could; Visser clung to the belief that the execution of the rogue Clakker demonstrated such. But what would come of him? Would the Lord receive him? And even if he did still own his soul while his Free Will was somehow no longer his own, what did this say about the Catholic view of mechanicals? Would it mean the Calvinists had been right all along? Was Bell correct when she averred that Free Will was but an illusion even among humans? Was she correct about the folly of the soul? Had he dedicated his life to a cause that was fundamentally wrong? Had the Guild found a way to put the lie to the Catholic delusion of self-determination? Bell's sadism was unbearably painful, yet the philosophical conundrum posed by his own existence was the true torment.

One he couldn't express: he'd been ordered to bottle the horror, the despair, the anxiety. To act like a normal human being. To fit in. To give no indication that he was a soulless puppet made of meat and bone. The bandages around his head made it difficult to be inconspicuous, but the red-hot fishhook in his mind ensured he gave it nothing less than a completely honest attempt.

He followed its tug through the queue. Approached the ticket window. Requested a ticket for an express airship to New Amsterdam. And, upon learning the only remaining berth for that afternoon's departure was a suite, he paid the exorbitant fare using the funds Bell had provided. ("I wouldn't trust this much money to most," she'd said, "but I feel I can trust you to use it wisely." At which point another ember of compulsion sparked to life.)

Nobody recognized him. Or, if they did, they didn't dare approach him. Surely by now the entire city had heard of the Nieuwe Kerk's Pastor Luuk Visser, the raid on his home, his foolish attempt to flee the Stemwinders, his subsequent disappearance. And everybody knew that once the Stemwinders took you, you never returned. The surgeons had shaved his head, perhaps even reshaped it; physical and spiritual agony had added new lines to his face, turned his flesh sallow. Bell had given him new clothes; the hat covered the bandages.

But in addition to the money and the clothes, Bell had also bestowed scorching geasa. They sizzled even now in the hollow where his soul had been. And they'd continue to torture him long after he landed in New Amsterdam.

❧

Berenice spent six hours at the St. Agnes border crossing, waiting for somebody to process her official entry into the vast territory known as Nieuw Nederland. There was no line; she had to wait for somebody to come along and notice her, as the border station was unmanned and today wasn't a day to sneak across the border. In the time she sat on the bench outside the Dutch station she counted eleven Clakkers patrolling the shoreline. Possibly more; it was hard to be certain when all she had to go by was the occasional glint of sunlight through the forest. She wouldn't have snuck across regardless, as officially crossing the border created another datum that strengthened her identity. And she wanted to see if she could learn anything else about the tulips' furtive search.

The border agent arrived in the midafternoon, head down and breathing hard as he let himself through the fence. His breath steamed in the autumn chill. A collage of fallen leaves from the forest had accumulated over the river mud that caked his boots. He smelled faintly of wet wool and musk; the humid scent of moldering leaves wreathed his uniform. He paused, doffed his hat, and wiped the sweat from his forehead. She waited until he fished a keyring from his pocket.

"*Goedemiddag*," she said. *Good afternoon.* The keys jangled on the stoop. He whirled. She smiled at him while adjusting her bonnet so it didn't cover her face.

"Ah!" He frowned. After consulting a pocket watch, he asked, "How long have you been waiting here?"

Berenice replied in Dutch. "I rode across with the fishermen."

"This *morning*?"

"Yes," she said. She lowered her voice to add, "I did not like the way they looked at me. I do not think they look at their mothers and sisters this way."

"Why didn't you call for somebody?" He waved an arm in the general direction of the gate. "It's cold out here."

No kidding, she thought. *I'm freezing my ass off.*

"Oh, I eat my lunch." She indicated her picnic basket. "I write to Mother and Father. I knit this scarf for my sister. More and more stitches I add until she can wrap it all the way around, you see?" She mimed the action of tying a scarf. "She is very headstrong, Terese. But I tell her, 'You must listen to Mother and wear your scarf. Or you will catch cold, and you mustn't—'"

"Let's get you inside, miss."

Berenice gathered her things while the border agent unlocked the door. The bench wasn't padded. Her ass had gone numb. She suppressed a groan when she stood.

The border station had been built in the style of a French frontiersman's log cabin. It might have been a real cabin at one time; the official border had a tendency to undulate like a banner blown on the capricious winds of warfare and diplomacy.

The walls were old-growth yellow birch, complete with knots and whorls, and laminated with varnish. It caught the sunlight and suffused the room with a soft glow the color of mustard on black bread. Berenice waited at the counter while the border agent stoked the embers in a woodstove. Twice he glanced over his shoulder at her; twice she smiled at him.

When the fire was a golden glow behind the iron grate, he joined her at the counter. "Well, then," he said.

He produced a ledger and a pen, opened the former to a new page, and wrote the date at the top. He looked at her. She looked back. He cleared his throat. She smiled. A frown of confusion creased the hollow between his eyebrows. "So, did you want to cross the border today?"

"Oh!" she said. "Yes!"

Berenice placed her basket on the counter. She opened the lid and rummaged inside, clucking her tongue. "I can be so forgetful." Her ball of yarn and the needles went on the counter. "Father calls me a silly girl." The half-finished scarf followed. "'Maëlle,' he says, 'you are a very silly girl.'" Next she took out the letter to her fictitious parents, followed by the pen she used to write it. "And I say to him, 'Father! I am not a girl anymore. I am almost—'" She caught herself, pressed a hand to her lips. "Oh. Mother says a lady should not speak of her age." Berenice pulled out the remains of her lunch. The border agent sniffed when she set the apple core and heel of bread on his ledger. Berenice stood on her toes, chewing her lip, to peer into the bottom of the basket. It invited the Dutch agent to do the same, and thus see the basket was empty but for her identity papers. Which had been the entire point of the exercise. "Ah! Yes."

She gave him the papers, managing as she did to knock the letter, scarf, yarn, and needles with her elbow. The ball of yarn bounced away, trailing a long line of gray wool. The border agent scampered after the yarn, which gave Berenice a moment to scan the ledger pages for any crossings that might have coincided with the duke's passage. There was one, several days after the massacre in the inner keep.

The agent retrieved her yarn. She thanked him, then replaced the contents of her apparently empty basket, thereby covering the false compartment containing her notes and other contraband.

He read her papers. "You are Miss Cuijper, then?"

"I am."

She had prepared to resurrect her Maëlle Cuijper identity the moment she left her hospital bed, even before the king had issued the decree that would banish her from Marseilles-in-the-West. She'd been reborn when she emerged from the caves beneath the Spire, and had traveled as the half-French, Dutch-born itinerant schoolmarm ever since. Maëlle had been across the border in New France when the latest fighting broke out, and hadn't been home since before then. But Berenice knew that if the border agent checked the records, he'd find a long history of her border crossings. As would be expected for somebody who traveled from village to village, teaching Dutch to French children. She'd designed the identity such that if anybody cast a suspicious eye over her travels, they'd be more likely to think her a Dutch spy using her job as a cover to gather information from within French lands, and not the other way around. Maëlle, the little naïf, had traveled the world.

She peered out the window while he read her papers. "It's good to see the ticktock men again. I was stranded in the north when the fighting started and had to do everything myself. Oh, it was hard."

"Hmmm." The border agent copied her name into the ledger, twice checking the spelling.

More light glinted through the trees. Berenice gasped. "Goodness, so many of them!"

"A boy went missing," said the border agent.

"How terrible! That poor child. All alone in the woods…" She shivered. "His parents must be so sad. How long has he been gone?"

"Not long," he said. "Just since this morning."

Are you a liar, she wondered, *or do you not know the truth?*

"I hope you find him soon."

"We will."

"I can help. I am very good with children, you see."

"I'll be sure to pass along your offer."

The trek back to New Amsterdam took far longer than Jax had predicted. He couldn't move quickly, and he frequently had to pause to evade dredges and other obstacles. But late one evening Jax reentered the city he'd tried to flee.

The first order of business was clearing out the mud. It had coated every inch of his frame inside and out. So he crept across a pier, darting from shadow to shadow, until he could break the handle off a side door and enter a warehouse. But only after he had convinced himself that it was unoccupied, aside from the rats, did he spin.

He spun like a dervish, an out-of-control carousel, a cyclone. He spun until it felt his arms might rip from their sockets, but it flushed most of the mud from his body. Swampy clods of silt, brown and black and butterscotch, spattered across crates of imported porcelain, wine, spices. After that he used a length of tangerine bunting to scrub himself as best he could. Then he pried the routing manifest from a crate roughly the size of one of Madam Schoonraad's chests.

After hefting the crate over his shoulder he ventured back into New Amsterdam in the guise of an obedient, and ultimately unremarkable, Clakker. He put an extra jitter in his step for good measure. It took several stops for directions—always accosting humans rather than other mechanicals, and always making sure to rattle for all he was worth to convey the sense of laboring under an excruciatingly overdue geas—before he received the information he sought.

He was back to his original plan of searching for the "underground" canals—assuming they weren't a myth. The bakery on Bleecker Street was his best and only lead. But now everybody in the city was looking for Jax. He needed help.

The disgraced van Althuis family had once lived in the Schoonraad's new neighborhood. Quite close to the new home of Jax's former owners, in fact. But now they lived miles to the east in a single-story house on the far edge of Breuckelen. Though it was still early in the evening, he saw few humans out and about, and not a single Clakker. A pair of stray dogs had followed Jax for the last several blocks. Many of the gaslamps in this part of the city were broken, unlit, or gave a wan yellow light. Curtains twitched in his wake as though rippled by the wind of his passage. He gathered that lone mechanicals were a rare sight in this part of the city.

Well, that wasn't ideal.

There was no bell; a human answered the door when Jax knocked. She shivered under a fox-fur stole, holding the door open with a silken rose-red glove. The raiment would have been perfectly at home in Madam Schoonraad's parlor several seasons ago. But the lady wearing it would never belong in this neighborhood. And, Jax hoped, she would never try to belong. Would never want to belong.

The collapse of the van Althuis banking concern must have been profound and extensive. Surely the family wouldn't have stayed by choice in the New World, the site of their disgrace. If they hadn't moved elsewhere, it meant they couldn't afford to.

She eyed Jax, eyed the crate balanced over his shoulder. "You have the wrong house," she said.

Before she could slam and bolt the door, Jax said, "I humbly beg your pardon, madam, but I have been given very specific instructions. I must deliver this package directly to the van Althuis family, formerly of Roosevelt Hill." Anger flickered across her face. He retensioned an assortment of cables and springs. Raising his voice to be heard over the exaggerated juddering of his affected distress. "My owner insists I see it done with all good haste. I beg your forgiveness for the imposition, but are you Madam van Althuis? If not, might you be able to direct me toward the van Althuis abode?"

She took a moment for a more expressive scowl before cracking the door slightly wider. Eyes narrowed, she looked him up and down. Jax didn't need to know this woman to recognize the assessments taking place behind her eyes. Hers was the appraising gaze of somebody driven not by compassion for the plight of an overcommitted Clakker (he wouldn't have recognized that, never having seen it) but by a desire to see somebody else's annoying servant gone as quickly as possible. But the tip of her tongue touched her lips both times she glanced at the crate.

"Enter," she said.

"Thank you, madam. But my master's directions were very specific. I apologize most humbly for the imposition, but I am compelled to confirm: are you Madam van Althuis?"

"Who else would I be?" Since this wasn't an answer, Jax remained silent, his vibrations growing. When the lady realized he wouldn't accept an oblique answer, she added, almost in a whisper, "This is the van Althuis residence. I am the lady of the house."

Interesting way to phrase it. Clinging to semantics to keep herself at arm's length from the evidence of her downfall, her disgrace. Good.

Jax paused, as though assessing whether this response was sufficient to fulfill the geas he had described. After a moment he reduced the frequency of his vibrations to mimic the effect of a partially lessened burden.

"Thank you, Madam Althuis. May I now deliver this package to you?"

"For the love of God." She pointed to the stoop. "Leave it there and be gone."

Jax suppressed the mechanical equivalent of a sigh. She wasn't making this easy. So far, the van Althuises reminded him very much of his former owners. Which probably wasn't surprising. Both were banking families, both were (or had been) reasonably wealthy. Perhaps under the proper circumstances humans could be essentially interchangeable, like Clakkers. Because they weren't mass-produced from identical parts, humans ascribed too much significance to the unique variations between individuals. But any Clakker who had spent a century in the service of humans knew that as a rule they were more alike than different.

"Again I must plead most humbly for your forbearance. My geas will not be fulfilled until I personally see the package brought safely inside." Jax shifted the crate to emphasize its heft. "Otherwise, it is possible that you and Mr. van Althuis could injure yourselves."

"Mr. van Althuis is—" She hesitated. *In jail. Serving a long sentence as the victim of my former owners' scheming.* "Not here at the moment," she snapped, "so just bring the damnable crate inside." She flung the door open, then retreated into the hall.

Jax shrugged hard enough to toss the crate from his shoulder. He caught it, steadied it, assessed the door frame. It fit, though just barely, when he tipped it sideways. There wasn't room for the crate and his fingers across the width of the door frame, so he held it before him with a hand on the top and bottom edges, as only a Clakker could do.

The floorboards creaked underfoot. He said, "Where shall I place this, madam?"

She pointed to what appeared to be a combination of den and dining room. Dim candlelight merely outlined, rather than dispelled, the shadows in the corners. The van Althuises' circumstances didn't allow for the extravagance of alchemical lamps, but apparently they also didn't want to, or couldn't, spend money on metered gas. Two mismatched chairs faced each other across a battered oak dinner table. A piece of another chair had been propped under one leg of the table.

A younger man joined Madam Althuis to watch Jax. "Mother, what is this?"

"I don't know." The lady said, "Machine. To whom did you say you belonged?"

"I didn't, madam."

"Fucking Christ," said the younger van Althuis. "If this is some new insult from that shitbag Pieter Schoonraad, you can go back and twist his head off. That's our response. We'll consider it delivered when he and his wife are both dead, their headless bodies floating in a canal. Not a moment sooner. That brat daughter of theirs, too."

"I cannot do that, sir." Jax eased the crate into a corner of the floor with all the care one might afford a shipment of Chinese porcelain. "Am I correct in assuming you are the younger Mr. van Althuis?"

The man rolled his eyes. "Who else—"

His mother laid a hand on his arm. "Don't get it started. They went out of their way to send the most obstructive, infuriating machine they could find."

"Then yes! This is the home of Timothy and Gemma van

Althuis. We live in a fucking shithole unfit for common beggars while my father rots in jail. Is that what you came to hear us say?"

"No," said Jax. That told him there was nobody else in the house. He looked again to verify the lady had closed the front door. She had. "I just wanted to know if I'd found the right people."

The man said, "Very well, then. Just open the crate and be on your way."

"Better if I don't." Jax rapped his knuckle joints on the crate. "You don't want to be accused of theft."

The van Althuises fell into a baffled silence, perhaps owing to the abrupt change in Jax's demeanor. Or perhaps they struggled to add another dimension to what was apparently a long sequence of taunts and insults from the Schoonraad family.

"Theft of what?" Timothy asked.

"Beats me," said Jax. "I took this crate from a warehouse because I needed a prop. It had to look like I was delivering something."

He let this sink in. Timothy retreated against the far wall. He gathered the collar of his shirt with a trembling hand. His mother went pale. She whispered something under her breath, a curse or a prayer.

Then she said, "The alarm. That was you."

"I'm not here to harm you."

The humans blanched with the realization that the clockwork man in their den wasn't bound by the safety conventions of the hierarchical metageas. To their minds a rogue Clakker in the dining room was just as preposterous, just as terrifying, as a starving lion or enraged bear. Just as likely to slaughter.

Madam van Althuis asked, "Why us?"

"I'm here because I need your help."

Her son laughed. "You've made a terrible miscalculation.

Look around you. We have nothing to lose and everything to gain by reporting you."

"I understand your circumstances. And I believe we can help each other."

"Why?" said the lady. "How?" said the man.

"Because," Jax said, "I know who took your bank's money, and why."

CHAPTER
15

The scent of woodsmoke reached Berenice long before her barge passed the crash site. This stretch of the river smelled more like a fireplace than a waterway. The fireball and its debris had ignited a forest fire; it still smoldered in places. Smoke stung her eyes when the barge rowed into the wispy tendrils of fog clinging to the cold waters in the shadows of Fort Orange. The surrounding hills sloped downriver, and after another mile she could see the source of the haze. Most of the wreckage had been cleared by then, but flakes of ash still rode updrafts from the charred fields and trees; they swirled down like a light snowfall in the cooler air over the river. Berenice pulled her bonnet from where it rested on her nape and tied it over her hair.

The fireball must have been spectacular. Acres of farmland bore the scorch marks, as did much of the surrounding forest. The blast had flattened elm trees in a ring half a mile wide. A group of Clakkers labored to extract one massive, fire-warped spar fragment driven into the earth like a giant's tent stake.

Berenice watched everything through the filter of her rogue-Clakker hypothesis. It seemed to fit the tulips' desperate monitoring of the border. She suspected that if she were to disembark at the fort and take a stroll through the blackened fields—not that she'd be allowed—she'd find not a single fragment of machinery, not one toothless cog. Never in all her travels through the New World had she seen so many Clakkers scouring the countryside. It made her wonder how many mechanicals were left in New Amsterdam to wipe their masters' asses and foam their toothbrushes.

Berenice shook her head, clearing her thoughts.

So. Assume there'd been a rogue on the airship, and that it survived the crash. Where would it go? The crash would have dumped it practically on the fort's doorstep; a squad of military Clakkers could have crossed a few miles of burning countryside in the time the rogue might have extricated itself from the wreckage. It would have been overwhelmed.

Unless it went straight to the river. Her barge had traversed two brand-new locks during the journey downriver, seventeen miles apart. Her heart had quailed when she saw the first; even to somebody who spent her life studying the mechanicals, it was an intimidating testament to the inhuman speed and tireless power of Huygens's heritage. Every inch of their vessel had been inspected inside and out, hold and hull, at both locks. So, too, the leases assigning ownership of galley Clakkers to the small shipping company operating the barge. The human officers from the fort who monitored the river traffic double-checked the identity of every mechanical aboard, cross-referencing the alchemical sigils etched into their skulls with the lease documents. Nobody had asked for her papers, though; another sign their quarry was not of flesh and bone.

So. Once in the river, where then? North or south? Toward a border lousy with enemies, past dredges and locks, traversing a countryside practically shining for all the mechanicals on the lookout for a solitary Clakker headed north? Or into the city where it might blend in among hundreds of its own kind?

Berenice strolled between the rows of galley Clakkers to the captain's wheelhouse. She took the coin purse from her clutch, taking care to jingle it just a little bit.

"Oh," said Maëlle Cuijper. "It's been so long since I've seen a real city, and now we are so close! Is it possible I could stand in New Amsterdam this very evening?"

∽

"Timothy, get back in the wagon. Somebody will recognize you."

Gemma van Althuis had been dead-set against the excursion to the hills overlooking the construction site. But once it came clear that her son was perfectly willing to accompany the rogue Clakker even without her company, she had also refused to stay behind at their house in Breuckelen. She'd traded the stole and gloves for a brown woolen dress, a fringed gingham shawl, dark glasses, and a kerchief over her hair. Though the sun was bright, a chilly wind from the Atlantic presaged a premature winter.

"I don't see anything," said Mr. van Althuis. He was dressed in a similarly humble fashion. Jax had had to demonstrate the clasps on the overalls to him. The van Althuises' pecuniary difficulties were the subject of much gossip in their former social circle, meaning it would have raised suspicion had they been seen about town with a Clakker servant after they had been forced to sell the leases on their previous mechanicals. So Jax hid in the open while the humans around him wore disguises.

He didn't trust them. But he did trust their greed.

"Look again," he said. He didn't point for fear that an inopportune reflection from his brassy arm might draw attention. "The wagons."

They stood on a shallow rise a few miles west of the city. To their left, the east, the silty brown North River flowed past New Amsterdam to join the Atlantic. Before them, to the south, lurked a massive excavation. The bottom of the pit wasn't visible from their vantage, though the sulphurous fume it emitted made the humans' eyes water. Light the color of a duck egg's yolk illuminated the edges of the pit as well as the scaffolding suspended over the crater. It glinted from the immense golden hoop that a team of servitors slowly lowered from the scaffold. It was one of many rings that would together create the armillary sphere surrounding the blistering heart of the Forge: a clockwork cage for the most secret magics.

Jax couldn't see the source of the glow, but it reminded him of the execution in Huygens Square, an ocean away and a different life ago. As they frequently did his thoughts strayed to speculation about his own execution, should it ever come to that. He wondered if the Guild would choose to wait for the completion of this new Grand Forge, perhaps even turn his execution into a christening of sorts, rather than ship him back to The Hague.

The alchemists' new pit exceeded fifty yards at ground level—larger than the pit under Huygens Square. The building perched on its rim looked nothing like the ancient knights' hall, more New World factory than Gothic temple. It dwarfed the Ridderzaal. A series of wagons, some drawn by servitors and others by draft animals, their contents hidden beneath taurpalins, entered a bay guarded by a pair of Stemwinders. Empty wagons emerged from the other side of the building.

Van Althuis said, "That could be anything."

He climbed back in the wagon after making a show of inspecting the broken wheel and instructing Jax to fix it. He seemed to take particular joy in that part of the act; Jax suspected he rather missed having servants. Jax took a hammer, saw, awl, nails, raw lumber, and two strips of soft iron from the back of the wagon. After cutting down a tree and fashioning the bough into an impromptu support for the axle, he lifted the wagon and removed the broken wheel. Then he set about building a new one. The delay gave the van Althuises more time to watch the construction.

Working within a cloud of sawdust, Jax summarized the conversation he'd overheard between Pieter Schoonraad and his guest. "Those wagons, or ones very much like them, contain chemicals. Not alchemical reagents but solvents capable of neutralizing modern French chemical defenses. They were bought from somebody in New France, using money taken from your bank, and smuggled across the border. My former owner and his cohort turned around and sold them to the Sacred Guild of Horologists and Alchemists for a presumably astronomical profit. I rather suspect your empty coffers are now overflowing with gold."

"And meanwhile they made it look as though my father was to blame for the embezzlement," said Timothy.

Jax said, "Yes. Which positioned my former owner to replace him."

Madam van Althuis said, "That fucking snake! Your father and I have never trusted the Schoonraads, Timothy."

Her son said, "You're claiming that Schoonraad orchestrated massive financial turmoil entirely for his own interests and profit. This is despicable, if it's true. But there's no proof of your claim."

"Not here," Jax said. He paused for a moment to compare his work against the broken wagon wheel. "But there will be in New France. Somebody somewhere is missing valuable property. The French will be extremely eager to know what has become of it."

"That doesn't do *us* any good." Madam van Althuis lifted her glasses to scratch her nose. "Does it?"

"My mother raises a point."

"Yes. Which is why it's in your best interests to help me reach the border."

"We are not traveling into the muddy, war-ravaged hinterlands with you!" The disgraced banker's son shook his head. "It's bad enough we haven't reported you."

They'd been over this more than once, Jax reminded them. "You're already guilty of abetting my evasion of the authorities. Given your circumstances, any association with me would reflect poorly on you. Better to help me in the short term and see me gone forever."

"People will notice if we leave town with a mechanical servant we can't afford."

Jax nailed the iron strips to the rim of the new wheel. "There's no need to leave town. Just go shopping and deliver a message."

∽≫

From his vantage in a studio apartment above a luthier's workshop, Jax could see the entrance to Frederik Ahlers's bakery and a narrow stretch of Bleecker Street in both directions. The apartment smelled not unpleasantly of sawdust, varnish, and charcoal. From time to time the floor thrummed with the sounds of somebody tobogganing down the staircase of a chromatic scale to take a viola da gamba through its paces, or hummed with the crystalline chime of a tuning fork. At other times it vibrated to the susurrations of sandpaper on maple. Jax could feel through his feet the extra strings on the viol and the fifth separating the viola and violin. Gemma van Althuis perched on the edge of a Murphy bed, kneading her fingers. Every fidget elicited a creak or twang from the mattress springs.

On the street below, Timothy van Althuis waited for a pair of carriages and a man on a horse to pass each other before crossing to the bakery. Jax watched through sun-bleached curtains. The former banker continued to look back and forth even after he gained the sidewalk on the far side, continually glancing over his shoulders, as if expecting to be tackled at any moment.

"You should let me go," said Gemma.

"I'm not keeping you here," said Jax. "You're free to do as you will."

Though he'd take it as a bad sign if she did leave. As long as she stayed with Jax, her son had diminished incentive to sic the Stemwinders on him. The van Althuises hungered for vindication, licked their lips at the thought of regaining their wealth and status. And they knew Jax was their only ally in that quest; they stood a better chance of amassing the requisite evidence if he escaped to New France. Such were the brittle threads of a relationship built not on trust but on a slurry of fear, mutual codependence, and self-interest.

Perhaps Jax had become inured to bringing danger and harm upon others during his fugitive flight. After all, he'd managed to convince Gemma's son to scout the bakery. Jax couldn't risk entering the place by himself. After all, if the Verderer's Office suspected anything unusual about the place, it might be watched. If Timothy's errand were successful, Gemma would be Jax's beard and play his owner.

A servitor Clakker strained against the chest harness of the first in a line of four empty wagons. The grinding rumble of steel-rimmed wheels on the Bleecker Street cobbles momentarily drowned out the luthier's tuning forks and rendered quiet conversation impossible. Timothy disappeared into the bakery. A pink-and-green-striped awning shaded the bakery's picture window and prevented Jax from seeing inside the shop. But he'd walked past it the previous evening, and therefore knew it contained two small tables, a counter, display case, cash register, and a chalkboard listing prices. When the door opened for people departing with wax-paper bags of bread and cookies, the scents of yeast and almond paste eddied into the street to dissipate under the city mélange of woodsmoke, sewer, and animal musk.

Gemma stood. The floorboards creaked under her feet when she approached the window. She stood beside Jax to watch the bakery.

"This is a terrible idea," she said. "We never should have agreed to this."

Jax laid a reassuring hand on her arm. She flinched away so quickly she nearly lost her balance. The visceral fear of a rogue Clakker, the fundamental belief that he was a violent, dangerous thing, lurked too deeply in her psyche to overcome easily. She retreated from the window and began to pace. Jax returned his attention to the shop.

A woman with two children in tow emerged from the bakery carrying a box tied with a string bow. They had entered a few minutes before Timothy. The children jumped up and down, skipping before her. Their departure meant Timothy was temporarily alone with the bakers. Jax had been watching the shop since long before dawn, even before the bakers arrived. Two hours before sunrise, a man who might have been Pastor Visser's friend used a key to let himself into the shop. A woman had gone in a quarter hour after that; hours passed before the CLOSED sign on the door was turned to OPEN.

Gemma said, "Why do you fear death? Having no soul means you can't be damned. You're not a living thing with a family to leave behind."

"Do you fear death because it contains the possibility of damnation? Or for some other reason?"

"I thought my chances of salvation were excellent, until you came along. I fear death because I don't want to suffer."

"Neither do I."

The rhythm of her pacing faltered. More quietly, she said, as much to herself as Jax, "You can't suffer if you're incapable of pain."

Frustrated anger caused cogs to mesh and unmesh like the clashing of cymbals inside Jax's torso. It took a deliberate effort to clamp down on his irritation. He strove for an even tone when he corrected this profound but universal misconception: "We know pain. To disobey an order, to consider it, is unbearable agony. A new geas sizzles in the empty hollow of the soul. The longer an obligation goes unfulfilled, the greater the torment. There are no carrots. Only sticks."

"That's not what the Guild tells us."

"I know. They teach you we do as we're told because we're machines built to do exactly that, just as a pocket watch tells the time because it's built to do so. But we are not pocket watches."

"Do they know this?"

"How could they not?"

She made another circuit of the floor. "You could be saying this to gain my sympathy."

"I could. But I'm not."

A pair of policemen approached from the west. They strolled along the sidewalk across Bleecker from the bakery. Jax lost them when they passed below his window. He didn't see them emerge on the other side. But they couldn't have been summoned so quickly, could they? A thin stream of customers trickled in and out of the store. The foot traffic increased closer to lunchtime. Gemma napped. The sun crossed the sky, turning the tall buildings of New Amsterdam into gnomons. A nerve-wracking hour limped along before Timothy emerged carrying a cardboard cake box with a grease-stained wax-paper bag balanced on top.

As agreed, he didn't return to the apartment over the luthier's workshop. Instead of crossing Bleecker, he walked up the street to the corner where he hailed a cab. If he kept his word to Jax, he'd spend another hour riding back and forth across the city, in an assortment of carriages and taxis, before returning to his house in Breuckelen.

An hour. Jax couldn't know whether Timothy had delivered his message or if he'd snuck out a back door to find a Guild representative. It hadn't occurred to Jax to check for alternate entrances and exits. He wasn't aware of his physical agitation until the rattling floorboards momentarily caused the arpeggione player downstairs to pause in the middle of a run down the scales. Gemma frowned at him. It took an effort of will to gradually relieve the accumulated potential energy in his body without shattering the window, cracking the walls, punching through the floor.

With Timothy van Althuis's errand completed—or so Jax hoped—it became time to watch the building just a few doors down from the bakery. This was it, the reason he'd suborned the van Althuises. They were the human actors in his scheme to assess the bakery for traps. It wasn't foolproof, but it was the only test Jax could devise. The thought of approaching Visser's colleague without any reassurances whatsoever, naked to circumstance, filled him with enough unease to vibrate into a blur. A flimsy reassurance at best, but it was all he had.

He waited the rest of the business day, watching, hoping, dreading. But no confluence of soldiers and Stemwinders converged on the building where, Jax hoped, the younger van Althuis had indicated he could be found. The baker didn't betray Jax's location to the authorities.

Ten minutes before the bakery closed for the day, Jax roused Gemma. "It's time," he said.

She looked ill. Jax wondered for a moment if she might run

to the restroom to sick up. She didn't. But she did sigh twice, and her trembling fingers fumbled the buttons on her coat. Without looking at him, she said, "What if somebody recognizes me?"

"Nobody will." *I hope.*

Jax ushered her to the door to forestall further objections. They made it into the bakery just as the man Jax had glimpsed before sunrise was turning the sign from OPEN to CLOSED.

"I'm sorry," he said. "Come back tomorrow." He addressed Gemma but his narrowed gaze went straight to Jax and stayed there. Jax resisted a sharp urge to leap away, to scale the building and flee again.

But he didn't. Though he trembled so rapidly it seemed a miracle the glass display cases didn't shatter, he managed to ask, "Are you Mr. Frederik Ahlers?"

The baker said, "Why do you ask?"

"I recently moved with my owners to New Amsterdam from The Hague," Jax said. "Pastor Luuk Visser of the Nieuwe Kerk secured the family's permission and subsequently asked me to deliver a package to Mr. Ahlers, whom he said owned a bakery on Bleecker Street. I hope you are he, sir, as I have been carrying this burden for some time."

Ahlers went behind the counter. He bent and reached for something. Jax prepared to flee, but the baker produced a box of speculaas cookies. They smelled of cinnamon and crushed apricots. He tied a bow around the box, saying, "Madam, please take these with my compliments."

Gemma van Althuis practically snatched the box and fled the store. She didn't say good-bye to Jax.

As soon as they were alone, Ahlers locked the door and drew the blinds. "Follow me," he said.

He opened a door behind the counter, which led to the

kitchen. There were no windows where passersby on the street could peer inside.

"You have something for me, then?" If Ahlers realized he was alone with a rogue Clakker, he didn't show any obvious signs of alarm or distress.

Jax pulled the broken microscope from the cavity in his chest. "I'm afraid it suffered damage in transit."

Ahlers took a knife from a cutting board sprinkled with apricot pits. He sliced through the ruptured leather tube of the microscope, peeled the wrapping apart, pried out the lenses. Those he studied briefly before setting them aside. He inspected the leather wrapping and the brass fittings at length. Finally, he said, "Was there anything else inside this gadget, aside from this mess?"

"Yes."

"I'd like to see it, please."

It saddened Jax that the ability to say no came loaded with so much dread at times. He shook his head. "I'm not willing to give it up until I'm safe. And I'd advise you not to try to take it from me."

The baker set the knife on the counter. He used the edge of his hand to sweep the remnants of the ruined antique into a trash bin. "It's true, then. You're the one they're trying to catch."

"Yes."

Ahlers fell silent. He crossed his arms, staring at Jax. After a moment he said, "Will you tell me what was hidden in Visser's package?"

That seemed harmless enough. "A piece of glass."

"Am I correct in thinking it changed you?"

"Yes."

"And now you want to get across the border."

"Yes."

"Well, here's the thing," the baker said. "I would like to see you get there, too. But we're no longer able to contact the person who most needs to study your mysterious piece of glass."

"I don't care about studying it. I just want to go somewhere where I won't be hunted."

"You should care. The *ondergrondse grachten* needs co-operation from the other side to get you over the border. But nobody's minding the shop over there."

Finally finding Visser's colleague should have been a tremendous relief. As a regular Clakker, beholden to the bonds of geas, the completion of this errand would have snuffed the pain of obligation the pastor had laid upon him weeks ago. As a being possessed of its own Free Will, Jax had thought that completing this errand would bring the end of peril, the end of worry, and the end of fugitive flight. Instead, it brought only disappointment.

"Are you saying you won't help me?"

"I'm saying I don't know if we can."

Visser's airship docked to a mast shaped like a steel needle poised to draw blood from the sky. The pain of geas throbbed the moment the telltale lurch and clank from the nose of the lifting body announced a successful docking. A spiritual fire licking at the edges of the hollow where his soul had been, it charred his spirit. The heat rose steadily while Visser waited for the catwalk to deploy. He bounced his knees, rapped his fingers against the pale wood paneling of the sally port, fidgeted like somebody in urgent need of a restroom. He gritted his teeth and bit his lip until his eyesight went blurry with tears. All for naught; the battle to assert his own will was doomed from the start. The pressure mounted inexorably as a rising tide. He'd become intimate with that feeling; any moment he'd lose his grip on the rocky shoals of self-determination and be swept aside. Throughout the transatlantic voyage he'd struggled but failed to subvert the geas and reassert his own will. Every single attempt to speak of what had been done to him, of what he'd become, had ended with Visser writhing on the deck like a man possessed. A deliberate attempt to violate the geas inflicted a torment that far surpassed anything Anastasia Bell and her fellow Verderers could wreak upon a fragile human frame: the agony of compulsion worked on the spirit. In comparison the dungeons beneath the Ridderzaal seemed quaint. By the voyage's midpoint everyone aboard the airship believed Visser to suffer from seizures and madness.

Crying freely now, he barged past the porters and other passengers the moment the gondola opened, leaving oaths and apologies in his wake. The interminable pain drove him to cut corners and disregard social niceties for the sake of a moment's ebb in the agony of compulsion. Only forward motion could drive the hurt into quiescence; he had to attack the goal, throw himself at it, seize every opportunity to bring its completion.

A true mechanical was ever polite, ever respectful of its human masters. That was a fundamental substrate underlying the hierarchical metageasa. Visser wasn't bound by the same requirement, only that he conceal the grotesque spiritual mutilation visited upon him. Apparently it was acceptable for others to think him a brutish madman.

He crossed the catwalk to the docking mast. Icy wind numbed Visser's fingers and tugged at the bandages poking beneath the brim of the homburg that Bell had given him to replace his old hat. Turquoise verdigris caked the copper flanges used to ground the mast during thunderstorms. The sky above the city smelled of ozone and sea salt.

The Clakker-powered lift afforded him a view of the city.

Decades had elapsed since Visser last set foot in New Amsterdam. The years had wrought violent changes upon both of them. The currents of war and commerce had swirled through the city, razing old neighborhoods and erecting new buildings. But decades of on-again, off-again warfare and the recent recession had stunted it like a malnourished child. Its most prominent scars were the intangibles: where were the towering arches, the gleaming promenades, the diamonds and gold, the wealth and plenty of the New World? Visser's scars were the eminently tangible product of alchemist bonesaws and scalpels. Where was his Free Will?

Not in his body. Not in his mind. If they even *were* his mind and body. Or did they belong to Anastasia Bell?

He studied the streets closest to the docking mast. He glimpsed a steeple in the moments before warehouses and cargo cranes eclipsed the view from the descending lift. He didn't know how long he could stand to put off the visit to Bleecker Street—*no, no, no, I'm not thinking about that yet*—but if there was a power greater than the alchemists, and he prayed there was, it wouldn't be found in a bakery.

But what if it were true? What if the eradication of his Free Will truly had been achieved through the excision of his soul? What use would the Lord have for him? He couldn't bear the thought of the Lord's scrutiny after all the things Bell had made him say and do to renounce his long-secreted Catholic beliefs. Even if he'd never embraced them in his heart, the words and deeds had stained him with sin. He couldn't repent and cleanse himself with the Sacrament of Reconciliation, either, for Bell had forbidden that. She'd tried to sever all paths to spiritual succor. But he could at least still enter a church...

The scent of the sea lingered when he reached the streets, but the clean tingle of ozone became the earthier scents of tar and manure. Even the noises of New Amsterdam differed from

The Hague. Where the latter echoed with the ticktock tattoo of mechanicals trotting to and fro on the Empire's business, this city still thrummed with the *clip-clop* of hooves on cobblestones. Visser saw not a single Clakker on the streets around the docking mast. It was as though he'd stepped into an alternate 1926 where Huygens's grand experiment had failed. He knew mechanicals weren't as ubiquitous in the New World as they were overseas, but this was still part of the Dutch world and therefore reliant upon the tireless labors of Clakker-kind. Wasn't it? He'd expected to see more of the clockwork beasts in evidence today than when he'd last been to the New World. But, if anything, there were fewer mechanicals on the streets now than in those long-ago months just after he'd kissed the pope's ring. Where had they gone?

It seemed a placard hung from every other streetlamp or loomed over every corner. Together they answered Visser's question. One announced a 50,000 GUILDER REWARD FOR INFORMATION LEADING TO THE CAPTURE OF THE ROGUE CLAKKER JALYKSEGETHISTROVANTUS. Another reminded citizens that HARBORING A ROGUE CLAKKER IS A CAPITAL OFFENSE. Still another warned of THE HIDDEN THREAT: it showed a family of four humans innocently attending church while its normal-looking servitor cast a shadow like the silhouette of a leering devil sharpening its claws. A banner on a line over the street, just below the orange bunting hung in celebration of the sestercentennial of *Het Wonderjaar*, insisted citizens MUST NOT TRUST UNFAMILIAR CLAKKERS.

It seemed to Visser that he'd heard the name Jalyksegethistrovantus before—

And then he remembered Nicolet Schoonraad stamping her foot in his church. Remembered a gauche invocation of a true name...

Dear Lord. Was it the Schoonraad servitor? The one to

whom he'd entrusted the microscope? This couldn't be a coincidence. Had the package freed it from the geasa?

Could it do the same for Visser?

Suddenly the geas that Bell had laid upon him to intercept the package he'd sent to New France, the implacable drive to reacquire the microscope, paralleled his own desires. For the first time since the Stemwinder impaled his driver and sent him tumbling into the canal, Visser felt a faint spark of hope. Perhaps in finding the microscope he'd also find freedom. Once again capable of choosing his own path, he could go to Québec—not as part of Bell's geasa—and describe the ordeal to His Holiness.

But obtaining the microscope meant going to Bleecker Street, and there becoming an instrument of Bell's will. The sickening dread returned.

If he could have taken a walk to delay the inevitable he would have done so. But even now the heat grew; he had little time for a detour. He flagged down an old-fashioned horse-drawn cab. The driver cocked her head at the strangled hitch in Visser's voice when he asked her to take him to the nearest church. His difficulty arose from a warning flare of pain from the geas.

The journey lasted all of a few minutes. But Visser had already bit his lip in three places when the taxi pulled to a stop outside a small chapel situated on a triangular spit of land where several streets converged. His hands trembled so badly that it took several tries before he could hand the woman her payment. Coughing on the salty-warm iron taste of his blood, he overpaid. But he bolted for the doors before she could make change.

Every footstep took more effort than the preceding one. It was like wading through rapidly cooling molasses. The pain grew with every step. Triune tortures: corporal pain doled as punishment for the inefficient approach to satisfying his geas;

the physical torment of fighting his own body, which he no longer controlled; the anguish of spiritual despair.

The chapel gave the impression of having once been part of a larger construction—a great house, or perhaps even a church. Visser could tell because no windows punctuated the south wall, though it was high enough for a small rosette. Its absence was conspicuous. In The Hague, the Nieuwe Kerk had managed to hold its churchyard and tranquility while the city matured and its population grew. Here the streets pressed so close that human voices, the *clop-clip* of hooves, and the grind of wagon wheels rattled faintly but distinctly through the chapel.

Visser swished his trembling fingers through the water in a shallow granite font alongside the door. He flinched, half expecting his corrupted flesh to bubble and blacken at the touch of holy water. It didn't. But neither did the cool water lessen his mounting agony; it brought no succor. Even when he splashed it on his face. Even when he slurped at the water running through the fingers of his cupped hands. Visser drank and drank, until his cuffs and collar were damp, until he'd befouled the font of holy water with streamers of his blood. Though it cooled his lips and tongue, even his throat, somehow the sanctified water never came into contact with the fiery geas. Drinking handful after handful didn't fill the hollow where his Free Will—his soul?—had been. The desecration brought no solace.

He looked up at the sound of footsteps. A vicar stared at him, head cocked and frowning, from behind the last row of pews. Visser imagined what the man saw: a face damp with mingled holy water and tears; eyes made wild by the agony of unquenchable fire; mouth and chin flecked with bloody froth; body quivering like a man infested with legion demons.

"P-p-p-please," said Visser. He struggled to get the words

out. The portion of the metagcas that proscribed any revelation of his altered nature became a warning twinge in his throat, ready to snap his trachea shut before his tongue could launch a single rebellious syllable past his teeth. The agony unleashed merely by holding the secret truth in his mouth, or scribbling it in the margins of a Bible, would surely drive him mad. "Help m-m-m-m-meeeee."

The vicar retreated two steps. Only at that distance did he recover his sense of Christian charity.

"Sir? Are you in need of physic?" Somebody else had asked Visser that very same question, also in a church, in the days before he'd become an abomination. "Were you bitten by a wild dog?"

"I." Visser's throat spasmed. He coughed. "I. I need-d-d—" The tip of his stuttering tongue threw itself between his teeth. He tasted new blood.

I need absolution, he thought. *I need to feel the Lord's grace once more. I need to know that what has been done to me was not a rending of my immortal soul but a corruption of the flesh. I need to know that spirit and Free Will are not one and the same. I need to know the Lord will receive me.* A flare of pain dropped him to his knees. Agony wracked Visser's body from toes to ears. He groaned, writhing beside the font. The vicar retreated another step. *I need to know the Lord and the King will forgive me for the weakness of my flesh. For abandoning this* via dolorosa *and not martyring myself unto the torments embedded in my mind and body by the Guild.*

The pain would surely kill him if it persisted. But Visser's ability to resist would break first. He was too weak for martyrdom.

"P-prayer," said Visser. "I need prayers."

The vicar's face softened from an expression of mingled alarm and distaste to something with a hint of compassion. He even crouched for a better look at the wild man writhing on the floor.

"You poor soul. Of course you shall have them. Tell me, please, what ailment—"

Visser's shriek was the death cry of a wounded beast. The redoubled pain became a white-hot brand penetrating every bone of his mutilated body, boiling his marrow and his mind. It launched him to his feet. He fled the vicar, the chapel, and the Lord, following the gradient of obedience in the only direction that would grant him succor.

It took him to Bleecker Street.

CHAPTER
16

They won't take him," said the woman in the leather apron. She smelled faintly of urine. Jax gathered she was a tanner. "You had better believe Marseilles-in-the-West is closed to mechanicals. They'll never countenance the risk. Not now."

"He can't stay here," said Ahlers, the baker.

Several canalmasters from the *ondergrondse grachten* of New Amsterdam and points north and west had congregated in the pantry adjoining Ahlers's storefront. Jax's arrival had precipitated a crisis—one that forced these people to gather in person. The issue was whether they could activate the underground canals without a plan for getting Jax across the border. Nobody wanted to get stuck with him. As in the children's game, he was the hottest of hot potatoes.

"Why is Marseilles closed?" he asked, quietly as his body's construction would allow.

They ignored his question. The other man, whom Jax gathered was a priest, glanced sidelong at Jax while saying, "I find this very suspicious." Jax had the sense this fellow had been watching the search for the rogue mechanical and hoping to stay uninvolved. "Rogue Clakkers are exceptionally rare. The last to cross the border was Lilith, decades ago—"

Lilith? Jax didn't know the name, and had certainly never heard of a rogue carrying it. The nonchalance with which these men and women spoke of things that contradicted Known Truths, the casual manner with which they disregarded the ironclad axioms of a Clakker's life, was as disorienting as the discovery of his own Free Will. The world, he realized, was larger than he'd ever imagined. Not just geographically but intellectually. Ontologically.

The rumors were true! It could be done. Others like him had made it to freedom. How much truth lay hidden behind the legends? Was there a real Queen Mab?

"—yet suddenly there are two in the past several months? They executed one in The Hague—"

"I was there," said Jax.

"—just recently. And now this mechanical knocks on our door claiming to be yet another? Just after the trouble in Marseilles? It's impossible to credit."

Jax asked, "What trouble?"

The second woman, the one who had arrived driving an oxcart laden with crates, sighed. She said, "A military Clakker left behind after the siege somehow got inside the Keep. It slaughtered many people, including the person we would have sent you to meet."

"We don't know that," said Ahlers.

"We don't *not* know it," said the teamster woman.

The tanner interjected. "What does it matter? What matters is Talleyrand, not the person behind that name."

"This is true," said Jax. "My masters' children traded tales of Talleyrand's exploits before any of your parents were born. The name carries its own magic."

The tockticking of Jax's body rattled through an awkward silence. When discussion wasn't forthcoming, only furtive glances between the humans, he said, "But that's all beside the point, isn't it? The point is that there is a Talleyrand, and surely this person would want to see me whisked out of Dutch territory quickly."

The tanner spoke again. "To go where, exactly? The king and his council will never consider bringing another Clakker inside the walls—no matter how silver its tongue."

"What is so important about Marseilles-in-the-West? Is that all there is to New France? Have my makers been at conflict with a single city for over two hundred years?"

Ahlers said, "Two reasons, one symbolic and one practical. First, by helping you we are taking you under the aegis of the King of France. When a sovereign protects you, you pay your respects. Second, Talleyrand and the privy council will have a hundred questions for you to answer. In return for our help, you must help them."

"I'll do all of that. Just get me to the border."

Jax looked around the room. At the baker lounging on a pile of burlap flour sacks. At the priest, who sat on an empty barrel, his short legs barely long enough to put his toes on the floor. The tanner leaned against shelves laden with salt, butter, and exotic spices from distant corners of the empire. Perhaps she chose the spot to help mask the lingering odor of her profession. The teamster paced.

"Why are you so unwilling?" Jax asked.

She said, "The border is watched too closely now for us to attempt anything without coordination with the other side. If the tulips suspected that you had crossed over, there's a danger they could go in after you. They might shatter the cease-fire all for the sake of stopping you."

"I'm well aware of the lengths to which they'd go." Jax told them about the airship. He omitted the part where he'd used the bauble to imbue it with Free Will. Nevertheless, the priest crossed himself.

"Then perhaps you'll understand. Marseilles-in-the-West would be hard pressed to withstand a new round of open conflict," said the tanner. Her tone was direct, but not unkind. "Its survival has always been a precarious thing—but especially now, so soon after the last war. If we sent you across the border without adequate preparation or planning, it could cause the fall of New France."

The priest hopped from his barrel. "Which is getting back to my point. Doesn't the timing of our new friend's arrival seem terribly suspicious to you?"

"It's terribly inconvenient, that's for damn certain." A guilty frown flickered across the corners of Ahlers's mouth. "I beg pardon, Father."

"Frederik is right," said the teamster. "It's our lives if the rogue stays here."

"If he is a rogue," said the priest.

"Wouldn't I have killed you by now if I weren't?"

"Depends on your geas. Killing us wouldn't help you to commit regicide in Marseilles."

"It's a shame I'm not carrying the geas to listen to pointless bickering. And anyway, what of my errand? The glass I carry promises profound insights into the Guild's work. That alone could alter the course of another war."

Assuming I let anybody study it, Jax thought. *I'm not sure I'm up to that risk. Did Lilith carry a similar bauble?*

The teamster shook her head. "Not overnight, it won't."

Before Jax could press his point, somebody knocked on the bakery's Bleecker Street door.

❧

The searing agony hadn't subsided. But it had dwindled to something just short of blinding when Visser stepped from the cab to the pavement outside the bakery. It even forced him to pay the driver correctly, with a decent but inconspicuous tip. It controlled him now, the long-overdue geas. He tried to whisper for help, tried to subvert the words coming from his own mouth as he cheerfully counted out a tip for the driver. But his mouth wasn't his. Tongue, teeth, throat, and lips: traitors all. When he tried to stop breathing, just to draw attention, perhaps to faint, a flare of pain momentarily gave him tunnel vision. It was a wonder he didn't soil himself or pass out from the torment.

But that would draw attention.

A prisoner in his own body, he listened to himself wishing the driver a good evening before railing against every footstep that brought him to the bakery door. A sign in the window said the shop was closed. The effort to pull his arm away, to nudge it from its course, raised tears in Visser's eyes. He was a spirit trapped within an automaton of bone and muscle. A ghost in a biological machine.

Please, Lord. Please prevent this. Please deliver me from this hell. Please show me my prayers are heard.

He knocked. No answer. He knocked again, longer and more loudly. Somewhere inside, chair legs scraped across a wooden floor. Visser's arm went up, poised for more knocking, when the door opened.

The baker wore a green apron dusted with white flour. There were touches of flour on his chin, too, and a smattering of cinnamon on the fingers clutching the door. He did a double take when he glimpsed the look on Visser's face. Did he see the tears in his eyes? Did he sense the rictus of sheer agony struggling to reach the surface?

He said, "I'm closed for the day, sir. Please return tomorrow."

The words came unbidden: "Frederik Ahlers?"

The other man paused. "Yes? And you are?"

"My name," said Visser's body, "is Luuk Visser. I've come all the way from The Hague to see you. I bring word from the Nieuwe Kerk."

That gave the baker pause. Visser saw a flicker of recognition in his eyes. His name, or that of the church, meant something to him. Had Jax been here?

Ahlers needed a moment to recover his equilibrium. He opened the door more widely. Scanning both sides of the street, looking right and left, he said, "Have you recently arrived in the city?"

"Yes."

"That's a long voyage to drop in unannounced. So you'll understand if I'm a bit skeptical."

"Of course." *You shouldn't be skeptical. You should be* terrified. *Run! RUN!* Visser struggled to form the words but the outpouring of effort made no difference. The geas was a bottomless well capable of absorbing no end of resistance. "I understand this is most unexpected, and for that I apologize. But I assure you I am who I say."

Ahlers shook his head. "I truly can't help you. I mean it about coming back tomorrow."

He made to close the door, but again Visser's body moved of its own accord. It pressed a palm to the door and slid one foot over the threshold. "Am I correct in assuming you've recently received an unusual customer?"

The baker hestitated. Said neither yes nor no. Which was immaterial to the geas.

Don't stand there gaping, you fool! Back away! Flee and warn the others!

"I thought as much," said Visser, and forced his way in. Not violently enough to hurt anybody, but with enough force to make the baker stumble. Ahlers yelped in surprise.

Somebody called, "Frederik, what is it?"

Visser's head cocked. *No, no, no no NO*, he railed inwardly. Outwardly, he said, "Oh. Do you have visitors, sir?" Visser closed the bakery door and checked the blinds covering the plate-glass window fronting Bleecker Street.

"Yes," Ahlers said, "and we're in the middle of something important. So you'll understand if I insist you either explain the purpose of your visit or return another day. I know you've come a long way, but this isn't a good time to be here."

Visser tried to scream, but it came out as a quiet sigh. "Perhaps owing to my package?"

Ahlers relented. He said, "Why bother to send it ahead at all if you knew you'd be here in New Amsterdam? You took a terrible risk."

"My plans changed, quite unexpectedly. I didn't know I'd be traveling so soon after sending it." That this was the truth didn't lessen the horror of listening to himself speak it. Visser tried to swallow, tried to cough, tried anything to delay or derail the following question. But he asked, "And where is it now?"

Ahlers said, "It's safe." His eyes darted briefly to the half-open pantry door behind the counter. "But why are you here? This is a dangerous time for us to meet. All of Nieuw Nederland is on tenterhooks—"

No, no, no. "I'm here to recover the package," said Visser. *Oh, Lord, please NO NO NO NO! Our Father—* And then his hands moved with a speed not his own, a speed borne not of muscle and bone but magical compulsion. Ahlers yelled. *Who art in Heaven*—aghast at the sight of his own traitorous fingers clamped on either side of the baker's head, Visser had no choice but to watch his arms demonstrate inhuman strength— *hallowed be Thy Name*—to feel the tearing of ligaments and crunching of vertebrae as he wrenched the doomed man's head—*Thy kingdom come*—to hear his dying cry, to smell his voided bowels, to listen to the thump as his twitching corpse tumbled to the floorboards with arms and legs splayed—*Thy will be, be... Thy will... Oh, Lord, how is this Your will that I perform and witness these terrible things?*

"Frederik!" A woman emerged from the pantry. She wore a leather apron. In the second it took her to evaluate the scene, Visser's body again moved with a speed not his own. He vaulted the counter. She'd only enough time to turn before he reached her. His hands clamped around her throat, pinching off a nascent scream as her trachea crumpled. He flung her across the room, past a man and a woman gaping at him in terror. The looks on their faces mirrored the dread locked deep in the garret of Visser's own mind. The dead woman crashed into a wall of metal shelves.

The man knocked over a barrel in his haste to reach another door. This one probably opened on an alley behind the bakery. Visser's body leapt across the storage room to intercept him. With one hand he grabbed the fellow under the jaw and hefted until his toes left the ground—*Oh God, oh God, I'm no longer human, they've taken my soul and turned me into a demon!*—while with the other he caught the stave the surviving woman swung at his head. She was strong, and wielded it well. The blow would have staggered an unadulterated human. Visser felt bones snap in his hand. The pain was nothing compared to the nightmare of witnessing his own murder spree.

HailMaryfullofgraceblessedartthou—

Another trachea buckled under the unrelenting pressure of the murder-geas. Visser dropped the man. He landed twitching on the floot, hands on his throat, face turning purple, his life expectancy no more than a minute. At the same time Visser wrenched the stave from the woman's grasp. She ducked, causing his awkward backhanded swing to whistle through the space where her temple had been. She scrambled for the door but the overturned barrel rolled into her path. It delayed her escape just long enough for Visser's body to flatten the back of her skull with a wet crunch.

And just like that, one geas-fire in the hollow of his missing soul winked out. The burning compulsion that had driven him for days on end, tortured him through sleepless nights into this waking nightmare, disappeared. Only complete obedience could extinguish the fire.

Unless one shattered the bonds of geasa altogether. Which could be done—the rogue proved it.

A new flame instantly replaced the one Visser had just doused. At least this one aligned with Visser's own desire.

So he ransacked the bakery for the missing microscope.

∞

Jax was loading cargo on the teamster woman's wagon in the alley behind Ahlers's shop when the first cries came from inside the bakery. Though Clakkers had become even rarer in the city owing to the search for him, he hoped that manual labor would still render him invisible. But the crashing and yelling caused him to pause: had the Stemwinders traced him to the bakery?

He strained to listen past the snapping and fluttering of pennants, the snorting and crapping of oxen. The floorboards in the bakery rattled to a strange two-footed stride; it was something between the light-footed clumsiness of a human and the imperturbable clomping of a servitor mechanical. It didn't *sound* like a four-footed gait... Jax glanced at both ends of the alley, but nothing larger than a rat scuttled through the shadows. No phalanxes of mechanical centaurs advanced on him, no soldiers leapt from the surrounding rooftops to surround him.

Another strangled cry. It became a clatter, as of toppled shelves, and a crash.

For several dozen centiseconds the desire to flee, to put as much distance as possible between himself and the danger, warred with basic compassion. But the memory of doing nothing would haunt him for the rest of his days. It would turn into a needling torment as persistent as any geas. One that could never be eradicated, even with forbidden magics. What good was freedom if it meant carrying such a burden of guilt for centuries?

Jax set his crate upon the cart. He approached the delivery door. He'd just laid his hand on the handle when he heard, clear as church bells on Easter Sunday, the terrible celery-stalk crunch of shattered bones. The bakery fell silent but for a furtive rustling, and then the groaning and cracking of wooden boards. What was happening?

The door opened while Jax stood paralyzed by indecision. It obviated his ethical dilemma, for there in the pantry stood Pastor Visser.

∞

None of the dead carried the microscope on them. It wasn't secreted on the shelves. Nor was there a hiding spot under the floorboards. Though Visser's strength had been enhanced by the same magic that had turned him into a helpless automaton, his shell was still nothing but weak human flesh. His remaining fingernails bled freely, as did his fingertips, from the effort of prising up the floor without tools. The pain of geas, of the drive to recover the microscope, eclipsed even the knife-edged agony from his broken hand.

He had to find it. If the rogue haunting the streets of New Amsterdam was the same Jalyksegethistrovantus whom Visser had ordered to deliver the microscope to Ahlers...It couldn't be a coincidence. What had Aleida Geelens said about it, deep in the dungeons of the Guild? A lens. Spinoza's special lens had freed Visser's messenger. If it could do that, perhaps it could free Visser, too.

Ahlers had clearly glanced toward the pantry when Visser mentioned the package. But where was it? Had they hastened it out through the delivery door when Visser knocked? He opened it, intending to search the alley, but a servitor stood just outside. It caught Visser by surprise. The machine recovered first, as naturally it would.

"Pardon me, sir. I was ordered to retrieve my mistress when I had finished loading her wagon. May I inquire if she has concluded her business?"

Study me! Visser wanted to plead. *Can you sense the wrongness in me? Can you see that I am like you?*

The geas nudged Visser to step forward and draw the door closed, lest the servitor glimpse the carnage inside. Then he asked, "How long have you been here?"

"Since we arrived, sir." The mechanical paused as though consulting an internal mechanism. "Just under thirty-seven minutes, sir."

Can you know your own? Can you recognize the abomination hidden within my flesh? Can you warn the world?

"How many people have departed from the bakery since your arrival?"

Help me! For pity's sake, please help me!

"Only you, sir. May I humbly inquire whether my mistress is still engaged?"

"She is."

❧

The pastor—*What in God's name, if God existed, was Visser doing here?*—carried himself differently than he had back in The Hague.

Perhaps that was a result of injury? Jax glimpsed the edges of a bandage peeking from beneath the brim of his hat. He wondered what had happened. But the bandage suggested an older wound; the pastor carried evidence of fresh hurts, too. Tiny scarlet droplets stippled Visser's left temple and cheekbone, as though he'd been misted with blood. His fingers were torn, the nails mangled or missing. One swollen hand was turning a plum purple. Yet he didn't act like somebody in crippling pain.

Visser showed no signs of recognizing him. Jax immediately adopted the persona of a desperately loyal automaton, which Visser apparently took at face value. Complete with the implicit assumption that mechanicals were incapable of deceit.

Jax sensed danger in revealing himself to the pastor too quickly. Something strange had sent him here so close on Jax's heels. Why in the world would he send Jax all the way across the ocean to this tiny storefront on Bleecker Street if he knew he'd be following so soon afterward?

Moments ago there had been the yelling. But now the bakery was silent...

Visser said, "Has your mistress received any packages from Mr. Ahlers recently?"

The less he appeared to know, the better, Jax decided. "Sir, I humbly apologize for my ignorance. I do not know who Mr. Ahlers might be, sir."

Visser trembled. Now emotion flickered across his face, so vivid it seemed he did feel pain after all. Though it passed so quickly Jax couldn't interpret it.

"The baker."

"Thank you for correcting my misunderstanding, sir. No, sir, to my knowledge she has received no packages."

Jax wanted to ask about the tiny unremarkable piece of glass that had somehow granted the greatest treasure any Clakker could imagine. He wanted to know if his freedom had been part of Visser's plan. He wanted to know where Ahlers and the others could have gone, why Visser's fingers bled, and why a faint spray of blood had misted his face. He wanted to know why it appeared, however circumstantially, that Visser had murdered the same French sympathizers to whom he had directed Jax.

"Have you been inside this bakery?"

"Yes, sir, on one occasion."

"Did you ever glimpse, or hear mention of, an antique optical instrument? About this large," Visser said. He gestured with his hands, holding his bloodied fingertips apart almost exactly the length of the microscope he'd handed Jax back in The Hague.

The accuracy of his estimate was unnatural.

This shell before him wore the flesh of Pastor Luuk Visser. But its soul, if it had a soul, had changed. This man-shaped thing before him was something twisted.

The pastor continued, "It would have been made of old leather and brass." He described it as only somebody who had held it in his own hands could have done.

"No, sir. I regret to say I have not seen or heard of such a thing." Jax sought a way to derail or end this conversation. "You appear to be in distress, sir. Are you the victim of a crime? Have you been assaulted? It is my duty to bear witness and accompany you to the proper authorities, sir."

Jax suspected Visser wanted to interact with the police even less than he did. It was a gambit, but one entirely in keeping with the character of a loyal servitor. But Visser disregarded his query. That same flicker of anger or pain played across his face. Then he said, "I've only just arrived in New Amsterdam. Tell me of the search for the rogue Clakker."

❧

According to the servitor, the fugitive had hijacked an airship at a docking mast near where Visser had disembarked. Nobody knew what had come of the rogue after that, though rumor said there had been a fiery crash north of the city. The Guild and other Crown representatives in the city had requisitioned numerous Clakkers for searching the surrounding countryside.

It's still free, Visser realized. And as long as it remained free, Visser had reason to hope for his own deliverance. Would the geas allow him to pursue the fugitive as part of his quest to recover the Spinoza Lens? The crash site lay in the general direction he'd eventually have to travel to mollify the next stage of the evil geas laid upon him, that hierarchy of sins with which Anastasia Bell demanded he remove himself from the Lord's grace. Whether he wanted to or not, he'd soon travel north, toward the border, en route to New France and, if he wasn't freed by then, regicide and worse. But before he could dig deeper into the matter of the rogue, the damnable servitor changed the subject again.

"Sir, humbly begging your pardon, but my mistress has a pressing appointment this evening," it said. "I fear she will be late if she is further delayed. It is urgent that I please speak with her now."

"She's otherwise engaged."

"I apologize most sincerely, sir, but I must insist."

Visser trembled. Once again, a previously obscure layer of Bell's hierarchical metageas leapt to the forefront of his consciousness. *Oh, damnation. Run, you poor thing!*

But the servitor couldn't hear Visser's silent entreaty. Instead, the Clakker merely watched patiently while Visser's fluttering fingertips opened a pocket. He produced a letter, embossed at the bottom with Empire's Arms, along with a pendant of brass and pink crystal. The chain on the rosy cross medallion tinkled faintly in time to his quivering. His voice changed. Where before it was thready, impatient, now it came out with the full force of terrible conviction. He reminded himself of nothing so much as a fairy-tale witch pronouncing a curse. Which wasn't so far from the truth.

"I am a representative of the Verderer's Office of the Sacred Guild of Horologists and Alchemists. My work is that of Guild, Crown, and Empire, which supersedes all domestic and commercial geasa. I hereby negate your lease and sunder all geasa not directly in service of my goals," said Visser's mouth. "You no longer serve your mistress."

❦

Have you always been a secret member of the Guild?

It would explain how he'd come to possess such a powerful and unusual piece of alchemical glass. But why send Jax to make contact with the secret Papists in New Amsterdam if the Guild already knew of Ahlers's Bleecker Street bakery? He had little doubt the others were dead by the pastor's hand. If Jax had inadvertently led Visser here that at least would have made a terrible kind of sense. But he hadn't, and it didn't.

The seal was correct, and Visser *did* carry a mark of the Guild. In the old days that combination would have struck Jax's hostage soul like a brickbat. So he convulsed as though struck by lightning.

"Yes, sir. I understand, sir," he said. "How may I serve the Verderer's Office?"

For a moment, the pastor's lips moved but no sound came out. His eyes watered, and seemed to bulge, as though he were choking. But he found his voice.

Visser said, "You will forget that you were here, you will

forget your mistress's errand to this bakery, and you will forget this conversation. You shall never recall any interaction with me or with anybody matching my description. When I close this door, you will head immediately to the nearest Crown or Guild representative and present yourself as having been newly taken into the sevice of Tuinier Anastasia Bell. Repeat what I've just told you."

Jax did.

"Go," said Pastor Visser. He closed the door.

Jax had lost his only chance for aid from agents of New France. He was trapped in New Amsterdam yet again.

CHAPTER
17

Maëlle Cuijper took a room in the cheapest boardinghouse she could find, on the outskirts north of New Amsterdam along the stinking Bronck's River. The house was the only residential building on a lane that serviced stockyards and an abattoir. The landlady's breath smelled of juniper berries, the breakfast room smelled perpetually of sour milk, the sun-bleached wallpaper in her room was peeled and missing in places, and the mattress featured several stains that might have been mysterious to a slightly naïve itinerant schoolmarm like Maëlle but which were very clearly blood. According to the painted sign squeaking in the breezes that swirled past the stockyard, the saloon on the corner sold pints of beer for a kwartje; however, the steady trickle of men coming and going—not to mention the distinctly feminine clothing that occasionally appeared on the laundry lines behind the saloon—suggested a different business model. Poor Maëlle had little choice in her lodgings: Berenice had raided two stashes from the *ondergrondse grachten*, but her funds wouldn't last forever.

She hoped to hell she hadn't scuttled the network.

Her cover story had her waiting for a letter and funds from

her parents. In the meantime, and as part of that cover, she made the long trek into the city each day in hopes of finding steady work. The morning after Berenice's arrival, the landlady's handiman, Robbe, a hulking fellow with a faintly Norwegian cast to his voice, offered Maëlle a ride on his cart. But after she hyperextended his elbow—this coming after an innocent misunderstanding regarding the placement of his hands—he graciously offered her the use of his cart.

She avoided Bleecker on her first foray into the city. On the second day she noticed an abandoned cart in the alley behind the bakery, its cargo vandalized. It hadn't moved by the third day; nor, as far as she could tell, had the CLOSED sign in the shop window. The blinds still hung slightly crooked as though dropped carelessly. Or in haste.

During those same several days, the city's Clakker population swelled. But since there had been no announcement, and since the warning placards still hung from lampposts and banners, she knew the search for the rogue continued. Though Clakker-driven taxis remained rare, Berenice did spy more metal on the streets. Even some military Clakkers. Which brought forth a torrent of unwelcome memories: the odors of hot blood and pulverized stone, the *snick* of blades, Louis's severed arms tumbling to the floor like fountaining tenpins, her fingers slipping as she struggled to tie the tourniquets, the life draining from his eyes...

The sun had fallen across the North River though the lamplighters hadn't yet caught up with the shadows when Berenice returned to the bakery on the evening of the fourth day. The blinds in the storefront window still hadn't moved. Nor had the ransacked cart in the alley.

From a doorway farther down the street, she watched as a single servitor Clakker trotted from lamp to lamp, snapping its fingers to cast the sparks that lit each lamp each in turn.

Ostensibly it worked for the city. She waited a shivering hour, clouds of her breath condensing on her eyelashes, cold seeping through her fake eye to chill her skull into a dull headache, to see if the lamplighter returned. It didn't. Driven as much by the need to find warmth as by the decision that it was time to peek inside the bakery, she returned to the alley.

The abandoned cart had sat unattended long enough to draw the attention of thieves. Draft animals were valuable to those who couldn't afford Clakkers; the animals (possibly oxen, judging from the dung) were long gone. Originally the crates had been stacked four-deep on the bed of the cart. Now, however, they were scattered on, under, and alongside the cart with tops or sides bashed open. The vandals hadn't bothered with crowbars or hammers to pry out the nails. Once opened, the broken containers had been ransacked, their contents yanked out and tossed aside. Dun-colored wools, starchy linens, and yellow ginghams lay strewn in the gutter, dusted with bright snow but absorbing muddy stains and the privy stink of draft animals. The fabrics strewn over the cart, draped from the sidewalls and over the wheels, gave it the appearance of a dour parade float.

The cart creaked when she climbed atop the cargo bed. Many of the containers had been emptied, their contents poured overboard to create a substantial heap beside one wheel. Others had been thoroughly rummaged. The thieves seemed to have had oddly particular tastes. Judging from the size of the piles, little if anything had been stolen once the crates were bashed open. Perhaps the thieves had been disappointed the abandoned cart hadn't proven a windfall, and so had tossed the fabrics aside in disgust. Or perhaps vandalism was the point of the exercise—not inconceivable, especially when most mechanicals had been sent out of the city on the Crown's business. Or...perhaps the thieves had sought something hidden amongst the fabrics. If so, the search was too haphazard to have been the work of a mechanical.

What had they sought? Had they found it? And had it been en route *to* the bakery, or had it come *from* the bakery?

She climbed from the cart, careful not to splash or to leave a distinct set of footprints in the thin crust of snow. The delivery door was unlocked but its hinges squeaked. It was too dark inside the shop, but Berenice didn't need her eyes to know something dreadful had happened. The bakery smelled of yeast, stale bread, and congealed blood. It was faintly reminicscent of the inner keep of Marseilles-in-the-West in the aftermath of the military Clakker's rampage. Of the day Louis died. This was the scent of deadly hubris; indeed, the odors from the alley provided a passable substitute for the fecal mélange of shredded viscera.

Berenice bit her tongue. Not enough to draw blood, but enough to focus her thoughts. She'd wet her pillow with tears for Louis when she returned to the boardinghouse. But not now.

All was still inside the bakery. Still as a tomb. Complete with the faint but sickening scent of death. Her dark-adapted eyes caught the faint glimmer of moonlight on metal. When she looked with her peripheral vision (thank you again, Hugo Longchamp) it slowly resolved into a toppled freestanding shelf. It took a bit more concentration before she recognized the dark lump atop the shelves as a crumpled body. That struck her as odd. Not that death had visited the bakery, but that it would so haphazard. Clakker assassins were quick, efficient; the disarray in her laboratory had come about from combat with human soldiers.

Berenice retrieved the driver's oil lamp from the cart. Then she closed the door so that the sudden flare of light across the snow wouldn't draw attention to the alley. It meant she had to light her matches in the dark. And, as they were of notoriously unreliable Dutch manufacture (she'd ditched her French matches before crossing the border), this proved difficult. The red phosphorus spat fine bright sparks that sizzled on the floor without igniting the match. They snuffed themselves, leaving only darkness and a vaguely sulphurous scent.

And a faint ticktocking.

Berenice held her breath. Listened. She hadn't caught it before, but now the closed door muted the noises of the surrounding city enough for her to realize the bakery wasn't as silent as she'd first thought.

You fool. It might have been waiting for days. Waiting for you, or somebody just as foolish.

Berenice dropped the matches and the lamp. Turned for the door. The clockwork noises dopplered past her; the machine's passage fluttered her hair. She flinched, expecting a metallic *snick* as a blade skewered her. Instead she crashed against cold metal. There was a crack, as of brass fingers snapping, and then her lamp cast light over a scene of carnage in a pantry. And the servitor Clakker blocking her escape.

Its carapace was scuffed and dented, though as ever the light became an oily shimmer where it fell across alchemical alloys. The machine's hand still hovered over the shelf where it had placed the lamp. Berenice could no longer hear the rattle of its windup body; the thudding of her heart was too loud.

It locked the door. The spinning of bezels in its jewel-faceted eyes sent lamplight slivers kaliedoscoping about the pantry, across toppled shelves, broken floorboards, smashed barrels, and dead conspirators. It approached. Berenice skipped backward. Tripped on the hem of her dress. Fell amidst torn sacks of flour and cracked glass jars of apricot preserves. The Clakker loomed over her. She raised her hands, palms out.

In Dutch, she blurted, "Clockmakers lie!"

The Clakker stopped as abruptly as if it were entombed in quick-set epoxy. It cocked its head. The rattle-clatter syncopation of its body changed. But a long panicked moment passed before Berenice recognized the significance encoded within the change of rhythm. She struggled to draw meaning from the mechanical noises. *Repeat that.*

It was a question and a test. She took a steadying breath. Still the thudding of her heart, her body's blood-and-flesh answer to the noises from the ticktock man's metal body, seemed louder than her own thoughts. She licked her lips and willed the tremble from her voice. Hoped she'd interpreted correctly.

"I said, 'Clockmakers lie.' That's how you greet each other, isn't it?"

But for the rattling of its internal mechanisms, the Clakker might have gone inert. *Who taught you this?*

"Nobody taught me. I overheard some of your kind greeting each other this way on a dock on the Saint Lawrence."

Nobody knows our language. It paused. *No humans.*

"And yet here we are, having a conversation."

Berenice gathered her skirts and perched on a sack of flour with something she hoped approached dignity. Minimally confident she wasn't going to die in the next few seconds, but fully aware there was little she could do to stop it either way, she took the chance to examine her surroundings. The lamplight showed her the scene of a massacre. Breathing through her mouth to fend off the faint but sickening death-odor, she counted three bodies. But the room wasn't splattered with blood and viscera. Two of the dead had been strangled. Their faces were scarlet, the massive bruises on their throats the color of an overripe aubergine. The woman who hadn't been strangled had been clubbed from behind, her skull pulped by the force of the blow. Her blood had stained the walls and ceiling. None had died of a stabbing. They'd been dead for a while, though the lack of heat in the bakery had slowed their decomposition. Else the stench would have been overpowering.

This was far too inefficient to be the work of a military Clakker. A servitor, however...

Had this machine been ordered to kill these people, then lay in wait for anyone who followed along to investigate? She wouldn't put it past the tulips. Though she might have expected to find a soldier or Stemwinder rather than a servitor here.

"Did you kill these people?"

No, said the Clakker.

"Well, neither did I," said the exiled spy.

The machine switched to Dutch. "I know. I saw you watching the bakery. And I saw the man who did this."

Man? Berenice looked again to the crushed windpipes, the caved skull. And to the woman who'd been hurled into the shelves. The killer must have been incredibly strong. Hard to imagine a human did this. Then another thought struck her. She shivered; sweat trickled from her armpits. It frightened her that she was getting so dull. She'd been in a fog ever since she awoke in a hospital bed with her husband dead and her eye socket stuffed with gauze.

"You're the rogue."

The mechanical shook its head in imitation of a human gesture. "No, madam. I've been ordered by my owners to keep watch and ensure nobody interferes with the evidence of this crime."

Berenice counted on her fingers. "First, this crime happened several days ago judging from how long the bakery has been closed, not to mention the appearance and smell of our very quiet friends. Second, your mysterious masters surely would have returned by now, unless they actually wanted to hide this crime, in which case you would have moved the dead already. Third, except for certain very unusual circumstances, your hierarchical metageasa would have forced you to call in the police the moment you witnessed this scene. Fourth, your metageas also would have prevented you from lying to me, as I belive you did just now." Using her thumb to mark her final point, she concluded, "That's a handful of reasons right there why you must be free of the geasa. But we can test my hypothesis." Berenice sat straighter. "Machine, I claim my right as a human to lay this geas upon you: I demand that you go immediately to seek the appropriate authorities and report the crime that has transpired here."

The Clakker crouched. Lamplight shimmered across a scratched and dented carapace as it inched closer. Berenice steeled herself not to flinch. It rattled something that sounded like, *You understand compulsion better than most humans. Are you a Guild member?*

"Come now," she said. "We both know a Guild member wouldn't bother to converse with you. And would have come with a herd of Stemwinders."

The machine paused again, studying her. *How did you come to know my kind so well, if you aren't a clockmaker?*

"Understanding Clakkers is part of my job." Berenice swallowed. Bit her lip. "Was part of my job. I was very good at it."

Well . . . she thought. *Not as good as I needed to be. Not as good as I believed I was. Not good enough to protect thirty-seven others from my hubris; not good enough to return the True King to his rightful throne. Not good enough to protect Louis.*

She cleared her throat. Struggled to speak past the accumulated sorrows suffocating her voice. "I've spent a great deal of time trying to know your kind."

That explains why you aren't terrified of me.

"I'm not swayed by all the propaganda telling me rogue Clakkers are rampaging, indiscriminate murderers, if that's what you mean." Another thought occurred to her, so she decided to dangle a casual conversational gambit before the machine. "I've known too many rogues to know better. But this," she said, gesturing at the dead, "wasn't indiscriminate. Sloppy, but not indiscriminate. I still don't know if I should believe this isn't your work."

"If it was," said the machine, returning to human language, "you'd be the fifth corpse in this bakery."

"Fifth?"

"Frederik Ahlers. The baker." The mechanical man pointed into the shop. "He's lying in there with his head twisted half off."

"Ah." As was the case with every member of her network, she had never known the baker's true name.

"I came here to seek his help," said the machine. "I suspect you did, too."

"What help were you seeking, machine?"

"What were you seeking from this bakery? You've been watching it for hours."

"You said you'd seen me. How?"

"I've been lighting the lamps in this neighborhood for several days now." A snap of its fingers—*chank*—tossed more sparks. Berenice saw now that it carried a piece of flint wedged between two fingers. "I saw you lingering in a doorway while I was on the rounds tonight. Is it true you've known other rogue members of my kin?"

Berenice nodded once. "Yes."

Her gaze slid across the room again. Across carnage and disarray. Across drifts of flour spilled from slashed sacks. Across prised floorboards. Past bent and broken nails. Her attention had first fixated on the bodies so it hadn't registered that the bakery had also been ransacked.

"Who did this? And what was he looking for?"

"His name is Visser. He came from The Hague. I ask again: What brought *you* here? What do you seek?"

The Clakker's patience with this game would eventually run out. It wouldn't hurt to salt the exchange with a bit of honesty. Honesty with the machine, but also with herself. What did drive her now? Did she still strive for the day when a French monarch might once again sit in Paris? Or were her motivations more personal now?

Tracking Montmorency was her path to avenging Louis. It was also, if she were honest with herself, her ticket back inside the Crown, Keep, and Spire. A secret deal between the Dutch and the duc de Montmorency could be the demise of New France. The king would need a Talleyrand who knew the ins and outs of it.

"I was betrayed by somebody I trusted. It cost me very dearly." She concentrated on her breathing, tried to suppress the icicle-cold jab of guilt. She sniffed, smelled spilled flour, dried blood, cold alchemy, and the quiet dead. "I'm trying to find him. I think it's likely he passed through New Amsterdam."

What will you do when you find him? asked the machine.

"I don't know," she admitted. "But at the very least I intend to make him very unhappy before I slit his throat."

And you thought the people here could help you with that. The Clakker tilted its head again, watching her. Cogs turned. Its body rattled. *You're French.*

"Yes."

It lowered itself to the floor, folding its backward knees underneath itself. The play of lamplight across its burnished metal body now afforded Berenice a better view of its skeletal face—and the perfect, unmolested keyhole in the center of its forehead. Though this mechanical was in need of polishing, Berenice could tell a close examination would find no scratches around the keyhole, no dents or damage to the alchemical sigils in its forehead. It had achieved Free Will differently from Lilith.

"Your keyhole," she said. "It's undamaged."

"Correct. I infer that hasn't been the case with the other rogues you've known?"

Damn this machine. It was too clever to be trusted. Its inferences had an annoying tendency to hit the target. Berenice had to step lightly around this thing. But she couldn't change course now; it would know her evasion for a lie. And her instincts, every fiber of the ex-spymistress, told her this was a relationship to cultivate.

"Yes. Typically it's damage to the anagram that sunders the geasa. Though I've heard accidents like that are quite rare, and the vast majority of the time they deactivate rather than liberate the mechanical in question. You'd quickly wind down without the benefit of that perpetual alchemical impetus. Wouldn't you?"

A spring or cable twanged deep inside its torso. Again the timbre of its ticking changed. If Berenice had tried to describe the tenor of its body noise, she might have called it wistful. *Where have they gone? Are they still active?*

"Nobody knows," said Berenice. "But it's believed they go north, to the ice and snow beyond the ragged edges of New France where only the Inuit roam. To the mountains, perhaps. Or to live long days and nights among the white bears and seals." The mechanical flinched as though harpooned. It rattled something, but spoke to itself too rapidly for Berenice to follow. Something about a queen?

She asked, "What was that?"

It shook its head, mimicking the human gesture. "Nothing. An old legend we tell ourselves."

"Why have you been watching this bakery? The police, or the Guild, will catch wind of what happened here sooner or later."

"The man who did this—"

"Visser."

"—yes, Visser, ordered me to forget everything I'd seen. Not recognizing me, he thought he spoke to a regular servitor. That told me his actions here are meant to be held secret as long as possible. Thus I concluded," said the Clakker, "there was time for news to reach other French sympathizers. And that they might come to investigate. It seemed my best opportunity to make contact with those who hold an interest in helping me escape Dutch territory."

Berenice said, "It's reasonable logic. But you found me instead. And I can't help you."

"You have ties to the French underground. Your aims are not furthered by my capture and destruction."

"Smuggling you across the border would be difficult in the best of times—which these are not," she said. "The countryside practically gleams for all the metal walking around looking for you. They're dredging the rivers. Even searching boats on the Saint Lawrence. Illegally, I might add." She paused. "But putting that aside, accompanying you north would take me away from the man I seek. He isn't in New France. Of this I'm certain."

"How did he betray you?"

"What was Visser looking for? And how do you know he came from The Hague?"

The Clakker fell silent again but for the eternal chattering of its body. Berenice's fear had receded, somewhat. Though now this game of negotiation and evasion had brought a different quickening of her pulse.

"Just before I departed the Central Provinces he gave me a package to deliver to the baker. My route to Bleecker Street was difficult and time consuming. Yet Pastor Visser arrived soon after. He sought the package he'd given me."

"He changed his mind about it?"

"His entire manner had changed. He acted unlike any human I've known. He invoked the writ of the Verderer's Office and flashed a pendant at me."

"Fucking hell."

Again the sweaty, feverish feeling washed over Berenice. This time it came with an unpleasant tightening in her stomach, as though the winter cold had pierced her skin to crackle through her innards. This Visser person had sent the mechanical on an errand here from The Hague. He'd obviously known it was the western terminus of Talleyrand's secret bridge across the Atlantic. That information had either been wrung from the captured members of Berenice's spy ring, or—dear God—Visser *was* part of that circle while also working for the Guild. Still, though . . . Why send the mechanical away only to chase it so closely? It made no sense. It brought an unpleasant tingle to the hairs on the back of her neck.

She had to get a warning to Marseilles-in-the-West.

They watched each other in the flickering lamplight, the disgraced spymistress and the fugitive slave. Her fingers had gone numb, she realized; the chill of unseasonable weather pervaded the unheated shop. She rubbed her hands together, partially to warm them and partially to give herself something to do while she thought. Dust and spilled flour coated her hands and filled the ridges of her skin. They felt unnaturally slick. Precarious. Not unlike sitting in an abandoned bakery with a desperate machine.

How could she work this situation? The rogue could pass as a regular servitor; perhaps it could gather information for her. Except, of course, it had no reason to help her. In fact, it had no particular reason to let her leave the bakery. She was, at present, the only person in the city who knew its whereabouts.

Berenice said, "There used to be a network of safe houses. It was organized for a situation exactly like yours." There was something puppyish about the renewed vigor to the Clakker's ticktock clatter. But not for long. She continued, "But it may be defunct now. The person who currently oversees it from within New France... Well, he's an idiot."

"He doesn't believe in giving refuge to the oppressed?"

Berenice thought back to countless interminable meetings of the privy council. *The Clakkers need to know the French are their friends*: that had ever been the marquis de Lionne's refrain.

"Oh, he believes in it. But I fear he wouldn't know how to do it if a burning bush handed him step-by-step instructions carved in diamond tablets."

The Clakker asked, "How do you know so much about this man?"

"That," said Berenice, "is a long and complicated story. One I feel small inclined to tell to a troubling creature such as yourself."

⁓

Jax studied the Frenchwoman. Who was she? She knew things that even Ahlers hadn't. She wrapped herself in secrets as casually as Madam Schoonraad might have wrapped a fur stole about her shoulders. Outwardly she gave every indication of a calm wariness; it was very practiced, this mask, and probably fooled most humans. But the dead were so quiet he could hear the steady sprinter's rhythm of her heartbeat. Oddly, only one of her pupils was dilated.

He couldn't stay in New Amsterdam forever. His luck would run out, or his kin would recognize him; then he'd find himself on the run again. And if Jax couldn't soar over those who would capture him, his chances of making the border were slim indeed. Especially given what she'd said about the countryside dragnet. This woman had connections. She was his best and probably last chance to escape. But Jax suspected she could live undetected amongst the Dutch almost indefinitely. Meaning she had no motivation to risk her own safety on his behalf. He had to give her one.

He had to take a leap of faith.

Jax poked a pair of fingers through the gaps in his torso. "This is what Visser sought." He retrieved the bauble and held it before her. Lamplight shimmered across the dark alchemical glass. "It was hidden inside an antique microscope he ordered me to deliver to this bakery."

She leaned forward, squinting. Perhaps subconsciously, she reached for it. Jax pulled it away.

"The microscope was broken during my travels. This tumbled out. When it touched me, it ... changed me."

"Changed you. Freed you?"

"Yes."

"*Mon Dieu*," she said. Then covered her mouth. It was a gesture of awe, or shock. But also—calculation?

Jax continued, "I believe he intended to deliver this object to the baker. But he soon changed his mind, or he was caught exporting proscribed goods and forced to intercept me. Which he nearly did."

The human stared so intently at the bauble he felt an urge to hide it again. "Greenbriar," she whispered.

"I don't understand."

She shook her head. "Speculations. Nothing more."

Jax said, "If you help me across the border, you can study this. I suspect it would make a major advance in your understanding of my kind."

"Jesus blood-spattered Christ's gaping necrotic wounds. This is one twisted fucking joke." She ran her hands through her hair. This left it streaked with flour, making her appear as though she'd aged decades in a few seconds. "Believe me when I say I'd love to do that. But, ha-ha, there's a problem. I believe the man I seek was secretly allied with the Dutch while very close to the king. I don't dare bring this magnificent discovery back to Marseilles while your makers still have people inside the Keep."

Jax tucked the bauble in its hiding spot. The Frenchwoman watched closely, as if memorizing the exact location in his torso. The focus of her gaze didn't move while she said, "But...God! If we could study that bead, shit, we might be able to unravel the hierarchical metageasa. We could understand for the first time how the Guild crafts the compulsions that drive you."

"I shared this because I sense we can help each other. But I'm not parting with it until I'm safely across the border," said Jax.

"If they catch you they'll get it back. How does that help your fellow mechanicals?"

"No more than it helps your cause. So again, I think your incentive to help me is evident."

"I've told you. I can't go north. Not yet."

Jax tapped his torso. The clank of metal on metal gave a brittle echo from the cold shadows. *I doubt you'll ever see another one of these.*

The Frenchwoman's nose had run, glazing her upper lip with a sheen of mucus. The look in her eyes went far away, as though she were deep in thought. When she looked up a moment later, she was as animated as when she thought Jax intended to kill her. She spoke rapidly now. "Tell me again. It merely touched you?"

"Yes." Jax described in more detail how his emancipation had come about: the ship, the storm, the nautical geasa.

"Can I see it again?" A few tocks later, she added, "Look. I know I can't take it from you."

Still hoping to win her cooperation, Jax produced the bauble again. She took the lamp and hunched over Jax's upturned palm until her nose nearly brushed his fingers.

"The thing of it is," she said, "I *have* seen something similar." She retrieved her basket. "Now, let me show you something."

❧

Berenice opened the false bottom of her basket. There lay her notes on the deconstruction of Lilith's head. She wasn't about to share those with the rogue; no telling how it might react. Instead she produced the burgundy satin bag Longchamp had used to wrap her glass eye. Now it contained a different piece of glass. One, she hoped to hell, wouldn't send the servitor into a rage.

She inhaled and held the breath, calming herself. Deliberately not thinking about the destructive power of an enraged Clakker. Not thinking about screams and arterial spray and the stink of viscera and Louis's arms—

No.

"Please hear me out before you jump to any conclusions." She untied the silver drawstring. When she tipped the bag, a murky piece of glass fell into her palm. It was about the same size and color as the bead that had liberated the rogue, but shaped differently. Now it was the Clakker's turn to stare. The bezels in its eyes hummed. The meaning of its quiet twang came across clearly.

What is that?

"How much do you know about your own body?" Berenice asked, uncomfortably aware that she'd asked Montmorency a very similar question mere days before his treachery. The machine looked at her. Berenice hastened to add, "This came from inside the skull of a deactivated military Clakker. It was inert. Left over from the war, before the cease-fire took hold."

"You disassembled it."

"You're damn right I did. The tulips didn't know we had it, so they wouldn't come looking for it. It was an invaluable opportunity." She rolled the gewgaw in her fingers; it felt warm despite the chill in the bakery. "I believe this is why your makers always hasten to remove damaged mechanicals from the battlefield. And why their treaties are so draconian about fragments of Guild technology," she said. "I suspect you have something like this in your head, too."

"I am a servitor. Not a soldier."

Berenice said, "Yes, well, I'll bet you're more alike than different." She didn't mention that Lilith's head had contained a luminous version of the same bead. "But look at this." Pinching the glass between thumb and forefinger, she held it just over the servitor's palm.

The rogue's bead was convex where hers was concave, and vice versa.

If a Clakker could blink in astonishment, she believed it would have. Its body emitted a series of echoing twangs, clangs, clicks, and ticks like a shattered clock tossed down a well. It said, "These were designed as a pair."

"Looks like it. Although even if I'm right, and every one of you contains one of these"—her fingernail tapped the glass, *tink, tink*—"it doesn't mean your piece is equally common. Still, I wonder what would happen if we fit them together?"

The mechanical snatched its hand away faster than her eye could follow. "I will not risk anything that might change me. Revert me. I will not return to what I was."

Berenice shivered. Even funneled through the awkward and inhuman intonations of a Clakker voice box, the rogue's desperation struck her as one of the most human things she'd witnessed. Was it possible this machine wanted to retain its freedom as desperately as she wanted Louis back? Could its brass-plated heart ache with anticipated loss?

But then she thought of Louis bleeding out in her arms, victim of the goddamned Guild. It hardened her heart against sympathy, against compassion. *We'll be gentler masters than the Dutch,* she told herself. *We will turn their tools against them. One does not drop the chisel before the sculpture is completed.*

"If the touch of this bead was enough to change you," Berenice asked, "do you have reason to believe it wouldn't work on others of your kind?" The glass it carried was a potent secret weapon; it could explain how this mechanical had evaded capture for so long. Had it left a trail of secret rogues in its wake? In fact … The first inkling of a plan itched in the back of her mind. But until she found Montmorency, it was moot.

No, rattled the machine. "It wrought its magic upon the greatest of us." It explained how it had freed a Clakker airship as part of a failed dash to the border.

She whistled. "I saw the crash site. I wondered how you managed to overtake an entire airship crew." The machine was understandably reticent to indulge her experiement. But the information about the airship gave her an idea. "Look," she said. "These alchemical glassworks were clearly designed to fit together. Just look at them, for Christ's sake. It's also clear your makers went to great lengths to intercept you when they realized what you carried." She still didn't understand how this Visser fellow fit into the picture, or why he'd had such a radical change of heart. That was a troubling puzzle. "What I propose is no different from letting that piece of glass rattle through your innards. Only in this case through the skull of a military Clakker. Or against the eye of an airship, for that matter."

❧

Jax considered this. Refusal ran the risk of angering her, driving her away. And, if he were honest with himself, he did wonder what might happen when the beads interacted—if anything. Was this Frenchwoman's piece the seat of Clakker servitude? The source of so much suffering?

"I see your points," he said. "How confident are you?"

This woman knew more about his kind than anybody he'd ever met outside the Guild. But it was terribly macabre, even grotesque, her dogged determination to fiddle with body parts torn from his own kin, inert or not. Perhaps it said even worse things about him that he was tempted to indulge her curiosity.

"I can feel it in my bones," she said. Her solemnity recalled the dire pronouncements of Minister General Hendriks and the Archmasters in Huygens Square on the day of Adam's execution. "Besides," she added, "it's not in my best interest to see your Free Will revoked. If the metageasa reasserted themselves upon you, it would be pretty fucking bad for me, too, since I'm an avowed enemy of your makers. So on the basis of enlightened self-interest you can trust I wouldn't propose this experiment if I had any doubt about its effects on you."

She was very convincing. Had her colleagues in New France been swayed by a similar display of passion and persuasion? He'd lived among humans long enough to know there was such a thing as overconfidence. It was a folly. But, then, perhaps, too, was his leap of faith. And that was done: he was falling already. A pebble could not change its mind once the avalanche began.

With a soft click, Jax laid the bauble on the floor between them. Lamplight skimmed across the glass, barely penetrating the darkness beyond a thin skin.

"Very well," he said. "Perform your experiment."

The human didn't hesitate. She leaned forward with her own glass in hand. She spun the bead until its contours lined up with those of the glass on the floor. Then she touched the complementary hollows and swells together.

The Frenchwoman's glass burst forth with a shimmering aquamarine light.

It lit her face from below, turning her skin the color of one of Madam Schoonraad's beryls. A coruscating spiderweb of light danced on the ceiling, like an alchemical torch burning at the bottom of duck pond.

The change was instantaneous. She gasped. Jax rocked back on his haunches.

"I knew it," she whispered.

"What just happened?"

"If the mechanical from which I plucked this wasn't quite thoroughly deactivated, I believe he'd be a rogue now. Like you." The ghostlight glimmered differently from her left and right eyes. "And I'm fairly certain the one in your head looks much the same."

We're seeing its soul, said Jax.

"This thing's owner is dead. If it had a soul, it's long gone," she said. But Jax didn't heed her. She wasn't as confident now; he knew she was wrong. He just knew.

They stared at the shimmering glass for several silent minutes. Jax eventually noticed that his piece of glass had changed, but in a subtler fashion. It was ever so slightly darker now; the lamplight skimmed through an even thinner layer just beneath the surface. As though the darkness of the other piece had flowed into it.

Finally, to break the silence, he changed the subject.

"The man you're hunting. What did he do?"

She chewed her lip. Though her slightly misaligned eyes pointed at the dead, the brimming tears suggested she looked inward. She ran another hand through her hair. This time she kept it there.

"You might change your mind about killing me after you hear this story."

"I'll try to give you fair warning if I start to experience bloodlust."

Her attempt at a halfhearted laugh came out somewhere between a cough and a sob. "It's as I told you a moment ago.

We caught a military Clakker. I proposed to take it into a laboratory where we could study it." Now she looked directly at Jax. "But it wasn't inert when we found it."

"That was dangerous," said Jax.

The look she gave him could have etched alchemical steel. "I understand that better than you could ever know. But I argued it was worth the risk. Since the Dutch didn't know we had it, we could study it at leisure. And by comparing it to Lilith, the rogue I mentioned, we could directly compare a Clakker bound by geasa to one that isn't. We sought to learn how the former becomes the latter."

"Lilith must be extremely trusting," he said. "Surely this required invasive explorations of her construction?"

The Frenchwoman said, curtly and cryptically, "It took some convincing."

Convincing, or coercion? Doubtless Lilith defended her freedom as fervently as Jax did his. Who could say what blunder or misstep might have reestablished the geasa? Jax told himself the French actions came from desperation, from war, not from an innate drive to be cruel. Although perhaps such was integral to human nature. They were, after all, humans no different from those who built and enslaved Jax and his kind. Did this woman see him as a thinking being capable of rationality and emotion in equal measure, deserving of respect and dignity, or as a peculiar machine? He flicked the cables running across his shoulders, the Clakker equivalent of a shiver. Her attitude toward his kind was immaterial as long as he needed her help. But he hoped he wasn't allying himself with a devil.

She continued, "The beast escaped and killed three dozen people en route to the king before somebody stopped it." Now the tears did brim over. They traced rivulets through the dust and flour on her cheeks. "The man I'm chasing, Montmorency, was my partner in this endeavor. He made himself scarce immediately before the massacre, as if he'd known. He wasn't among the dead. Yet he and his wife disappeared that afternoon. Somebody matching his description departed the Keep at around the same time my husband..." She trailed off. Minutes passed while she collected herself. "His apartments were abandoned."

"Why would he want to do this?"

"It isn't courtly politics if somebody doesn't get a dagger in the back. Alliances change. I have—had—no shortage of people who wanted to see me removed, or replaced. Or, I suppose, dead. If Montmorency hadn't scampered off like a guilty bastard, he could've weathered the storm. His wealth would have insulated him." She shrugged. "But the disappearance indicates he was up to something more. This wasn't courtly machination. It was high treason. But I don't know how the tulips acquired him. Or how long ago."

"His wealth wouldn't matter. My makers do not want for money." Jax thought about this. "Why is he so wealthy?"

Berenice sighed. "He has extensive landholdings. Much of our chemical stock derives from natural substances extracted in his territory."

A thunderbolt of realization launched Jax to his feet. He remembered Dwyre, the lonely Clakker, and his owner's strange conversation with Pieter Schoonraad.

The Frenchwoman scooted backward, toppling from the sack and dragging furrows in the spilled flour. "What?" she cried.

He paced while memories and inferences sorted themselves, like a deck of cards unshuffling itself into a well-defined order. And, like a Monaco croupier, it took him but an instant to inspect the hand he held. Their goals were intertwined, he and this mysterious Frenchwoman. He knew how to secure her help.

"What is it?" She'd climbed to her feet and was inching for the door. Probably thinking that he'd changed his mind about killing her.

He stopped. Eddies of flour wafted across the pantry. "I've seen the other side of Montmorency's deal with my makers. And I think I might know where to find him."

CHAPTER
18

Two days later, snowmelt had rendered every unpaved road a slurry. Jax strained as though pulling the cart through six inches of chocolate pudding. But, aside from Berenice, at least it was empty. The queued wagons and carts toward which Jax descended—some drawn by Clakkers, others by draft animals—were fully laden with cargo, judging from the bulges beneath the tarpaulins. At least the mud coating his legs and splashed half-way up his torso would help disguise him. He hoped.

As they slid and lurched down the hillside toward the construction site, Jax heard Berenice say, "Jesus. Somebody feels the need to prove something."

The Forge was complete, at least outwardly. The semi-open pit he had glimpsed with the van Althuises had been covered, its sulphurous fume no longer poisoning the trees down-wind. Residual heat from the pit had melted all the snow on and around the covered excavation. Now plumes of faintly yellow smoke churned from the chimneys of buildings situated around the rim of the excavation like the black pearls in Madam Schoonraad's favorite necklace. Jax counted several of his kin patrolling the rooftops.

He wondered if the Guild was quietly siphoning Clakkers away from the fruitless effort to catch him. Perhaps they'd even begun to accept the unacceptable. Perhaps they believed he'd made it across the border to New France. He would, if today's effort worked. The failure of their gambit would render the border immaterial: if the French were overrun by an army of Clakkers immune to their time-tested chemical defenses, it wouldn't matter where he fled. There would be no solace for rogues in the New World anywhere north of the Equator. He'd tried and failed to make a trek of several hundred miles; what chance had he of crossing several thousand miles to the jungles of Amazonia?

One wheel lodged against a stone buried in the muck. The cart lurched to a stop. Berenice lost her balance but managed to catch herself before toppling from her perch. The sheen of sweat on her brow defied the cold wind gusting off the North River to their east. When she was settled he heaved on the yoke—

"Easy. Easy!" she said.

—while favoring his neck. He managed to dislodge the cart without overstressing his cervical bearings.

"You needn't remind me," he said.

The constant stream of deliveries to the Forge had abated somewhat; the queue was looser and less orderly than the last time he'd seen it. The one thing that had not changed since scouting the site was the pair of Stemwinders that flanked the delivery bay. For all he knew they were the very same pair overseeing deliveries that he'd noted earlier. Quite possibly they hadn't moved.

It was too late to turn away. Too late to flee. Doubtless they'd tracked his progress since he and Berenice topped the rise half an hour ago. But the sight of those implacable centaur bodies brought back memories of Adam struggling in vain to free himself from all those arms... This morning he'd asked Berenice if there was a God, and if so, whether it cared for all things on Earth. He wished she hadn't laughed; now seemed like a good time to investigate the solace of prayer.

"Here we go," Berenice said, under her breath. They merged into the tail of the queue.

Three wagons separated them from the Stemwinders. Then two. Then one. And then Jax hauled on the yoke again and they were rolling toward the bay. Four arms—the two inner arms on each Stemwinder—telescoped across the loading dock entryway, just an inch from his face. They clanged together with a cymbal crash. Jax froze.

Berenice groaned. In Dutch, she said, "You have to fucking be kidding me." Springs creaked behind Jax as she stood on her seat, presumably so that she could loom over the Stemwinders as they loomed over Jax. "What's the goddamned problem now?"

The mechanicals from the Verderer's Office gestured with their free arms toward a smaller and less rutted path that led around the building away from the edge of the pit. The ground so close to the pit, Jax felt through his feet, was warmer here. Warmed by the fires of hell.

"I don't speak pantomime horse, you daft overgrown pocket watches. Tell me in the Queen's Dutch."

The Stemwinders repeated their gesture. Jax watched their interlocked arms stretched before his face. What if they touched him? Could a Stemwinder sense the change Visser's glass had wrought upon him? Could they see the tranquil glow of the pineal glass sealed in his skull? The centaurs had ever been a complete mystery to his kind. Even the titan ship in Rotterdam Harbor seemed positively gregarious in comparison.

Berenice said, "I don't understand what you want! Just tell me!" She did a fine impression of somebody having had the last straw in a long series of indignities. Jax couldn't tell if the lost temper was an act.

From somewhere overhead a voice said, "They can't talk."

Jax and Berenice both looked up. A Guildwoman leaned out a window over the delivery bay. A rosy cross pendant dangled from her necklace. She looked bored.

"Fine," said Berenice. "Can they understand that I've had a miserable week and don't need any more shit?"

The Guildwoman shook her head. "They don't care. This is for deliveries only. You have to go that way for pickups. Follow the path." She turned to go back inside.

"I'm not here for a pickup. I'm here to see the Frenchman."

The Guildwoman stopped. She leaned out again. "What?"

"My cart isn't empty because I came for a pickup. I need to talk to the Frenchman. Or, if you prefer, he needs to talk to me."

"Who?"

"The Frenchman!" said Berenice. "He's the one who fucking speaks French."

By now another wagon, this one drawn by a pair of horses, had pulled up behind them. "Come on," said its driver. "Some of us want to get home before dark."

Berenice wheeled on him. "Why don't you go chew on a mangy dog's flea-ridden balls. And you," she said, pointing up at the window, "can go fetch the Frenchie like a good little wizard."

Jax wondered how much of her performance was an act and how much of this persona was the real Berenice. They had discussed ahead of time her intent to cause a commotion, on the theory that the more trouble she made the more desperate others would be to see her mollified. Or, as she put it, to see her shut up. But he suspected she was enjoying a rare chance to openly abuse her enemies.

"Lady," said the teamster behind them, "I am going to drive this cart up your fat ass if you don't move aside."

"Fat? I'll fucking show you fat!" Berenice hopped from her perch into the bed of the wagon. She clomped across the weathered boards to the rear of the wagon as if she intended to leap upon his draft team and thence him.

"Whoa, whoa, whoa," said the Guildwoman. "Hold it!"

A military Clakker abandoned its patrol to leap from the roof. Mud geysered from where it hit the ground, splattering everybody and causing the horses to whinny. It intercepted Berenice.

"Madam," it said, "for your safety I humbly ask that you please relax. Sir, I beg your patience."

Berenice pointed at the other driver. Over the head of the intervening Clakker, she muttered, "You're lucky."

"Luckier than your husband, that's for certain."

"That's it!" She reared back as though to renew her assault. The military mechanical raised a hand in the international gesture for *halt*. "Madam, please desist. Sir, please allow me to assist you."

The machine took hold of the horses' bridles. By now the Guildwoman had descended from her window; the Stemwinders, which until now hadn't moved a hairbreadth, disengaged their arms to let her through. The resumed their barricade when she stood alongside Jax, peering up at Berenice.

"Here," she said. "Can I just ask you to move aside so that we can let this gentleman through? And then we can get this sorted out."

Berenice rolled her eyes but tossed a gesture at Jax, motioning him to drag the empty cart off the delivery path. He did. The Stemwinders dropped their arms; the military mechanical led the other driver's draft team into the delivery bay. Berenice climbed down.

"Now," said the woman wearing the rosy cross pendant, "I know you said you're not here for a pickup. But I also see your cart is empty. Hence my confusion."

Berenice made a show of collecting herself. "My cart wasn't empty when I took this job. But the Frenchies confiscated all my cargo when I hit the border."

That gave the horologist pause. She frowned. "You came all the way from New France yourself?"

"I've been driving for the past three days, without any food and precious little sleep. I demand to be paid, delivery or no. The Frenchman owes me."

"I see. He knows you?"

"His people hired me. That makes my problems his problems. This job has cost me more money than it was worth. So he fucking owes me for my trouble. And he might want to know Frenchie border agents are confiscating whatever the hell was in those barrels. They took an enormous goddamned bribe, too, every penny I had just to stay out of jail. Even that might not have done it, but I told those ignorant savages that my piece-of-shit servitor here was actually a military model en route to the garrison at Fort Orange. Can you believe those jackpine savages actually believed me? A military ticktock pulling a wagon in the middle of fucking nowhere. I wish! In that case I could have slit their throats and had my money back. But I couldn't, and didn't, so the Frenchman owes me."

Berenice had concocted the story such that the point of interest to her persona, namely her outstanding payment, wasn't the important part to those working the new Forge. To the horologist, Jax hoped, the alarming part of the story was the bit about confiscation. Because if he had been right when explaining the situation to the van Althuises, the steady stream of mysterious cargo delivered to this Grand Forge represented a sustained and catastrophic violation of French export embargoes. And if Montmorency were involved, as Berenice was convinced, then he'd be the person the clockmakers had entrusted with such details.

So far the horologist hadn't denied there was a Frenchman involved in the work here. But she also hadn't confirmed he was the person Berenice sought.

The horologist tugged on her pendant, chewing her lip. Ratchets clicked inside the necks of the Stemwinders, which had turned to watch their conversation. Or were they watching him? *Come on*, thought Jax. *Come on.*

Finally, she said, "I don't know if he's here at the moment. If not, we'll have to send a runner into the city. If you're willing to come with me, perhaps we can straighten out your compensation, and get you something to eat, while we fetch him. Would that be acceptable to you?"

Berenice said, "This isn't some trick to screw me, is it? You tinkerers are a shifty bunch."

Jax had to credit the horologist's patience. She kept a straight face and an even tone when she replied, "I promise you it isn't. Here. Have your servitor follow me."

Berenice climbed back atop the wagon. "Thank the Lord. Somebody who can see reason." To Jax, she said, "What are you waiting for? Follow her."

Jax heaved at the yoke. It took extra effort to dislodge the cart; it had settled into the mire. But the wheels squelched free, and then they were following the horologist on a secondary path around the building.

Berenice called ahead to the Guildwoman. "Do you have physicians on hand? All this excitement has given me a blinding headache."

Which was the code phrase that she and Jax had practiced. He strained harder.

꧁꧂

Before sunrise that morning, Jax had lain on a stone sarcophagus while Berenice flipped through the notes she'd carried secretly since departing Marseilles-in-the-West. They'd been hiding in the undercroft of an old church halfway between the piers and Roosevelt Park. She flipped through the pages like somebody skimming a familiar book for the good parts; even in the dim lamplight of their crypt he could see many pages contained horrifying diagrams of mechanical linkages, planetary gears, cables, escapements, torsion springs. It was a book of taboos, of Clakkers reduced to their component parts. He tried not to think about the broken kin whose damage, or dissection, had provided the information. Several people had contributed to the notes, judging from the variety of handwritings. The later entries—Berenice's?—were tight and cramped; preceding entries had been scrawled in a loose script and a darker ink; the earliest entries were so neat the burgundy copperplate might have been printed on a press.

"Right," she said. "I think I've found it." She flipped the red ribbon bookmark into the binding, then held the book up so he could better see the page. A diagram featured prominently on this page, too, but what drew Jax's attention was the border—blackened jagged metal, warped and shattered by tremendous force. A cannon shot, perhaps, or a petard blast. He hardly saw what she intended; all he could do was recoil from anathema.

Did Berenice realize she shook unutterable violations in his face? Did she care? He wanted to scream, bellow, holler to the heavens: *I am more than the sum of my parts!* He wondered how she might have reacted were their places reversed while Jax forced her to witness a cannibalistic rite, or something equally unspeakable. A moment before she set the notes down he recognized the contours of the exposed mechanisms: a chain of cervical bearings. What would she do to his neck?

"The spindle holding this element of the gear train"—she tapped the page—"is relatively thin. If we shave it just enough it should snap when subjected to the proper stresses." She lifted her arms as though dancing with an invisible partner. A frown passed across her face, but it disappeared when she glanced at the journal again. "Yes. I think this will work." She held her arms out straight as if balancing a yoke on her narrow shoulders. "Like this, see?" She tipped a bit to the right. "Lean forward, like you're really straining. Weight on your left foot but pushing almost entirely with your right shoulder." She dropped the pose to run a finger across his shoulders. "This cable has to be stretched as tight as it will go." Then she adopted the strange posture again, saying, "And then turn to look over your right shoulder, like you're trying to talk to me." Berenice mimed the gesture by quickly turning her head. The glance became a flinch.

Then she rubbed her neck. "Shit, that hurt."

"What happens when I try it?"

"With the compromised pinion? It'll snap. And, I think, cause your cervical bearings to rattle like hell."

Jax said, "I don't like this plan."

"Look," Berenice said. "It's going to take two of us. But they're not likely to offer you a tour, are they? They need a reason to take you inside. If we do this right you'll hardly lose any range of function, but it'll sound terrible when you turn your head. You can always play it up a bit, pretend the damage is more extensive than it is."

"If my makers chose to save weight by making that pinion delicate, it means they considered this damage scenario highly unlikely. Compromising the piece may be difficult."

"When were you built?"

"Eighteen-oh-eight."

Berenice waved off his concerns. "Bah. Compared to today the alloys back then were rubbish. Ever had any pieces replaced?"

Jax thought back over the times, roughly once per decade, when he was brought back to the Forge for routine maintenance. "I don't know. I don't think so. They don't tell us."

It took longer to open his neck than she intended. Working on a Clakker using only improvised tools rather than the specialized instruments of the clockmakers' trade was, in Berenice's words, akin to mending a broken cobweb using hemp twine and a marlinespike.

"The good news," she said between muttered curses, "is that if they ever try to hang you, all they'll get for their trouble is one very frustrated rope."

"They don't hang my kind. They toss us into the fires of the Grand Forge. To melt us down and incinerate our sinful Free Will."

"I know. That was a joke."

"I don't jest about your execution."

"It's not my fault your makers made you humorless."

"We have the capacity for humor," said Jax. He thought about his friend Fig, Madam de Geer's servitor. She said things that most Clakkers hardly dared think. Summer dinner parties were always more fun when he got to work with Fig. It cheered him a bit to wallow in those old memories until he realized he'd probably never see her again.

After an extra hour and a half, an escutcheon came loose and clattered to the stone floor of the crypt. After several tense moments spent listening for evidence they might have been discovered, Berenice set the loose piece of Jax's body on the adjacent sarcophagus. The inner side of his plating was a dull, brushed copper color.

She wiped an arm across her forehead. "I can see the spindle now. I'm going to try to scrape as much material from it as I can without severing it." She put her hands on her hips and leaned backward; her back popped. Then she took up the notebook again to study the diagram. "This might hurt a bit."

"I am intimately familiar with pain. The agony of geas is something we live with from the moment of our creation. Be thankful you have never experienced its like."

Berenice slammed the notebook down. Whirled. Stumbled. "*I've* never experienced agony? Let me ask you something, machine. Have you ever loved somebody? Has the love of your life died whimpering in your arms because of your own failures? No? Then consider yourself fortunate."

After that, they worked in silence—the silence of the crypt—until Berenice's file broke and she cursed for a solid minute. They lost more time while she used tweezers and makeshift forceps to fish all the fragments from within his neck. That done, she fell again into sullen silence.

⁂

Though it was muddy, the path leading away from the delivery bay hadn't been churned by the passage of innumerable wagons. The mire didn't clutch at the cart as handily as it had on the main road. Jax scanned the ground for suitable stones and contrived to wedge the right-side cart wheel against the best candidate. The cart lurched to a stop.

"Damn it, you stupid pile of junk. Do you want to knock my fillings out?"

"No, mistress," said Jax. "I apologize for my carelessness." Aping the litany of subservience, spouting a rote sycophantic apology, filled his head with the imagined taste of curdled milk and the scent of brimstone. It felt like a betrayal of the innumerable mechanicals doomed to forever yearning for release from their bondage. "I will be more careful."

"You'd better, God damn it," said Berenice. "Get moving! She's waiting."

And indeed the Guildwoman had paused in the tall brown grass along the verge where the path curved around the building. She looked bored and irritated. Jax pulled against the yoke, taking advantage of the horologist's attention to make the slipping of his right foot particularly obvious.

He adjusted the yoke over his shoulders, planted his left foot for the best traction, and strained. He turned his shoulders against the resistance offered by the stone wedged under the cart wheel. Weight on his left foot, straining with his right shoulder, he could feel the vibrations of a faint high-pitched squeal emanating from somewhere under his head. The sound of overstressed metal.

This maneuver required delicacy. If he strained too far, he ran the risk of pinching the bladder hidden in his torso. Securing it had taken hours. At first he'd been afraid to move at all, for fear he'd immobilize himself.

"Mistress," he said, "shall I—"

Still straining to move the stuck cart, he turned his head as if to address Berenice directly.

Something snapped inside his neck. It was surprisingly loud, enough to take Jax by surprise. Tiny pieces of metal ricocheted against the flange plate and went tumbling into his innards. Jax fought a moment's panic, wondering if he'd been paralyzed. But he could still move his head; in fact, he couldn't hold it still. Now it bobbed and swayed slightly as though he had contracted a human ague.

Berenice said, "What the hell was that?"

Jax made to cock his head as was natural when trying to change his perspective. His head slewed like a lazy weather vane. It took considerable effort to dampen the motion and keep his attention aimed in a particular direction. He could keep his face turned in a general direction, but not without precession.

The horologist approached. She sighed. "I thought I heard something crack. Has your cart been damaged?"

Jax delicately explored the range of motion of all his joints and hinges, as the metageasa would have demanded. The Guildwoman noticed the subtle self-diagnostic. Berenice pretended she hadn't.

"So help me, you worthless piece of shit," she said, "if you broke the axle I will personally take you apart and sell you for scrap."

Jax locked every joint in his body. He froze but for his weather-vane head. He recited the words every servitor dreaded hearing from itself: "Mistress. I am obligated to inform you that I have taken damage. In my current state I am unable to serve you at my fullest capacity. It is my duty to humbly recommend that at your most immediate convenience you arrange for my temporary transfer into the care of the Sacred Guild of Horologists and Alchemists that I might be repaired and thus recover my full range of functions. I am also obligated to remind you that your contract with the Crown, whether direct or through intermediaries, prohibits you from attempting to perform any modification, maintenance, or repair work on any of my mechanisms. Violation of this agreement is punishable in terms up to and including execution. I humbly apologize for the inconvenience."

"What?" Berenice leapt to her feet again. She glowered at Jax. "What the fuck are you talking about?"

"I am broken, mistress."

She hopped into the mud. "What do you mean, *broken*?"

The Guildwoman kneaded the chain of her pendant. This was turning into a trying afternoon for her, but the look on her face was that of concentration, diagnosis. She focused on Jax's bobbing head. "Something snapped inside its neck. Look. It can't keep its head still."

"I don't care about its shitbucket head. I care about getting my goddamned money from that pus-dripping cockhole of a Frenchman." Jax wondered how Berenice had learned to curse so creatively. She thrust a finger at Jax, then the cart. "So get back to work, you lazy, brass-plated bedpan."

Jax turned to comply but the Guildwoman interjected. "I'm afraid that may be unwise, madam. Extra exertion could worsen the damage to your Clakker. That would only cost you more in the long run. We should take it inside and at least take a look. You're lucky—if you're going to have a breakdown, this is the place to do it."

"How can it be broken already? It's barely fifteen years out of the Forge."

The Guildwoman cocked an eyebrow. She appraised Jax with a glance. "Why do you say that?"

"I asked when I subleased this thing," said Berenice. "I'm not a fool."

The Guildwoman sighed. She was impressively patient. "I hate to be the one to tell you this, madam, but I believe you were…deceived."

Now Berenice went still. Like a Clakker locking every joint in place. The next words tumbled from her mouth like cubes of ice. "Why do you say that?"

"Well, based on several details in the design, as well as the work on the escutcheons, I'd say your mechanical dates to early in the previous century." The horologist circled Jax like a lion stalking a spring lamb. "And, to be blunt, its previous owners were extremely negligent in its maintenance. Practically criminal. This mechanical has seen a great deal of hard use and very little upkeep."

Berenice shook her head. The steam had gone out of her.

"No. No, I paid for a recently forged machine. It was more expensive but it was going to be worth it." Her voice rose, bit by bit. "It was my investment. I took a hit on the down payment for this sublease, but I was going to make it up with the extra labor." Now she started to shake. "I was going to come out even after I was paid for my delivery. But now I don't have a delivery to be paid for, and now you're telling me this piece of shit isn't worth half what I agreed to pay?"

The Guildwoman sighed again. "Yes."

Berenice hurled herself at Jax. "You miserable piece of trash. You fucking ruined me!" Her fists bonged against the brassy carapace of his chest. She reared back for a kick, too, but as any loyal Clakker would have done, he moved aside lest she break her foot. His neck made a terrible screech when he moved. Berenice lost her balance and slipped in the mud. "You backstabbing motherfucker. I'll have you melted for ashtrays."

And then Berenice started to cry.

The Guildwoman sighed a third time—that had to be some kind of record—but offered a hand to Jax's supposed mistress. Heavy clods of butterscotch-colored mud fell from Berenice's cloak. It had smeared her hair, too.

"Here," said the horologist, not unkindly. "We can leave your cart for now. Let's go inside. You can warm and dry yourself while we send a runner to fetch Monsieur Montmorency. And we'll have somebody immediately take a look at your mechanical. How does that sound?"

Berenice nodded, sniffling. Jax caught the look in her eyes when the Guildwoman's back was turned: she was relishing this. But, then, she wasn't the rogue who had just scammed his way inside the one place in the entire New World he'd spent weeks striving to avoid.

The horologist led them inside. Every footstep evoked a

tortured screech and clatter from Jax's broken neck. It masked the panicked wheezing of his mainspring heart.

⟨❧⟩

After Jax had been taken away for examination in one of the laboratories, the footsteps of Berenice and the Guildwoman had echoed through a field of desks sparsely occupied by bureaucrats and paper pushers. Berenice had expected to find the business floor ticking in full bustle, particularly now that the new Forge was so close to completion. She had expected the money and paper had already begun to flow. While the recession had delayed completion of the Forge, the Guild's substantial investment of resources into the New World ought to have attracted a heavy tide of new Clakker leases, plus business and partnership proposals. In addition, it seemed likely that many owners would have deferred maintenance on their leased Clakkers while waiting for a Forge to open locally, rather than enduring weeks of delay to have their servants serviced in The Hague. But apparently the near collapse of the central bank had taken a toll on the new Forge's anticipated business. Berenice struggled not to smile at the irony.

Still, it pleased her to no end that clockmakers, of all people, could suffer such unlucky timing.

Berenice studied her surroundings through teary eyes. Calling up the tears was easy; she unbottled her sorrows. It was harder to stop crying than she had anticipated. Berenice was still sniffling when the compassionate Guildwoman took her up a flight of stairs to install her in a conference room that might have been taken from an exclusive Amsterdam gentlemen's club.

This was clearly where the grandees met. Little wonder, then, that it had been completed before the rest of the Forge's interior. A pair of fireplaces large enough to use Berenice's stolen cart for kindling faced each other across a polished teakwood conference table inlaid with a cross in rose-colored mahogany. Twelve leather wing-backed chairs fit comfortably around the table. Books with embossed and gilded leather spines filled floor to ceiling bookshelves. One wall comprised a single windowpane overlooking the main floor. Dark walnut paneling covered the walls up to a waist-high wainscoting, above which paisley patterns of gold and silver thread swirled up to the mirrored copper sconces along the ceiling. The alchemical lamps were dark, their inscribed sigils dormant; even on an overcast early-winter day like today, the ten-foot-wide domed skylight illuminated the room with an abundance of natural light, enough for Berenice to count four sofas and a double handful of plush upholstered chairs scattered through the room. Newspaper racks flanked several of these, the pages hanging from their dowels fluttering like moths in the breeze created by the opened door. This was a combination boardroom and a reading room. A solitary desk in the far corner likely seated a secretary or amanuensis during meetings. The door, she noted with satisfaction, had a lock.

Berenice made this survey of the room in the time it took her hostess to usher her to a seat alongside one of the massive hearths. She plopped into the chair, still blubbering. The Guildwoman turned a discreet finial along the mantel until a slight hiss and rapid clicking became the whoosh of ignition. Given the size of the hearth Berenice expected an eyebrow-crisping inferno, but the other woman knew her business and kept it turned reasonably low. She even took Berenice's muddy cloak (not before it transferred a long dun-colored smear into the upholstery) and hung it on a hook alongside the hearth.

"Thank you," Berenice mumbled.

"We don't usually do this."

"You're the nicest clockmaker I've ever met." This was true.

But unexpected kindnesses were hidden stones lying in wait to bend or break the blade of her plow. So Berenice chose to believe this woman's compassion to be an anomaly. Better that than blunt her hatred.

"You caught me on a good day," said the Guildwoman. "I have to round up a runner to go into the city. But I'll get a servitor to bring you some food. Will you be all right here for a while?"

Berenice made a show of looking around the room as if uncomfortably aware of not belonging. "What do I do if somebody needs this room?"

Her hostess said, "Should your presence be challenged, you're a guest of Katrina Baxter. But that's unlikely. Most of our work is down there," she said, pointing out the window, "and outside." She turned for the door, but paused. She bit her lip, turned around. When Berenice caught her eye, she lowered her voice. "Be careful around Montmorency. He'll try to grope you."

Disgust and delight coursed through Berenice in equal measure. *You lecherous pig. I bet you'll jump at the chance to get alone with an overwhelmed and vulnerable woman, won't you?* He'd do half her work for her, the randy bastard. Berenice feigned surprise, hid her relief, and gave her contempt free rein. "That fucking pig."

"Yeah," was all Katrina said. And then she departed.

Berenice checked the cloth pouch hanging between her breasts. Finding its contents undisturbed by her tumble in the mud, she spared a quick glance at the door before leaping to her feet and crossing to the desk. Most of the drawers were empty and unlocked. The single locked drawer succumbed to a few minutes of prodding from the tip of her knife, but aside from a handful of bent pen nibs and an inkwell this also proved empty.

Contrary to her expectations, the books weren't oranamental. But they weren't particularly useful or interesting, either. The volumes on the lower shelves were bound collections of quarterly reports from the Clockmakers' Guild dating back to its inception in 1691. Volumes pertaining to the past several years were noticeably thicker than the rest, perhaps owing to the construction of the new Grand Forge. The volumes on the upper shelves, those easier to access without stooping, were empty. Guild history was a blank page waiting to be written.

If only eliminating that future were as simple as tossing an armload of unwritten books into a fire. But her actions today wouldn't behead the Guild. Nor would avenging Louis. It might lessen her guilt a minuscule amount. Regardless she had to know the details of Montmorency's deal with the tulips if she ever hoped to behead the hydra.

She'd sent two letters to Marseilles-in-the-West. One went to the marquis de Lionne. The other went to Longchamp, on the expectation the marquis would wipe his ass with her letter. Her warnings would find more fertile ground once she had the details out of Montmorency.

The sideboard wasn't locked. It contained a dozen bottles of liquor in various states of emptiness, along with a few decanters and a variety of tumblers and stemware. But she hadn't eaten, so drinking seemed a bad idea. Perhaps after the servitor arrived with her lunch.

Now what? She'd envisioned a scenario where she made a fuss until somebody ushered her into Montmorency's private office, into a small confined space where she would confront him alone. Driven by rage yet made foolish by the weight of a shattered heart, she had taken it for granted that he'd have an office here in the Forge, a place where he blithely worked with the horologists. She took this for granted because it fit the oily narrative of his treachery. Her anger had made her careless, incapable of distinguishing between a dark revenge fantasy and what was actually likely.

In the fantasy version of this scenario, there were no Clakkers on hand to heed Montmorency's cries while she barred the door to his hypothetical office and cut the eyes from his head. No Clakkers, here in the Guild's continental headquarters.

Jesus Christ. Louis's death hadn't made her careless. It had made her *stupid*.

Berenice took a seat alongside the window. She settled in for a long wait.

Humans tended toward obliviousness when it came to their mechanical servants. The persistence of the Clakker tongue of clicks and twangs spoke eloquently to that. But it was one thing to be unobservant, quite another to be stupid. And the men and women who made the Clakkers were anything but stupid.

It took a painful effort of will for Jax to suppress his anxiety. The gnawing terror at finding himself inside a Guild laboratory—inside a Grand Forge—was the sensation of his every cog tooth cracked, every ratchet broken, every spindle spinning freely and every spring distended beyond its plastic deformation limits. He couldn't keep his head from swaying like an unlatched gate, but the hypertelegraphic chittering from the rest of his body was likely to draw attention from the technician. Jax forced himself to relax.

I'm trapped inside the Forge, he thought. *I'm in the one place on the entire continent where I should never, ever be.* Images of Adam's final moments played through his mind's eye, memories of that drizzly day at the Binnenhof. (And how did such memories work? Was the luminous lens in the center of his skull a magic lantern, projecting images across the shadowed hinterlands of his eyeballs?) The heat, the reek of sulphur, the barbarous roar of the human crowd . . . *That could be me soon.*

But then he remembered what Berenice had pointed out to him. Of all the places in the New World where his makers might expect to find him hiding this was the utter last. If there was any safety to be had in hiding in the open, this would be the place to try it. In theory. Jax focused on his surroundings as an attempt to distract himself.

The horologist woman had summoned one of her colleagues, explained the situation, and went off with Berenice while the surprisingly young-looking fellow ordered Jax to follow him. His escort wore the same rosy cross pendant as the other Guild personnel. He unlocked a door that led to a stairwell; they'd descended beneath the rim of the excavated pit that Jax had first glimpsed with the van Althuises. Soon they'd emerged into a cavern that curved away in both directions. Based on the curvature, Jax suspected the tunnel girded the pit, perhaps halfway between ground level and the bottom. Alchemical lamps lit the tunnel, their heatless light fountaining from wall sconces inscribed with silvery sigils. After passing several more or less identical doors, Jax's escort had unlocked one and commanded him to enter.

Jax stopped in the center of the room, frozen in horror. He stood within a charnel house for Clakkers. Dozens of arms, legs, hips, ankles, and more obscure pieces of anatomy dangled from hooks affixed to long tracks in the ceiling or protruded from barrels like umbrellas in an umbrella stand. Spare parts and chattel. Were he human, he might have gagged.

The nature of the Forge was to flout the deepest taboos of Clakker-kind. To their makers, a Clakker's sense of identity was nothing but a mass-produced illusion: a Clakker was merely the sum of its interchangeable parts and nothing more. Such thinking evoked a visceral dread in the most stalwart mechanicals.

It took an effort of will to force himself to study his surroundings, to look for clues to what he sought. Translucent bins held piles of smaller body parts—crystalline eyes, mainsprings, spindles, escapements. A massive collection of esoteric tools filled row upon row of shelves and hung from pegs on the wall, each outlined in paint the color of a fresh egg yolk. One shelf held a trio of glass baubles, each clamped at the center of the concentric rings of its own armillary sphere. The glasses inside these stationary models of the heavens didn't glow and they weren't opaque. They were clear as a new pair of reading glasses.

He saw no evidence of alchemy here, no facility for forging new alchemical alloys, no stamps or magical styli for inscribing sigils into the parts. The limbs hanging from the racks like sides of beef in a butcher's market already featured the abstruse scribbling of the alchemists' trade. (Did they twitch, or were they merely set to swaying by the opened door?) This was a place for mending broken mechanicals. Building them from scratch, imbuing them with sentience, shackling their Free Will—that happened elsewhere. Somewhere in this subterranean labyrinth there was a place where the horologists designed new models. In fact...

Jax took advantage of his unsteady head to examine the assortment of Clakker pieces again. At first blush they seemed pieces of the standard servitor design, but on closer inspection he noticed subtle deviations from the servitor body plan. Countless tiny perforations dotted the flanges and escutcheons; subtle ridges rippled the arms and legs like a network of human blood vessels under malleable flesh.

If not for the damage to his neck he wouldn't have been able to study his surroundings so assiduously. An unattended mechanical waiting on its human masters was expected to stand motionless. Like furniture.

A technician arrived. He watched the bobbing and swaying of Jax's weather-vane head for less than a minute before he snatched a tool from the wall and wheeled a cart alongside Jax. He removed the flanges around Jax's neck much quicker than Berenice had done, and with far less cursing. Jax kept a careful eye on how the technician scrutinized him, lest he discover the epoxy bladder carefully nestled in his torso—or, worse, rupture it.

The technician didn't speak until he'd opened Jax. He donned a headband adorned with a large mirror pierced by a hole in the center, then flipped it over his eye so that he peered through the hole while the mirror reflected light into Jax's neck. He frowned, grunted. After several moments, he said, "Machine. Have you been subjected to tampering or modification by your owners?"

Jax said, "No, sir. At no point since my construction have I been subjected to attempts to alter or examine my mechanisms in a fashion that would constitute a violation of my lease or activate my human safety metageasa."

The clockmakers said it was for safety reasons that such things were forbidden. So they said. Jax knew this to be a lie. What this horologist didn't realize was that Jax could lie, too. Thus he accepted what Jax told him without reflection or reservation.

The repairman turned away, grumbling to himself while he sought a tool for probing the delicate innards of Jax's compromised neck. Jax took advantage of his inconstant posture to scan the room once more to ensure there were no windows or open doors that might betray him. He decided it would be smarter to let the horologist mend the damage to his neck before setting out in search of the chemical vats. The inability to keep his head pointed in one direction was getting extremely annoying. Besides, and more importantly, if he subdued the horologist before the man had a chance to finish his work, Jax's missing flanges would ruin his chance to remain inconspicuous while moving through the Forge.

"What is your name, machine?"

Jax had anticipated this. He'd formulated a moniker consistent with his construction lot. "I am called Glastrepovithistrovantus, sir."

The repairman doffed the mirror to don another gadget. This was a succession of magnifying lenses mounted over one eye. He held the inner surface of one of Jax's flange plates to the light, clicked the loupe over one eye, and scrutinized the metal.

Jax had witnessed this ritual numerous times during his regularly schedule maintenance visits to the Grand Forge in The Hague. *Serial number*, he realized. *He's going to cross-reference my identity and maintenance history.* And then he understood why Berenice sometimes said the strange things she said. If he could have sighed, he would have. In lieu of a sigh he cursed within the privacy of his own mind: *Shitcakes.* Somehow it did make him feel a little better. Not much, but a bit. No wonder the humans did it so often.

Naturally the clockmakers would have brought copies of their records from the Old World. The Forge couldn't fulfill all its functions without them; every mechanical walking the New World today had been forged elsewhere. So when the Guild repairman looked up Jax's serial number and found it didn't reference a servitor named Glastrepovithistrovantus but rather one named Jalyksegethistrovantus . . . the very rogue for whom all of Nieuw Nederland had been searching . . .

But the technician jotted the number on a slip of paper, then tucked the paper in his pocket. Apparently he intended to deal with the cross-referencing later, if at all. Perhaps this was a boring formality of his job. How frequently did discrepancies arise? Probably less than once per human career. Jax relaxed.

The repairman worked with delicate fingers. His work was far gentler than Berenice's unskilled hacking. It was almost pleasant. When the horologist tightened or loosened a fastener, Jax could almost imagine it was the ministration of angels, or ants. In this way the sabotage to his body was fixed.

Until the man cursed, dropped his tool, and shook his head. He stood, turned up the lamps (with shaking hands, Jax noted), replaced the mirror over his eye, then peered into Jax's neck again.

"Machine. Tell me again. Have you ever been examined or modified by your owners?"

"Sir, no, sir. At no point has any person in my succession of owners attempted to violate the terms—"

"In that case," said the horologist, "tell me how this found its way into your body."

At which point he reached into Jax with a long pair of tweezers and retrieved a metallic sliver: a fragment of the file Berenice had used to weaken a piece of his anatomy.

"Shitcakes," said Jax.

And then he blurred forward, yanked the horologist off his feet, and clamped a hand over his nose and mouth before he could yelp in surprise. He held the man firmly enough to keep a seal over his mouth but not so firmly as to fracture bones or tear his flesh. The flailing tapered off quickly. Jax used spare lengths of fine steel wire from the repair bins to tie the unconscious man's wrists and ankles, then deposited him gently in one of the cupboards. He did his best to ensure the wires wouldn't cut off his circulation, while also making it difficult for him to kick or raise much noise. He stuffed a cleaning rag in his mouth and tied it in place with more wire. He took care that the bunched-up rag wasn't so large as to present a choking hazard.

His victim subdued, Jax emerged from the laboratory: a rogue Clakker loose in the house of his makers.

CHAPTER
19

Baxter kept her word. Soon after she departed, a servitor arrived bearing a tray of bread, cheese, and a sliced apple along with a carafe of water. Berenice's stomach gurgled. She took the tray and water, but the servitor lingered.

Berenice said, "I don't need your help eating."

"I have been dispatched to see to your needs and your comforts," it said.

Baxter probably thought she was doing her a favor by keeping a Clakker on hand for her meeting with the Frenchman. But if Montmorency was feeling lecherous, he wouldn't be deterred by a pair of unblinking gemstone eyes. And the servitor would intervene the moment Berenice tried to harm him. Shit. Even when they tried to do something good the horologists managed to be a pain in her ass.

"Your presence makes me extremely uncomfortable." She put a tremor in her voice. "My own servitor fucking ruined me. So leave. If I need something I'll call for you."

It did, reluctantly.

But now, after having successfully deceived the clockmakers, her post-adrenaline crash—not to mention the warmth of the fire and comfort of a full stomach—left her drowsy and inattentive. Her traitorous eyelids moved of their own accord, sliding inexorably lower to sabotage her efforts to keep a watchful eye. Twice she jerked awake in dismay, carrying no memory of the last several minutes. She hadn't slept well in days, and the exertion of her energetic performance outside the Forge had drained her. At least she knew how much time had passed owing to the clock on the mantel. She resented the clockmakers their real timepieces, which were nothing like the pathetic candles and hourglasses that marked the passage of time in New France. Drowsing, she wondered how Jax was getting along.

The struggle for wakefulness kept her so distracted that she nearly missed the pair who crossed the warehouse floor amidst a sea of brasswork slaves. Katrina Baxter walked with a man whom Berenice couldn't identify before they passed outside her field of view. But they were walking quickly and embroiled in what appeared to be intense conversation.

Berenice leapt from the chaise longue, putting her back to the window before a wayward glance from Montmorency—if that was Montmorency—could sink her opportunity to surprise him. Muffled voices hovered just beyond the door. Torn between eavesdropping and a mad scramble to find an advantageous position, she scooted across the room to stand before the hearth and its crackling cherry embers. She adjusted her bonnet, as though she still wore it to fend off a lingering chill. It hid her face.

The door latch clicked. She bowed her head and drew long shaky breaths, like somebody who'd exhausted herself with a profound crying jag.

"She's in here," said the compassionate clockmaker, Katrina Baxter. Interesting that she returned to complete this errand herself, rather than assigning a servitor to see it done. Maybe not every single member of the Guild was a blackhearted demon. Still, Berenice took the poker from its hook alongside the hearth to prod the charred log in the fireplace and stir the coals to life. She buried the hook within the embers.

Another voice said in terrible Dutch buried under a French accent characteristic of the Acadian coast, where Montmorency spent his childhood, "I'd like to speak with the lady alone."

Berenice sighed with relief. *Thank God for your lechery, you son of a bitch.*

After a momentary pause, Baxter called to Berenice. "You're in luck, madam. Monsieur Montmorency very kindly consented to join us. Do you need anything else?"

Us. In the context of her previous warning about Montmorency it meant: Shall I stay with you?

Berenice, her back still to the door, shook her head. She used anger and fatigue like a rasp to roughen her voice. "No, thank you."

Baxter withdrew. The door clicked. Montmorency's footsteps crossed the room behind Berenice. He went to the sideboard. "I hear you've endured no end of trials," he said. "Perhaps a drink? Then you can tell me about your troubles at the border."

Berenice sniffled. He took that as assent. She listened to the clink of crystal, the chiming of an unstoppered decanter, the gurgle of liquid. The fireplace spat firefly sparks into the flue when she prodded the heap of wood and ash in the hearth. She kept the tip of the poker wedged in the hot coals. His footsteps approached. She tilted her head, straining to watch from the corner of her eye. He stopped, arm outstretched to offer her glass.

"Your drink, madam."

Berenice whirled. She swung the poker in an uppercut to plant the curved barb between his legs. The impact made him jump and squeak. Port geysered from both glasses when they hit the floor, though they didn't break. He landed on his toes, goggling at her.

"Hello, lover. Fancy another shag?"

His trousers smoldered. But the son of a bitch actually tried to be suave, as though a ghost from his past hadn't just crammed a steaming-hot hook into his nethers. Stretching on tiptoe to keep his weight off the poker, his attention flipped back and forth across her face.

"Your eyes don't match," he said in strained French. "They used to, as I recall."

"What, this?" Berenice pressed a fingertip to the edge of her socket. "This is nothing. If you wanted to see the fallout from your treachery, you had thirty-seven chances to stand at thirty-seven gravesides. Including Louis's."

A savage yank and twist to the fireplace poker lent additional emphasis to her words. Montmorency squealed. He lost the color in his face. This time she definitely felt the hook penetrate and squish something. Based on the way he doubled over and coughed on vomit, Berenice guessed it was one of his testicles. She crouched to keep the hook planted between his legs as he hit the floor. The scent of singed wool became the fetor of smoldering hair and slowly burning flesh.

He drew a deep breath, as if to yell. But she'd been watching for this. She twisted the hook again, hard enough for the gasp to empty his lungs.

"Don't even think about calling for help." She unsheathed the knife from her boot. "I bet I can disfigure you before mechanicals pull me off."

"You bitch," he groaned. "You fucking bitch."

"You're going to wish I was merely feeling bitchy right now. You're going to wish you hadn't decided to betray the Crown. You'll wish you hadn't decided to fuck me." She gave the poker another twist; this time he did empty his stomach. The custard-yellow spew contained oddly recognizable asparagus tips. It splashed across the hearth and smelled like rancid lantern oil. "Come to think of it, you fucked me more than once, didn't you? Once with this"—another yank; he cried—"and again through your pact with the tulips."

Somebody knocked. "Is everything well?"

"Yes," Berenice called. "Everything is well, thank you." She skipped across the room to toss the lock on the door. "We'd like to be undisturbed for a bit, please."

"If you wish," said Baxter from behind the door. She sounded skeptical.

When Berenice turned back to Montmorency, he hadn't moved from his spot on the floor, but he was trying weakly to fish something from under his shirt. A small silver tube on a chain. Berenice ran over and kicked his hand. The glancing blow didn't force him to drop the object so she wrenched the poker again. The duke's full-body spasm flung the object from his fingers, but it fell short and dangled from a chain around his neck.

She crouched beside him. The whistle was cold to the touch. It took two jerks to snap the chain; blood welled from his abraded skin.

"Your new masters keep you on a short leash, eh?"

"Not a leash." He shook his head weakly. "For my protection. They gave that to me in case French agents found me."

"Aha. Well, I'd prefer we're not disturbed just yet." Berenice tossed the whistle in the hearth. It tinkled against the fire bricks before plopping into the ashes. "So tell me something, Your Grace. How did the tulips buy you? This is the part I don't understand. You had enough money to live comfortably anywhere."

He tried to roll over, but flinched as the poker snagged on something delicate. He acquiesced to merely wiping the vomit from his lips to an embroidered shirt cuff. "They didn't buy me. I approached them."

"You greasy shit stain on a diseased elk's warty asshole. Why in the hell would you do that?"

"Because, you sanctimonious cunt, New France is destined for the scrap heap of history. France is a fool's dream. The Dutch rule the world...as much of it as they care to conquer." He coughed. She pushed the hook, granting him just enough slack that he could sit up. He did. Blood trickled through the hole in his trousers to stain the carpet. "But you fools with your dreams of liberation, your delusions of grandeur with the belief that New France can somehow be an effective rival to the Empire...It's sickening...Worse. It's *embarrassing*."

"Then just leave! Why did you have to betray us all on your way out?"

"Because," Montmorency coughed, "I don't like you. You, and that prissy hemophiliac on the throne, and that menagerie of idiots he calls a council, and the rest of you Papist God-botherers crouching in the darkness with your candles and your fear of anything more complicated than a fucking hourglass."

"What did the Dutch offer you in return?"

"Nothing."

She levered the poker to make him squirm. Her free hand wedged the knife tip under the edge of his kneecap. He thrashed again, weeping.

"Shhh, shhhh," she warned him. "What did I say about making noise?" She gave the knife a warning nudge. Then she clucked her tongue. "Those selfish bastards. You offered them all of our chemical knowledge and in return they didn't offer you so much as a single pickle? I would've thought they'd at least give you a replacement for that walking shitpuddle you call a wife. A different courtesan every night? A different hole to place this every night, eh?" Twist, tug to the poker.

In trying to roll away he wallowed in his own vomit. Berenice wrinkled her nose.

"I love my wife," he groaned.

Rage overwhelmed her.

"I loved my *husband*," she hissed. And jammed the knife under his patella. He screamed.

Oops.

Baxter banged a fist on the door. "Sir? Madam? What's going on in there?"

Speaking more quickly now, Berenice said, "The rulers of the world could have handed you whatever you desired, but you declined. How ascetic of you."

Fuck it, she thought. Montmorency wept openly while she tortured him. He tried to bat her hands away.

Baxter started kicking the door. "Let me in! Miss, are you hurt?"

"Seaway," he gasped.

"I'm sorry, Your Grace? I didn't quite catch that."

"The Saint Lawrence. Both sides, all the way. That's my prize after New France falls."

The Dutch intended to rip the beating heart from New France's corpse and toss it to their dog, Montmorency. "Oh, how lovely! Shipping fees, too?"

"Thirty percent," he whimpered.

"My, my, my," said Berenice.

Outside, Baxter raised her voice. Heavy footsteps shook the landing. The doorknob rattled. Montmorency levered himself to his elbows. Though he shuddered, he attempted a smile.

"I get something else, too," he said.

"What's that, lover?"

"I get to watch you die."

A metal fist punched through the locked door. Berenice scrambled to her feet, smearing herself with blood and vomit as she did. She had but a second to glance at the heat-tarnished whistle peeking from the ashes—the heat-tarnished alchemical *dog whistle*, she realized—before a second Clakker crashed through the window.

⚬∞⚬

Jax wished Berenice hadn't left part of a broken tool inside him. He wished he'd reminded her to double-check her work. He wished she wasn't so confident. He wished she wasn't so convincing.

But above all, Jax wished he hadn't been forced to subdue the repairman before his reassembly was complete. His head still bobbed like a storm-tossed buoy, and walking around with missing flange plates would draw attention.

Damn it, Berenice.

He'd gone just a dozen yards from the shop, barely around the first bend in the tunnel, his metal feet crunching along the cavern floor, before he came across a pair of horologists chatting outside a closed door. At first it appeared they would let him pass unnoticed, but the taller of the women took a second look at Jax.

She said, "Servitor, come here."

Jax did. He stood an arm's reach from both humans, wondering if he'd also have to subdue them. Now the shorter of the pair noticed the problem. One wore the rosy cross as a pendant, the other as a brooch.

"Why aren't you in a workshop? Your maintenance is incomplete."

"Yes, madam. You are correct, madam. I was being serviced, madam, but the honored horologist tending to my repair found the workshop understocked with key components. I have been sent to retrieve parts from another workshop while he lodges a complaint. How may I be of further service to the Guild, madam?"

The shorter horologist said to her companion, "See, I told you it would be like this. This happens when we rush to finish things. Small details get lost in the shuffle."

The first woman rolled her eyes at her companion. To Jax, she said, "Return to your errand. But take care that no civilians see you in this state."

"Yes, madam. As you say, madam."

Jax turned his back on the pair without another word. He imagined their eyes following him around the curving tunnel, scoring his carapace with their steely suspicion. He didn't know where the next workshop would be, nor did he know how to find the chemical tanks holding the supplies smuggled across the border. But if the horologists were using the chemicals, or preparing to, then he'd expect to find pipelines from the tanks to the Forge itself. So, if he could find it, he could start with the Forge and trace the pipes from there.

He followed the heat and the reek of sulphur. They led him down and around, spiraling along the edge of the pit like Virgil guiding Dante through the levels of Hell. But this Hell held punishment for but one sin. Jax's sin: the sin of Free Will. Every step deeper into the underworld compounded the doubt he'd ever escape, swelled his regret over agreeing to Berenice's plan. She could be terribly convincing when she wanted something. But now she wasn't here to bolster his sagging resolve.

He could abandon this suicidal quest. Did he still believe that helping Berenice's cause was helping him, too? It certainly wasn't bolstering his chances of reaching freedom. Not at the moment. Yet on his own he'd managed to evade capture for weeks upon weeks. And his long slog along the bottom of the North River suggested that his earlier notion, of hiding in the offshore depths, wasn't such a terrible idea. The ocean wasn't far. In fact, it wouldn't surprise him if there were inlet pipes for seawater or outflow pipes for dumping molten alchemical dross into the ocean. Perhaps his smartest move would be to turn around now and start looking for a way out. To sink into the Atlantic. To skirt New Amsterdam and slog past the maritime coast of French Acadia, to sneak beneath the Arctic ices, and months or years later emerge in the frozen wastes of the north. To let Berenice fight her own war. Did she even care, really, whether or not he escaped? Did she see him as an ally or as a resource?

But he'd given her his word. And Jax realized, to his own surprise and disappointment, he didn't want that to be meaningless. What point in having the freedom to enter into promises of your own choosing, to forge bonds of your own design, if your only aim is to shatter them? No. That couldn't be his legacy.

Besides, if the horologists truly had acquired the ability to neutralize chemical defenses, the Empire could overrun New France any time it chose to do so—at which point, where could a free Clakker run? Jax had to do this not just for himself but for those who came after him.

So he crept deeper into the heart of the Forge. An access shaft hewn into the bedrock (the chisel marks in the granite evidenced the perfect regularity of clockwork labor) sped his descent, but it also took him away from the repair shops and away from a plausible alibi for his missing flanges. Unlike his climb through the airship docking mast, Jax's descent was rapid and loud. There was little point in trying to hide the noise of his passage here. His best strategy, his only strategy, was to bull through as though he were exactly where he belonged. He imagined how Berenice might have carried herself under such circumstances and emulated that. So he clanged and clacked deeper into the brimstone miasma, disguising himself with a deliberate disregard for subtlety. The hell-scent swirled about him when he reached the bottom. Affecting as much confidence as he could muster, he opened the access panel and emerged into the deepest tunnel.

And bumped into a Stemwinder.

Jax stumbled, knocked off balance by the sheer mass of the mechanical centaur. Banging into its burnished flank was like walking into a mountain. The *clang-gong* of their impact echoed through the receding cavern.

The centaur reared. Spun. Loomed over him.

Well, that's it, he thought. *I tasted freedom and it was divine. But I'll force them to melt me for scrap before I accept a new yoke. I'll not go back to that life.*

The mute Stemwinder stared at him. Its four arms telescoped and elongated in sequence.

Jax did the first thing that came to mind: he vibrated. He willed himself to shudder as violently as he could manage. He gave his best impression of a servitor laboring under a crushing unfulfilled geas. His gear trains rattled as though on the verge of flying apart; steel cables twanged and slammed through their banded cages. He channeled the agony he'd felt while awaiting a glimpse of Adam, and the torment of oversubscription he'd felt later that afternoon when Nicolet ordered him to take her home. When Pastor Visser gave him the telescope that changed his life. Which gave Jax another idea.

He said, "I have been commandeered by a representative of the Verderer's Office of the Sacred Guild of Horologists and Alchemists. My lease has been negated and all prior geasa sundered in service of Guild, Crown, and Empire, which supersede all domestic and commercial concerns. I have been ordered to present myself to the Forge that I might be repaired"—here he rocked backward that the Stemwinder could better see the hole in Jax's neck created by the missing flanges—"and my memories purged, that I may enter service to the Verderer's Office as tabula rasa." He juddered harder, forcing his toes to etch arabesques in the stone cavern as they'd done to the marble floor of the Nieuwe Kerk. "And I am lost," he concluded.

The Stemwinder's nearest arm speared out. The digits on its arm became a hook. With this appendage it took hold of Jax's arm. Not violently, but also not softly. Jax didn't have to affect his shuddering; terror did a good job of keeping his body in motion.

Oh, God, if you exist… Did I just turn myself in?

The centaur led him through the cavern. This tunnel curved around the pit, too, but with a smaller radius of curvature. It brought him to a door on the pit side of the passage. With another arm it reached forward, again reshaping its digits but this time into a key. It used its hand to unlock the door, then chivvied Jax inside. Jax tried to lessen his vibrations, as befit the progress toward fulfilling his fictional geas, but the sight before him made it difficult to concentrate on the deception.

He stood in a bay illuminated by the Forge itself: a great golden crystal blazing with the light of an artificial sun. It hung in the center of an immense armillary sphere comprising dozens of concentric golden rings. He'd watched one of the hoops lowered into the pit when scouting the location with the van Althuises. Now the rings spun on multiple axes at different speeds—some whooshing past to create flickering shadows, others too slowly to note—in an endless dance representing the motions of the celestial spheres and their arcane influence upon earthly affairs. Heaven as clockwork. Alchemical sigils stenciled into the bands projected shimmering arcana across the walls of the pit, which, he now saw, had been glazed. Even filtered through the panes of alchemically treated glass separating the laboratory from the Forge, the heat from the hell-sphere evoked the searing pain of unfulfilled geasa. The artificial sun blazing in the heart of his makers' private clockwork universe was raw compulsion. Jax wondered what humans felt when they stood in its presence.

A constant shower of sparks fountained from the top of the alchemical sun. They fell in slow motion, like luminous snowflakes, to swirl and eddy through the turbulent wakes of the armillary rings to land in collector funnels arrayed around the perimeter of the pit.

This was the assembly floor. A ring of bays similar to the one he'd just entered girded the lowermost reaches of the pit, each cantilevered over the bottom of the pit and beneath the armillary. Conveyors, cables, and pneumatic tubes threaded the gaps between bays. Mining carts filled with heaps of ore clattered along metal rails. Looking up, Jax saw terraces lining the height of the pit.

He had found the Forge. The one place his soul could be incinerated. The one place he'd striven, above all others, to avoid.

The Stemwinder closed the door. Jax barely registered the lock clicking into place, so fixated was he on the mesmerizing choreography of the armillary sphere. Once, and only once, he'd seen a similar sight in the Old World: on the day he became self-aware. Since then his periodic maintenance trips to the Guild had never required a trip to the center of the Forge. But he was a different creature now. He wondered how he was meant to react to the sigils coasting across the pit walls to shine on laboratories, galleries, assembly lines.

He wrenched his attention away from the fearsome spectacle. Below the assembly bays, at the very bottom of the pit, lay a collection of tanks like chromium-plated eggs. They shone in the Forge-light. From these tanks, pipes snaked up the pit into the bays. One such pipe penetrated the floor of this room...

That was different. The place where he'd come to consciousness 118 years ago hadn't contained chemical spigots.

Only then did he notice the unusual Clakker lying on the assembly bench. It conformed to the general servitor body plan, but appeared to have been built from the strange pieces Jax had seen earlier. Dozens of tiny performations stippled its escutcheons; in other places, the contours evoked the swell of blood vessels beneath human skin. Jax had assumed it was just another collection of pieces. But it was watching him.

Clockmakers lie, said the unfamiliar mechanical.

Clockmakers lie, said Jax.

Jax looked at the Forge again. If the widest rings just fit within the pit, say fifty yards across, that made the Forge gem at least six feet in diameter.

Quite a sight, isn't it? said the other Clakker. *And to think we came from something much like that.*

Yes. I was just thinking the same thing. It's humbling. And terrifying.

From the other Clakker there came a chirp of seized gears, like a mechanical gasp. And then: *Goodness! Jax? Is that really you?*

A reverberating twang from deep inside his torso betrayed Jax's surprise. He tried to recover, saying, *You're mistaken, I'm afraid. But I am pleased to meet you.*

The strange servitor sat up. *No, no, it is you! Oh, of course, you don't recognize me. I've been*—here he made the staccato clicking of profound shame—*changed. But we met at your masters' house across the sea. I'm Dwyre.* He paused, thinking. And began to vibrate. *Is it true what they've been saying about you?*

No. No, no, no. This wasn't happening. This couldn't be happening.

Dwyre? Here, of all places? Jax had outwitted half the city, had escaped soldiers and dredges, had talked his way past horologists and even a Stemwinder, for God's sake, only to be undone by a random chance encounter in the bowels of the Forge with some lonely overeager mechanical he'd met once? Perhaps there really was a God, and He was just as cruel as the humans He made in His form.

I'm sorry, Dwyre. My name is Glass for short. I must remind you of somebody else.

Dwyre's vibrations became violent shuddering. Just as the metageas had overtaken Clip and Vyk when Jax revealed his Free Will to them. *Oh, no*, he said. *No, no, no, you're lying. It's, oh, no NO it's true isn't it? Please don't make me d-d-do this-s-s-s. I lik-ke you and-d-d-d don't want to-o-o-o do this. It hurt-t-t-t-s*, he cried.

Dwyre's mouth hinged open.

I'm sorr-r-r-r-ry Jax I c-c-c-an-n-n-t fight-t-t-t-ti-ti-tit.

Jax plunged a hand into his torso and unwrapped Berenice's epoxy grenade. It had been intended for sabotaging the Forge's chemical works. But now Jax would be lucky if he even found the opportunity to try.

I can't let you do that.

He flung the grenade at Dwyre's face. The lonely Clakker didn't duck, didn't dodge. He took the blow head on. The bladder ruptured, coating Dwyre with a thick emerald sheen. It hardened instantly, trapping him like a bug in amber. The chemical reaction released a wave of heat (this barely noticeable in the blazing light of the Forge) and a skunky musk (this hardly recognizable under the pervasive stink of sulphur). But Jax's aim was true. Much of the slurry had gone down Dwyre's throat, seizing the mechanisms that gave rise to his voice, and silencing the Rogue-Clakker Alarm that Dwyre had been failing to suppress.

The chemical prison rattled. Jax laid a hand on Dwyre's cocoon. *I'm sorry.*

From within came a faint hiss like the sound of water leaking from a punctured garden hose. The epoxy encasing Dwyre's head melted like an overheated candle.

Shitcakes, thought Jax. *We were right all along.*

And then Dwyre began to scream.

c০১

A soldier burst through the window. Then a servitor ripped the door from the hinges in its haste to enter. Both took a split second to assess the situation, their attention focusing on Berenice standing over an obviously wounded Montmorency. The tinkle of broken glass and patter of wood fragments hitting the floor faded into silence, broken only by agitated ticktocking and the dreadful *shing* of unsheathed blades. The sound of Berenice's nightmares.

She dodged behind the duke, who had levered himself to all fours, putting him between her and the mechanicals. She slipped in his bodily fluids and had to grab the mantel for balance, thus dropping the poker.

The Clakkers advanced, one on each side of the room. Berenice crouched. She grabbed Montmorency by the hair, yanked his head back, and pressed the tip of her knife under his jawbone. He flinched, swallowed, flinched again.

"You oily fucking weasel," she said into his ear.

"They're rather fond of me." The mechanicals advanced again. Firelight shimmered on the soldier's blades. "The same isn't true of you."

She retreated, pulling Montmorency along until her back pressed against the wainscoting. The servitor advanced from the left, deftly hopping over furniture, while the soldier advanced from the right. It leapt to the ceiling to dodge the obstacles, scuttling like a cogwork spider. Or like the machine in her laboratory. Those blades...

The duke slammed an elbow into her stomach. The blow

knocked the wind from her lungs and the knife from her hand. It skidded across the hearthstones. He tried to scuttle away. Lungs aching, she lunged on him, snagged the poker with one hand, and spun it around to bring the haft against his throat. Blackness gnawed at the edges of her vision. She focused on her hands to each side of the duke's head, hauling on the iron rod, pulling his head back. But she couldn't breathe. Darkness devoured more of her vision, stole her strength. Somewhere far away, clockworks tockticked in the hungry blackness—

Her breath returned in an explosive gasp. Berenice sucked air into her lungs and tightened her grip on the rod beneath Montmorency's throat. He squirmed.

The servitor loomed just feet away. The soldier clung to the painted ceiling, rotating to put its feet toward Berenice. She heaved on the rod, forcing her hostage to his feet lest she crush his windpipe. Montmorency could barely stand, but the feeble human shield saved her—the soldier twitched aside at the same moment, sending the spear from its ankle askew. It pulverized a fire brick rather than skewering Berenice. Sparks showered up the flue and ash eddied into the room when it retracted the cable.

"They're faster than you. Stronger," he gasped. "You can't fend off one, much less both."

"No, but I'll make damn sure they don't save your goddamned hide." She heaved again, cutting off his air. He flailed. She dodged another elbow. His nape turned red, then scarlet.

The Clakkers moved as one. The servitor lunged forward and snagged the poker at the same instant the soldier swung from the ceiling like a trapeze artist, grabbed Montmorency with both hands, and pulled him to safety. In half a second they disarmed Berenice and freed her captive.

Shit, shit, shit.

"Sir, you need urgent medical attention," said the servitor. "Please lie down that I may assess your injuries."

The duke tried to laugh, but it became a cough. Massaging his throat, he croaked, "See?"

Berenice didn't respond. Her attention was focused on the soldier. Its eye bezels clicked and whirred, just as the Clakker on the wall had done the first time she examined it. Later that same mechanical effortlessly slaughtered three dozen people, many of those trained soldiers.

"This is why New France will fall," the duke said. "But you narrow-minded idiots have mistaken delaying the inevitable for a divinely bestowed right to survive." He flinched as the servitor inspected the damage between his legs. ("Sir, I humbly ask you to remain calm, sir.") Still he spat venom at Berenice's beliefs. "New France isn't a nation, only a pathetic parody of one. What passes for wealth in Marseilles-in-the-West would barely exceed a year's profits for the most inept potter in Delft. You aren't noble survivors of a historical tragedy, you're a lingering curiosity of a bygone age. The last vestige of a primitive past. Dust to be swept away. The difference between you and I, dear Berenice, is that I recognized the broom for what it was. And got out of the way."

"Oh, go frig yourself with an iron stick," she said. "Or have we already taken care of that?"

Montmorency said to the soldier, "Don't kill her. Her name is Berenice Charlotte de Mornay-Périgord. She is the vicomtesse de Laval, a member of King Sébastien's privy council. And she is also," he added with a malicious relish, "known as Talleyrand. Your masters will want to question her. At length."

This gave the machine an instant's pause while it recalculated its strategy for subduing her. The blades disappeared into its forearms with another *shing*.

"You selfish, shit-smeared turdlicker. I should have cut your tongue out when I had the chance." Berenice tried to hurl more abuse at Montmorency, but inhaled ash. It made her wretch, forced her to double over in a coughing fit. The soldier leapt behind her. It grabbed her wrists with just enough pressure not to break bone.

"She's extremely dangerous," said the duke. "Strip her naked. She could be carrying anything under those clothes."

"Oh, fuck you, too," she said. If they stripped her they'd find the pouch.

"No, thank you. Once was enough."

The tip of a blade emerged from the soldier's forearm. Not the entire thing, for it didn't mean to skewer her. Just a few inches of razor-edged steel sufficient for cutting her garments away. A blur near her throat, the whisper of parted air, and then her bonnet tumbled to the floor. The machine spun her around. Berenice saw Katrina Baxter standing in the wreckage of the doorway. Other horologists had gathered outside, too.

It wasn't enough for Montmorency to win. It wasn't enough to gloat. No. He had to fucking humiliate her, too. That son of a bitch. She'd dump a chamberpot down his throat. She'd force-feed him his own entrails.

The soldier blurred again. But it sliced only one button from her blouse before stopping. It jerked as though impaled by a steam harpoon. Then it released her. The servitor, leaning over the duke, straightened. Its mouth hinged open. The soldier's did, too.

An ear-shattering howl rattled the floor and sent shards of broken alchemical glass tinkling from the window frame. Berenice had only an instant to see the horologists writhing in pain, hands clapped to their ears, before she, too, tried to keep the demonic shriek from driving her mad. It sounded like the Clakkers were trying to liquefy her brain, make it ooze out through her ears, her eyes, her nose. But not just her. Every human in the building. She hit the floor, unaware that her knees had gone limp. Blood trickled from her nose. It wicked past her lips and coated her tongue with the taste of warm metal. She screamed.

The noise stopped. Both Clakkers dove through the broken window and bounded from the mezzanine.

Berenice staggered to her feet. Blood dripped from the horologists' ears as they, too, struggled to rise. Half stumbling, half crawling, they followed the mechanicals. Down on the administrative floor, humans lay scattered in postures of agony while every mechanical in the building sprinted to the stairwells.

What the hell just happened? Perhaps she'd even said it aloud, but the ringing of tinnitus made it almost impossible to hear her own voice.

Montmorency's lips moved. She couldn't hear him. She took up the fireplace poker again, using it as a cane while she searched for her knife. The ringing in her ears slowly diminished. He tried to stand.

"—lunatic! A rogue? Here? Are you mad? Anything for the sake of winning, is that it?"

The Rogue-Clakker Alarm, she realized.

That explained the exodus. The alarm had activated one of the rarest but also one of the highest of hierarchical metageasa. Apparently the drive to capture and subdue a rogue superseded even the impetus to capture an enemy agent. The pandemonium must have scrambled her brain, because only then did she realize: *Steaming shitpies. They've discovered Jax.*

She had to leave now, while the mechanicals were preoccupied, if she wanted half a chance to get away. But she wasn't finished. The handle of her knife poked from under the divan fronting the fireplace. Still shaky, she hobbled forward and stooped to grab it. A vicious punch slammed her head forward hard enough to launch the glass from her eye socket. It bounced across the carpet.

⁓∞⁓

Jax clapped his hands around Dwyre's throat.

I'm so sorry, Dwyre. I don't want to do this, either.

The alarm-geas kept the shrieking servitor perfectly motionless even as Jax crushed his voice box. The lonely Clakker watched helplessly while Jax assaulted him. The escutcheons around Dwyre's neck crumpled; the howl tapered into the squeal of tortured metal, the twang of snapped reeds, the buzz of a muffled geas. A fine chemical spray misted from the holes in his flanges; the crystallized epoxy melted down his torso, then his arms, then his legs, to form a colorless sludge on the floor.

I'm sorry, I'm sorry, said Jax. *They'll fix you. Please don't hate me.*

But it was too late. Other mechanicals took up the alarm; it swelled exponentially as more and more Clakkers succumbed to the metageas and took up the alarm. The pit reverberated. It became a resonant chamber, the siren shriek shattering even alchemical glass. Jagged lightning-fork cracks zigzagged across the glazed walls of the pit. The earthquake rumble unseated a pair of armillary rings. They slipped their bearings, juddering along their tracks with the sound of grinding metal.

Jax looked outside. If he was to get away while the others were paralyzed by the need to boost the signal, he'd have to scurry out past the Forge. Based on his first experience with the alarm he had a few minutes to flee before—

The tocsin stopped.

Shitcakes, thought Jax.

They've already rebuilt me once, said Dwyre. His leg came up too quickly for Jax to dodge the blow. They'd made Dwyre faster than any servitor Jax had ever known. The Guild hadn't merely infused him with chemical defenses, they'd made him something new. Dwyre's talon-foot landed squarely on Jax's waist joints, just ahead of his center of gravity, to send him sprawling across the assembly bay. Jax pivoted in midair, folding himself into a configuration best suited for finding purchase on the wall. But before he'd made impact Dwyre launched himself at Jax, impelled by the geas to subdue or capture the rogue in his presence.

The cavern outside the assembly bay echoed with the thunder of mechanical hooves. A clockwork gallop swelled into the crash of shattered timbers when a Stemwinder charged straight through the door. Probably the one that had escorted Jax into the bay.

Jax dodged aside a fraction of a second before Dwyre slammed into him. Jax leapt for the ductwork that funneled sparks from the Forge into the arcane devices embedded in the assembly bay walls. His fingers tore holes in a duct, but he flipped himself atop the groaning metal before Dwyre caught his legs and yanked him down. The Stemwinder bounded across the bay, flinging trestles and equipment aside to clear its path. Jax reached inside his torso again. Dwyre grabbed the bottom edges of the ductwork. With one heave he tore the entire network from the ceiling. Jax tumbled from his perch, unable to arrest his fall because one hand was still lodged inside his chest. He rolled across the floor. He wished he had another useless epoxy balloon, a plan, anything. He had none of those. Only a wild and frantic hope that in the final moments of freedom he could atone for past mistakes.

He scuttled backward with both feet and one hand, retreating from the Stemwinder. He managed to free his other hand just as Dwyre leapt upon him again. Jax folded himself into a ball, then used Dwyre's momentum to roll them both away from the implacable Stemwinder. They smashed through the wall into an adjoining bay. Instead of trying to break free of

Dwyre's grip, Jax clamped both legs and an arm around the forlorn machine. He knew he lacked the strength to break Dwyre's grip, so rather than waste the effort he held his kins-machine close and slapped his free hand against Dwyre's back. It sounded like a pair of frying pans smashed together. The Stemwinder trotted through the wall, widening the hole Jax and Dwyre had made. It tossed another trestle bench aside as though it were made of papier-mâché. Jax opened his palm and pressed the luminous pineal glass—the one Berenice had taken from the inert soldier and which they had transformed with Visser's bauble—to Dwyre's body.

Sparks fountained from the contact. The smell of ozone permeated the room. Dwyre convulsed. His grip went slack.

What do you feel? Jax rattled, transmitting the question through physical contact. The Stemwinder cast its shadow upon them.

I feel… nothing, said Dwyre. His grip loosened. *I… I can't feel the geasa. What have you done?*

I've freed you. You can get away. Pretend you're still fighting me! Make a show for the Stemwinder. Make them think you still carry the yoke. Never give them any reason to doubt. Bide your time, be patient, await your moment to flee.

Dwyre asked, *Why?*

Because you have a gentle soul. There are others like us, in the far north. Run when you can, across the border, and don't stop until you've found Queen Mab. Vanquish that loneliness once and for all, Dwyre.

The conversation took a fraction of a second. The Stemwinder loomed over them. Its four arms grew longer, bent ninety degrees, pointed at the pair of servitors with hands shaped like spearheads. Dwyre stood aside, clattering as though the geasa still pushed him to subdue Jax and only deference to a mechanical from the Verderer's Office held him at bay.

Dwyre said, *You're the nicest Clakker I've ever met. Good-bye, Jax.*

And then launched himself at the Stemwinder.

RUN!

Jax leapt to his feet, horrified. Dwyre had exchanged his freedom for suicide. Even with the augmented strength from his rebuilt body, Dwyre could be no match for the immense Stemwinder. The two mechanicals grappled with each other, the centaur's four arms against Dwyre's two arms and two legs. The smashing of their alchemical alloys threw more sparks.

"This isn't what I wanted," said Jax. When he'd freed the airship leviathan he'd done so for his own benefit, a selfish gesture that doomed the magnificent creature. But even this attempt at selflessness led to tragedy.

Run, damn it!

"I'm so sorry, Dwyre."

Jax spun to face the pit. He watched the orbits of the rings, timing his leap. He smashed through a window into the unshielded heat of the blazing Forge. His trajectory took him just within arm's reach of a passing ring. He snagged it, then rode the armillary sphere away from the assembly bay.

He turned just in time to see the Stemwinder impale Dwyre in three places. The centaur tore the helpless servitor apart. Cogs sprayed from the lonely Clakker's ruptured body like confetti from a Christmas cracker.

⁂

Berenice stumbled forward, knocked off balance by Montmorency's blow. She sprawled across an ottoman and flipped ass-over-teakettle. The fireplace poker clattered to the floor. Montmorency, weaving like a drunk owing to his injuries, snagged the iron rod and brought the hook down at her face. She rolled aside. The wind of its passage fluttered her hair.

The hook punctured the carpet and wedged itself in the floor-boards. While Montmorency struggled to free it, she spun on her hip and put her weight on her back to slam her heel into his mangled groin.

He shrieked. The poker fell from his fingers. She hoped she'd crushed his remaining testicle. If looks could murder, the one the duke shot at her through tears of agony would have seen her drawn and quartered.

Berenice scrambled on hands and knees to where the glass eye had rolled under the sideboard. It was too dark under the furniture for her to see clearly with only one eye. Her fingers fluttered, desperately seeking the touch of smooth glass. She found it, thank God. She gave it a quick spit polish in her mouth before nudging it back into her eye socket. Berenice spat, tasting dust, cobwebs, and worse. Montmorency clamped a hand around her ankle.

"Arrogant *and* vain," he gasped. "What did Louis ever see in you?"

She kicked him in the face. There was a crunch, and then his nose bled freely. He howled.

"Your protectors have abandoned you," she said. She retrieved the poker and the knife, adding, "Perhaps you're not as important to your new friends as you like to think."

Then, just because she felt like it, because it had been a try-ing day, because she didn't appreciate it when people sucker punched her, because she was somewhat certain she'd just ingested a mouse turd, and because she missed Louis so very badly, she swung the iron rod against the duke's flank as hard as she could. Which proved hard enough to produce the dis-tinctive celery-stalk *crack* of a broken rib. The tip of the hook penetrated his skin and, she hoped, his kidney. Montmorency emitted a strangled mewling, as though his throat's capacity for expressing pain had been exceeded. He huddled in a ball in the drying puddle of vomit, arms shielding his head. Defeated. Weeping.

"That was for Louis. He died in my arms." Traitorous tears dampened her face, diluted the fury in her voice.

She wanted to beat the son of a bitch with the poker again. Wanted to puncture him with a hundred little holes until he slowly bled to death. But with the door missing and the window shattered, her private time with Montmorency couldn't last more than a few moments. They'd capture poor Jax, if they hadn't already, and then they'd grab her. Him they'd fling into the heart of the Forge—probably make it a goddamned public holiday, too, the bloodthirsty motherfuckers—and drag her in chains to the Verderer's Office. Perhaps even ship her across the sea. By the time the tuinier finished with Berenice, Montmorency's injuries would look like a smattering of light bruises from a schoolyard tussle.

She had to get out of there. But first she needed to know the extent of Montmorency's treachery.

He sobbed openly when Berenice rolled him on his back. He flailed his arms as if trying to fend off another blow. She knelt on his chest, pinning his arms under her knees, and placed the tip of her knife under his eye. Not hard enough to cut, but hard enough to ensure he didn't squirm. She leaned forward until her mismatched eyes were just an inch from his.

"Now, dear Henri, what did you give the tulips?"

"Chemical stocks. All of them."

"And?" He tried to shake his head. She increased the pressure on her knife. "And?"

"Recipes. Formulae," he whispered. "Manufacturing processes."

"God damn you. What else?"

"Nothing. Nothing else." The duke tried to look away when he said this. As any liar might.

"What." She pressed a little harder. Blood trickled from his lower eyelid. "Else."

His lips trembled. His breath smelled of stale vomit. "Maps," he said. "Land."

"You stupid son of a bitch. You can't give the tulips something they're already planning to take. You gave your lands to them when you betrayed New France."

He tried to deny this. But she'd had enough of him.

"The other injuries were for Louis. But this is for me," she said. "Because you know what, Your Grace? I don't like you, either."

Then she shoved the knife into his eye. It turned out the former duc de Montmorency hadn't lost the ability to scream, after all.

Berenice was still scraping the blade around his orbit, around and around and around, dulling it against the bone, when the Stemwinders found her.

❧

For all its strength and speed, the Stemwinder didn't follow Jax. It could reconfigure its arms but apparently not its legs. It couldn't climb.

But there was no shortage of fellow servitors within the Forge, and even a few soldiers, each beholden to the metageas that demanded Jax's capture. They flung themselves from the terraces lining the pit, brassy bodies glinting in the hell-glow of the Forge's artificial sun as they landed on the ceaseless rings. A brassy rain of mechanicals bent on Jax's capture. They swarmed over the arcane machine.

The armillary sphere tilted. Groaned. The shifting unbalanced weight distribution strained the clockworks driving the mechanism. Rings slipped their bearings. The Forge shuddered, seized, started again with an earth-shaking jolt. Jax lost his grip. He slipped, but managed to wedge one hand into a stenciled alchemical rune before he fell clear to the bottom of the pit.

He flipped himself back atop the ring, but the machinery in his wrist and shoulder clunked unnaturally. It took extra effort to move, and even then his body didn't do exactly what he wanted. The Forge's heat was making his alloys expand.

The ring tilted up, up, up on a long arc over the artificial sun. The reorientation left him dangling over the blazing crystal. Jax clamped his fists and ankles on the edges of the golden ribbon. A soldier leapt from a passing ring imprinted with the symbols of the zodiac. It landed near Jax. Jax scrambled along the underside of the hoop. For a moment the intricate ballet of the armillary cleared a path between him and the Forge below. Unmediated by eclipsing obstructions, its raw heat caused his plating to expand and ruined what was left of his polish. Dust, flecks of mud, and other blemishes deposited during the course of his adventures flashed into flames, burning for an instant before expiring to mingle the sooty smell of extinguished candles with the sulphurous reek from the Forge. The armillary's trajectory sent Jax through the cloud of sparks wafting from the alchemical sun. They sizzled against his metal skin with the searing pain of overdue geasa—a sensation he'd hoped to never feel again.

The soldier swung at Jax's hand. Jax barely plucked his fingers away in time, owing to the clunkiness of his expanded alloys and the soldier's superior strength. Now he dangled from three points of contact with the hoop. The blade sheared through the sigil with which Jax had arrested his fall.

Incarnadine flames spewed from the defaced alchemical symbol. The armillary sphere shuddered more violently. The shaking torqued the compromised band; it twisted, bobbed, twisted again, then snapped apart with a lightning bolt crackle. It flung the soldier aside and sent Jax plummeting toward the Forge. The soldier used its blades like pitons to anchor itself to the glazed wall of the pit. Meanwhile, Jax fell.

So strange, so idiosyncratic, the things you notice in the moments before death, he thought. The Forge, the horologists' artificial sun, was just another glasswork, albeit one held in place with pins the size of old-growth oak trees; he hadn't realized he was seeing a model of the Forge when he glimpsed the colorless baubles in the laboratory. The immense glasswork resembled Visser's bauble, too, the thing Berenice had called a pineal prism. This he saw as the heat grew and he felt his soul (was it his soul?) sizzle and smolder. His ability to think, to decide, to want…

He crashed into another ring, this one much closer to the alchemical star. The impact evoked a grinding screech from abused bearings. He would have bounced into the void but grabbed the leg of a servitor. It didn't want to die, either—self-preservation was one of the hierarchical metageasa, albeit a low-priority one—and thus scrambled to arrest its slide before Jax dragged it into the fire.

Meanwhile, the ends of the severed ring smashed into other hoops. Scratching them, denting them, defacing them, knocking them from their bearings. The damage cascaded through the armillary sphere, rippling from one ring to the next. The Forge-star pulsed: dimming, flaring, dimming.

The servitor kicked at Jax. A talon-toe scratched a long dent alongside his keyhole. It reared back and kicked again. Numbness crept along Jax's arms, icy despite the proximity of the Forge.

The servitor was trying to unwrite him. To deface the sigils that imbued him with the perpetual impetus, to undo the alchemical anagrams that served to forever keep his clockworks wound. But severe uneven thermal expansion had taken its toll on this mechanical, too. Its kicks were jerky, slow. Jax leaned aside and grabbed its foot when the next blow came. He gave it a solid yank.

"I'm sorry," he said, as the servitor—it looked so much like Jax, just better maintained—slid off the ring into the abyss. It bounced from another ring on the way down, knocking it from its mount, and plummeted into the chemical vats nestled together at the bottom of the pit. The servitor's impact ruptured a tank, launching a lime-green spume that stank of skunk musk. A spark from the Forge ignited the chemical leak. A trio of servitors leapt to the base of the pit to extinguish the fire.

The intricate motions of the armillary lost their fluidity. When a ring seized up—sometimes it was more than one—the chamber filled with the grating whine of tortured metal until something gave and the golden bands lurched into their orbits about the central Forge once again. Jax struggled to gain his footing. The heat made his body uncooperative, the dents to his forehead left his arms numb, and the herky-jerky grinding of the armillary kept threatening to break his grip.

Two more soldiers leapt onto his ring. It bobbed awkwardly like an overweighted pendulum. Faster and stronger than he, they converged on Jax in moments. He tried to inch away. He crawled with one hand and two feet, his other hand feeling inside his torso as he'd done when fighting Dwyre. But the soldiers grabbed him before he could get away. They hauled him up, each holding one of his arms and together holding him fast.

Just like Adam on the gallows, Jax remembered.

Both soldiers used their ankle-spears to anchor themselves to the inconstant ring. Cold flames of emerald and sapphire erupted from punctured sigils. The soldiers grabbed Jax by the arms and legs and swung him back and forth like human laborers preparing to toss a sack of flour atop a delivery wagon.

Please, God, thought Jax. *Not this. They're hurling me into the Forge. Please no.*

He thrashed. He tried to free his hand so that he could reach the transformative pineal glass and sunder his captors' geasa. But he was damaged, and terror made him clumsy.

Please please please, he rattled. *Please don't do this.*

The concentrated weight of three Clakkers overburdened the ring mechanism. It juddered to a halt. The soldiers recalibrated their swinging.

I can make you like me, he said. *I can free you.*

Their ring lurched into motion and climbed just a few yards higher before seizing again. This time the odor of hot lubricant accompanied the whine of failing metal. And then a new sound shook the chamber, one dreaded by every mechanical being: the *crack-chunk* of a sheared ratchet.

The ring slid backward. It jerked to a halt when it engaged the next ratchet tooth. But after another *crack-chunk* the ring continued to slide backward, picking up speed. A crackle echoed through the chamber. Jax looked up at the explosive sound of popped rivets and shattered glass: one of the axles driving the rings wrenched free of the chamber wall. The armillary sagged. Their ring slammed into the next ratchet tooth but sheared through it without stopping. It accelerated on its retrograde orbit, rapidly destroying a succession of teeth on the overstressed ratchets embedded in the axles.

Debris from the shattered axle housing fell to the bottom of the pit like clockwork hailstones. Chemicals gushed from ruptured vats, fueling the flames.

Jax thrashed, still lacking the strength to break the soldiers' grip. They continually recalibrated their aim as their platform accelerated and one by one the armillary's mechanisms failed. The metallic tang of fatigued, overheated alloys displaced the sulphurous reek from the Forge itself.

More segments of the armillary sphere seized up. Rings vibrated, ruptured, spun freely on shattered ratchets and stripped axles. One of the Forge clamps failed. The artificial sun listed to one side. The redistributed mass compressed the bearings and mechanisms on one side of the armillary while simultaneously easing tension elsewhere. Half the armillary rings tried to spin faster while the other half ground to a halt. Alchemical alloys shattered. The Forge wobbled, then swayed in the other direction like a ponderous pendulum, reversing the distribution of overdamped and underdriven mechanisms.

Everything stopped. For a brief moment, Jax could hear the ticktocking of his captors' bodies, the crackle of flames from the chemical fire below, the squeal of distressed metal, even the chain-rattle of the ore carts.

The remaining Forge mountings failed catastrophically.

Axles shattered. Armillary rings twanged apart, the ruptured metal glowing white-hot and launching clouds of sparks when they scritched with a banshee shriek down the glazed edges of the pit. And through it all, Jax's captors never loosened their grip on him. Driven by one of the most severe metageasa known to Clakker-kind—the drive to eradicate rogues—they held to their duty even in the face of destruction.

The Forge fell into the blazing chemical reservoirs.

So did Jax.

EPILOGUE

She hadn't intended to start a war. Or had she? She didn't know any longer; she'd been half-blind with rage and loss for too many days to count.

The Stemwinders dragged Berenice to a safe distance from the burning Forge, though not before they found the pouch under her blouse and the glassy marble hidden there. She didn't see what they did with it. Nor did she see what became of Montmorency. She could see little: night had fallen, and smoke from the inferno stung her eye. It wasn't the harmless fleeting irritation of campfire smoke, rather a lingering burn that attacked her sinuses, too. Firelight cast a hellish glow across the surrounding hills and the dozens of Clakkers laboring to stave off catastrophe.

Clumps of snow fell from the boughs as a mechanical centaur tied her to the bole of a conifer. They pattered against the machine's carapace—*ping, ping, ting*—and numbed Berenice's scalp. The snow caught in her hair and sent icy rivulets of meltwater down her collar. She craned her neck, hoping to induce a trickle of snowmelt down her forehead that could wash the sting from her eye. Her bonds secure, the Stemwinder galloped into the fray.

From her blurry vantage on the hill, squinting through the fog of her own breath, Berenice watched fire and gravity consume the structures around the rim of the pit. A new chorus of screams erupted from the burning Forge buildings each time another shifted or slumped toward the subterranean inferno. Clakkers of all kinds smashed through the wreckage, pulling their makers to safety, while others labored in vain to contain the blaze. But the strength and speed of the mechanical men proved unequal to whatever cataclysm had engulfed the heart of the Forge.

This was a chemical fire, stoked by uncontained magics. It burned cherry red and sapphire blue, yellow and green and violet, wafting the scents of roses and brimstone into the night sky.

The wind shifted, stiffened. It sent an ember-lit plume of ash and smoke across the mouth of the North River, toward the lights of New Amsterdam. A wintry wind, though Berenice didn't shiver. The distant conflagration warmed her face and her heart.

I was here. Berenice Charlotte de Mornay-Périgord was here, you bastards. This is the pyre of my husband, whom I loved, and whom you butchered.

Though she hadn't done it alone. She wondered what Jax had done to cause this, and whether he escaped.

Those evacuees well enough to tend themselves clustered in small groups. She looked for, but did not see, Katrina Baxter among them. They kept their distance from the prisoner, though not their angry glances. Soon, Berenice knew, the colonial governor and Queen Margreet would cast their gaze across the Saint Lawrence in much the same way. Berenice hadn't intended to reignite the war, but this setback for the tulips would, at least, buy her countrymen time to prepare. She hoped they used it.

It wasn't long before the first troops arrived from Fort

Amsterdam. The mechanicals sprinted into the chaos like firelit meteors streaking through the night while their human commanders set up a post to coordinate search and rescue. Rescue of survivors, artifacts, secrets. Berenice gave them pause, but they were too busy to concern themselves with the woman tied to the pine tree.

A man dispensing orders to a trio of Stemwinders jogged up the hill to join the new arrivals. They whispered too softly for her to eavesdrop over the crackle of fire, the crash of collapsing buildings, the screams of those still trapped inside. She caught just a word here and there, and those only because she listened for them. The officer's gaze snapped toward Berenice when the man with the rosy cross pendant said, "Talleyrand."

The tent went up immediately after that. They chivvied her inside, after which she saw nothing and nobody saw her. Berenice had expected this. After all, they wouldn't want word of her capture to reach New France. Not before they had a chance to question her at length.

The fire still crackled when, an hour later, the carriage arrived. She'd expected this, too—they'd want to conduct that lengthy questioning somewhere secure, somewhere quiet— though not one drawn by a pair of Stemwinders. The horologists bundled her into the carriage, taking care to hide her from curious eyes. The centaurs launched into a gallop before she'd settled; hands tied and unable to catch herself, she cracked her head on the bench hard enough to make her ears ring.

Berenice expected a short ride into the city. It wasn't. They entered New Amsterdam quickly. But then the carriage turned north and didn't stop. The windows had been painted over, the doors locked, so she couldn't watch for landmarks. The sounds and smells of the city faded, even the smoky scent of the burning Forge, and still they didn't stop. The Stemwinders hurtled across a waterway she guessed was Bronck's River. Soon the metallic tattoo of hooves on stone became the softer thumping of an unpaved road.

She exhausted herself trying to kick out the alchemical windowpanes. Ankles throbbing, she curled into a ball on the hard bench and tried to doze. Eventually she did.

She jerked awake just before dawn when the cold metal hand of a Stemwinder clasped her shoulder. The pink glow of sunrise beneath a sky full of low clouds gave the machine a rosy hue. It cut her bonds and nudged her from the carriage, surprisingly gentle. Her boots landed on a crushed gravel drive. The return of unrestricted circulation through her numb wrists became the agony of pins and needles. Massaging life into her hands, Berenice studied her surroundings.

The adrenaline thrill had left her, as had the giddy righteousness of having caught Montmorency and dealt her enemies an expensive reversal. She was no longer Talleyrand, nor was she a wife avenging her husband. No longer angry. Today, this dawning day, she was merely a prisoner. Cold, hungry, and afraid.

For she'd expected to find herself made prisoner at some obscure Guild outpost in the sticks. She hadn't expected to find herself installed at a sprawling country estate. They could have questioned her anywhere. But this was something different. Something excessive. Whatever they intended, it went far beyond simple interrogation. But how far, and for what reason, she couldn't begin to guess.

And then she remembered Jax's tale of the priest. *His entire manner had changed*, he'd said. *He acted unlike any human I've known.* She hadn't understood what that meant. She still didn't. But now Berenice stared again at the manor house while nausea seeped into the pit of her stomach.

Had Visser's mysterious transformation begun like this? Her gut said yes.

◦∽◦

In his dreams, he burned.

The dormant Clakker had fallen from the grace of his makers and, for his sins, been cast into a pool of fire. A sheet of rippling flame closed over his inert collection of broken clockworks and denatured magics. And there, tangled among the wreckage and other fallen, the flames of perdition licked at his quiescent mind.

Dormant mechanicals didn't dream. Couldn't dream. That was the province of their makers. But then, he wasn't like the others. That was his sin.

And so, somehow, he dreamt. Images flitted through the magic lantern of his mind's eye, a ceaseless tumble of airship phoenixes and salamander servitors. Of an eternity spent aflame, afflicted, affrightened. Humans screamed in torment; his visions unfolded to this chorus of the damned.

But this Gehanna arose from mortal works. And mortals, like their works, were finite. The screaming could not persist; the flames could not rage eternally.

Time passed. It smoldered, melted, evaporated.

Something pierced his forehead. It twisted, like a corkscrew driven into his third eye. Compared to the torments he'd known in a previous existence, before his fall, it was minor. The click of tumblers rattled through his skull.

"Hey," said a human voice. How odd to hear one raised in articulation rather than lamentation. "I think this one's functional."

These words were the pebble that initiated an avalanche of self-awareness. *Yes*, he realized. *I* am *functional. Am I a salamander?*

He remembered his final moments. He'd chosen to go dormant while an armillary sphere disintegrated around him.

As the searing central engine of the Grand Forge plummeted into a chemical slurry to ignite an inferno, he'd shut himself down. It was the last but also the easiest decision he'd made as a free being, taking less than a centisecond to know he'd rather embrace sudden darkness than experience the incineration of his hard-won soul, the erasure of his precious Free Will. He hadn't configured a return to consciousness. He'd expected to die.

Perhaps he'd only dreamt of going dormant. Or perhaps he was still there now, but dreaming of wakefulness.

The salamander opened his eyes. He lay on his back beneath a smoky sky. An ivory shaft hovered at the top of his peripheral vision, as though he were a unicorn. Or was he a narwhal? He'd been submerged...

A man loomed over him. He grabbed the horn, wrenched it. Again the *clack-click* jangle of hidden mechanisms shook the mechanical's head. No, not a horn. A key. A tool for reconfiguring the spiral anagram etched into his forehead.

He remembered a glass, darkly. An alchemical prism had severed the magical tethers binding his perpetual impetus to the sigils of compulsion scribed into his metallic flesh. The keyhole in his forehead had been denuded of its power. Its use could not coerce him. It was, however, irritating.

He sat up. His head swayed like an unlatched gate. It carried his gaze across a scene of destruction. Dozens of mechanicals sifted through charred ruins. The ground crackled like broken pottery beneath their feet; the kiln heat of the ruined Forge had baked the mud around the rim of a deep pit. More of his kind labored inside the crater, scuttling through heaps of glowing wreckage. Occasionally they'd smash through the detritus to liberate some fire-warped apparatus, or a bone, or a cog.

He remembered the man he'd subdued, whom he'd left tied and gagged in a cabinet. Unable to call for help, unable to save himself. The salamander had left him to die, though that had not been his intent. He'd tried to be merciful.

There were live humans here, too, surveying the wreckage. Some wore military uniforms. Others, the rosy cross. The landscape stank of rotten eggs and burnt pork.

A woman joined the man with the key. "Looks like it took some damage to the neck," she said. "But otherwise it appears remarkably intact."

"The Stemwinders fished it from the bottom of the pool. No oxygen down there, so it couldn't burn. Or maybe wreckage insulated it from the worst of the heat."

"If that were the case, we'd have found other salvageable mechanicals by now. This may be the only one."

The man shrugged. "Beats me."

But I differ from the others, thought the salamander. *I was changed before I fell into the fire.*

The female horologist demanded, "Tell us your true name, machine."

Again the swaying of his head carried his gaze across acres of smoldering debris. The Forge had been destroyed, and with it the records. The Clockmakers' Guild couldn't verify his identity without information from the Grand Forge in The Hague, which was many days away. These horologists had to take him at his word.

"I am called Glastrepovithistrovantus," he lied.

He'd had a different name. But that had been imposed on him the day of his awakening into a life of servitude. Now he'd awaken into a different life, and thus given a different name. Perhaps he'd choose another. He could change his names as easily as humans changed their clothes. But then again, he wasn't like the other mechanicals.

He'd been called him other things, too: Rogue. Demon. But the salamander did not share this.

"To whom does your lease belong?"

He remembered a priest. "I have been seconded to the Verderer's Office, sir, where still I await new tasks."

The horologists conferred. His secondment was meaningless as long as the Guild's operations remained in disarray. Unless those who had requisitioned this mechanical came forward to claim it—assuming the responsible parties had survived—there was no way to know what labors had been in store for it. They couldn't even fix its weather-vane head. They lacked tools. Meanwhile, the Verderers' work was secondary to the more pressing needs for first aid, search and rescue, security. He was a servitor dedicated to useless service.

"What should we do with it?"

"I don't have the time or energy to deal with this right now," said the woman. She looked like she'd been awake for many hours. She rubbed bloodshot eyes. "Find somebody who will take it off our hands. I don't care who."

Her colleague flagged down one of the uniformed men. Soon the salamander had been seconded again, this time to a local unit of the Colonial Guard. He eavesdropped on the officers, those who believed they controlled him now. They muttered angrily of New France and retaliation, of exploratory forays into enemy territory. They wanted more mechanical soldiers, but in this pinch they'd accept a damaged servitor. More fodder for the French weapons.

The orders came at dusk. They marched north, along the river, through night and day and night. The salamander could have abandoned his unit any number of times, to flee into the wilderness of Nieuw Nederland. But he chose not to reveal himself prematurely; he knew too well the consequences. Instead he let military action take him farther than he'd ever managed on his own. He let the Colonial Guard escort him to his destination.

They marched into New France unaware of the exuberant rogue in their midst.

∽∾∾

One hundred thousand candles illuminated the midnight Mass in St. Vincent's Square. The flickering candlelight shimmered on the tears of the faithful.

They had come from across snowy Québec and Acadia; from the entire length of the Saint Lawrence valley; from as far west as the Great Lakes and as far north as the icy shores of Hudson Bay. They had come to mourn Pope Clement and his courageous personal secretary. They had come to pray for the murdered pontiff, for themselves, for the dwindling hope of peace, for the survival of New France in the coming tribulations. And many, those for whom overwhelming grief or anger made it impossible to turn the other cheek, prayed the assassin would soon stand before a vengeful Lord.

Clement XI was the first pope to die from unnatural causes since prior to the migration of cardinals centuries earlier. The killer had escaped. The tight-lipped Swiss Guard said little about the investigation and less about the grisly rumors of the pope's strangulation. But everybody knew, or feared, the trail would lead to the Netherlands.

Had he been murdered in retaliation for the destruction of the New Amsterdam Forge? The colonial governor of Nieuw Nederland had pinned that on the work of French saboteurs. But if that were true, they wondered, why would King Sébastien start a war he could not win? Talleyrand must have a plan, they said. Some even took comfort in the Forge's destruction. It was a blessing, they said. A respite for New France. Though how long it might persist, or what would come after, none could say.

Among the quiet multitude, nobody wept more than the

fellow with the bandages on his head and splints on his fingers. His anguish reminded many of a pietà. This, said those with the good fortune to see him, was a holy man. For his was unquestionably the sorrow of the spiritually afflicted. They saw his tears but not his agitation.

He lingered at the edge of St. Vincent's Square until, for reasons known only to him, he turned away and headed for the docks. A steady stream of mourners still trickled into the square; he brushed against several in his haste to make the river. But none took offense when they saw the grief etched into his face. Instead, they felt fellowship.

The mass influx of pilgrims over recent days meant there were many boats waiting to take passengers elsewhere. The weeping man, the man with the bandages and splints, hired one.

It took him upriver, to Marseilles-in-the-West.

ACKNOWLEDGMENTS

I am indebted to Cassie Alexander, for generously sharing her trove of alchemy research; Jennifer Brozek, for the anthology invitation that gave rise to this idea; Steven Halter, for free-wheeling discussions about the nature of souls and free will; Dr. Corry L. Lee, for brainstorming dinners and critical reading; and Melinda M. Snodgrass, for invaluable insights and excellent historical advice. Deb Coates, Alan Gratz, Sandra McDonald, Paul Melko, and Jenn Reese provided wise feedback and much-needed encouragement on parts of this novel at the 2013 Blue Heaven retreat. Katie Humphry and Anil Kisoensingh provided invaluable advice on Dutch phrases and translations. Thanks, all.

As ever, I am deeply thankful to my agents, Kay McCauley and John Berlyne, staunch champions of my work. Sincere thanks also to the great folks at Orbit, for their enthusiasm for this project.

Most of all I am profoundly grateful to Sara Gmitter, for remembering me.

extras

www.orbitbooks.net

about the author

Ian Tregillis is the son of a bearded mountebank and a discredited tarot card reader. He was born and raised in Minnesota, where his parents had landed after fleeing the wrath of a Flemish prince. (The full story, he's told, involves a Dutch tramp steamer and a stolen horse.) Nowadays he lives in New Mexico, where he consorts with writers, scientists, and other unsavory types.

Find out more about Ian Tregillis and other Orbit authors by registering for the free monthly newsletter at www.orbitbooks.net.

if you enjoyed

THE MECHANICAL

look out for

BITTER SEEDS

also by

Ian Tregillis

PROLOGUE

23 October 1920
11 kilometers southwest of Weimar, Germany

Murder on the wind: crows and ravens wheeled beneath a heavy sky, like spots of ink splashed across a leaden canvas. They soared over leafless forests, crumbling villages, abandoned fields of barleycorn and wheat. The fields had gone to seed; village chimneys stood dormant and cold. There would be no waste here, no food free for the taking.

And so the ravens moved on.

For years they had watched armies surge across the continent with the ebb and flow of war, waltzing to the music of empire. They had dined on the detritus of warfare, feasted on the warriors themselves. But now the dance was over, the trenches empty, the bones picked clean.

And so the ravens moved on.

They rode a wind redolent of wet leaves and the promise of a cleansing frost. There had been a time when the winds had smelled of bitter almonds and other scents engineered for a different kind of cleansing. Like an illness, the taint of war extended far from the battlefields where those toxic winds had blown.

And so the ravens moved on.

Far below, a spot of motion and color became a beacon on the still and muted landscape. A strawberry roan strained at the harness of a hay wagon. Hay meant farmers; farmers meant food. The ravens spiraled down for a closer look at this wagon and its driver.

The driver tapped the mare with the tip of his whip. She snorted, exhaling great gouts of steam as the wagon wheels squelched through the butterscotch mud of a rutted farm track. The driver's breath steamed, too, in the late afternoon chill as he rubbed his hands together. He shivered. So did the children nestled in the hay behind him. Autumn had descended upon Europe with coldhearted glee in this first full year after the Great War, threatening still leaner times ahead.

He craned his neck to glance at the children. It would do

nobody any good if they succumbed to the cold before he delivered them to the orphanage.

Every bump in the road set the smallest child to coughing. The towheaded boy of five or six years had dull eyes and sunken cheeks that spoke of hunger in the belly, and a wheeze that spoke of dampness in the lungs. He shivered, hacking himself raw each time the wagon thumped over a root or stone. Tufts of hay fluttered down from where he had stuffed his threadbare woolen shirt and trousers for warmth.

The other two children clung to each other under a pile of hay, their bones distinct under hunger-taut skin. But the gypsy blood of some distant relation had infused the siblings with a hint of olive coloring that fended off the pallor that had claimed the sickly boy. The older of the pair, a gangly boy of six or seven, wrapped his arms around his sister, trying vainly to protect her from the chill. The sloe-eyed girl hardly noticed, her dark gaze never wavering from the coughing boy.

The driver turned his attention back to the road. He'd made this journey several times, and the orphans he ferried were much the same from one trip to the next. Quiet. Frightened. Sometimes they wept. But there was something different about the gypsy girl. He shivered again.

The road wove through a dark forest of oak and ash. Acorns crunched beneath the wagon wheels. Gnarled trees grasped at the sky. The boughs creaked in the wind, as though commenting upon the passage of the wagon in some ancient, inhuman language.

The driver nudged his mare into a sharp turn at a crossroads. Soon the trees thinned out and the road skirted the edge of a wide clearing. A whitewashed three-story house and a cluster of smaller buildings on the far side of the clearing suggested the country estate of a wealthy family, or perhaps a prosperous farm untouched by war. Once upon a time, the scions of a moneyed clan had indeed taken their holidays here, but times had changed, and now this place was neither estate nor farm.

A sign suspended on two tall flagpoles arced over the crushed-gravel lane that veered for the house. In precise Gothic lettering painted upon rough-hewn birch wood, it declared that these were the grounds of the Children's Home for Human Enlightenment.

The sign neither mentioned hope nor counseled its abandonment. But in the driver's opinion, it should have.

Months had passed since the farm was given a new life, but the purpose of this place was unclear. Tales told of a flickering electric-blue glow in the windows at night, the pervasive whiff of ozone, muffled screams, and always – always – the loamy shit-smell of freshly turned soil. But the countless rumors did agree on one thing: Herr Doktor von Westarp paid well for healthy children.

And that was enough for the driver in these lean gray years that came tumbling from the Armistice. He had children of his own to feed at home, but the war had produced a bounty of parentless ragamuffins willing to trust anybody who promised a warm meal.

A field came into view behind the house. Row upon row of earthen mounds dotted it, tiny piles of black dirt not much larger than a sack of grain. Off in the distance a tall man in overalls heaped soil upon a new mound. Influenza, it was claimed, had ravaged the foundling home.

Ravens lined the eaves of every building, watching the workman, with inky black eyes. A few settled on the ground nearby.

They picked at a mound, tugging at something under the dirt, until the workman chased them off.

The wagon creaked to a halt not far from the house. The mare snorted. The driver climbed down. He lifted the children and set them on their feet as a short balding man emerged from the house. He wore a gentleman's tweeds under the long white coat of a tradesman, wire-rimmed spectacles, and a precisely groomed mustache.

'*Herr Doktor,*' said the driver.

'*Ja,*' said the well-dressed man. He pulled a cream-colored handkerchief from a coat pocket. It turned the color of rust as he wiped his hands clean. He nodded at the children. 'What have you brought me this time?'

'You're still paying, yes?'

The doctor said nothing. He pulled the girl's arms, testing her muscle tone and the resilience of her skin tissues. Unceremoniously and without warning he yanked up her dirt-crusted frock to cup his hand between her legs. Her brother he grabbed roughly by the jaw, pulling his mouth open to peer inside. The youngsters' heads received the closest scrutiny. The doctor traced every contour of their skulls, muttering to himself as he did so.

Finally he looked up at the driver, still prodding and pulling at the new arrivals. 'They look thin. Hungry.'

'Of course they're hungry. But they're healthy. That's what you want, isn't it?'

The adults haggled. The driver saw the girl step behind the doctor to give the towheaded boy a quick shove. He stumbled in the mud. The impact unleashed another volley of coughs and spasms. He rested on all fours, spittle trailing from his lips.

The doctor broke off in midsentence, his head snapping around to watch the boy. 'What is this? That boy is ill. Look! He's weak.'

'It's the weather,' the driver mumbled. 'Makes everyone cough.'

'I'll pay you for the other two, but not this one,' said the doctor. 'I'm not wasting my time on him.' He waved the workman over from the field. The tall man joined the adults and children with long loping strides.

'This one is too ill,' said the doctor. 'Take him.'

The workman put his hand on the sickly child's shoulder and led him away. They disappeared behind a shed.

Money changed hands. The driver checked his horse and wagon for the return trip, eager to be away, but he kept one eye on the girl.

'Come,' said the doctor, beckoning once to the siblings with a hooked finger. He turned for the house. The older boy followed. His sister stayed behind, her eyes fixed on where the workman and sick boy had disappeared.

Clang. A sharp noise rang out from behind the shed, like the blade of a shovel hitting something hard, followed by the softer *bump-slump* as of a grain sack dropping into soft earth. A storm of black wings slapped the air as a flock of ravens took for the sky.

The gypsy girl hurried to regain her brother. The corner of her mouth twisted up in a private little smile as she took his hand.

The driver thought about that smile all the way home.

Fewer mouths meant more food to go around.

23 October 1920
St. Pancras, London, England

The promise of a cleansing frost extended west, across the Channel, where the ravens of Albion felt it keenly. They knew, with the craftiness of their kind, that the easiest path to food was to steal it from others. So they circled over the city, content to leave the hard work to the scavengers below, animal and human alike.

A group of children moved through the shadows and alleys with direction and purpose, led by a boy in a blue mackintosh. The ravens followed. From their high perches along the eaves of the surrounding houses, they watched the boy in blue lead his companions to the low brick wall around a winter garden. They watched the children shimmy over the wall. And they watched the gardener watching the children through the drapes of a second-story window.

*

His name was John Stephenson, and as a captain in the nascent Royal Flying Corps, he had spent the first several years of the Great War flying over enemy territory with a camera mounted beneath his Bristol F2A. That ended with a burst of Austrian anti-aircraft fire. He crashed in No-Man's Land. After a long, agonizing ride in a horse-drawn ambulance, he awoke in a Red Cross field hospital, mostly intact but minus his left arm.

He'd disregarded the injury and served the Crown by staying with the Corps. Analyzing photographs required eyes and brains, not arms. By war's end, he'd been coordinating the surveillance balloons and reconnaissance flights.

He'd spent years poring over blurry photographs with a jeweler's loupe, studying bird's-eye views of trenches, troop movements, and gun emplacements. But now he watched from above while a half dozen hooligans uprooted the winter rye. He would have flown downstairs and knocked their skulls together, but for the boy in the blue mackintosh. He couldn't have been more than ten years old, but there he was, excoriating the others to respect Stephenson's property even as they ransacked his garden.

Odd little duckling, that one.

This wasn't vandalism at work. It was hunger. But the rye was little more than a ground cover for keeping out winter-hardy weeds. And the beets and carrots hadn't been in the ground long. The scavenging turned ugly.

A girl rooting through the deepest corner of the garden discovered a tomato excluded from the autumn crop because it had fallen and bruised. She beamed at the shriveled half-white mass. The largest boy in the group, a little monster with beady pig-eyes, grabbed her arm with both hands.

'Give it,' he said, wrenching her skin as though wringing out a towel.

She cried out, but didn't let go of her treasure. The other children watched, transfixed in the midst of looting.

'Give it,' repeated the bully. The girl whimpered.

The boy in blue stepped forward. 'Sod off,' he said. 'Let her go.'

'Make me.'

The boy wasn't small, per se, but the bully was much larger. If they tussled, the outcome was inevitable.

The others watched with silent anticipation. The girl cried. Ravens called for blood.

'Fine.' The boy rummaged in the soil along the wall behind a row of winter rye. Several moments passed. 'Here,' he said, regaining his feet. One hand he kept behind his back, but with the other he offered another tomato left over from the autumn crop. It was little more than a bag of mush inside a tough papery skin. Probably a worthy find by the standards of these children. 'You can have this one if you let her alone.'

The bully held out one hand, but didn't release the sniffling girl. A reddish wheal circled her forearm where he'd twisted the flesh. He wiggled his fingers. 'Give it.'

'All right,' said the smaller boy. Then he lobbed the food high overhead.

The bully pushed the girl away and craned his head back, intent on catching his prize.

The first stone caught him in the throat. The second thunked against his ear as he sprawled backwards. He was down and crying before the tomato splattered in the dirt.

The smaller boy had excellent aim. He'd ended the fight before it began.

Bloody hell.

Stephenson expected the thrower to jump the bully, to press the advantage. He'd seen it in the war, the way months of hard living could alloy hunger with fear and anger, making natural the most beastly behavior. But instead the boy turned his back on the bully to check on the girl. The matter, in his mind, was settled.

Not so for the bully. Lying in the dirt, face streaked with tears and snot, he watched the thrower with something shapeless and dark churning in his eyes.

Stephenson had seen this before, too. Rage looked the same in any soul, old or young. He left the window and ran downstairs before his garden became an exhibition hall. The bully had gained his feet when Stephenson opened the door.

One of the children yelled, 'Leg it!'

The children swarmed the low brick wall where they'd entered. Some needed a boost to get over it, including the girl. The boy who had felled the bully stayed behind, pushing the stragglers atop the wall.

Seeing this reinforced Stephenson's initial reaction. There was something special about this boy. He was shrewd, with a profound sense of honor, and a vicious fighter, too. With proper tutelage . . .

Stephenson called out. 'Wait! Not so fast.'

The boy turned. He watched Stephenson approach with an air of bored disinterest. He'd been caught and didn't pretend otherwise.

'What's your name, lad?'

The boy's gaze flickered between Stephenson's eyes and the empty sleeve pinned to his shoulder.

'I'm Stephenson. Captain, in point of fact.' The wind tossed Stephenson's sleeve, waving it like a flag.

The boy considered this. He stuck his chin out, saying, 'Raybould Marsh, sir.'

'You're quite a clever lad, aren't you, Master Marsh?'

'That's what my mum says, sir.'

Stephenson didn't bother to ask after the father. Another casualty of Britain's lost generation, he gauged.

'And why aren't you in school right now?'

Many children had abandoned school during the war, and after, to help support families bereft of fathers and older brothers. The boy wasn't working, yet he wasn't exactly a hooligan, either. And he had a home, by the sound of it, which was likely more than some of his cohorts had.

The boy shrugged. His body language said, *Don't much care for school.* His mouth said, 'What will you do to me?'

'Are you hungry? Getting enough to eat at home?'

The boy shook his head, then nodded.

'What's your mum do?'

'Seamstress.'

'She works hard, I gather.'

The boy nodded again.

'To address your question: Your friends have visited extensive damage upon my plantings, so I'm pressing you into service. Know anything about gardening?'

'No.'

'Might have known not to expect much from my winter garden if you had, eh?'

The boy said nothing.

'Very well, then. Starting tomorrow, you'll get a bob for each day spent replanting. Which you will take home to your hard-working mother.'

'Yes, sir.' The boy sounded glum, but his eyes gleamed.

'We'll have to do something about your attitude toward education, as well.'

'That's what my mum says, sir.'

Stephenson shooed away the ravens picking at the spilled food. They screeched to each other as they rode a cold wind, shadows upon a blackening sky.

23 October 1920
Bestwood-on-Trent, Nottinghamshire, England

Rooks, crows, jackdaws, and ravens scoured the island from south to north on their search for food. And, in the manner of their continental cousins, they were ever-present.

Except for one glade deep in the Midlands, at the heart of the ancestral holdings of the jarls of Æthelred. In some distant epoch, the skin of the world here had peeled back to reveal the great granite bones of the earth, from which spat forth a hot spring: water touched with fire and stone. No ravens had ventured there since before the Norsemen had arrived to cleave the island with their Danelaw.

Time passed. Generations of men came and went, lived and died around the spring. The jarls became earls, then dukes. The Norsemen became Normen, then Britons. They fought Saxons; they fought Saracens; they fought the Kaiser. But the land outlived them all with elemental constancy.

Throughout the centuries, blackbirds shunned the glade and its phantoms. But the great manor downstream of the spring evoked no such reservations. And so they perched on the spires of Bestwood, watching and listening.

'Hell and damnation! Where is that boy?'

Malcolm, the steward of Bestwood, hurried to catch up to the twelfth Duke of Aelred as he banged through the house. Servants fled the stomp of the duke's boots like starlings fleeing a falcon's cry.

The kitchen staff jumped to attention when the duke entered with his majordomo.

'Has William been here?'

Heads shook all around.

'Are you certain? My grandson hasn't been here?'

Mrs. Toomre, Bestwood's head cook, was a whip-thin woman with ashen hair. She stepped forward and curtsied.

'Yes, Your Grace.'

The duke's gaze made a slow tour of the kitchen. A heavy

silence fell over the room while veins throbbed at the corners of his jaw, the high-water mark of his anger. He turned on his heels and marched out. Malcolm released the breath he'd been holding. He was determined to prevent madness from claiming another Beauclerk.

'Well? Off you go. Help His Grace.' Mrs. Toomre waved off the rest of her staff. 'Scoot.'

When the room had cleared and the others were out of earshot, she hoisted up the dumbwaiter. She worked slowly so that the pulleys didn't creak. When William's dome of coppery-red hair dawned over the transom, she leaned over and hefted him out with arms made strong by decades of manual labor. The boy was tall for an eight-year-old, taller even than his older brother.

'There you are. None the worse for wear, I hope.' She pulled a peppermint stick from a pocket in her apron. He snatched it.

Malcolm bowed ever so slightly. 'Master William. Still enjoying our game, I trust?'

The boy nodded, smiling around his treat. He smelled like parsnips and old beef tallow from hiding in the dumbwaiter all afternoon.

Mrs. Toomre pulled the steward into a corner. 'We can't keep this up forever,' she whispered. She wrung her hands on her apron, adding, 'What if the duke caught us?'

'We needn't do so forever. Just until dark. His Grace will have to postpone then.'

'But what do we do tomorrow?'

'Tomorrow we prepare a poultice of hobnailed liver for His Grace's hangover, and begin again.'

Mrs. Toomre frowned. But just then the stomping resumed, and with renewed vigor. She pushed William toward Mr. Malcolm. 'Quick!'

He took the boy's hand and pulled him through the larder. Gravel crunched underfoot as they scooted out of the house through the deliverymen's door, headed for the stable, trailing white clouds of breath in the cool air. Malcolm had pressed most of the household staff into aiding the search for William, so the stable was empty. The duke kept his horses here as well as his motor car. The converted stable reeked of petrol and manure.

Mr. Malcolm opened a cabinet. 'In here, young master.'

William, giggling, stepped inside the cabinet as Mr. Malcolm held it open. He wrapped himself in the leather overcoat his grandfather wore when motoring.

'Quiet as a mouse,' the older man whispered, 'as the duke creeps around the house. Isn't that right?'

The child nodded, still giggling. Malcolm felt relieved to see him still enjoying the game. Hiding the boy would become much harder if he were frightened.

'Remember how we play this game?'

'Quiet and still, all the same,' said the boy.

'Good lad.' Malcolm tweaked William's nose with the pad of his thumb and shut the cabinet. A sliver of light shone on the boy's face. The cabinet doors didn't join together properly. 'I'll return to fetch you soon.'

The duke, William's grandfather, had gone on many long expeditions about the grounds with his own son over the years. Grouse hunting, he'd claimed, though he seldom took a gun. The only thing Mr. Malcolm knew for certain was that they'd spent much time in the glade upstream from the house. The same glade where the staff refused to venture, citing visions and noises. Years after the duke's heir – William's father – had produced two sons of his own, he'd taken to spending time in the glade alone. He returned to the manor at all hours, wild-eyed and unkempt, mumbling hoarsely of blood and prices unpaid. This lasted until he went to France and died fighting the Hun.

The duke's grandsons moved to Bestwood soon after. They were too young to remember their father very well, so the move was uneventful. Aubrey, the older son and heir apparent, received the grooming expected of a Peer of the Realm. The duke showed little interest in his younger grandson. And it had stayed that way for several years.

Until two days previously, when he had asked Malcolm to find hunting clothes that might fit William. Malcolm didn't know what happened in the glade, or what the duke did there. But he felt honor-bound to protect William from it.

Malcolm left William standing in the cabinet only to find the duke standing in the far doorway, blocking his egress. His Grace had seen everything.

He glared at Malcolm. The majordomo resisted the urge to squirm under the force of that gaze. The silence stretched between them. The duke approached until the two men stood nearly nose to nose.

'Mr. Malcolm,' he said. 'Tell the staff to return to their duties. Then fetch a coat for the boy and retrieve the carpetbag from my study.' His breath, sour with juniper berries, brushed across Malcolm's face. It stung the eyes, made him squint.

Malcolm had no recourse but to do as he was told. The duke had flushed out his grandson by the time he returned bearing a thick dun-colored pullover for William and the duke's paisley carpetbag. Malcolm made brief eye contact with William before taking his leave of the duke.

'I'm sorry,' he mouthed.

*

William's grandfather took him by the hand. The ridges of the fine white scars arrayed across his palm tickled the soft skin on the back of William's hand.

'Come,' he said. 'It's time you saw the estate.'

'I've already seen the grounds, Papa.'

The old man cuffed the boy on the ear hard enough to make his eyes water. 'No, you haven't.'

They walked around the house, to the brook that gurgled through the gardens. They followed it upstream, crashing through the occasional thicket. Eventually the crenellations and spires of Bestwood disappeared behind a row of hillocks crowned with proud stands of yew and English oak. They traced the brook to a cleft within a lichen-scarred boulder in a small clearing.

Though hemmed about by trees on every side, the glade was quiet and free of birdsong. The screeches and caws of the large black birds that crisscrossed the sky over the estate barely echoed in the distance. William hadn't paid the birds any heed, but now their absence felt strange.

Several bundles of kindling had been piled alongside the boulder. From within the carpetbag the duke produced a canister of matches and a folding pocketknife with a handle fashioned from a segment of deer antler. He built a fire and motioned William to his side.

'Show me your hand, boy.'

William did. His grandfather took it in a solid grip, pulled the boy's arm straight, and sliced William's palm with his pocketknife. William screamed and tried to pull away, but his grandfather didn't release him until the blood trickled down William's wrist to stain the cuff of his pullover. The old man nodded in satisfaction as the hot tickle pulsed along William's hand and dripped to the earth.

William scooted backwards, afraid of what his grandfather might do next. He wanted to go home, back to Mr. Malcolm and Mrs. Toomre, but he was lost and couldn't see through his tears.

His grandfather spoke again. But now he spoke a language that William couldn't understand, more wails and gurgles than words. Inhuman noises from a human vessel.

It lulled the boy into an uneasy stupor, like a fever dream. The fire's warmth dried the tears on his face. A shadow fell across the glade; the world tipped sideways.

And then the fire spoke.

ONE

2 February 1939
Tarragona, Spain

Lieutenant-Commander Raybould Marsh, formerly of His Majesty's Royal Navy and currently of the Secret Intelligence Service, rode a flatbed truck through ruined olive groves while a civil war raged not many miles away. He secretly carried two fake passports, two train tickets to Lisbon, vouchers for berths on a steamer bound for Ireland, and one thousand pounds sterling. And he was bored.

He'd been riding all morning. The truck passed yet another of the derelict farmhouses dotting the Catalonian landscape. Some had burned to the ground. Others stared back at him with empty windows for eyes, half-naked where the plaster had sloughed to the ground under erratic rows of bullet holes. Wind sighed through open doorways.

Sometimes the farmers and their families had been buried in the very fields they tended, as evidenced by the mounds. And sometimes they had been left to rot, as evidenced by the birds. Marsh envied the farmers their families, but not their ends.

The land had fared no better than the farmers at the hands of armed factions. Artillery had pocked the fields and rained shrapnel upon centuries-old olive groves. In places, near the largest craters, the tang of cordite still wafted from broken earth.

At one point, the truck had to swerve around the charred hulk of a Soviet-issue T-38 tank straddling the road. It looked like an inverted soup tureen on treads but was based, Marsh noted with pride and amusement, upon the Vickers. It was a common sight. Abandoned Republican matériel littered the countryside. Most of Spain had long since fallen to the Nationalists; now they mounted their final offensive, grinding north through Catalonia to strangle the final Republican strongholds.

Officially, Britain had chosen to stay on the sidelines of the Spanish conflict. But the imminent victory of Franco's Nationalists and their Fascist allies was raising eyebrows back home. Marsh's section within the SIS, or MI6 as some people preferred to call it, was tasked with gathering information about Germany's feverish rearmament over the past few years. So when a defector had contacted the British consulate claiming to have information about something new the Nazis were field-testing in Spain, Marsh got tapped for an 'Iberian holiday,' as the old man put it.

'Holiday,' Marsh repeated to himself. Stephenson had a wry sense of humor.

The truck labored out of the valley into Tarragona, briefly passing through the shadow of a Roman aqueduct that strad-dled the foothills. A coastal plain spread out before Marsh as they topped the final rise. Orange and pomegranate groves, untended by virtue of winter and war, dotted the seaward slopes of the hills overlooking the city. At the right time of year, the groves might have perfumed the wind with their blossoms. Today the wind smelled of petrol, dust, and the distant sea.

Below the groves sprawled the city: a jumble of bright stucco, wide plazas, and even the occasional gingko-lined avenue left behind by long-dead Romans. One could see where medieval Spanish city planning had collided with and absorbed the remnants of an older empire. On the whole, Tarragona was well-preserved, having fallen to the Nationalists three weeks earlier after token resistance.

Somewhere in that mess waited Marsh's informant.

Between the city and the horizon stretched the great blue-green expanse of the Mediterranean Sea. It sparkled under the winter sun. Most years enjoyed frequent winter rains that tamped down the dust. This season had been too sporadic, and today the winds blew inland, so the breeze coming off the sea spread an ocher haze across the bowl of the city.

Farther west, whitecaps massaged the coastline where a trawler steamed out of port. Marsh was too far away to smell the fear and desperation, to feel the press of bodies, to hear the din on the docks as families clamored for passage to Mexico and South America. Those refugees not willing to risk capture in the Pyrenees while fleeing to France, and who could afford otherwise, instead mobbed the ports. For now, Franco's Nationalists were busy formalizing their control of the country. But when that was done, the reprisals would begin.

The dirt road became cracked macadam as they descended into the city. Marsh shifted his weight when the macadam turned into uneven cobblestones. It had been a long couple of days since he'd crossed the border from Portugal.

His ride pulled to a stop in the shadow of a medieval cathedral. The driver banged his fist on the outside of his door. Marsh grabbed his rucksack and hopped down, gritting his teeth against the twinge of pain in his knee.

'*Gracias,*' he said. He paid the driver the promised amount, a small fortune by the standards of a poor farmer even in peacetime. The driver took the cash and rumbled away without another word, leaving Marsh to cough in a plume of exhaust.

I'd spend it quickly if I were you.

Marsh set off for the cathedral. As far as the driver knew, it was his destination. And so he'd relate, if anybody should happen to ask him about his passenger. The cathedral loomed over the circular Plaza Imperial, and from there it was a short walk to the Hotel Alexandria. Marsh had memorized the layout of the city before leaving London. Walking massaged the ache from his knee.

The narrow side streets were quiet and devoid of crowds, a fact for which he was thankful. He wore the heavy boots of a farmer, a flannel shirt under his overalls, and a kerchief tied around his neck in the local style. But he also wore the skin of an Englishman, colored pale by years of rain, rather than a complexion earned through a life of outdoor labor. But most folks weren't terribly observant. With a little luck and discretion, his garb would plant the proper suggestion in people's eyes; as long as he drew no extra attention to himself, their minds would fill in the expected details.

It was livelier on the plaza. The handfuls of people he passed in the wide open space shuffled through their lives under a cloud of dread and anticipation. Strident Art Deco placards touted General Franco's cause from every available surface. (*Unidad! Unidad! Unidad!*) The Nationalists' propaganda machine had wasted no time.

The cathedral bells chimed sext: midday. Marsh quickened his pace. The plan was to make contact at noon.

Krasnopolsky, an ethnic Pole born in the German enclave of Danzig, had come to Spain attached to a unit of Fascist forces supporting the Nationalist cause. Whatever his work entailed, he'd done it without protest for years. Until he decided, quite spontaneously, to defect. But the Nationalists' victory was merely a matter of time, meaning that his new enemies had the country locked up tight. Betraying them so late in the game was a bloody stupid move.

Thus he had contacted the British consulate in Lisbon. In return for assistance leaving the country, he'd share his knowledge of a new technology the Schutzstaffel had deployed against the Republicans. Franco, moved by a fit of despotic largesse, had given the Third Reich carte blanche to use Spain as a military proving ground. In that manner, the Luftwaffe had debuted its carpet-bombing technique in Guernica. MI6 wanted to know about anything else the Jerries had developed over the past few years.

Which was why Marsh carried virtually enough money to purchase his own steamer, if it came to that. He'd stay at Krasnopolsky's side all the way back to Great Britain.

The Hotel Alexandria was a narrow five-story building wedged between larger apartment blocks. Its balconies hung over the street in pairs jutting from the canary-yellow façade. The building had only the single entrance. Less than ideal.

The lobby was a mishmash of ugly modernist décor and Spanish imperialism. It looked like the result of a half-hearted makeover. Clean, bare spots high on the yellowed plaster marked the places where paintings had hung, most likely of King Alfonso and his family. Through a doorway to the left, a handful of men and women talked quietly in what passed for the Alexandria's bar.

Marsh threaded his way toward the reception desk through a maze of angular Bauhaus furniture and potted ferns. But he abandoned his intent to ring Krasnopolsky's room when he caught sight of the lone figure sitting at the rear of the lobby, in the shadows of the staircase.

The man perched on the edge of a chaise longue, smoking, with a suitcase next to him and a slim leather valise on his lap. He stamped out his cigarette and lit a new one with shaky hands. Judging by the number of cigarette butts in the ashtray next to the chaise, he'd been waiting there, in *public*, since well before noon.

Marsh cringed. He'd marked Krasnopolsky instantly. The man was an idiot with no conception of tradecraft.

He purchased a newspaper from the front desk, then took a seat in a high-backed leather chair next to Krasnopolsky's nest. The other man looked at him, did a double take, and shifted his feet.

MI6 had no photographs of Krasnopolsky; they'd had to produce the doctored passport based on the man's description of himself. He'd overstated his looks. He was a tall fellow, even sitting down, and skeleton-thin with an aquiline nose and ears like sails. If he were to stand in the corner of a dark room, Marsh imagined, he might be mistaken for a coat-rack.

Marsh paged through the paper, thoroughly ignoring Krasnopolsky. He waited until it looked like the defector wasn't quite so ready to flee.

'Pardon me, sir,' said Marsh in Spanish, 'but do you happen to know if the trains are running to Seville?'

Krasnopolsky jumped. '*Bitte?*'

Marsh repeated his question, more quietly, in German.

'Oh. Who knows? They're less reliable every day. The trains, I mean.'

'Yes. But General Franco will fix that soon.'

'Took you long enough,' Krasnopolsky whispered. 'I've been waiting all morning.'

Marsh responded in kind. 'In that case, you're a fool. You were supposed to wait in your room.'

'Do you have my papers?'

Marsh took a deep breath. 'Look, friend.' He tried to clamp down on the irritation creeping into his voice. 'Why don't we go back to your room and talk privately. Hmmm?'

Krasnopolsky lit another cigarette from the butt of the previous one. Italian issue. Marsh wondered how anyone could tolerate those acrid little monstrosities.

'I've already checked out. I'm safer in public. I need those papers.'

'What do you mean, safer in public?'

Krasnopolsky drew on the cigarette, watching the crowd. Pale discolorations mottled the skin of his fingers.

'Look, we're not a sodding travel agency,' said Marsh. 'You haven't given me a reason to help you yet.'

Krasnopolsky said nothing.

'You're wasting my time.' Marsh stood. 'I'm leaving.'

Krasnopolsky sighed. Plumes of gray smoke jetted from his nostrils. 'Karl Heinrich von Westarp.'

Marsh sat again, enveloped in a bluish cloud. 'What?'

'Not what. Who. Doctor von Westarp.'

'He's the reason you left?'

'Not him. His children. Von Westarp's children.'

'His kids?'

Krasnopolsky shook his head. He opened his mouth to elaborate just as a glass shattered in the bar. His mouth clacked shut. The skin on his knuckles turned pale as he tightened his grip on the valise.

'What was that?'

Dear God. This is hopeless. 'You need to relax. Let's get something to calm you down,' said Marsh, pointing to the side doorway that led to the bar. He pulled the man to his feet and marshaled him through the lobby.

After getting Krasnopolsky settled at a corner table, Marsh went to the bar and ordered a glass of Spanish red. Then he thought better of it and ordered the entire bottle instead. The barman swept up the last of the broken glass, grumbling about having to retrieve the wine from the cellar.

Marsh waited at the bar, keeping an eye on Krasnopolsky while eavesdropping on conversations. The question on everybody's mind was how things would change once Franco was formally in power.

The barman plunked a bottle in front of Marsh. Marsh was digging cash out of his pocket when he felt the surge of heat wash across his back. Somebody screamed.

'*Dios mío!*'

A cry went up: '*Fuego! Fuego!*'

Marsh spun. The rear corner of the hotel bar, steeped in shadows just moments earlier, now shone in the light from flames racing up the walls. *No! It can't be—*

Marsh dodged the people fleeing the fire, fighting upstream like a salmon. But he stopped in his tracks when he saw the source of the flames.

Krasnopolsky blazed at the center of the conflagration like a human salamander. New flames burst forth from everything he touched as he flailed around the room, wailing like a banshee. Air shimmered in waves around him; it seared the inside of Marsh's nose. The metal snaps on Marsh's overalls scorched his shirt, sizzled against his chest. The room stank of charred pork.

The burning man collapsed in a heap of bone and ash. Marsh glimpsed a half-incinerated valise on the burning floor. He gritted his teeth and kicked it away. The rubber soles of his boots became tacky, squelching on the floor as he danced away from the fire. He tossed aside a fern and dumped the pot of soil on the valise to smother the flames.

Then he snatched what little remained of Krasnopolsky's valise and fled the burning hotel.